SURRENDER TO A CHEAT

"Oh, Aimee, your lips are sweeter than honey," Mano's deep voice sighed softly. "Tell me you liked my kissing you. Tell me, *chiquita!*"

Oh, how his masculine heat consumed her! Aimee could not deny the truth. "I loved your kiss, Mark. You know that," she told him in a near whisper. Could he feel her heart pounding as hard and fast as it felt to her right now? she wondered.

Pressing her even closer, Mano breathed, "I want you, Aimee. I want you as a man wants a woman. I want to make love to you in the most intimate way," he huskily declared as his firm body pulsed eagerly against her. "Stop me now, if you must, or it will be too late!"

The force and power of him were too much for her. Aimee was too intoxicated by the spell he'd cast over her. For Aimee, nothing existed at that moment but herself and Mark in their own private paradise.

She gave him her answer by raising up her lips to meet his in a kiss—and that was all the answer Mano needed. . . .

SUMMER SPLENDOR

WANDA OWEN

ZEBRA BOOKS
KENSINGTON PUBLISHING CORP.

ZEBRA BOOKS

are published by

Kensington Publishing Corp.
475 Park Avenue South
New York, NY 10016

First printing: August, 1988

Printed in the United States of America

I wish to thank my daughter Sheila Northcott, for the wonderful poetry she created for this book. With pride and gratitude, I thank you!

I wish to thank my daughter Cherie Owen, for her constant support and encouragement. You were the first one to encourage me to write that first book. This is my tenth book so I certainly thank you!

Part One

Fury of the Past

The rage of the past,
when first eyes did meet,
gave way to a future
of love bittersweet.

Sheila Northcott

Chapter 1

The golden palomino galloped swiftly across the countryside with its arrogant head held high and its almost-white mane flowing. The swishing white tail swung back and forth with spirit and fire. But Mario Mateo's eyes were focused on the girl astride the magnificent beast. She had the same fire and spirit as the handsome animal she straddled. Never had he seen such beautiful blond hair on any lady's head. It was almost as white as her fine palomino's mane and tail. Her eyes were as gloriously violet as the sunset he'd been observing when she happened to ride by on her way back to her home a short distance away.

Why did his cantankerous father have to have a feud going with old Paul Aragon, who just happened to be the beautiful Aimee's father? Mario yearned so to court her; he had since the first moment his eyes had beheld her breathtaking loveliness.

Now if he were like his happy-go-lucky younger brother, Manuelo, he would not have let a mere little family feud stop him from pursuing the lovely Aimee. God, how he wished he were like Manuelo! Oh, he'd tried being like him with that wild, reckless air, but it seemed he only ended up looking silly and foolish. There was no way he could be like that.

Their stern, reserved father might rant and rave, shouting his disapproval about Manuelo's ways and his refusal to conform to old Carlos Mateo's demands, but Mario saw the admiration in his father's eyes for his headstrong younger son.

Mario envied Manuelo's strength and determination even when they were young lads. He would never forget the day their father had been so distraught with him that he'd called him a miserable handful to deal with. Ever since then, Manuelo had been called by the nickname his father had given him— Mano.

It would not have bothered Mano that he put the whole countryside around San Jose in a furor if he'd wished to call upon and try to woo and win the lovely Aimee Aragon. It was rumored that her father, Paul Aragon, intended her to marry into the very wealthy, affluent Bigler family.

His lovely daughter had just returned from two years of schooling back in the East and a tour of Europe. Now she was ready to make the proper marriage—so the gossips of the region were saying.

Mario considered the young Bigler bachelor to be a lucky son-of-a-gun!

But he questioned what the lovely Aimee thought about all this if the rumors were true. Somehow, he had grave doubts that she would be bent to anyone's will other than her own.

He'd only seen her three times since she'd returned to California, and each time he'd been impressed by the arrogance he saw in the stubborn set of her chin and the assured way she carried her body. While he'd never been close enough to her to drown himself in those lovely violet pools of her eyes, he knew there was the brilliant fire of determination and strength there.

The way she sat astride that palomino of hers reminded him of that same daring recklessness of his brother, Mano. *Madre de Dios*, the two of them together would prove to be utter

10

havoc! Aimee Aragon had a wild streak in her, Mario suspected.

Perhaps it was a good thing that Mano was away right now. But then, who ever knew when he might suddenly show up some night, with that big broad grin on his handsome face, and jauntily march into the parlor as he'd done so often in the last four or five years. How many times had Mario sat and listened to his father vow to disown his brother when unexpectedly Mano would march into the house with that winning smile on his face. Carlos would always rush to embrace his youngest son, elated to see him back home.

Quite honestly, Mario understood his father's feelings. It was impossible to resist Mano's charm. There was a certain charisma about his brother that always ignited attention and excitement. Mario had realized that since the time they were both youngsters. Mano was like their lovely, hot-blooded mother, Theresa, who had that magnetic warmth that always drew people to her. Mario had inherited the quiet, reserved nature of his father, Carlos.

Oh, he recalled the furious fights he had overheard during the years between the two volatile Latin tempers of his parents. His mother was not the typical Latin lady with a sweet docile nature, subservient to her lordly husband.

Carlos did not like it, but he worshipped his lovely wife. Mario knew, as he grew older, that his overbearing father finally realized that he'd never change her. The lovely Theresa would never be tamed by Carlos Mateo or any other man. Mario also realized that there were many men in their valley who would have loved to have stepped into Carlos Mateo's shoes. His father was a wise man and he surely had to know this, too.

Now, as Mario spurred his fine Arabian mare into action to go homeward, for the lovely sight of Aimee Aragon had faded with the sunset, he wondered how different life would have been had his mother not died when she did. Reflecting on the past as he was now doing, he recalled that that was when the

11

turmoil had broken loose in the valley.

The feud of idiocy between the Mateo family and the Aragon family had sparked the year that the Mateo bulls had ravaged the grapevines of the Aragon vineyards. Paul Aragon's prized grapes that he'd brought from his native country of France were trampled and ruined by the two fine prized Mateo bulls. Angry words were spoken by both powerful, strong-willed men. Both were justified by their accusations and their demands. Both were unrelenting as the months and years passed. The barrier grew higher and higher.

It had not mattered to Mario until recently, but now it did. As he rode toward his home, he pondered what he could do to ease the tension between the two families. The bulls his father raised had never broken through the fences again, but neither Carlos nor the arrogant, proud Frenchman had ever humbled themselves to be neighborly. It seemed a shame to Mario. More to the point, it seemed foolish and childish.

In this region of San Jose, the names Mateo and Aragon both drew great honor and respect. A Mateo bull was prized and demanded a most handsome price. The same could be said about the Aragon grapes and fruits. Aragon's wines and their fruits were constantly sought. Both gentlemen had prospered over the years and by 1852 had made quite a name for themselves in this California valley.

Crazily, their lives had many parallels that could have bound them together but for their headstrong, stubborn natures. Carlos Mateo, with his proud Spanish heritage, would not bend to the will of the aristocratic Frenchman Aragon.

Paul Aragon had never allowed Carlos Mateo to intimidate him with his fierce, powerful demeanor. It did not impress him that the Mateo family had lived in the region long before the Aragon family arrived in California and were subsequently considered the outsiders. The wonder of this new country was that it was made up of a hodgepodge of all nationalities.

Both men swelled with an enormous conceit that could not be dented by the other, and each of them was prideful about his heritage. Both harbored a private disappointment that their lovely wives had produced so few heirs to carry on for them as they'd grown older.

Carlos's wife, Theresa, had died so very young, leaving him with only two sons. He had yearned for a much larger family. But he had found out shortly after Mano was born that she wished to have no more children by him. No longer did she welcome him into her boudoir.

Paul Aragon suffered the same dilemma, but the doctor had warned him that his wife Lisette should never again bear a child after she had given him two husky sons, Armand and Emile. She had gambled with her life to give him a beautiful daughter, Aimee. After Aimee's arrival the doctor had warned Paul, with most strong terms, that he would be responsible for Lisette's death should she become pregnant again. Paul had accepted his fate and turned all his energies toward his vineyards, working from sunup to sunset.

Amazingly, Paul found his cross not so heavy to bear, for he was exhausted at the end of the day and he found such joy in his two handsome sons, a most beautiful daughter, and a devoted, loyal wife. What more could a man want out of life? he asked himself.

Good fortune was his, for he prospered, shipping his fruits all over the world. Each year he sought to perfect his wines, and the demands were now overwhelming. This was most gratifying to Paul Aragon. Always, his lovely Lisette was by his side, encouraging him. He dared not be selfish and think only of himself, for she was as denied as he was but she never complained. He knew Lisette to be a woman of strong passion.

As startling as it might have seemed to him when he was younger, there was a glorious feeling to just holding the woman he loved in his arms and feeling the sweet warmth of her flesh close to his. To know this woman loved him so much that she was willing to gamble her life was enough to demand his loyalty and respect the rest of his life, Paul considered.

He'd never be unfaithful to his beloved Lisette, for there

was no woman who could give to him what she already had.

Since his daughter Aimee had returned from the East and her tour of Europe, Paul pondered the absence of any of Lisette's traits in her. She was certainly not like her mother, nor could he see himself in her. Was it from that frivolous sister of his in Paris that Aimee had inherited her bold, reckless ways? he wondered. God forbid! He prayed that wasn't so.

His two robust sons were easy to handle compared to Aimee, and he'd certainly found that out the last six weeks since she'd arrived back home.

Yet, he was probably the only one feeling this way about her. Her two older brothers pampered her slightest whim and Lisette was utterly happy to have her daughter home. Aimee had captivated all the house servants with her charm and winning ways. Paul was the only one who found her so stubborn and determined that she was going to have her way. Yet he could not help admiring the way she could so effortlessly and innocently beguile anyone around her.

Did she know she had this power? he wondered. Was she as naive and innocent as she appeared? All he could say to himself was he felt sorry for the man she married. He'd better be a strong-willed individual to cope with her. From observing young Fred Bigler, he rather doubted that. Yet he knew he was the best choice of a husband for Aimee, and a young lady like her needed to be married now that she was eighteen.

She was a young lady in full blossom, lovely of face and figure. She would draw men's attention like bees are drawn to the nectar of flowers. So Paul could not chance the wrong man coming into her life. The truth was she did remind him of his younger sister, whom he knew to be a woman of passion. He wanted Aimee to do more with her life than Denise had done. He knew that women like Denise were ruled by their hearts and not by their heads. This was the fear prodding at him where Aimee was concerned right now.

If Paul were having his doubts that he could rule his daughter, his two older sons were sure that their younger sister

14

was not going to be told what she could or could not do. Already, they were amused and jesting about the fact that the petite Aimee was frustrating their father.

The evening meal at their home was a formal occasion, as it had always been for as long as Emile and Armand could remember. Now they came in from their day's labor in the vineyards to bathe and discard their work garb. When they came down to dine in the evening, they were dressed in snowy white linen shirts and fine tailored woolen pants.

A delectable dinner was served at the long dining room table, which was draped in a white cloth, and there was always a centerpiece of flowers or candles. Lisette had picked a particular wine to enhance whatever the cook had prepared for the meal of the evening. The evening meal was an Aragon ritual, which was always a pleasant occasion arranged by Lisette.

Tonight it was not as sublime or serene as usual. Armand and Emile had to admit that it was amusing to hear Aimee disagree with their father. Few people had ever done that.

Both admired her boldness and her guts. They both agreed with her that young Fred Bigler was a milksop.

But Paul Aragon pointedly tried to impress on his willful daughter that Fred just happened to be the nephew of the governor of the state of California. "Most young ladies would be elated that he wished to court them, *ma petite*," Paul Aragon told her.

Her two doting brothers stood, admiring the way she whirled around in the center of their parlor to declare to her father, "But I'm not like most young ladies, Papa. Surely you suspected that a long time ago. Never will I be." Her violet eyes locked into his with such firm determination and honesty that Paul was left speechless, for he knew she spoke the truth.

Like her two sons, Emile and Armand, Lisette sat by the fireplace doing her needlepoint, daring not to voice her

15

opinion. Never did she question that her husband was the lord and master of his castle. Rarely did her two husky, robust sons venture to question their father's words or demands. Only their fragile-looking, delicate sister Aimee dared to do that! Like her brothers, her mother admired her. But Lisette also worried about such a headstrong miss as Aimee. Such daring boldness was bound to get her in trouble, her mother feared. Perhaps the year spent in Paris had not been wise, Lisette pondered, knowing the ways of Aimee's *Tante* Denise, but that had been Paul's decision and not hers!

Lisette watched her husband fold and unfold his newspaper, the *Mercury-Herald,* and she knew his frustration with his eighteen-year-old daughter. A part of her compassion went out to him, for she knew how hard he'd worked to establish his vineyards when they'd come from France to this new, wonderful country of America.

On September 9, 1850, when California was admitted as a state, no one in the region was prouder than Paul Aragon. That was the year the Aragon family and the Mateo family of Spanish descent began their feud. Paul had told his wife that the Aragons were as much Americans as the Latin family whose land bordered theirs.

She recalled the tone of his deep voice on that occasion, and he was as sincere this evening as he told his daughter, "I see you as a grand lady, Aimee. A young lady with your charm and grace is destined to fulfill a role in history. Always, it has been that way. This is destined to be a great state in this country. Think about it, my darling. This was a lonely Spanish outpost with some fifteen thousand people, and now it has grown in four years to two hundred fifty thousand. The future of this great state will be left to young men and women like you, Aimee. You could be a most influential, grand lady."

She turned to smile at her father and there was a flippant air about her, but she spoke softly as she replied to him, "But what if I do not wish to be a grand lady, Papa?"

In utter despair, Paul Aragon threw his hands up in the air to declare, "Then I do not understand you, Aimee."

"Obviously you don't, Papa." She whirled around, the soft, flowing material of her muslin gown swishing to and fro as she moved to leave the room. Her long tresses of spun gold swayed around her shoulders. Suddenly, she stopped to look back at her father and there was a twinkle of mischief in those blue-violet eyes as she smiled and said, "But you will understand me, Papa. You see, I would never give my love to a man just because he could make me a grand lady. The man who wins my love and my heart will make me feel like no other man could possibly make me feel. You understand, Papa?"

Paul Aragon stood speechless, watching his lovely daughter leave the room. Emile and Armand exchanged amused grins and their mother bowed her head to hide the smile on her face, too.

It would take a rare breed of man to conquer the beautiful Aimee's reckless heart; they all agreed about that!

Chapter 2

Aimee Aragon was like most young girls her age when she envisioned the handsome Prince Charming who would come marching into her life to steal her heart away and make her feel wonderful and excited. The image of the man of her dreams was always the same, with his hair as black as a raven's wing and his eyes to match. His male figure was tall and trim, with broad shoulders but a smaller waist and hip line. His deep voice would thrill her when he spoke to her. At least, it always did in her dreams. The touch of his hands made her titillate as he stroked her flesh in the dark privacy of her bedroom late at night when she lay there thinking about this man—her lover she'd meet someday soon.

Her brothers were right to think he would be a rare breed of man. This certainly did not fit the image of Fred Bigler, with his expressionless face and ordinary plain looks. As far as Aimee was concerned, Bigler's expensive, fine-tailored suits did nothing to enhance his attractive appeal as a man. He just did not impress her at all. It was as pure and simple as that.

Aimee did not understand this new attitude of her father's.

He seemed so different now that she had returned home after an absence of two years. They seemed to constantly be having disagreements. Aimee found it impossible to fault herself for the fury always exploding between them. She found her relations with her mother and brothers exactly as they had been in the past. It was only with her father that she seemed to have this problem. Why? she asked herself. Why could it not be as it had been before she'd left to go to school in the East?

She knew not what the answer was. But she did not like being in her father's disfavor.

Rarely did Lisette Aragon question her husband's wisdom about handling any situation. But tonight she felt she must say something. As clever as Paul was, he was handling Aimee all wrong. He was never going to get her to do as he wished the way he was going about things.

She sat at her dressing table, unwinding the long coil at the back of her head. Her husband was already in bed, propped up against the pillows and staring thoughtfully. She watched him, his image reflecting in the mirror of her dressing table.

"Paul, you are pushing Aimee far too hard. She'll not agree to see Fred if you keep this up. I'm telling you the truth. For once, you'd do well to listen to me and not be so stubborn yourself." She ran her silver brush through the long tresses of her dark hair that were streaked with silver-grey strands. She watched his heavy dark brow arch with a displeased reaction about her remarks. But she knew he was giving them due consideration, too.

"I want what is best for Aimee, too, Paul. You must know that. But Aimee is no ordinary young lady. I think we've both known that since she had her fourteenth birthday, haven't we? It is almost frightening to have a daughter be as beautiful as she is. It can not be simple. I—I always knew this. You must not be impatient with her, Paul."

This was all she would say to her husband before dimming the lamp and crawling between the sheets of the bed to lay beside him. Let him absorb her words of wisdom about

19

their daughter.

Paul Aragon lay silently, knowing that his wife had spoken the truth. But he had a dream for his daughter and nothing must stand in the way of its coming true. He knew he could make it all happen for Aimee, if only she would listen to him. When it did happen, she would be grateful for his clever planning, Paul knew. Oh, yes, he had no doubts about that at all!

Once she truly became a mature young lady and moved out of this frivolous adolescent time, Paul knew she would be glad he'd taken charge of her life for this short period.

Headstrong young ladies like Aimee needed a firm hand to direct them, Aragon was convinced. It was a devoted father's duty to do so. This attitude of her father's was utterly confusing to Aimee after she'd been allowed the freedom and independence of living several months with her *Tante* Denise in Paris. Aimee could only wonder if her father were unaware of the lifestyle his younger sister lived. Surely, he must be!

Her wealthy husband's untimely death had left her a young widow with the funds to live lavishly, and her *Tante* Denise denied herself nothing. She did not live by the conventional hours of the days and nights like here at the Chateau L'Aragon. Aimee had to admit she rather liked the irregular hours of her existence at her aunt's townhouse.

She found the constant parade of handsome gentlemen coming to her aunt's home always exciting and interesting. Denise's attractive lady friends were equally interesting, and Aimee noticed the air of gaiety that always seemed to engulf the luxurious surroundings of her aunt's home.

Never were there worries or concerns about the crops or the weather, which caused her parents to go around with long faces and frowns. More than ever, Aimee had been aware of how hard her father and brothers worked to earn their living. It seemed to her they had little time for lightheartedness and laughter. She did not wish her life to be nothing but work nad drudgery.

The truth was she could have been very excited about the Governor's Ball to be held the next month if her father were not so determined to matchmake her with the governor's nephew, Fred.

She loved the lovely silk gown of hyacinth blue that Madame de Gier had designed and was making for her. There would be a pair of satin slippers for her dainty feet in the same shade of hyacinth blue and a reticule to match. In case there was a chill to the air the night of the ball, Madame was making a cape to drape over her shoulders. The lining was the same shade of hyacinth blue as the gown, but the velvet was a deeper shade in the outer liner. It was a gorgeous ensemble and Aimee knew it must be costing her parents a handsome price.

When she mentioned this fact to her mother, Lisette's reply to her daughter was, "Ah, *ma petite,* it is worth everything to your papa for you to be the most elegant young lady there."

Aimee gave her mother a slow, uneasy smile, for she wished never to be a disappointment to her parents. But she could not help questioning if her father were going to be asking more of her than she was willing to give.

He would not be pleased to know that a man she found most attractive was the son of her father's bitter enemy, Carlos Mateo. Such a stupid feud it was to have lasted so long and deprived two families of a neighborly association over all these years. It was ridiculous, Aimee thought to herself.

Nevertheless, she had already made her mind up about some things where the Mateo family was concerned. She'd seen the handsome Mario Mateo astride his black stallion riding over the countryside and she also knew he'd been watching her ride wildly into the valley to return to her home. She thought he was very good-looking and he certainly appealed to her more than Fred Bigler. He reminded her of the handsome gypsy flamenco dancer she'd seen when her *Tante* Denise had taken her to the theater in Paris.

*   *   *

Mario Mateo would have been the happiest man in the whole state of California if he had known the lovely Aimee Aragon found him so handsome. She had been constantly in his thoughts since he'd seen her riding into the sunset toward the Chateau L'Aragon and had reined his fine black stallion around to go toward his own home, La Casa Grande.

The golden-haired Aimee was a delightful fantasy, Mario realized. Never would he have her except in his daydreams. He would be his father's dutiful son and marry the young lady Carlos wished him to marry, carrying on the family traditions of many years in the past. But nothing could stop a young, virile man from dreaming, Mario consoled himself. Absolutely nothing!

Obviously his preoccupied thoughts were noted by his father as the two of them sat at the massive dining room table to have their evening meal.

It was a nightly ritual that they dine in this spacious room with its dark, rich panelled walls. The table was always draped with a fine white linen cloth, and two large silver candelabra holding numerous tapers gave forth a sparkling, brilliant light.

Now it seemed ridiculous to Mario when it was only he and his father dining. It had been different a few years ago when their mother and Manuelo had joined them. Often in those years, there were friends present for the evening. Such was not the case anymore.

Suddenly, that harsh, deep voice of Carlos Mateo cut through the silence of the room, bringing Mario out of his fantasy and back to reality. "You've heard not a word I've said to you all evening! Am I to have two Manos on my hands? God forbid! Shall I repeat what I've just said, Mario?"

"I'm sorry, Father. It is true, my thoughts were elsewhere. I make no excuses." He took a sip of the fine Madeira, hoping it would make him more alert.

"Thank you, Mario, thank you for not lying to me as Mano would have to try to cover up for himself. I respect this quality in you. I asked if you were ready to travel to Mexico in the next couple of weeks to oversee a shipment of our bulls to the Ortego rancho. We're talking about a vast sum of money, Mario, and that is why I'd like you to go along with Juan. You understand?"

"Of course I do, Father, and I will go," Mario assured him.

"You are a good son, Mario. I don't know what I would do without you. A man must have someone he can depend upon when he reaches my age and I would be in a dilemma if I was depending on my youngest, eh?" He gave forth a nervous little laugh.

"Oh, Mano will come around, Father. In due time, he will finish sowing all his wild oats, as they say." Mario laughed. He wasn't so sure he spoke the truth to his father.

"You really think so, Mario? Sometimes, I rather doubt that Mano will ever stop." Carlos's face took on a very serious air as he sat silently for a moment before speaking again. "I loved your mother dearly, Mario, but she had this same streak in her. From the time that I met her, this beautiful young girl, until the day she died as a lovely mature lady who had given me two fine sons, some things never changed about my Theresa. I fear the same is true of Mano."

"Maybe not, Father," Mario tried to soothe his father.

"Time will tell, my son. Time will tell as it always does about most things," Carlos declared.

"Mano has a good heart, Father," Mario said. It was the only thing he could say at this particular moment. But there was truth in his statement, for he knew no one more generous and giving than his brother.

There was an imposing air about Carlos Mateo, with his aristocratic bearing and formal dignity. His deep voice always reflected a stern, serious tone. It did now as he told his oldest son, "It is you, Mario, who has a good heart. Mano's heart is fickle and he is generous only when he is having things his own way."

Mario sat silently, making no effort to reply or comment, for what his father said was true. He watched as Carlos rose

23

slowly from the chair, signaling that the evening meal was over. As Mario suspected, his father was about to announce to him that he had some work to go over in his study. Otherwise, he would have requested his son join him in a game of chess.

"By the way, my son, I am assuming you are to escort Camilla Reyes to the Governor's Ball?"

"*Si*, Father. I am taking Camilla as I usually do," Mario replied. Carlos would have had to be blind not to have noticed the lack of enthusiasm in his son over the prospect of squiring Jose Reyes's daughter to the gala occasion at the Capitol.

Carlos decided it was best not to prod Mario this evening about his courtship with Camilla Reyes. She was the daughter of his oldest and dearest friend in the valley, and of course he and Jose had grand ideas of their two heirs marrying someday.

For over two years now, Mario had found himself Camilla's appointed escort at the social gatherings the two families attended or at their family dinners.

Of the two Reyes daughters, Mario would have preferred the company of Camilla's seventeen-year-old sister, Juanita. But he was paired with Camilla, while Mano had been chosen to escort the vivacious Juanita. At least, when he was home at the ranch he was the one picked to escort her to the family functions.

Mano was just a lucky son-of-a-gun and that was the truth of the matter.

Mario was glad he didn't have to be sequestered in the study with his father this evening, playing chess. It was too nice outside, he noticed as he ambled to the opened double doors onto the roofed patio.

A million sparkling stars seemed to be twinkling up in the dark California evening sky and the sweetest exotic aroma of the blossoms that grew in the gardens of the walled courtyard wafted to his nostrils.

He noted the dappled streams of the moonbeams shining through the swaying branches and he was reminded of the shining silver-blond tresses of Aimee Aragon as she rode by him as wild as the wind this afternoon. It was Aimee he would have desired to take to the ball instead of Camilla Reyes, but that was impossible. He could imagine how gorgeous she would look in her fancy ball gown! There would be no lady to compare to her.

He sat down on the grilled iron bench in the center of the courtyard garden, listening to the soft whispering flow of the fountain's water as it cascaded down from one tier to the other. To Mario, it seemed to be a melodious sound, murmuring the name of the lady intriguing him.

Aimee . . . Aimee . . . Aimee, Mario would have sworn it seemed to say.

Chapter 3

Two generations of the Mateo family had lived and operated the La Casa Grande Ranch before Carlos Mateo took the helm. The rich and fertile land was situated some ten miles from the southern tip of San Francisco Bay.

Always, the Mateos had raised and bred their fine cattle and prized bulls, and Carlos stubbornly refused to give up his cattle to grow and harvest the various fruit crops like so many of his rancher friends were doing. Mario knew the futility of arguing with his father about the possibility that they might try growing some fruit and vegetables on a small section of the vast acres of the ranchland. But Manuelo and his father had engaged in a very heated argument about this very thing the evening before he'd left the ranch to go on one of his impromptu trips.

Mano was never as far away from his home as Carlos Mateo imagined, nor was he indulging himself in a wild, reckless way of life as his father might have suspected. He had found the tranquil peace he sought, after such unpleasant scenes with his father, up at Half Moon Bay, a quaint little fishing village located on the coast between San Jose and San Francisco.

It was with a relative of his mother's that Mano stayed. He found old Phil Cabrillo a fascinating gent to be around. The more time Mano had spent up at Half Moon Bay, the more he understood things that had plagued him about his lovely mother who seemed to have died so young.

Now he wondered if it was that Portuguese heritage of hers that had caused the conflict between his parents. Perhaps it also explained the vast differences between him and his brother, Mario. Always, his father was telling him he was like his mother, Theresa. All his life he'd felt his father made the remark contemptuously, and this pained him deeply. Oh, never did Mano show the hurt or the pain, but it was there just the same!

Time spent in the company of Phil Cabrillo was sharing very simple things like fishing in the bay, helping plant a garden, or splitting wood to stack up for the winter so the small cabin would be warm during that damp, rainy period. The winter was a most miserable time of the year, with the constant daily rains coming in off the bay, accompanied by the dense, thick fog devouring the countryside.

Over the last few years, Mano had spent part of each season up at Half Moon Bay. Sometimes it would be a couple of weeks and sometimes he'd stay for a month or two. It never seemed to bother Phil how long he stayed. Perhaps it was this marvelous feeling of freedom that always beckoned Mano to return to the small fishing village.

Always, he enjoyed talking to Cabrillo about his mother, for Phil was the only one who could tell him the intimate little details about her early life. His father had not known her then. Only Phil Cabrillo had known Theresa when she was sixteen and went to live with her Aunt Tessa because her parents were killed in a carriage accident one foggy night as they were returning home from a fair.

This night at Half Moon Bay was like all the other times after dinner when Mano and Phil would be sitting around enjoying

27

their little thin black cigarillos, along with a glass of wine.

"Your mother slipped away from La Casa Grande a couple of times, Mano. Did you know that? She told no one where she was going—not even her trusted little maid. She stayed up here with me for over a week, enjoying the sweet freedom of going around in her bare feet and wearing a pair of my old faded pants. No fancy, frilly petticoats either! When she decided to return to La Casa Grande, she was glowing and radiant, as though she'd been rejuvenated. So refreshed and full of spirit she was, Mano."

Mano had listened intently to his relative speak about his mother. He supposed Phil had to be his second cousin if Cabrillo and his mother were first cousins.

"It would seem to me, Phil, from all you've told me about my mother, that most of the time she was not a very happy lady. It seems she was a woman of mercurial moods that changed within the blink of an eye. Obviously, her family was not enough to make her happy."

"Ah, she worshipped you and Mario. You are wrong—ah, so very wrong!" Cabrillo's dark eyes flashed brilliantly with the intensity of his feelings.

Mano's handsome face creased with a frown and he gave forth an uneasy smile as he replied, "I would hope so, Phil. But if that were so, why would she have left us back at La Casa Grande?"

"A Portuguese is a free soul, Mano. It can't be walled in or kept a prisoner. Would you not break out, eh?" He gave forth a devious little chuckle, which brought an immediate response from Mano, along with a gusto of laughter.

"I think you know me all too well, Phil," Mano confessed, sheepishly grinning.

"As I knew Theresa. She knew she was going back to her sons. She only wanted a brief time of freedom, Mano. That was all."

"From two demanding little brats like Mario and me, and our

father, who was also too demanding, eh?"

Old Phil's weathered face remained expressionless, for he'd always guarded himself from speaking too harshly of Carlos Mateo as he would have liked to do. After all, Mano was his son, and blood was thicker than water, so he'd always been told. "Something like that, Mano. It is as you've told me many times over the last few years that Carlos Mateo is a most congenial man as long as those around him conform to his way of thinking. Theresa could not bring herself to always conform any more than you do. Is that not so?"

"It is so. It will be Mario who will take over the operating of La Casa Grande when father is no longer able to oversee it. The two of us could never work together."

"And what will you do, my young man?"

"Will you not laugh if I tell you what really fascinates me, Phil? Something I think would be most exciting and challenging with each new year that passed with the yield of a new harvest—the wine vineyards of the valley." His dark eyes gleamed as he spoke to his elderly relative. Phil Cabrillo was struck speechless for a moment, for Carlos Mateo would be utterly devastated to hear his youngest son speak about grapevines instead of fine bulls. He would consider him an absolute idiot. Mano realized this and never had he dared to discuss it with anyone other than Phil. Not even Mario would have heard such remarks from his younger brother.

"I would never laugh at any man, Mano, for speaking from the heart as you just have. What is life if a man can't pursue the dream in his heart, eh?" There was a broad grin on the old Portuguese's face as he spoke.

Mano gave him an agreeing nod of his head. Cabrillo took the last puff on his cigarrillo, excusing himself for having to retire. "I promised my friend I would give him a hand with clearing out some timber on his land, so I must get up very early in the morning. You know you are free to stay as long as you want, Mano, whether I am here or not. My cottage is yours."

29

"I know, Phil, and I thank you. As always, I seem to find the peace I seek up here at Half Moon Bay. I—I might just meander up to the Santa Cruz Mountains for a couple of days before starting back to La Casa Grande. In fact, I might just get up early myself in the morning." He tossed his cigarillo out into the darkness and stood up, stretching his long muscled legs.

Suddenly, the hearty meal and wine, coupled with the cool night breeze as they'd enjoyed their pleasant conversation, found Mano serenely relaxed and ready to retire.

At dawn's first light, Mano reined his stallion up the winding lane into the Santa Cruz Mountains, and he stayed a couple of days in the small redwood cabin. He found that the silence and stillness of the forest calmed his restless soul. For the longest time, he enjoyed watching the gathering ducks flap on the pond or the small creatures of the forest scamper and play all around him. His presence did not seem to bother them nor did they act like he was an intruder in their domain.

Sometimes he napped in the afternoon until the shafts of sunshine broke through the roof to the dense forest. So very bright it was that he jerked up quickly from the intense heat searing his flesh.

On the third day up in the mountains, Mano was seized by the impulse to leave. La Casa Grande called out to him, and being a man guided by his primitive instincts, he knew he must obey.

The next morning he rode back down the eight-mile lane out of the Santa Cruz Mountains to travel southward, leaving Half Moon Bay back in the distance. But he had no doubt he'd be coming back this way. There was a magic about Half Moon Bay that drew him there and he knew it.

As he traveled across the California countryside that late spring day, it seemed everything was so gloriously alive with

30

activity. All the little villages along the bay were busy and prosperous with the constant flowing crowd of people coming into the state from other parts of the country in search for gold. All along the San Francisco Bay area, multitudes of ships had been abandoned because the crews had gone in search of the gold. It was a true form of madness, Mano decided, when he thought about the greedy obsession devouring the souls of men. To see all these magnificent schooners and ships left unattended while their crews went feverishly to seek their gold seemed foolhardy to him.

Could it be he felt this way because he was a wealthy man's son who'd never had to wait or want for anything? Maybe that was the answer.

When he left the small towns and fishing villages behind to ride into the fertile valley of the south bay, there was no doubt that the summer season was approaching. The fruit farms were in full bloom with a glorious array of pastel pinks and whites. Soon these colorful blossoms would become pears, apricots, and cherries, and would be shipped to ports all over the world.

It reminded Mano how very stubborn his father was not to understand this and change his thinking to go along with the times. Suddenly, he began to have grave doubts as to why he'd bothered to come back to La Casa Grande, but he knew there was a reason so he decided not to question it for the moment.

No place had a more beautiful sunset than California, he swore, He took the time to rein up on his fiery stallion to enjoy the sights of purples and roses, deep golds and rusts, over in the western sky.

Mano held a tight rein on the silver-grey stallion with its jet black tail and mane as the animal pranced nervously back and forth. In the next moment, Mano would realize why the stallion was so nervous, for he heard the shrill sound of a female's voice trying to be muzzled.

He patted the horse's mane, declaring, as he spurred him into action, "You've a sharper ear than me, Demonio." Like a

31

silver streak, he galloped into the small, secluded valley below to rescue the lovely girl with hair of silvery gold fighting valiantly to protect her honor. The odds were tremendously against her as she did her battle against the giant of a man atop her.

That was enough to make Mano's hot-blooded Latin temper explode into a wild rage. He detested such bastards as that. Black fire blazed in his eyes as he watched the beast of a man pound on the helpless beauty lying underneath him. His foul hands fondled and prodded her lovely satin flesh.

By the time Mano reined up on Demonio and leaped off his stallion, he was pulsing with hate and fully prepared to kill the man, a stranger he did not know.

The power and strength in his two hands were unbelievable as he yanked the man away from the lovely girl's body to fling him aside. As she lay there gasping, Mano yearned to bend down and take her in his arms to comfort her, but he had to assure himself that the animal lying there in the darkness no longer posed a threat. But when Mano bent down over the huge mountain of a man, he immediately realized the bastard was not breathing. A sharp boulder had obviously slammed the back of the man's head with a mighty blow.

Mano felt no remorse as he turned his back on the dead man to go comfort the lovely, sobbing girl lying a few feet away on the ground. In his soft, deep voice he tried to soothe her fears as he bent down slowly to cradle her in his strong arms, "It is all right, *chiquita*. You are safe with Mano. Mano will not let any harm come to you. Believe me!" He pressed her lovingly against him. As he looked down to see all the breathtaking loveliness of her face, he was stunned and amazed. "Ah, *bonita! Bonita!*" he drawled slowly as he appraised each exquisite feature his eyes beheld.

Such delicate, desirable loveliness he'd never seen before in any woman. As he protectively held her close to his broad chest, he wondered just who this alluring little enchantress was. Mano knew he'd never have overlooked a girl this beautiful if she'd lived here long in the region. Just before he'd become involved in rescuing her from that burly character attacking her, he'd recognized the familiar sights of the countryside telling him the ranch was just a short distance away.

As impressed as he'd been by her beautiful face as she accepted the consoling comfort of his arms, he was beguiled by the deep purple pools of her eyes, fringed with thick layers of long, curling lashes, staring up at him. In a soft, sweet voice, she murmured, "I thank you from the bottom of my heart."

Mano smiled, "Ah, senorita, the pleasure was all mine, I assure you." Selfishly, he would have liked to linger there in the deepening twilight much longer and just hold her in his arms as he'd been doing for a few brief moments, but he knew she must be escorted to her home after the ordeal she'd just experienced.

With a devious twinkle in his black eyes and an air of carefree lightheartedness, he inquired of her, "May I ask who you are, my fair young damsel?"

"You may, my knight in shining armor," she remarked, tantalizing him with the sparkling gleam of a coquette in her own eyes. "I am Aimee Aragon."

Dios, the French vintner's daughter, he silently mused!

"And who are you, monsieur?" she asked Mano.

"Me? Oh, I am—I am Mark Perez," he stammered out his hastily concocted lie to her. No family feud was going to ruin his chances with this ravishing beauty before he even had an opportunity to win her favor. He was not about to play the fool and tell her he was Manuelo Mateo.

"Well, Mark Perez, I thank you again, and may I ask one more favor of you since it seems my horse was frightened away. Could I impose on you to take me to my home?"

"Again may I say it will be my pleasure," he declared, letting his eyes devour the girl as he swung her up in his powerful arms as though she were as light a a feather.

Together, they rode Demonio toward the Aragon estate.

Mano thought to himself, as they rode along, that he was surely the only Mateo to ever set foot on Aragon land. He found himself curious about this Frenchman, Paul Aragon, because he knew of his father's intense dislike for him.

Already, Mano knew he was going to satisfy the insatiable curiosity gnawing at him where the lovely Aimee was concerned!

Chapter 4

Needless to say, the beauty of her face and the sensuous curves of her petite body were enough to excite any man, but Mano found her intriguing in another strange way. As they rode along atop Demonio with their bodies touching, she did not seem to mind in the least the closeness of him. She gave him no impression of being shy or innocent. He adored the way her violet eyes boldly challenged him when she looked at him.

Was it his wild imagination that she was leaning back against his chest now as though she were completely at ease and relaxed?

"Tell me, senorita, for I did not think I was blind, but have you been here in California long?" he asked of her.

"I've been away—if that is what you mean. My family has been here for several years and I was born and raised here. I've just returned from my schooling back East and then my father allowed me to tour Europe in the company of my aunt who lives in Paris."

"I see," Mano slowly drawled, deciding perhaps that

explained that certain sophistication he saw in her manner that was missing from most of the ranchers' daughters coming to his father's fiestas and barbecues. She was certainly not like those two Reyes sisters he and poor Mario were always stuck with. If his father had his way, Mario, his elder brother, was going to find himself married to the older Reyes girl. He kept warning Mario that he should speak up before it was too late.

"So that explains it then," Mano replied.

"And you, Mark . . . have you lived around here long, because I don't remember anyone named Perez living nearby?"

"Off and on. I spend a lot of time up around Half Moon Bay. I doubt that you've heard about it . . . just a little fishing village."

She confessed that she had not, and he was grateful she did not prod anymore about his background because Mano was usually sharp with a quick wit. However, he was too intoxicated by her breathtaking loveliness right now. His whole being pulsed with wild desire to kiss those honeyed lips and make love to her.

He'd known many women in his life but none had ever ignited him with such a hot, searing flame as the one riding with him right now. God, she was like nothing his eyes had ever devoured before!

This girl with her eyes of deep purple and her hair so fair with silvery highlights was a vision of how goddesses must surely look like, Mano concluded. She was the image of beguiling femininity that most men daydream about.

Having had a ravishing, sultry Latin mother, Mano had always considered the black-haired, black-eyed senoritas the most alluring ladies, but all of that had suddenly changed now that he'd met Aimee Aragon.

Unlike the tawny golden skin of his mother and most of the young women he'd been attracted to in the past, Aimee's satiny flesh looked like a soft gardenia petal. Her hair was not the golden shade of most fair-haired blondes. Hers had unusual silver tones, so shining and glossy.

When they arrived at the entrance gate to the wall-enclosed grounds of her father's estate, Mano had to admit that he hoped there was no one around who'd recognize him as a Mateo. He did not see how it would be possible, since the two families did not pay neighboring calls on one another.

Aimee was completely unaware of any misgivings he might be harboring as he lifted her down from the saddle. She *was* very much aware of his unhurried manner, though, as her body slowly brushed against his firm muscled physique.

He wore a devious grin on his handsome face, as though he could read her thoughts, and if he had not been so darned good-looking, she would have resented his arrogance. But he had such a charming way about him she found it impossible to dislike him.

Raising a fine-arched eyebrow, she returned his grin with one of her own and declared, "I think you are a rascal, Mark Perez."

His hand snaked around her tiny waist to hold her, and he gave out a deep chuckle, "I won't make you any promises about that, senorita. But I am a nice rascal."

"Oh, you!" she giggled as she matched her stride to his. Anyone observing them moving up the stone path to the front entrance would have thought they had known each other all their lives instead of a few brief moments. These were exactly the private thoughts parading through Aimee's mind as they approached the steps of her home.

Before they'd mounted the steps to enter the house, the massive heavy oak door flung open and Paul Aragon came rushing out to meet them. His face reflected the emotion and passion of a father's deep concern about his daughter arriving home in the company of a stranger. When her golden palomino, Lady, had returned to the grounds without her, that was enough to send her two older brothers, Emile and Armand, out to search for their sister.

They had insisted that their father stay at the house since he had been ill with a cold. Paul Aragon had done nothing but pace all the time his sons had been gone.

Now to see her arriving in the company of this dark, swarthy stranger filled him with mixed emotions. Dear God, he was happy to see that she was unharmed, but there was something about her disarranged hair and the torn skirt she wore that stirred up a quandary in Paul.

What was all this all about? Paul's impatient nature demanded to know. This was exactly the first question he asked his daughter as she approached him.

"Please, Papa, can we not get inside first and we will explain it all to you, *oui?*" Her eyes flashed brilliantly because she could see the disapproving look he was giving Mark Perez. He should be feeling gratitude for what Mark had done for her if only he'd give them a chance to explain.

But the situation was saved by the appearance of her mother, Lisette, rushing up to enclose her in her arms, declaring, "Oh, thank God you are all right, ma petite. We've all been so worried. Emile and Armand are out now looking for you."

"I understand, Mother, and if it had not been for Monsieur Perez coming along when he did, I could have been harmed. I—I am most grateful to him, as you and Papa should be."

Lisette graciously extended her hand to Mano and asked him to forgive them for their rudeness. "Monsieur Perez, I'm sure you understand that we were not quite ourselves. I am Aimee's mother, as I'm sure you've guessed, and this is her father. But please, let us all go into the parlor so you two young people can enlighten us about all this. Paul, why don't you take them into the parlor while I order us up some refreshments, eh?"

It was one of those rare times in the Aragon household when Lisette took full charge and Paul allowed her the liberty. He motioned the young couple down the long dark hallway toward the parlor, remaining silent as the three of them walked along.

It was only when they had entered the luxurious parlor of the Aragon home that Paul assumed his usual authoritative manner again. "Have a seat . . . Monsieur Perez? Was that not the name?"

Aimee saw how his dark eyes were measuring Mark once again, but what she was truly admiring was the way Mark's dark eyes were locking into her father's. There was boldness and strength there that intrigued her instantly. He was nothing like the nervous Fred Bigler her father had hoped to match her with. Paul Aragon did not intimidate Mark Perez.

"Yes, sir. My name is Mark Perez." He took a seat next to Aimee on the deep blue brocade settee and not the plush wedgewood-blue velvet chair Paul had motioned him to take. So instead Paul's towering body sunk down into the chair and he crossed his long legs as he clasped his huge hands together, which was his usual habit when he chatted.

"You live around here, young man?" Aragon inquired of Mano. Mano had to admit that this Aragon did have a most impressive face, with his greying dark hair, a mustache to match, and heavy sideburns.

"I live around here part of the time, sir," Mano told him, offering no more information than that about himself. He mused about where the delicate features of the lovely Aimee had come from. Paul Aragon's features were coarse and her mother was a rather plain-looking lady, even though she did have a warm, friendly way about her. Mano could see nothing about her face that hinted she had been lovely even when she was young.

By the time Lisette joined them and their servant trailed behind her, carrying a tray of hot chocolate with some dainty little iced cakes, Aimee was already relating to her father what had taken place just before Mano happened to be riding into the valley.

"Oh, you poor child!" Lisette gasped.

39

Paul forgot there was a strange young man in their presence as he barked angrily, "No, she is not a child, Lisette, and that is why she must take most seriously our warnings about her roaming the countryside now that California has all kinds of riffraff coming in for this gold. I fear it is a damnation instead of a blessing. Sane men seem to be losing their good sense."

At least, Paul Aragon was right that she was no child, Mano thought to himself. He would also agree with him about the gold fever driving men into an insane frenzy. When he saw the abandoned ships lining the San Francisco Bay, he considered the gold-seekers slightly crazy.

Somehow, he felt that the man who'd waited for Aimee to ride toward her home knew she'd be coming that way at a certain time in the late afternoon. Why he felt this so strongly he could not have explained. It was just a gut feeling he had. As old Phil Cabrillo would have explained it to Mano, it was that inborn Portuguese instinct.

But who would want to harm such a beautiful woman like Aimee, as that beast was trying to do? Mano knew one thing at this very moment, as he sat so close to her he could feel the sweet warmth of her firing him: He'd not allow it to happen again if he could prevent it.

At least, now that the whole story was told, Paul Aragon was looking at him in a kindlier way. It was at this moment that her two husky brothers rushed into the room with anxious looks on their two tanned faces.

Mano found Emile and Armand gave him a much friendlier reception than their father had, even before Aimee repeated her story. There was one detail of the story yet to be told, and Mano decided that before he took his leave he should tell them about the man he'd left back in the valley. "He was dead . . . hit his head on a sharp rock when I flung him off Aimee. I'll attend to that since it was my handiwork."

He stood up to take his leave, but Aimee's oldest brother, Armand, quickly spoke up, detaining Mano's departure. "Just a moment, *mon ami*. Emile and I shall go with you to see to this man."

Emile immediately echoed his older brother's sentiments by declaring, "*Oui*, Aimee is our sister . . . our concern. We owe you so much, Monsieur Perez." His eyes were dark like his father's, but they were warmer and friendlier than Paul Aragon's.

Mano was left with no doubt about the protective attitude these two older brothers felt toward their younger sister. He could certainly understand this, because if he'd had a sister like Aimee, he would have felt the same way.

The two of them joined him, but Mano turned to glance once more in Aimee's direction before he took his leave. His emotion-filled black eyes spoke the words he could not say in front of her parents and her brothers, but she knew what he was trying to tell her and she smiled at him. That was enough to please Mano as she softly and sweetly bid him good night. "I thank you again, Mark, for all you did. Please let the Aragons thank you properly. Will you come to dine with us soon?"

A slow, pleased smile creased Mano's face as he replied to her, "Ah, it will be my pleasure, Senorita Aragon." He turned to her parents and addressed them. "A pleasure to meet you, Senor and Senora Aragon. I wish it could have been a more pleasant circumstance." He gave them a gallant bow as he motioned to Emile and Armand that he was ready to leave.

Aimee's two older brothers were both sharing the mutual thoughts that this just might be the man to win their sister's heart. They'd seen the sparks of excitement in her eyes as she'd glanced his way. It was easy to see why any young girl would have been titillated by the presence of Mark Perez. He was a magnificent specimen of a man, with that firm muscled body of his and a certain magnetic charm that would certainly intrigue Aimee.

There was another trait in this Mark Perez that would please Aimee. It was that bold, daring manner of his, which would challenge Paul Aragon. This would appeal to Aimee.

Emile and Armand Aragon liked this stranger, Mark Perez, and Mano sensed it!

If they knew he was Manuelo Mateo, they would not have felt this way, he suspected. He was glad he had lied. He cared not what he had to do to win the favor of a lovely lady like Aimee Aragon.

He would win her, he had decided!

Chapter 5

Mano had seen many dead men, and he would have sworn that mountain of a man was dead when he'd left with Aimee. But when he arrived with the two brothers, at the spot where he'd rescued their sister and left the man he'd assumed was dead, there was no sign of his limp body. How could he have been so wrong? Mano wondered.

"He's gone! *Madre de Dios*, I would have sworn he was dead," Mano declared, completely befuddled and bewildered.

Emile and Armand exchanged glances with one another. Their sister had declared there was such a man, so they could not doubt that her friend was telling the truth.

"Obviously, he wasn't, *mon ami*," Emile replied.

"Obviously," Mano slowly drawled, still finding it hard to believe. "I guess that means we can call it a night, eh amigos, and get some sleep?"

A short time later, Mano was riding toward La Casa Grande. He had bid the Aragon brothers good night. They would have been shocked to know his destination and that where he would sleep this night would be the Mateo hacienda. A devious grin creased his face as he thought about the happenings of this night. Carlos Mateo would find it hard to believe that he was graciously served hot chocolate and iced cakes in the grand parlor of the Aragons.

The hour was late when he arrived at La Casa Grande. He settled Demonio in a stall and moved across the grounds from the barn toward the walled courtyard surrounding the spacious two-story house with its red tiled roof. It was shrouded in darkness as Mano expected at this late hour.

Quietly, he made his entrance and went up the winding stairway to his room. Once inside his bedroom, he pulled the draperies at the windows before lighting the lamp on the nightstand by his bed. As he surveyed the familiar surroundings of the room that since his boyhood had been his little corner of privacy in the hacienda, it seemed to him there had been no changes in the few weeks he'd been gone.

He smiled, knowing that the old housekeeper, Minerva, had made a daily inspection for any dust or cobwebs while he was gone. What would he have done without her throughout all these years? he wondered.

He owed this old Mexican woman so very much, for she had saved his hide many times during the years he was growing up. Carlos Mateo would have never believed that honest-looking face of hers to be lying to save Mano from getting a whipping. That was enough for Mano to love her forever, because his father's lashings were fierce.

When there was no way she could save him and Carlos had sent him up to his room, punishing him by denial of the evening meal, it was Minerva who had slipped him a tray of food.

It was she who soothed his tears when he'd fallen and hurt himself. It was her rough hands that had doctored those cuts and bruises with her special mestizo ointments she'd told him her Indian mother had passed on to her. They did work their wonders, Mano knew without any doubts.

Of all the people here in La Casa Grande, he most anticipated the sight of her in the morning. This was not to say that he did not have very deep feelings for his brother, Mario, or his father, Carlos. Mano had realized at a very early age that they were just different in their natures and he figured there was nothing to change that.

His older brother was a man to be admired, for he was intelligent and well-educated, and more important to Mano's thinking, Mario was a good man with a kind heart. The thing that galled the indomitable Mano was that Mario allowed their overbearing father to lord it over him. This riled Mano.

All his life, Mano had been aware that the name Mateo brought forth instant respect and esteem, but the imposing, formidable presence of Carlos Mateo had never intimidated him as it did most people. As a young boy, he'd dare to defy him and that was what had gotten him into so many problem situations that Minerva had to try to rescue and protect him from.

Yet, Mano felt a great depth of admiration for the fine-looking, aristocratic Latin gentleman who was his father. Like his father, he shared the pride of their illustrious heritage that their Spanish ancestors had settled here in California long before Mexico had ceded the province to the United States.

What Mano could not bring himself to accept was the future his father had planned for him, and this was the constant spark that fired their violent rages. He was not interested in raising cattle and their prized bulls as Carlos had found such gratification in during his lifetime.

For four years, Mano had gone searching in hopes of finding just what it was he wanted out of life. He'd searched like so many others for the gold hidden in the California earth and he'd shipped out on the packets leaving the California coast for faraway places. But the place that had soothed Mano's restless soul more peacefully was a smooth, out-of-the-way fishing village up on Half Moon Bay.

Since it was the tradition that the oldest son take over when the father decided to step down, Mano was glad Mario was the

45

older son.

Tonight he was glad to be at La Casa Grande and his comfortable bed was beckoning to him. He looked forward to the snowy white clean sheets, which would feel so good to him when he crawled into that welcoming softness. It had been a very long day and night and he was ready to enjoy some relaxing hours of sleep.

Without further ado, he undressed and dimmed the light. Slipping in between the sheets, his last thought before sleep swept over him was the lovely vision of Aimee Aragon coming to haunt him in the most pleasant way. How sweet it was to let his imagination run wild and pretend that her sweet nectar lips were kissing him good night!

The bright shining sun could not invade the heavy drapes drawn across the double windows of his bedroom, but Mano was one of those individuals who rarely slept more than six hours. As the hands of the clock moved to the hour of seven and even though it had been midnight when he arrived at La Casa Grande, he woke up.

Without any hesitation, he leaped out of bed to move to the windows, opening the draperies to allow the sun to shine brightly into his room. He stood like a magnificent cat, stretching his firm muscled body slowly and unhurriedly.

Lingering there at the window and looking out at the grounds of the courtyard below, he had to confess it was a glorious sight. The verdant splendor of the gardens below were a breathtaking sight, along with all the colorful blooming plants and flowers. The magnificent fountain in the center of the courtyard had been shipped all the way from Italy as a special surprise for his mother, Mano recalled.

Minerva had told him that his mother loved to sit there on the little iron grilled benches to watch the birds as they bathed themselves in the water and she'd toss them crumbs of bread to feast on.

As he stood there now at his window, he could envision her with her dark, sultry beauty sitting there tossing her crumbs of bread. She was a warm, loving woman, Minera had said. These very vivid descriptions of his mother were appreciated by Mano because it seemed his father found it difficult to discuss his wife. This puzzled the son.

As he'd become a man and known his first woman, Mano had wondered about the relationship between the woman Minerva had described to him and his very somber, stern father. He wondered how they'd been attracted to one another when they were young and if this had all changed after they were married.

Turning from the window, Mano decided he had spent enough time in his private musings about the past. So he went over to the long, low oak chest and opened the drawer to pull out one of the freshly laundered white linen shirts Minerva tediously ironed for him. With it, he wore a pair of the black twill pants that molded perfectly to his fine trim physique.

Now that he was dressed he wasted precious little time putting the brush to his thick mane of black hair. Mano's thoughts were occupied by that delicious food Minerva would be serving down in the dining room. That was enough to prod him into fast action to get downstairs.

As it would happen, he was ahead of his father and Mario, but his brother had never been the early riser. In fact, the whole dining room was deserted as he ambled in and took a seat at his usual place at the long table. He noticed immediately the lovely fresh-cut flowers in the colorful pottery container. Minerva never forgot that long-standing request of his mother's. Fresh flowers on the table to start the day off, she'd insisted of her housekeeper.

The delicate little purple flowers mingled with the white and yellow blossoms reminded him of the beautiful Aimee's gorgeous eyes. These were his thoughts when he heard a delighted shriek coming from the direction of the doorway, and he knew it was Minerva even before he turned around. He roared with laughter as he quickly leaped out of the chair to

47

help her support the tray she was about to drop.

"Picaro—Mano! You gave me such a start," she muttered. But a pleased smile was already coming to her face as he took the heavy tray out of her hands to carry it to a serving cart near the long table. Shaking her head, she gave out a light-hearted chuckle, declaring, "You will never change, will you, Mano? Here you pop up so unexpected this morning."

He smiled and bent to place a kiss on her cheek. "Now, don't you tell me that you aren't tickled to see me, Minerva? You know I can't stay away from you too long."

"You can't stay away from my good cooking, young man. This is Minerva—remember? I know all your little tricks," she said, giving him a playful swat on the back.

"But, Minerva, I'm learning new tricks all the time," he teased her as she turned to pour a cup of coffee for him. As she placed the cup by the side of his plate, she remarked, "Oh, I can certainly believe that, Manuelo Mateo!"

The two of them continued to have their pleasant chat as she prepared his usual breakfast fare from her dishes on the serving cart.

Rapaciously, Mano began devouring the food on his plate and swearing to Minerva that no one could cook like her. He was taking the last bite on his plate when Carlos came through the doorway, followed by Mario.

It took strong willpower to hide the exuberance Carlos Mateo felt when he saw his fine-looking younger son sitting at the dining table in the seat where he should be sitting every morning if Carlos had his way about things. In the privacy of his study so many late nights, Carlos Mateo had searched his mind for the answer and the solution to how he could convince his son that La Casa Grande was his future and he should be taking an active role now that he was past twenty years of age.

Instead of the warm, loving voice that would have reflected his true feelings, Carlos casually addressed his son, "Well, Mano, I see you've decided to come home."

Slowly, Mano's black eyes met with those of his father's and

48

that slow, easy smile creased his handsome face as he greeted him after a few weeks' absence from the ranch. "Couldn't stand it any longer, Father. Had to get back for some of Minerva's good cooking." He turned in her direction with a grin of mischief and a wink of his eyes. Then he turned in Mario's direction and greeted him with his usual brotherly warmth. "Morning, Mario."

Mario never could resist that happy-go-lucky brother of his, with that winning smile and friendly nature, and he went to him, giving him a warm embrace and telling him it was good to have him home again.

"Good to see you, too, Mario," Mano told him.

Mario moved around the table to take his seat; Carlos had already taken his place at the head of the table. He watched his two sons, marveling at them for they were sons any man would have been proud to have sired. No father could have asked for a more devoted son than Mario, and such a handsome young man he was.

How did he describe Mano, his handful from the time he was a small tot? Mano was a striking figure of a young man, the dashing caballero. He had a certain magnetic charm that made all the senoritas fawn over him, and men found him a most interesting, entertaining individual. This charisma had been Mano's since he was sixteen, Carlos realized.

Mano could be anything he wished to be and succeed, but Carlos had seen no signs yet that his younger son was making any goals for himself. This is what irritated the very serious-minded Carlos Mateo, ruled all his life by the conventional Latin customs of his ancestors.

Mano lingered there at the dining table while his father and brother breakfasted. Knowing that his father would soon be suggesting he go see the magnificent new bulls in the corrals, Mano made his hasty farewell to the two of them by using the excuse that he was going to take a morning drive over the countryside.

"Too beautiful a morning to waste," he declared, making his

swift exit before either of them could utter a protest.

It was not the lovely countryside Mano was interested in this morning. Since the previous night, he could not get the beautiful Aimee off his mind and it was the Chateau L'Aragon he was planning to visit.

The atmosphere around the Aragon breakfast table was not a pleasant one, and Aimee was making her own hasty excuse to be gone. As Mano had told his father and brother, she was telling her family that she was going for a ride on Lady. Before her overprotective father could voice his protest, she was assuring him she would stay close to the grounds of the estate.

She wanted some time to think, and to do that she knew she must get away from the house. Never did she like to displease her doting father, but she detested the thought of going to the Governor's Ball with that despicable Fred Bigler and maybe time would give her the answer.

Now that she'd met Mark Perez, the image of Fred Bigler was more repulsive. So before the subject of Bigler brought on a horrible, explosive fight between them, Aimee rushed from the dining room, leaving her mother, father, and two brothers still eating their breakfast.

"She eats like a bird," Paul grumbled in a disgruntled mood.

Lisette knew exactly why her daughter had made such a fast exit. "Best you not try to clip her wing, *mon cher*. She wishes to be as free as the birds flying there in the sky."

He knew she spoke with wisdom, but he did not wish his daughter to be as free as the birds in the sky. A girl like Aimee could get into horrible trouble. She had to be protected for her own good, he reasoned privately.

In that soft, sweet voice of hers, Lisette reminded him, as she did so often lately, "Aimee is not like other girls, Paul."

Chapter 6

Once she sat astride Lady and rode away from the stable, Aimee felt unhampered by the demands of her father. She felt free, like a heavy burden had been lifted from her back. Her long silver-blond hair was blowing back loose and free, for she wore no hat nor had she tied it back with a ribbon as she often did.

It was one of those glorious California days, with the sun shining down brilliantly on the rolling verdant valley. Just outside the walled courtyard fence that enclosed the grounds of their house, she reined her horse into the open field flourishing with its numerous varieties of wildflowers. Perhaps it was the climate here that made everything grow so marvelously.

This was what she needed, she told herself as she rode alone over the countryside. If her father thought she was going to be kept a prisoner in the house or inside the walls of the courtyard, then he had better change his thinking. She knew what had happened to her last night was going to make him even more protective now, and she had to admit she had been

51

utterly shocked and unprepared when that ferocious-looking man accosted her.

Neither was she prepared or expecting to meet the dashing, exciting stranger who'd come to rescue her and take her safely home. Mark Perez had had a strange effect on her, and when she was in her bedroom later that night, she questioned just how safe she'd be with him if they were alone for any length of time. She'd seen the devious look in his eyes, and she had to confess how wild and reckless she felt with his overwhelming maleness so close to her.

It was even obvious to her maid, Jolie, that she was exhilarated and stirred up with a fever heat about something. The two of them being so close in age, Aimee confessed to her, "Oh, Jolie, I met the most exciting man tonight."

"You did, mademoiselle?" The petite little maid came alive with her own excitement and curiosity.

"*Oui.* The blackest eyes I've ever seen and the most devilish look out of them. I'd have sworn he was undressing me as they moved from my head to my toes, Jolie." She gave out a girlish gusto of giggles. Jolie joined her by laughing too.

"No wonder you are so radiant, mademoiselle. He sounds *magnifique!*"

"He looks *magnifique,* too." Aimee quickly started giving her maid a very vivid description of Mark Perez.

"Perhaps the Chateau L'Aragon will not seem so dull to you now, eh?" Jolie smiled and gave her a wink of her eye, for she knew more than anyone here at the Aragon residence just how bored Aimee had been since returning from Paris. It was this that formed the unusual bond of friendship between the two of them. Often they'd talk when Jolie prepared her baths or turned her bed down at night.

"Perhaps you are right, Jolie," Aimee declared. A short time later, the little maid had left her room for the night.

But Jolie was quick to point out to Aimee the next morning, before the young girl had gone downstairs to have breakfast with her family, that the glow was still on her face. It was still there and that was why the subject of Fred Bigler was so repulsive to her. She could not bear to think about being courted by that man. She couldn't care at all that he was some relative of the governor of the state. Just because her father was favorably impressed did not mean she had to feel that way. But how did she convince him?

Maybe she would speak to her mother and seek her help in interceding on her behalf about this thing with Fred Bigler. For now, she wished to forget about him and just daydream about that handsome devil, Mark Perez.

When she and Lady came to a spot where a grotesque-looking old oak tree stood and the earth had a thick covering of grass, she pulled up on the reins and the palomino came to an abrupt halt.

"Ah, Lady, it looks inviting here. Shall we take a rest?" She gave her silver-white mane a gentle pat of affection and the mare bobbed her head up and down as though she understood exactly what her mistress had said.

She gave out a little laugh. "I see you agree." She leaped off Lady to secure the reins to a small sapling nearby before she sunk to the ground to lean up against the trunk of the oak. She snaked her hands around the back of her neck, lifted her long tresses and tossed them to one side of her shoulder, and gazed up at the cloudless blue sky. A sublime, serene feeling washed over her and she closed her eyes to give out a deep sigh of complete contentment.

There was no serene contentment within the hot-blooded virile man observing her a short distance away. He was tantalized by the sight of her and he wanted her. God, did he want her!

As he spurred his thoroughbred to move, he was a man driven by the force of those desires swelling within him, desires he knew would not be satisfied until he took the honey from those tempting lips and held that sensuous body close to his, as he had done last night. Mano was drawn to the spot where Aimee Aragon sat under the old oak, so devastatingly tempting and tantalizing.

Aimee was thinking of her aunt in faraway Paris. So often they'd spoken of romance and men, for her *Tante* Denise was a very sophisticated, worldly-wise lady. She talked freely and easily about certain subjects that Aimee's mother would have found difficult and embarrassing to discuss.

Aimee knew why she was thinking about her vivacious aunt today. She was remembering a late night conversation they'd shared after all Denise's dinner guests had left her townhouse. As they'd sat leisurely listening to the rain pelting against the window panes, Aimee had asked her aunt how she'd known when she was in love with a man.

The very attractive older woman smiled at her niece, and while she did not mind discussing men and the affairs of the heart with her, she'd dare not tell her how many lovers she'd had. However, she did tell her, "Ah, *cherie,* when you are in love with a man, it is like nothing else in the whole world. He makes you feel like no other has ever made you feel before. His kisses are so much more exciting. *N'est-ce pas?*"

"*Oui, Tante* Denise," Aimee had replied to her aunt.

"I thought you would. You see, my pet, I know a few young gentlemen who have stolen a kiss or two from you since you've been here with me in Paris. I saw that rogue Andre kiss you that night in the foyer, and if he would have thrilled you, there would have been stars in your eyes the next morning. I would have seen them and you would have been asking me some questions. Am I not right?"

Aimee answered her with a giggle, declaring she was right.

What would her aunt have seen in her eyes this morning? Aimee wondered as she sat under the oak tree, and she thought she knew the answer. She would have seen a young woman alive, fascinated by the irresistible charm of Mark Perez. Never had a man thrilled her so!

Her violet eyes opened wide to see the grey horse with its black tail and mane galloping toward her. She knew who the rider was even before she could make out his handsome face. It

54

was as though her secret wish had been granted.

Aimee felt herself trembling with the wild excitement churning within her, because she knew soon he would be here beside her. A giddiness engulfed her as she sat there waiting for him to cover the distance dividing them. By now, she could see the unruly hair falling down over one side of his forehead and the broad grin on his tanned face. Already, his arm was raised up in the air and his hand was waving to her.

She remained there on the ground as she returned his wave, the reason being she feared her legs might not hold her up because she knew they felt like jelly. In that brief moment she had before he was leaping off the thoroughbred, she chided herself harshly for being such a silly dunce. So he was tall, dark, and handsome, she told herself, but that didn't mean she should act like a fool.

She quickly reminded herself of all the debonair gentlemen, gracefully charming, that she'd met at her *Tante* Denise's home. But all her lectures did no good when he agilely leaped off his horse and sauntered toward her.

He looked different this morning, in his tight-fitted black pants and the thin white shirt opened at the neckline to display an exposed cluster of curly black chest hair.

"Good morning, senorita. May I say you are as gloriously beautiful as the day itself?" His black eyes slowly savored the sight of her sitting there on the ground. He thought to himself that it was the perfect setting for her here under the oak tree with the sun shining brightly. Little purple wildflowers dotted the thick green grass she sat upon. He noticed that she did not wear the usual divided skirt but an extra-full, gathered floral one, with a soft sheer batiste blouse of white, which had delicate embroidery around the neck and puffed sleeves. He liked the fact that she wore no hat to hide her lovely flowing hair nor did she have it rolled in a coil.

"Nice to see you, Mark, and a surprise, too, I might add," Aimee replied.

"May I join you?" he asked, only to appear gallant because

55

nothing would have made him leave the spot.

"Of course. Please do!" She gave him a sweet smile.

He sunk down on the grass beside her, making a point of sitting close to her. If it were possible, she looked more beautiful in the daylight than she had the previous night, he thought as he gazed at that face.

"A favorite place of yours?" he quizzed her.

"Not really. Lady and I were just out for a ride and it looked inviting, so we stopped. Besides, I promised Papa I would not go too far from the grounds."

He heard the spark of rebellion and resentment reflected in her voice as she spoke and he sensed instantly she did not like being ordered or demanded to obey rules. Perhaps they were two of a kind.

"Well, you can hardly blame him for wanting to protect you, Aimee. Last night will leave a fear in him for a long time to come, knowing his beautiful daughter could have been harmed."

"Oh, I understand, but I can't smother inside the house day and night. I just couldn't!"

A crooked grin came slowly to his face as he watched her every expression as she spoke. She was a divine little creature! His arms ached to take her right then and there but he knew that would not be too smart. After all, he'd had a fair share of women and he knew it was only the fool who rushed in too fast, giving vent to his amorous intentions. It could spoil everything.

He gave out a hearty laugh, "No, I can't see you restrained on anything you really wanted to do, Aimee Aragon. That is what makes you so enchanting and delightful."

She tilted her head with a coquettish air about her that she was not aware of as she taunted him, "Now tell me, Mark Perez, you just met me last night, so how would you know so much about me?"

He moved closer until his lips were almost touching hers, and she felt her heart pounding wildly from such nearness. His eyes gazed into hers, as though he wished to drown in them, and he murmured softly, "Ah, *chiquita*, I have strange powers. Have you not suspected it?" She knew he was teasing her but she could believe it to be the truth. He did have a strange effect on her.

When her half-parted lips were about to speak, Mano gave way to the overwhelming urge to kiss her and his lips moved to capture hers. Oh, so sweet it was as their lips met in that first glorious kiss! It was a long, lingering kiss, with Mano's sensuous lips gently teasing and coaxing her with tender persuasion.

When his mouth finally released her lips, she felt breathless and gasped his name. His heated lips were still caressing her flushed cheek and his hands pressed her back, urging her closer to him.

"Oh, Aimee, your lips are sweeter than honey," his deep voice sighed softly. "Tell me you liked my kissing you. Tell me, *chiquita*."

Oh, how his masculine heat consumed her! She could not deny the truth. "I loved your kiss, Mark. You know that," she told him in almost a whisper. Could he feel her heart pounding as fast and hard as it felt to her right now? she wondered.

That was all Mano needed to hear to seek her waiting lips again. This time his kiss was fired with more passion, and when he felt her sweet response, he was pleased. Ardently, his mouth and hands caressed her now. His tongue tantalized her lips and she tingled with the wild excitement of this new, wonderful experience. Mano sensed that she'd never known such a kiss as this before with any man, and it thrilled him to no end.

Her lovely body moved so naturally with an abandoned surrender that Mano was burning with the heat of desire. He was a man driven by a force he could not control. His hands had caressed the warm flesh of her breasts and he'd felt her arch fiercely against him, so he knew the sensations he'd stirred within her. He removed the barrier of the batiste blouse as well as the cumbersome floral skirt.

Now that his bared chest could press against her naked flesh the heat and flames soared higher and hotter.

"I want you, Aimee. I want you as a man wants a woman. I want to make love to you in the most intimate way," he huskily declared as his firm body pulsed eagerly against her. "Stop me now, if you must, or it will be too late."

The force and power of him were too much for her. She was too intoxicated by the spell he'd cast over her. As far as Aimee was concerned, at that moment nothing existed except her and Mark in their own little private paradise. It was not like anything she'd ever imagined in her wildest dreams, and she could not bear to stop it all now.

She gave him her answer by raising up her lips to meet his in a kiss, and that was all the answer Mano needed. So as their thighs entwined, his hands played the same magic and ecstasy around the velvet softness he must soon invade to usher her into that world of rapture where he wished to take her.

Once he took her through that threshold, he would give her the most wonderful pleasure she'd ever know, he vowed silently.

So gentle and patient he was, even though it took all his strong will to restrain the raging fires consuming him. But when he felt the time was right, he moved to bury himself between her thighs and enter her. There was only one brief moment that she stiffened and trembled, but he gentled and soothed her with words of love.

As he'd hoped, she quickly joined him once again, feeling that height of ecstatic pleasure, and together they soared to a peak of that strange, wonderful world of lovers. They lingered there in that rapturous splendor for a few precious moments before descending back down to this world.

Mano would have yearned for the wonderful interlude to have lasted longer!

Chapter 7

The peace and serenity of the lovers' paradise was interrupted by the sound of approaching riders. The beating pounding of horses' hooves moving across the valley was enough to bring Mano alive and alert. "Aimee, someone is coming! Get yourself put together as quick as you can!"

It was not exactly how he'd planned to bid her farewell, but if the riders should be her father and brothers, it could prove to be a most embarrassing scene. As far as he was concerned, he didn't give a damn. By the time she was sitting up, slipping the blouse over her head, and scrambling to yank up her floral skirt, he had led Demonio from the sapling where he'd been secured, so he could ride into the nearby forest.

All he had to hear her say was that it was her brothers, Emile and Armand, to urge him to quickly mount Demonio and make a hasty departure toward the concealing woods a short distance away. He put the spurs to Demonio's side to go as fast as he could. It was only when he reached the dense cover of the trees that he slowed his pace.

Madre de Dios, it was not going to be a simple thing to court the beautiful Aimee! But any price he paid was surely well worth it. Never had he felt such exaltation as he had this day, but now he had to wonder how she was feeling about it all. If they had not been forced to separate so quickly, he'd hoped to get her reaction. Now, she'd probably consider him a horrible cad who'd tucked his tail and ran, fearing to face the dangerous sight of her brothers. That was not it at all.

He would not have minded to face the whole Aragon family and tell them how he felt about their daughter. After today, he worshipped her even more. She was a dream come true, the ravishing love goddess he'd always imagined to find.

He would never forget this day that she surrendered to him, giving him her gift of virginity. How proud he was to know this! Being a Latin, he could not deny that this was very important to him. A man might conquer many women, but one lady was the wife and the mother of a man's children. Mano saw in Aimee Aragon a woman of fierce fire and passion, as well as a lady he'd claim as his wife.

From a spot in the woods, he watched the riders approach the old oak where Aimee was. She was standing up with all her clothes on by the time they arrived. If he could have seen her lovely face, he could well imagine that she was looking up at her brothers astride their horses in wide-eyed wonderment of one so innocent as to what all the furor was about. She was a sly little fox, he was sure of after last night, listening to her older brothers praise her. They adored their younger sister.

He continued to watch the group gathered there by the oak tree until Aimee mounted her palomino, Lady, to ride with them in the direction of her home. Only then did he rein Demonio in the direction of La Casa Grande.

How long could he keep up this charade of being Mark Perez instead of Mano Mateo? That happy-go-lucky nature of his told him not to worry, but to play it one day at a time. So that was what he decided to do.

Had she not affected him so deeply he could have been

satisfied by the fact that he'd done what he had yearned to do. He'd possessed and conquered her, but Mano wanted so much more from Aimee. She was not like the other women he'd bedded. He could not turn his back and walk away. He didn't want to walk away, even though he knew she was an Aragon and he was a Mateo. That was enough to be a hell of a challenge! He was prepared to face it and fight it to the bitter end.

When he rode onto the grounds of La Casa Grande, he spotted his father and Mario out by the corrals. Mano instinctively knew they were viewing the prized bulls to be shipped very soon to Mexico. Since there was no way he could escape encountering them, he reined Demonio up toward the corral fence.

Mario turned to see him first and called out to him, "Mano, come here! You must see this one!"

Carlos responded now to his younger son and gave him a nod of his head as Mano led Demonio up to the place on the fence where they perched.

Mano saw the animal they were so enthused about and did as they both expected him to do, by declaring, "Ah, *si,* he is a fine one! He should put them on a fine showing in the *corrida de toros.*"

Carlos Mateo looked at his younger son in a most sober, serious manner as he spoke, and his deep voice reflected the depth of his emotions. "This is a part of you, Mano, even though you seem to ignore it. This is your heritage—the raising of our fine Mateo bulls."

How often he'd heard those words! How many times they'd been drilled into him since the age of twelve Mano could not remember.

He was not wishing to fuss with his father and he certainly was not ready to leave La Casa Grande again so soon. But that stubborn streak in him would not allow him to remain silent as Mario would have chosen to do under similar circumstances. In that usual headstrong, firm air of his, he replied to his father, "I have two heritages, Father. I am Spanish and I am

61

Portuguese. Perhaps I will become a fisherman up on San Francisco Bay." He reined his dappled grey stallion on toward the stables. Demonio swished his black tail with the same arrogance as his master as he pranced toward the stables.

Sensing his horse's mood, Mano rubbed the silky black mane and declared, "At least you understand me, Demonio. We do not need the bulls or the bullfights to excite us, do we?"

He was barely through the huge double doors of the stables, leading Demonio by the reins to his stall, when he heard the accented shriek of a young Mexican named Paco.

"Senor—Senor Mano, I did not know you'd returned," the young man called out to him as he came hastily down the ladder of the loft.

"Ah, amigo, how are you?" Mano greeted the young man who he'd taken an instant liking to from the day his father had hired him on here at the ranchero. The young Mexican had seemed to form an instant hero worship of Mano.

"I am fine, senor," he responded with a broad grin on his face. He walked forward toward Mano, wiping his hands on the tail of his faded blue shirt before he extended his right one to shake Mano's.

There was a certain humility about the young man that impressed Mano. Paco's fine features had a certain quality to them that made Mano question his background. He could have been the son of a fine Mexican family, like so many of the Latin ranchers living there in the valley. Paco could have been dressed in the same proper attire and put in the same proper surroundings as Mano had been brought up in, and then he could have been a Mateo. Fate had been unfair to Paco.

"I think I'll leave Demonio in your hands, Paco. I think he likes you. How is your young colt coming along by now? Is he out of that awkward stage yet—all legs?" Mano gave out a hearty laugh.

"Ah, *si*, senor. He is becoming as graceful as a dancer," Paco declared proudly.

"Must take after his master then, because I remember our

last fiesta here and I saw you dancing with the pretty senorita, Paco. You have the grace of a dancer," Mano pointed out to him. It was true, for Paco had the trim, slim body of a dancer, and the grace and movement of a flamenco dancer.

"Ah, *mucho gracias*, senor! You are always so kind to me and I appreciate it." He bowed his head, overwhelmed with the senor's praise.

"I am only speaking the truth, Paco. Kindness has nothing to do with it." He spoke for a few more minutes with the young man before bidding him good-bye and giving him the promise that they would share some time together now that he was home again. That was enough to delight Paco.

Aimee was glad that her brothers could not see the hard pounding of her heart as they arrived at the spot where she stood under the old oak. She sent up a silent prayer that she'd managed to get her blouse and skirt back on. Her dainty hands played the part of the brush as they ran through her long, loose hair.

As Mano had suspected, she stood, fluttering her long thick lashes and looking up at her brothers with her lovely violet eyes reflecting surprise as to why they were there seeking her out.

With wide-eyed innocence, she greeted them, "Emile, Armand, what are you up to?"

"What are *we* up to? Dear God, Aimee! What are *you* up to? Papa was concerned after you were gone so long," Emile angrily barked at her. After all, he and his crew of men had been pulled out of the fields to hunt for her.

"I am up to nothing other than a pleasant ride on a delightful day, Emile. Papa will have to learn to accept this. What is the matter with him, Emile?"

Emile gave her an understanding smile, because he appreciated her feelings as well as his father's. "He just doesn't want something happening to a daughter he adores, Aimee.

63

Last night was a most harrowing experience for him."

"But I had such freedom in Paris, Emile," she protested.

"I know, little sister. I truly do. Come . . . shall we get you home and ease an old man's mind?" he urged with a gentle persuasion she could not refuse.

Emile was such a good person and such a devoted brother, she realized. She was a most fortunate young lady to have two fine brothers ready to fight her cause. Realizing this, she gave him no fuss as she moved to mount Lady and ride with him and his men back to the house.

Many thoughts paraded through her mind as she rode with Emile and his workers from the Chateau L'Aragon. It was obvious that there were no visible changes in the sister that he adored and she was grateful for that. Guilt did wash over her when she thought about the liberties she'd allowed Mark Perez to take. Emile and Armand would probably think she had acted wantonly with this man who was a stranger she'd known for less than twenty-four hours. How could she ever explain it to them when she could not explain it to herself?

There was only one person who would have possibly understood what she had done this afternoon. It was *Tante* Denise.

Emile had instantly noted a certain air about his sister that he questioned. He was far more intuitive than his brother, Armand. Somehow, he felt Aimee was at this particuliar spot for a rendezvous with the young man, Mark Perez, and he and his men had spoiled it all for her. Never did he figure that the meeting had already taken place. Her quiet mood was because she was disappointed, he figured, as they rode toward the estate.

Emile's thinking was so wrong. Her quiet mood was a reflection, as she mused each and every moment of the time she'd spent with Mark. It was glorious! She did not regret a thing, and if that made her a wanton, she did not care.

If she were in Paris and she told her *Tante* Denise what had happened between her and Mark Perez, she was certain she would have heard her aunt exclaim with most dramatic delight, "Ooh, la, la." She surely wished she were there right now instead of California!

Now that she'd experienced a different way of life with her aunt, which blended more with her rebel thinking, Aimee knew she could never conform to the conventional ways of her parents anymore. It was as if fate had deemed she meet Mark Perez at this time in her life. Once again, she recalled her aunt's comments on the subject of love and romance. Aimee knew her mother and father would not have approved of Denise's very liberal lifestyle. But after all, it was her father's idea that she live with his sister all those months. However, the sophistication he'd hoped she'd acquire being in Paris all those months was probably more than he'd bargained for when he allowed her this privilege.

Maybe he'd forgotten his own sister, Aimee concluded, and her way of life. Perhaps Paul Aragon would not allow himself to admit that his own sister was a courtesan and he turned his head, pretending it were not true. Aimee might have been naive, but she'd understood Denise's ways shortly after her arrival in Paris.

It did not matter to Aimee that her aunt was a whore because she adored her. As far as she was concerned, a whore was a whore. Denise was a high-classed whore!

The thing that had enraged Aimee the night before, when she'd seen her father look down his aristocratic, snobbish nose at Mark Perez, was something she abhorred. She yearned to cry out to him that he should know about his own sister. Did it cleanse you just because you mingled with the elite and wealthy? She could not accept that!

That was why Fred Bigler repulsed her so. Just because he was the relative of the governor of the state did not make him acceptable to her as he seemed to be to her father. She planned to fight him all the way about that!

It mattered not to her about Mark Perez's background. She'd prefer a cottage with Mark Perez to a palatial mansion as

Fred Bigler's wife. Like it or not, that was what her father must understand about her, Aimee Aragon felt. That was the way it would be!

To be a grand lady meant nothing to her. To be a lady loved as Mark had loved her this day meant everything to her! This was her heart's desire!

Chapter 8

On the ride back to the Chateau L'Aragon, Aimee surveyed the verdant hillsides of California. Never had they looked so beautiful to her, for now she was in love for the very first time in her life. She knew she would always see that live oak tree back there in the valley in a different way after today. Those sinuous branches had cast a net of seclusion for that romantic interlude with Mark.

No longer did she have to wonder or imagine what it was like to have a man make love to her. Now she knew, and it was so much more than she'd expected that she was still in a state of giddiness. Those lofty heights of ecstasy she'd shared with Mark Perez had made her feel like she was up in the blue, cloudless sky above.

As her brother Emile had chanced to glance in her direction, he saw the glowing loveliness of her face. He had to admit that she'd never looked more beautiful. But he knew, too, that their mother would admonish her when they returned for not wearing her wide-brimmed hat to shade her lovely gardenia-white skin. She was always cautioning Aimee about that.

"You forgot your hat again, little sister," he shouted over to her as they rode along side by side.

"I know, because I detest a hat as you well know, Emile," she smiled with a twinkle in her violet eyes.

He wondered how this gay mood of hers would change when they arrived at the house and she found out they had a guest there. That was one of the reasons their father had sent him out to search for her. More and more, he found himself in league with Aimee about Fred Bigler. Something about the man rubbed him wrong, but he could not put his finger on it. Armand did not agree with him.

As their mother was always saying about such things, time would tell. He would agree with that and wait to see. But he had to confess that he hoped his father did not push Aimee into a marriage with the man too hastily. He rather suspected that if Bigler was not a relative of the governor of the state, his father would not have been so impressed by this young man.

As far as Emile knew, Fred held no position nor did he put in a day's work in an office or a business. He recalled how his father had always advocated that it was honorable for a man to labor and sweat to make his living. God knows, he and Armand had worked and sweated in his vineyards to make their fortune this family now enjoyed. But neither of them had much time left to enjoy themselves. Lately, Emile had been thinking about this, for he would soon be thirty years of age and he'd known very few women. The same was true for Armand.

So why did his father find this Bigler the ideal suitor for their sister Aimee? Emile had been wondering. Was his age affecting his thinking, perhaps?

As she and Emile rode toward the stables and the workers veered off in an opposite direction to go back to the fields, she did not notice Fred's buggy. Emile realized this as they turned over their horses to the stableboy.

Emile had to make up the hour he'd taken off to go out looking for her and he did not accompany her from the stables. "I'll see you later, little sister. Just let Papa know that you're home safe and sound, eh?" he playfully admonished her.

"I shall, Emile. I—I'm sorry if the trouble of going to find me will cause you to have to work longer this evening."

"Do not worry about that. It was not all that long. Now, I don't intend to do this everyday, I must warn you, *ma petite*. I will turn you over my lap and give you a firm whipping, I promise," he chuckled as he sauntered away.

She never doubted for a minute that her husky brother could have done it with ease, but he would not have dared to lay a hand on her and she knew that, too.

As she left the stable, she broke into a jaunty, swaying pace. Never had she been so aware of her femininity before, and the look on her face and the movements of her curvy body were expressing this wonderful new feeling that possessed Aimee Aragon.

At that moment she would have sworn that nothing could dent her high spirits, but a few seconds later that was exactly what happened as her eyes recognized the fancy little buggy and the roan mare. Fred Bigler was paying one of his calls at the Chateau L'Aragon.

Dear God, she didn't want to put up with his dismal company this afternoon! But what could she do to avoid it? she pondered.

Cautiously, she moved through the gate and around to the side of the house. Like a thief in the night, she slipped among the camellia bushes and the green and yellow japonica plants to get to the side door. If she could manage to get upstairs without being seen, she'd stay in her room without letting her return be known until he finally left, she reasoned.

As she entered the kitchen, she motioned to the two servants not to speak or address her. They seemed to understand that she did not want it known she was in the house. Because she'd become the darling of all the house servants, they obeyed her, giving a soft giggle. She gave them one of her sweet, charming smiles as she went on toward the back stairs.

When she reached the second landing and was making her

way down the carpeted hallway, she heaved a deep sigh of relief. She figured she'd spared herself a wasted hour or two in the company of Fred.

As she slipped through her bedroom door as quiet as a mouse, Jolie's voice startled her as she addressed her, "Mademoiselle, you are back and expected downstairs."

"Shut up! I know it, but I do not wish to be downstairs," she cautioned in a whisper-soft voice to her maid.

A slow grin came to Jolie's face, for she understood what her young mistress was about. "So you know you have a guest?"

"I do. I plan to stay right here until he leaves, and I pray it is soon." She requested that Jolie prepare a warm bath for her because she felt the need for it. After all, she could hardly be expected to rush downstairs to greet Fred if she was in the middle of a bath.

"*Oui*, mademoiselle. I will put some of the jasmine oil in it you like. A lady cannot be disturbed when she is attending to her toilette," she grinned, winking her dark eye.

Aimee broke into a girlish giggle, for they understood one another so well. As her maid turned to do as she'd requested, Aimee began to undress.

It was one of the longest and most leisurely baths Aimee had ever taken. As Jolie was helping her into her silk robe of robin's egg blue, a commotion caught their attention. It seemed to be voices below Aimee's bedroom window, and Jolie rushed to see what it was all about. She motioned frantically for Aimee to come to the window. There was a smile of delight on the little maid's face.

Aimee knew why when she looked down at the garden area below. Her father was ushering a disgruntled Bigler down the stone walkway as he was obviously making his departure. She watched as her father bid him farewell and walked back toward the house. Ah, what a displeased look he wore on his face! There was no doubt that Paul Aragon was angry.

The sly little Aimee knew she must be prepared for an unpleasant encounter when she went downstairs for their evening meal, but at least she was not unaware of what she faced. There was time to plot how she would tactfully try to soothe his ruffled feathers, she thought to herself, watching him move to the entrance. A smug smile creased her pretty face. As much as she adored him, he could not mold and bend her to his will. This would be hard for Paul Aragon to accept!

Paul Aragon was the lord and master of his household and his lands. He expected that his orders should be carried out without question. They were obeyed by his dutiful sons and his devoted wife, as well as the workers in his vineyard.

As Aimee sat thinking about this, she guessed she was the only person who defied him by disobeying his demands of her. Oh, she knew there were times when her mother did not agree with him, but Lisette rarely spoke up to tell him so. Often when she'd witnessed such a scene it had vexed Aimee and she'd wanted to scream out at her mother to say what she truly felt, but of course she hadn't. She would not do anything to hurt that sweet, gentle mother of hers, who was just too nice for her own good.

She was the first to admit that she'd not inherited her mother's nature. But neither was she like her father. Perhaps it was her *Tante* Denise she was like.

Later, she picked out the frock she wanted to wear downstairs for the evening meal—the plum-colored one with the white lacy ruffling around the squared neckline and the short puffed sleeves. The calculating little conniver had a very definite reason for selecting that particular one. She knew her father liked the dress. He always remarked about it making her look like a little girl. And that was the image she intended to project this evening.

She did not wish him to see her as his blossomed grown-up daughter, to be courted by that boring, dull Fred Bigler. But there in the privacy of her bedroom she could not suppress a mischievous giggle, knowing after this afternoon she was certainly no little innocent girl.

When she called on Jolie to style her long hair, she gave

careful consideration to that, too, and had her put a lovely white ribbon around the long tresses pulled to the back of her head. Small tendrils curled at her temples, and Aimee was well pleased with the final results.

To be sure that she would have all the time it would take, she'd begun to dress earlier than usual. Looking at the clock over on the chest, she realized, now that she was ready to leave her room, it was almost an hour before dinner would be served.

It did not startle her when she heard the soft rap on her door and she knew before she opened it that it would be her mother. It was always about this time that Lisette came upstairs, once she'd given the final orders for the meal, to refresh herself before joining her family at their dinner table. For as long as Aimee could recall, this had always been her mother's routine.

As her daughter's door opened and Lisette was intending to inquire where she'd been all afternoon and inform her what a rage her father was in, she was distracted by the girlish loveliness of her fair-haired daughter. "Ah, *ma petite*, how very, very pretty you are. Why, you remind me of the lovely pink and purple fuchsias down in the garden."

"Why, thank you, Mother. I consider that a lovely compliment because they are such beautiful flowers."

"Oh, Aimee, you probably aren't going to be too pleased to hear what else I have to tell you, but your father is most unhappy that you made no appearance when Mr. Bigler came by this afternoon. He felt that he left feeling very insulted, and this disturbed your father very much. Where were you so long, dear?" her mother inquired in that soft voice of hers.

"Oh, Emile found me and Lady down in the valley. I had not ridden so far. I'd promised you I wouldn't. But I heard father and Fred talking there in the parlor and I saw no sight of you, so I just came on upstairs, feeling the need of a bath after my ride. I hardly looked like greeting a guest." She played a most convincing role.

Lisette listened to her excuse and was convinced by the sincerity of her words that she was truly concerned about the way she had looked. "Well, you must tell your father this so he will understand, dear."

"Oh, I shall, mother. By the time Jolie had prepared my bath and it was taken, I heard Fred's buggy leaving, so I just stayed on up here in my room."

Giving her a warm smile and a pat on the cheek, Lisette told her daughter she would see her later at dinner and left to go to her own bedroom.

Aimee turned to go back over to her dressing table to dab some of the jasmine water behind her ears and on her wrists.

Her mother's response was exactly what she'd hoped for, and now she was feeling very assured and confident that her father's mood would mellow, too.

She was soon to find out!

Chapter 9

Emile was an easygoing young Frenchman who'd known nothing all his life but the hard work and long days in his father's vineyards, and never had he complained. But tonight when he had joined his father in the parlor, as he usually did to enjoy a glass of wine before their meal, and was so harshly rebuked for not carrying out Paul's request, he felt anger— an anger like he'd never known before.

"I brought her back home, Papa. Now where she went or what she did after I escorted her as far as the stables I do not know. I had work to attend to so I did not escort her into the house," Emile retorted in a tone Paul was not familiar with from his son.

Paul Aragon was wondering, as he gazed into Emile's eyes, if he was to end up with a rebellious son as well as a daughter. "I—I am not angry with you, Emile. It is your young sister. Here, have a glass of wine with me and forget that I tossed my bad temper on you. Aimee is proving to be a handful. I fear I made a big mistake exposing her to my younger sister for such a long stay in Paris. Denise is a reckless sort and she obviously

74

was not the best influence on a young girl like your sister."

There was no point in trying to tell his father that Aimee had been a headstrong little vixen long before she'd gone to stay with their *Tante* Denise. So he took the glass of wine his father offered him and took a seat, allowing Paul to talk as he usually did.

When Paul quizzed him as to the time he'd gotten her back to the house, Emile did not try to cover for his sister. By now, he figured the little imp had cleverly concocted a story to tell their father when she joined the family for dinner. Aimee was a sly little fox and no one knew that better than he and Armand, being her older brothers. She'd always been able to get what she wanted out of the two of them. It was impossible to refuse her when she was so cute and adorable.

As he sat sipping slowly from the glass of wine, he was amused that she'd obviously outfoxed her father and Fred Bigler by not making an appearance in the parlor. Good for her, he thought to himself.

Armand was the next one to join them in the parlor. Shortly, Lisette came through the door, and Emile sensed that his father was growing impatient for Aimee to make an appearance.

The luxurious opulence of Lisette Aragon's parlor was influenced by her French background. She was constantly reminded of her native France when she sat in her lovely parlor, which always had vases of fresh-cut flowers to enjoy. The blue velvet overstuffed chairs by the fireplace and her settees covered in the soft shades of blue, lavender, and white provided a soft, serene setting for the evening gathering of her family, the one time they were all together.

The room was a reflection of the dainty little French lady Lisette Aragon was. Her handiwork was everywhere in the room, from the fresh flowers she picked daily to the silk and velvet pillows she made. Always, her family had been her whole life. That was why she planned the delicious foods for the cook to prepare for her family and carefully chose the right wine to enhance the meal.

Now that she had arrived in her parlor to find her sons and her husband there but no sign of her daughter, she was slightly disturbed. She knew Aimee had been dressed to come downstairs because she'd been to her room and seen her. What was the little imp doing now? she pondered as she took the glass of wine her husband served her.

Suddenly, she appeared as gloriously lovely as Lisette remembered seeing her before she went to her own room to refresh herself and change her gown. Sometimes she wondered how she and Paul were so blessed with such a lovely child as Aimee. Seeing her now walking so gracefully into the room, Lisette thought she looked like a lovely, adorable child. She glanced in Paul's direction to see his reaction as he looked at her.

In that austere manner of his, he addressed his daughter, "Good evening, Aimee." Truthfully, he was finding it very hard to be so stern with her, for she looked like the cute little monkey he'd known years ago, before she became so grown-up with such a strong will of her own.

"Good evening to you, Papa. Mother, you look awfully pretty tonight in your blue gown." Her twinkling bright eyes danced over in the direction of Emile and Armand. With the two of them, she always enjoyed playful teasing. Tonight was no exception. "You two look too handsome to be true."

Armand broke into a husky laugh, "Come on, Aimee, neither of us look that good after the day we've put in. Just two big gents you like to tease."

"Of course I do, Armand. That is the horrible dilemma of having a brat younger sister," she gave out a soft lighthearted laugh.

Emile stood silently beside his brother, listening to their casual cajoling, and he knew exactly what she was up to as she directed her conversation to Armand. When would his father demand an answer from her about her unseemly conduct this afternoon? he wondered. Right now, she was giving Armand her full attention. In fact, she could have been an actress. Watching his sister, Emile found himself amazed about her self-assured air for one so young. Perhaps his father was right that the months spent in Paris with their sophisticated aunt had had a great influence on Aimee.

There was something about this younger sister of his that filled him with brotherly pride. She was as radiant as the brilliant California sunshine and as intoxicating as their finest vintage wines. Dear God, she was like a breath of fresh air now that she'd returned to the Chateau L'Aragon! Emile had to admit he was glad she was back home again.

By now, Paul Aragon had served his daughter a glass of wine, which she'd graciously thanked him for placing in her hand.

No one was more stunned than Emile by the mellowed tone his father used when he addressed her. There was no harshness in his voice as he told her, "Fred Bigler was very disappointed that he did not get to pay you his respects, Aimee."

"I was not presentable after my ride, so I went directly upstairs to have a bath. When I finished, I heard Fred's buggy going down the drive. It was as simple as that," she replied quite casually. An afterthought urged her to add, for Emile's sake, "Emile found me without any trouble. I was down there by that old live oak. Lady and I were enjoying the day. Ah, what a wonderful day it was in this valley!"

Armand was unaware of his sister's manipulating her father, but Emile realized it all the time they lingered there in the parlor and later as they went into the dining room for their evening meal.

In fact, the whole subject was forgotten after Aimee had given him her convincing explanation for her absence that afternoon. He wondered if Aimee realized what a clever little liar she was. More than ever he was convinced that Fred Bigler was not the man for her, but neither were any of the neighboring ranchers' sons that he knew of.

Aimee was feeling quite smug about her little performance this evening by the time she'd finished the delicious dessert and the last sip of her wine. She'd had a ravenous appetite tonight and the meal had been a pleasant time, since her father had not been in a grumpy mood. For the rest of her family's sake, she was glad that her actions had not caused them any discomfort.

Paul Aragon could not refuse her when she sweetly asked him, "I could just take a stroll in our gardens, couldn't I, Papa? I feel the need for a walk after eating so much."

A grin came to Emile's face, because it was as if she was taunting him. As he figured, Aragon did not refuse her. Aimee gave him a nod of her head and moved out of her chair to leave the table.

Gone was the warm day in the California valley. A cool night breeze wafted through the opened dining room door leading out onto the railed terrace. Aimee stood by the railing for a moment before moving down the two steps of the pathway that would lead her toward the center of the garden where the fountain was situated. Sago palms flourished nearby, their glossy fronds cascading like the waters of the fountain.

As soon as she leisurely swayed down the stone path, her nose smelled the pleasant, sweet aroma of the star jasmine's clustered white blossoms. As she had always admired and praised her father for taking this rich California soil and growing his vines of grapes, she admired her mother's skill and expertise for creating such a garden paradise surrounding their two-story stone house. To think that they'd come to this strange new world and realized their dreams was wonderful, Aimee thought to herself.

Where would she be when she was their age? she wondered. Who would be the man she'd share a lifetime with as her mother had shared hers with her father, Paul Aragon? Would it be the handsome Mark Perez she'd surrendered herself to this afternoon under the live oak tree? Now that she thought about it, she did not know anything about him nor what he did with his time. He did not wear the fine clothes of a man like Fred, so was he the son of a rancher or maybe a hired hand?

So absorbed was she with her thoughts, that she had strolled the full hundred and fifty foot length of the garden before she sought to sit down on one of the little benches placed at various places along the path.

She did not hear the catlike movement coming from behind the concealing sago palm a few feet away. The tall, towering figure moved closer and closer until he was directly behind her and close enough to clasp his huge hand over her mouth to muzzle the scream he knew she'd make.

Aimee was rendered helpless to yell for help and she knew it, but she did not wish to when she heard his deep voice murmur in her ear, "Shhh, *chiquita,* it is only me—Mark." She watched his impressive figure move around the bench. His black attire made him blend in with the dark night surrounding them at this far end of the garden. He'd helped himself to one of the clusters of star jasmine and moved to slip it behind her ear as he sat down behind her with a grin on his face. "Forgive me for giving you that minute of fright but I couldn't let you give me away."

"I should, Mark Perez. This is twice in one day you've frightened me."

His arm was now encircling her shoulder and his hand was holding hers. "I did not frighten you when we made love, did I? I wish not to believe that, Aimee. I want to think you were feeling like I did."

"What frightened me was that I couldn't get all my clothes back on before my brother arrived on the spot, Mark. That could have been embarrassing to say the least." There was such a cool honesty about her that he was impressed by this unusual young lady.

"So you will admit that you liked my loving you, eh *querida?*" he whispered softly in her ear, letting his lips gently caress her.

For one brief moment she did not answer him, for she noted an air of conceit about this charming devil sitting beside her dressed in his black pants and black shirt. His overwhelming

79

sensuous maleness was already intoxicating her and she knew it. But he could have been a scoundrel for all she knew and she had to face that possibility.

"I will admit nothing, Mark Perez," she gave out a soft giggle. Like the flirting coquette she'd seen in her *Tante* Denise so many times, she taunted him, "I will let you wonder about that, I think."

Arching his dark brows, he gave her a crooked grin, "Oh, you will, will you? Oh, my little *violeta*, I am a most impatient man and a most inquisitive one." To prove that he spoke the truth, his lips came down to meet hers in a searing, persuasive kiss. He felt her eager response and it pleased him because her lips did not lie.

Her soft body yielded to him as well, as she leaned against his broad chest and the flames of desire engulfing him were spreading to her. When finally his mouth released hers, she gasped, "Oh, God, Mark! Please, I cannot breathe!"

"Oh, sweetheart, I can't help myself when I'm near you. I swear it!" he gave a husky laugh.

Before he had her so spellbound she could not control the reckless emotions and wild desire he'd stirred this afternoon, she pushed away from him so her pulsing breasts were not pressed against his chest. "Mark, you speak words I do not understand and you make me feel in a way I do not understand. Everything is moving too fast for me."

He felt the instant stiffening of her supple body and he allowed her the space she seemed to need. His black eyes fired with the depth of feeling he declared. His deep, slightly accented voice spoke with such sincerity she had to believe him, "I speak words of my love for you, Aimee, in Spanish. I am very proud of that heritage, as you and your family are of yours. I called you my little *violeta* because your lovely eyes remind me of the deep purple violets that grow in the gardens. Such a delicate little flower but yet so very beautiful! I've never seen such eyes as yours, Aimee."

She was overwhelmed and affected by the beauty of his

words. He was a most unusual man, who fascinated her and also frightened her at the same time because of the strange forceful power he'd held over her from the first moment they'd met.

She gave him a smile and shook her head to confess, "I've never known anyone like you, Mark Perez."

He wished he could tell her who he really was but that would have to wait, he knew. He returned her smile with one of his own as he vowed, "Nor will you, *chiquita*. That, I promise you!"

Chapter 10

When Mano Mateo would have ardently attempted to prove the vow he'd just made to the beautiful Aimee, his dark eyes caught sight of a flickering light over in the distance of the gardens. As he held her close to him, his keen eyes continued to observe the sight, which seemed to move slowly closer. When the bright moonlight focused in on the figure through the branches of the trees, he realized that the flickering light was the cheroot the imposing Paul Aragon was puffing on as he strolled through his gardens.

Damn the Frenchman! He knew he must once again rush away from the lovely lady he was holding in his arms. It seemed that courting this delectable little senorita was going to be a taxing, nerve-racking task, but he was so enthralled by her he was willing to take the gamble.

"Aimee, I—I have to leave you, as much as I regret it. This time your father is the one, instead of your brothers. You are a very protected lady," he told her with a devious smile on his face.

Aimee looked in the direction he was motioning and she saw

the formidable figure, who was most assuredly her father. She gave a disgusted sigh of her disapproval because it seemed she was to have no privacy here at the Chateau L'Aragon. If it wasn't her brothers watching her every move, it was her father checking her out. It wasn't fair to come back to this after the freedom she'd been allowed in Paris which, ironically, had had her father's approval.

By now she had reluctantly freed herself from the encircling arms of Mark Perez and he was telling her that he must slip back over the garden wall just as unceremoniously as he had made his entry earlier in the evening. "*Adios*, senorita—for now. Until the next time we meet, remember I adore you." By now, he was hastily moving to the back of the bench, heading toward the huge, widespread branches of the sago palm to get to the wall a short distance away.

Aimee was left there on the bench all alone, wondering how she might slip through the dense greenery and miss an encounter with her father, which was the last thing she wanted right now.

She wasted no more time just sitting there on the bench. Her petite body could move in and out through the shrubs with ease, and she made her way toward the massive cover of the bougainvillea bush with its deep magenta blossoms. Her lovely frock would blend in perfectly with those huge clusters of flowers. Her father could walk right by her and never detect that she was standing there, her cunning brain told her. This was exactly what she did, and she stood to watch him as he ambled slowly down the pathway.

There was no doubt in her mind that he was out there searching for her as she oberved that head of his held so high in that aristocratic air, looking from side to side of the garden pathway.

She muzzled her own mouth as she giggled like a child playing games with her parents, which she had done many times in the past. Standing there in the night's darkness, Aimee recalled those times, but now it was different, even though she was resorting to this maneuver. What galled her was that she had to resort to such tactics at her age.

How could her father urge her to allow Fred Bigler to court her? If he approved of Fred as her husband, then he had to consider her no child, but he was treating her like one. Perhaps she would point this out to him the next time the subject of Bigler came up.

Right now, she was left with a consuming need that could have been fulfilled by the black-eyed strange man she knew as Mark Perez if her father hadn't interfered. Now she could only wait and yearn for the time when they would meet again.

She'd known an unbridled passion with this dark, rugged-looking Perez and never would she settle for anything less, she told herself as she now moved through the garden to go into the house. Her little maid Jolie would have a chuckle when she told her about the incident in the garden tonight, she knew.

As she went toward the house, Mano rode toward La Casa Grande, having his own thoughts about the brief interlude in the Aragon gardens, remembering those ruby lips that tasted as sweet as wine and her satiny, flawless skin. God, she was divine!

He knew it was not just his male ego telling him that she truly cared for him and found pleasure when his arms held her. No, she did feel about him the same way he felt about her.

Life was surely crazy, he thought as he rode along the hillside on Demonio. Of all the girls in the world to steal his heart so completely, he would have to pick his father's bitter enemy, Aragon. Was that the wild and crazy streak of Portuguese in him? he questioned. What would old Phil Cabrillo say if he asked him?

But right now, he had no desire to go to Half Moon Bay and leave Aimee. No, he had obeyed his impulse to leave the ranch tonight because he didn't intend to put himself through the long, boring evening and dinner with the Reyes family, especially those two daughters.

He considered Camilla and Juanita Reyes a big pain in the behind, and he had made a hasty departure before they were due to arrive. He did feel a little guilty about poor Mario being stuck with the two of them tonight, but then his brother must stand on his own two feet, Mano figured. Oh, his father was going to be indignant and angry when they next encountered one another. But Mano was accustomed to that.

At least, he was pleased to see the lights at the ranch were dimmed, which meant that the Reyeses were gone and his father had retired for the evening. So Mano figured he could enter without making his presence known, but he did intend to see what Minerva had left for him to eat. She knew that he was not planning on sharing the evening meal there at the ranch and she had admonished him for it as he rushed through her kitchen while she was preparing dinner for their guests. She slapped his hand as he helped himself to a huge slice of the golden roasted chicken she had placed on a huge platter.

Nevertheless, he knew he would find himself a tasty feast awaiting him there on the counter of the cupboard. As he moved around the dark kitchen toward where he knew Minerva would have left a late night snack, he suddenly realized just how famished he was.

As usual, he was not disappointed when he found a plate covered with a napkin on the counter. There in the dark he sat at the old oak table, eating in solitude but enjoying himself far more than if he'd had to endure the evening meal with the Reyes family hours earlier.

He left nothing on the plate and helped himself to another piece of Minerva's delectable cherry pie. Only then was he sated of his hunger and did he leave the kitchen to go upstairs to his bedroom. By the time he'd ridded himself of his clothes and slipped in between the sheets, sleep came swiftly.

A few miles away at the Chateau L'Aragon, in Aimee Aragon's bedroom, the fair-haired Aimee and the dark-haired little French maid Jolie sat together on the canopied bed laughing and giggling as Aimee told her about the garden incident earlier.

"Ah, mademoiselle, he sounds like a most romantic gentleman, climbing over the huge wall just in hopes of getting a glimpse of you. I'm most curious to see what this paragon looks like that you speak of in such glowing terms."

"I've no doubt that you'll get that opportunity, Jolie, sooner or later. At least, I hope so. You will, if I have my way."

There was a twinkle in Jolie's dark eyes as she replied, "Oh, I've got a feeling you will have your way against all odds, mademoiselle. You are a most determined young lady, I think."

Aimee grinned and reached over to give Jolie's hand a friendly pat, finding it nice to have someone to confide in here at the Chateau L'Aragon. Many times she could have been lonely but for her little French maid to chat with and share confidences. "You've come to know me quite well, Jolie," she admitted to her. "I think I must be very determined if I don't wish to end up married to that Fred Bigler. That I will not do!"

"*Oui*, mademoiselle, I—I understand," Jolie said, nodding her head.

The two bid one another good night, and Jolie left the room to go to her own quarters. Aimee moved to pull back the coverlet and crawl into her bed. As she propped her head against the pillows and stared out the window into the starlit darkness, she wondered where Mark Perez lived in this California valley. She promised herself that the next time they met she was going to make a point of asking him about that.

Some fifty miles south of Sacramento, in Whiskey Flats, one of the small mining camps in San Joaquin County, two rugged-looking individuals sat inside a tent lit by one hanging lantern, drinking greedily from their jug of whiskey. One of the fellows was a giant of a man, with an unruly mane of black hair that matched a thick, heavy beard. There was a ferocious look about

86

him, with those piercing jet-black eyes and dark, swarthy complexion. The other man was as thin as a reed, with ruddy leathered skin and a pinched expression on his face. He had a hawklike nose, far too large for the rest of the features on his face. He was drinking his whiskey with as much zest as his huge companion, and cautioning him, "You better think twice, Bear, about crossing Ross. You know he can be a goddamn bastard when he's riled."

"Tired of all this shit, Joe. Don't intend to play his stupid games like he's doing now. He was different when we were back in Texas. Out here, he's something else."

Joe gave out a slow drawl, "Hell, I know that, Bear. Knowed it since the day we arrived and he set upon this crazy scheme of his. Just ain't the way we always did things."

The big man shook his mane of hair and declared, "He'd have been better off if we'd not happened on that young, dumb kid coming here to California to see his relative."

"Yeah, I agree with you, Bear. Didn't mind robbing the kid nor Ross killing him, but sweet Jesus, I never figured he'd come here and pretend to be him. God!"

"Old Ross's ears really perked up when that stupid kid told him he was a close relative of the governor of the state of California. When Ross found all that money on him after he shot him, that was all he needed to set him off, I guess."

The wiry Joe Latham had been around a long time and he'd done a lot of things in his lifetime that he wasn't exactly proud of. He'd be the first to admit that he was an unsavory character, and the fact that he was honest was the one star in Joe's crown. "It's never going to work, Bear. I know this and you do, too. But I think we better go along with him for a while for our own good. Do you get my meanin', Bear?"

He might be a mountain of a man, but Joe knew Bear wasn't too smart and he reacted like an impulsive child most of the time. As threatening as he might look, Joe knew that Ross could easily arrange for a bullet to make its mark in Bear's back, as he could in Joe's.

"But I'm tired of all this, Joe. I want to get back to Texas. Don't like California. Don't like it at all! Can't say I liked what I did to that pretty little lady 'cause Ross made me do it and, besides, that sonofabitch that tore into me almost killed me. Ain't going to do it again." The expression on the burly man's face was like that of a pouting unhappy child.

"All I can say is that dude must have been some man to have done that to you, Bear. I'd be damned curious to see that son-of-a-gun."

"The truth is, Joe, I couldn't tell you what the hell he looked like. I could pass him and I wouldn't even know it."

Joe poured himself another glass of whiskey as he listened to his buddy talking. The wiry Latham was an uncomplicated, easygoing man, always ready with a simple answer to most problems in life. "Then, Bear, you better damned well hope that you don't meet up with him again. Next time you might just end up dead, my friend."

Bear scratched his head as he absorbed the sage wisdom of his old friend. He took a generous drink of his whiskey as he sat there silent for a moment before he spoke.

His huge hand slammed the table and he declared, "Damn, I'm goin' back to Texas! That settles it!"

The next morning Joe found Bear's cot was empty and all his gear was gone. He'd meant what he'd said the night before. Ross Maynard was going to be madder than hell, but there was not much he could do about it.

Perhaps Bear was the smart one, Joe thought to himself.

Chapter 11

Joe Latham found himself pondering just how foolish he was to remain up here in Whiskey Flats, and now that Bear was gone, he felt rather lonely. He wished the big bastard had told him what he was about, and then he might have just taken off, too. This searching for gold was a form of madness. Joe realized this as he'd watched the occupants of the tents surrounding his. They'd rushed here from every part of the country, working their guts out in search of that pot of gold they were so sure they were going to find.

Blankets sold for the small fortune of a hundred dollars and he'd seen bread sell for a dollar a slice. Now, that was utterly ridiculous! No, he could not fault Bear for yearning to get back to the more realistic, down-to-earth living back in Texas.

As he thought about it while his coffee brewed, it had been he and Bear who'd been living in the primitive conditions of this damned tent, while old Ross was high-living it up by pretending he was this relative of the governor and spending time up at his fancy mansion, enjoying all the luxuries.

The more he thought about it, the madder he got, and by the

time he'd finished his black coffee and had had a bite to eat, Joe had made his decision. Maybe if Bear weren't riding too fast, he might just catch up with him in a day or two. Knowing the simple-minded oaf, he'd take the trail they'd taken when they came from Texas with Ross.

By the time he'd packed the gear he could use along the trail and saddled up his horse, Joe had convinced himself that he was deserving of the extra horse that belonged to Ross. He was still being cheated, and the animal would serve as a pack-horse for his gear. Ross could have the damned tent and the cots.

He mounted his horse and led the other one down the rutted dirt road that veered around the numerous tent dwellings of Whiskey Flats. There seemed to be no activity there, for the occupants were already gone for their daily routine of working and sweating from sunup to sunset in search for their "fortune." He knew now that very few would ever find that fortune.

When Whiskey Flats began to fade back in the distance as Joe looked over his shoulder, he found his spirits soar higher and higher. He had a feeling he was never going to miss California, but he was certainly looking forward to seeing those wonderful blue Texas skies again.

He gave out a raucous roar of laughter when he thought about Ross Maynard. God, he'd love to see his face when he came to Whiskey Flats and found that deserted tent.

Now that he was riding away from it all, Joe questioned why he and Bear had ever allowed Ross to appoint himself the boss and start giving out orders. It hadn't been that way when they were back in Texas. He could understand how old Bear would have allowed it, but *he* shouldn't have, so Joe blamed himself. But when he and Bear met again—and he knew they would—he would have to thank him for taking the lead, which he sought to follow. Yes, he'd sure have to do that!

Ross would have to find himself some new boys to do his

dirty work and he wasn't going to like that, Joe thought to himself as he rode along the California countryside.

Mano was not expecting to find his father and Mario already up and in the dining room when he casually sauntered through the doorway. However, he soon found out the reason for all the activity and intense conversation going on between his brother and his father.

"I would not put anything past Paul Aragon if the bull wanders into his prized vineyards. He or one of those sons of his would shoot him without blinking an eye."

Mano watched as Mario shook his head and declared, in defense of Aragon, "I don't think so, Father. Senor Aragon is not a cruel man."

"*Madre de Dios*, Mario," Carlos Mateo dejectedly moaned. "You—you find it impossible for anyone to be different than you. You *would not* do it, but Aragon would!"

Mano could not resist the devious impulse to enter the room, saying, "And you would not, Father, if it was your grapes the beast was destroying with its hooves? Like it or not, Senor Aragon's grapes draw as much praise as your bulls. His wines are shipped all over the world now."

Never had Mano seen such a look on his father's face as his cutting black eyes turned on him. But this did not intimidate Mano or cause him to tremble with fear as it would have Mario.

It seemed for a minute that the arrogant Carlos Mateo was at a loss for words. When he did speak, his words were so sharp and painful they cut like a knife. Mano knew he would remember them the rest of his life. His father's deep voice declared, "A son who would equate a grape to a fine bull is a damnation, Mano." He turned away from him, as though he could not stand the sight of his son. Mario and Mano were left there alone in the dining room to exchange glances with one another. Each was having his own private thoughts. Manò had to exert a strong will not to reveal the hurt to his brother Mario.

Never would Mario have suspected from that cocky, devil-may-care air about his younger brother that he was hurting. Since he had been a small lad, Mano's way had always been to conceal the pain Carlos Mateo could inflict upon him.

"Go with me, Mano. I have a need to talk with you while we look for the bull, eh?" Mario urged.

A slow, easy grin came on Mano's face as he agreed, "I will go, Mario, and we shall talk if you like."

"I would like that, Mano." There was an eager excitement Mario did not often exhibit, as he suggested that Mano sit down to eat before they left.

Mano ate a hearty breakfast and indulged himself with two cups of coffee, as Mario had suggested before they left the dining room. Once Minerva had peered through the door to observe the two Mateo brothers sitting there at the table alone. How compatible they were when the stern, overbearing Carlos Mateo wasn't around, enjoying themselves as they laughed and talked lightheartedly.

How different the atmosphere would have been around this hacienda if the vivacious Theresa had not died. She would have shared her sons' laughter and joys, and they would have enjoyed and cherished those times with her that they were never to know. How sad it had all been, Minerva thought as she watched those two handsome boys she adored so much.

How completely different the two of them were, and yet she found special things about each young man that endeared him to her. No one was sweeter and nicer than Mario, who was always so mannerly and considerate of everyone. She was sure that a harsh word had never been spoken about Mario in this California valley.

Minerva knew that any of the neighboring ranchers of Spanish descent would have more than welcomed the prospect of Mario being their son-in-law. The same could not be said about Mano, she thought with a grin of amusement on her dark face. She also knew that Mano could not have cared less that this was the opinion about him.

Ah, she might be an old woman now, but there was nothing wrong with her memory, and if she were that young senorita again, she would find Mano irresistible. That handsome face of his had a certain rugged, reckless charm that Mario did not possess. She knew it was the way he used those devilish black eyes of his and the cocky swagger of his fine muscled physique that made him so magnetic.

There were many people who did not know about that gentle streak in him and that kind heart of his, but Minerva did. Oh, yes, he was thoughtful, too, for she had a multitude of presents he'd given to her over the years. She treasured each and every one of them, from the pressed flower he'd brought her one day from the garden when he was only five years old, to the exquisite lace shawl he'd brought her from some faraway place during the six-months period when he'd shipped out on a packet ship making runs up and down the California coastline.

Minerva closed the door, returning to her kitchen and attending to her morning chores, but she still lingered with her wonderful memories of Mano and Mario as she puttered around the room.

The two young men knew nothing about the fond thoughts being enjoyed by the old Mexican woman in the next room. However, they were happily sharing one of those rare, infrequent periods of each other's company.

They left the house, proceeding toward the stables to have their horses saddled up so they could be on their way to search for the missing Mateo bull. As they rode their fine thoroughbreds through the gate and down the drive, they made a striking pair sitting straight in the saddle, their flat-crowned, wide-brimmed black hats atop their heads. Both wore thin white linen shirts opened at the necks, with colorful kerchiefs tied around their throats. Mario usually chose a deep, dark blue for his twill pants and Mano always wore black.

Mano asked of his brother, as they passed through the high arched entranceway, "Which direction do we go, Mario?" Mario pointed to the north and Mano gave him a nod, following his older brother's lead. By the time they got to the lane that led out of La Casa Grande, four of the hired ranch hands were waiting to join them to track down the wayward bull.

Mario greeted the men, knowing all of them and addressing each by his name. Mano knew only one of them but gave each man a friendly smile and greeting. "*Buenos dias,*" he said.

They all returned his greeting, harboring their private thoughts about this youngest Mateo heir. Each had heard the tales and gossip about Mano Mateo. All found him a friendly hombre as they rode along together that morning, sharing casual conversation as they surveyed the vast hillside area and scanned the landscape.

Nowhere did they see the big black beast roaming the rich, green valley, but a thick forest could easily conceal the animal and they all knew this. The dense woods led from the land belonging to the Mateo family into the hillside. Where the forest ended and the clearing began was the land of the Aragon family.

"Father better be praying that that damned bull isn't in the Aragon vineyards as it was in the past. This time I suspect we'll find him dead," Mano remarked to his brother. Now that he'd met Paul Aragon, he knew the man would not hesitate a moment to destroy anything that belonged to him.

Mario gave out a dejected moan, "Oh, God, we don't need any more animosity between those two."

"Don't know about you, Mario, but I've always felt it was a rather foolish state of affairs. I wonder if Aragon's family holds such a grudge against us as their father?"

"Never had the chance to find out, Mano, and I don't guess you did either. I've seen the two sons a few times in San Jose and they didn't seem to be as overbearing as their father. Then there is the daughter, Aimee Aragon. But she has been away for a few years, going to school back East, I've been told."

94

Mano could have assured his brother that Emile and Armand Aragon were nothing like their father, with his lordly ways. In fact, now that he thought about it, Paul Aragon and his own father were a lot alike. In a similar fashion, Mario was like Emile and Armand, carrying out his father's demands, daring not to question or defy.

No, he could not yet tell Mario that he knew Aimee's brothers. Perhaps he might one day, but for now, it was best to keep the little secret that he was pretending to be Mark Perez to himself.

But Mario's next comment made him consider confiding the little game he'd sought to play in order to be around the gorgeous Aimee. It was obvious to Mano that she had made a tremendous impact on Mario for him to speak so glowingly about a young lady. It was just not Mario's way to discuss young women, Mano had realized. Whatever his private thoughts were he kept them to himself, and it had been this way from the time they were in their teens. Mano, on the other hand, had talked eagerly about the beautiful ladies who'd caught his eye and attention.

The sparks in Mario's black eyes as he described Aimee Aragon made Mano raise a skeptical brow. There was no smile on his face, either, a certain sober, tense demeanor creasing his features as he listened to Mario praise her, "Never have you seen a face like that one, Mano. Never! Now, I know you've had your share of the beautiful senoritas around the valley, as well as many other places you've traveled, which I haven't. But I'd wager you've never seen a lady to compare to Aimee Aragon."

A slow drawl came from Mano, "Really? That breathtaking—*si?*"

"I don't lie, Mano. That is the way she affected me when I saw her riding home one day along the top of the hill. She came galloping from down in the valley and up the slope on that golden palomino with that silver-blond hair of hers flying back, and God, she took my breath away."

Mario did not see the fire blazing in Mano's eyes nor sense

that he was annoyed. The bright sparkle he saw was probably the curiosity he'd whetted speaking about this young lady Mano had not met yet, he figured.

He tried to play the cool, calm individual he usually was, but Mano was a man whose emotions ran deep. He was sorely tempted to snap back at Mario and tell him to forget any ideas where Aimee Aragon was concerned. She was his woman! He had decided that the first time he laid eyes on her.

That golden moment of splendor they'd shared under the live oak tree had settled that when she sweetly surrendered to him.

"I must meet this golden goddess you are so enamored with, Mario," he mumbled, faking that devil-may-care attitude of his, which was not how he was feeling at all.

Mario chuckled, "Ah, Mano, if you and Aimee Aragon met, that could prove to be a great misfortune."

Mano's fists clenched and a strong will had to be exerted, for he was almost tempted to sock that handsome, grinning face of his older brother.

Never had he felt that way about Mario!

Never had he felt so intense and serious about a woman!

Chapter 12

Nothing could have pleased Mario Mateo more than the sight of his men leading the reluctant bull out of the woods a short distance away from the spot where he and his younger brother had been sitting down to have a cigarillo. Perhaps it was lucky for Mario that they appeared when they did with the way Mano was feeling.

But Mario was so elated that the bull was not in the Aragon vineyards he did not notice the subdued, quiet mood of Mano as they walked side by side to mount their horses and join the men who were laughing lightheartedly about their conquest of the cantankerous bull they called Pillo. Knowing the bull's nature, Mario had to agree that he was a rogue. They'd had their problems with this one before at the ranch, so when his father told him that one of their bulls had broken out he knew it was old Pillo.

During the ride back to the ranch, Mario was engrossed in conversation with the men. Mano was not included in their conversation but he did not wish to be, for he cared nothing about the damned ugly bull they led back to La Casa Grande.

He kept thinking about Mario's conversation, and that was enough to ignite his jealousy and his anger. Never had he experienced this kind of irritation over any woman and this displeased Mano about himself. He was always in control of his emotions, so he thought. Up to now, it had always been so.

Oh, he'd heard the tales of the lovely ladies who could make a man weak in his knees and a slave to his passion, but he never considered that he could be such a man. Secretly, he vowed to himself then and there that he would fight such a weakness. He would not allow his fascination with Aimee Aragon to make him a weakling.

By the time they arrived back at the ranch and the bull was secured inside the corral, Mano was his old happy-go-lucky self once again and Mario was never the wiser that his brother's hot-blooded temper had mounted when he'd spoken about the woman Mano was infatuated with.

As the two of them walked from the corrals toward the house, Mario laughed as he declared, "Glad history didn't repeat itself and we'd be at odds again with the Aragons."

"Yes, we need no more trouble with the Aragons over one damned bull," Mano barked, finding it impossible to admire the ugly beast. In an effort to change the subject, he inquired of his older brother, "You said you had a need to talk to me, Mario. Has it something to do with Father?"

Mario gave him a slow and easy smile as he replied, "I think it was just to have a brotherly chat with you, Mano. I enjoyed the time we shared together today. It happens so rarely." He hesitated for a brief moment before he added, "There was something else I guess I had on my mind and I wanted your opinion about, Mano. I've thought about this for the last few weeks but I've come up with no answer. I'd like to mend this ridiculous misunderstanding between our family and our close neighbors, the Aragons."

Mano froze in his tracks and turned sharply on his booted heels. "Why don't you attempt to do it then, Mario? What's stopping you?" There was a harsh, challenging tone to his voice.

Mario looked embarrassed, for he should have expected such a reaction as this from Mano, who feared nothing or no one. "I—I guess I am not as bold a man as you, because God knows, I've wanted to. You see, I would not hesitate about calling on Aimee Aragon if things were different between our two families. As it is now, that is impossible for me."

Mano's teeth clenched tightly and the nerve in his jaw twitched as he pointed out to his brother, "Nothing is impossible, Mario—not if you want it bad enough. Nothing would stop me if I wanted to see this Aimee Aragon. Nothing!"

He was not aware that he began to make longer striding steps, leaving Mario behind. Mario sought to catch up with him, for he recognized that Mano was having one of those mercurial mood changes of his. Why, he did not know. The morning they'd shared had been a pleasant one up to this point, but that volatile personality of Mano's was now upon him. Maybe that was the mystic charm about his younger brother, Mario thought to himself as he rushed up to his side.

Like an eager youth addressing his superior, Mario mumbled in a faltering voice, "I—I know this, Mano, and that is why I spoke to you about it. I am not the courageous person you are. *Madre de Dios,* I wish I were!"

A strange look was in Mano's black eyes as they turned to pierce Mario, and there was a ferocious fury on his face that reminded Mario of their father. He'd never seen this side of Mano before.

"Being my older brother, I thank you, Mario, for your tribute to me. But I cannot give you guts or courage, for that must come from you. We are different types and breeds. We always have been."

It was obvious to Mario that he had offended Mano, but he didn't know what he had done. Realizing this, he knew not what to do or say, so he followed his younger brother into the courtyard. He walked in silence, searching his mind for the wrong he'd committed but coming up with no answer. Mano walked beside him in silence, too, every fiber of his body tensed. Each of the brothers was going through his own particular turmoil and hell.

Of all the men in the world, Mano could not have imagined vying for a lovely lady's affection by competing with Mario. This afternoon had given him things to think about if he wished to woo and win the lovely Aimee. In his heart, he'd already laid his claim to her as those who'd laid their claims to the precious gold in the California land. Now he suddenly realized that was not enough.

Mario moved through the entrance of the sprawling ranch house with a new awareness about his younger brother, a most complex young man. Something seethed within Mano and he had sparked it, Mario concluded. It made Mario realize what a very simple, uncomplicated person he was.

Knowing that it was best for both of them if he went his own way, Mano bid him farewell. He was in a foul, ugly mood and he knew it.

Mario returned his farewell as he went toward his father's study to inform him that the bull was found and back at the ranch.

Mano did not have to be told where Mario was going. He was glad he was not the oldest son, as he recalled the tradition of the Mateo family. He had no desire to fall heir to La Casa Grande and carry on that tradition.

Besides, Mario was better suited for it and he probably yearned for nothing more than this. He would marry when his father decided it was the right time, then bring his new bride here to the ranch to become the new mistress. Only one thing concerned Mano after their brotherly talk this morning and that was that it would not be Aimee Aragon. By heaven or hell, it would not be her! Mano was firmly determined about that.

It went against Mano's nature to lie as he had to her. It was not his way. Whatever his faults might be, Mano was honest and straightforward, and those who knew him would agree about that. There were times when his candid honesty had gotten him into trouble and a little lie could have saved him a big headache later. But that was not Mano.

Whether he liked it or not, he realized he must continue this masquerade he'd initiated with Aimee and her family. But it was repulsive to him, for he felt a tremendous pride in who he was and to not declare it was frustrating.

Soon, he promised himself, he could confess the truth to the woman he loved, and he had to believe that she would accept him as Mano Mateo.

The day had been an endless one for Aimee, because her mother had insisted she not leave the house today since she was expecting the couturiere from San Jose to come out to the Chateau L'Aragon. The gentle-natured Lisette pointed out to her daughter, "She is a most obliging lady to bring her patterns and samples of material to our home. Madame Corrine Devore is a sweet, sweet lady and you will like her, Aimee. You will see."

Aimee had no doubt that she was a nice lady and that she was obliging, as her mother had said, because Madame Corrine knew Paul Aragon was the wealthiest man in the valley. Had her mother not stopped to think about that? As much as she loved her, Aimee could not help comparing her darling, naive mother to her clever, sharp-witted *Tante* Denise.

"I'm sure she is very nice, Mother, and I promise you I will not wander off the grounds for the whole day," she smiled sweetly, hoping to soothe any apprehensions her mother might be harboring. God, she wanted to get away from the house by mid afternoon and Madame Corrine had not made an appearance as yet.

She shared a light lunch with her mother out on the terrace

just outside their dining room. It was a delightful day. The garden area was alive with birds seeking to bathe themselves in the waters of the fountain spray. The intriguing little hummingbirds sought the nectar of the multitude of blossoms in her mother's garden. Aimee found it a most pleasant, private time they were sharing together without her father or her two brothers around as they usually were. She realized that there was a gay, lighthearted side to Lisette Aragon she did not witness during those evening meals when the family gathered together.

They were just two ladies indulging themselves in the glorious day and the surroundings as they lunched on the cold sliced chicken with the light flaky little rolls the cook had prepared. Aimee loved the fresh green peas smothered in that special rich cheesy sauce. By the time she'd devoured the strawberries with cream and sugar, she felt like she'd want no evening meal and she confessed this to her mother.

Lisette gave forth a gale of laughter and declared, "Ah, we will see, *cherie*. I have noticed since you've returned home you have a hearty appetite for one so tiny."

When Aimee would have made a reply to her mother, her eyes caught the sight of Lisette's tiny lapdog chasing a squirrel across the grounds. "Look at Poupée, Mother. The squirrel was about to get the crumb of the roll I'd thrown down to Poupée."

Lisette laughed as she watched the wee dog exert such a fierce temper at the intrusive squirrel. These magnificent grounds were her territory, so Poupée thought.

Their pleasant mother-daughter interlude was interrupted when the Aragons' housekeeper came out on the terrace to announce to Lisette that the Juan Melita family had come to call on her.

"Have them join us out here, Hetty. It is so nice out here today." She turned from the housekeeper to inform Aimee, "They are one of the rancher families of Spanish descent who seem to not resent us Frenchmen invading their valley.

102

Whether you know it or not, Paul and I were always considered outsiders coming into this valley when we did. Ooh, la, la, they did not like it that we were French, for this was a Spanish province. They did not want us foreigners coming in."

Aimee listened with intensity, for she'd never realized this as she was growing up. Perhaps her parents had shielded her from this. Being the youngest child in the family, she would not have had an awareness of such things like her two older brothers did. Aimee had always suspected that her birth had been an unexpected event, since there was such a gap of the years between the boys and her.

She had no knowledge that a doctor had forbid her mother to ever have another child after her two brothers were born. Such intimate details were never discussed with Aimee. This would have been unthinkable to the very private person Lisette Aragon was.

As shy as she was, Lisette was always the gracious lady though. She made a point of telling Aimee that the Melita family had a daughter about her age. "I think you might like her, dear. I know how lonely you must be here with so few people your age to share your time with. It has always been a grave concern of mine. The boys always had one another to share their time with, but you have not."

"Oh, Mother, I have not been that lonely," Aimee said, trying to console her and ease her concern. But it was true that the California valley did not offer the excitement and interesting times she'd known in Paris with her aunt. Now that she'd tasted that sort of lifestyle, she was finding it most difficult to adjust to her former way of life here in the valley. Two years had made a vast difference!

There was no time for her to say more to her mother because the Melita family emerged out of the double doors onto the terrace, and a most impressive group they were. They were true aristocrats of Spanish descent, with their dark, swarthy features. Their daughter was a sultry-looking, beautiful young lady about Aimee's age, as her mother had told her. Her mother was the image of subdued elegance and the father was an arrogant, lordly gentleman with a most debonair air about him.

After Lisette had introduced them to her daughter, they were seated and invited to join her and Aimee with some refreshments enhanced by a special bottle of Aragon wine. Juan Melita gallantly directed his comments to the lovely Aimee. "It is a pleasure to have you back in our valley again after such a long absence. I can imagine how delighted your parents are to have you back home after two long years. I can't imagine being parted from my beloved daughter Gabriella that long." He gave a light little chuckle.

Aimee gave him a lovely smile as she responded, "Thank you, Monsieur Melita, and it is a pleasure to be back home. It is also a pleasure to meet you and your family."

As the senor and senora engaged themselves in conversation with Lisette, Gabriella sought to chat with Aimee. She was delighted to find another young woman her own age in the valley. As Aimee was lonely, so was she.

Aimee found Gabriella Melita a stunningly beautiful young lady and a most friendly one. After they'd chatted for a while, Gabriella asked her, in a most excited voice, indicating to Aimee just how much she was anticipating the occasion, "Are you going to the Mateo fiesta? I just can't wait now that I've heard Mano is back!"

"Please forgive me, Gabriella, but I know nothing about a fiesta and I know nothing about this Mano you speak about," Aimee confessed.

Gabriella Melita's eyes flashed with fire and feeling as she answered Aimee's questions, "Mano is Mano Mateo, the son of Carlos Mateo. He is the owner of La Casa Grande. Their land borders your father's, Aimee. If you have not met Mano, then you have a treat coming, I can tell you."

"You make him sound like some kind of god, Gabriella. You have me most curious," Aimee gave out a soft little laugh.

"Ah, wait until you see him. He is *mucho* hombre!"

"*Mucho* hombre?"

"*Si*, he is a most magnificent man," Gabriella declared.

Aimee's inquisitive nature could not deny that she was very curious about this young man who could draw such praise from such a sultry young lady, and she was hoping that they had received an invitation to their neighbor's fiesta.

She doubted that this Mano Mateo could measure up to Mark Perez though!

Chapter 13

The Juan Melita family spent a pleasant hour visiting at the Chateau L'Aragon with the always-charming Lisette Aragon, but the topic of conversation as they traveled back to their own ranch was the strikingly beautiful daughter, Aimee, they'd not seen in almost three years.

Senora Melita was quick to point out the miraculous changes in the young lady since she'd last seen her. Knowing that Gabriella was almost two years younger than Aimee, she realized that her daughter was blossoming much sooner than most young ladies. So many problems would probably be faced sooner, the senora thought to herself.

Stealing a glance at Gabriella, with her voluptuous figure and that sultry dark loveliness, she sent up a silent prayer that she and Juan would be spared heartaches over a daughter with such seductive looks. Senora Melita had not been blind about Gabriella's manner with certain young men lately and her sparkling, flirting dark eyes when she was around them. The thing that disturbed her the most was that some of those men were the hired hands around their ranch.

Only one young gentleman met Senora Melita's approval for her Gabriella, and that was Mario Mateo. He was exactly the type of fine Latin gentleman she would hope for her daughter to marry when she was of marriageable age.

At least, Lisette Aragon had a daughter who was of an age for marriage, she thought to herself as they moved down the dirt road, away from the hillside estate of the Aragons and into the valley.

These were the thoughts parading through her mind when Gabriella drew her attention by asking, "Why are the Aragons not invited to the Mateo fiesta, Momma? They are so very nice. I don't understand that, and to think they are close neighbors."

"I—I did not know that they weren't, Gabriella. Who told you this?" her mother responded reluctantly. So it was obvious that the stubborn, overbearing Carlos Mateo was insisting on holding his grudge of some twenty years. The man was as unflinching as he'd always been. Senora Melita knew Carlos far longer than they'd known the Aragons.

Long ago, when she'd tried to be neighborly with Carlos's beautiful young bride, she remembered the husband as a cold, unfeeling individual. She'd felt very sorry for his sweet, vivacious wife with her outgoing friendly nature. She also recalled how stunned she'd been that one so lively and full of spirit had suddenly died.

"Well, they aren't, because Aimee told me so," Gabriella said. "I think it is shameful of the Mateos."

"This is the business of Carlos Mateo who he invites to his home, daughter," Juan Melita informed Gabriella in that very eloquent air of his, as his dark eyes exchanged glances with his wife. All the older generation knew the story about the Frenchman's feud with the influential, powerful Mateo family. Personally, Juan Melita had always admired Paul Aragon for daring to challenge the wrath of Carlos Mateo, even though he, too, was of Spanish descent.

Gabriella was a true Latin daughter who never questioned

her masterful father, but today she declared, "I understand this, Father. I can still wonder why."

"Yes, dear, you can do that," he told her. But the subject was then dropped as they journeyed the rest of the way to their home.

Gabriella was not the only one curious about the snubbing of the Aragon family. Aimee made a point of inquiring of her mother, after the Melitas had left, why they were not invited to the gala occasion taking place at the neighboring ranch whose land bordered theirs. There was furious indignation in her voice as she asked Lisette, "I find it an insult, Mama. Father is a most respected gentleman in this valley and a very wealthy one, too. Why would we be ignored? I felt very embarrassed when Gabriella Melita spoke about it and I had to act so dumb."

Lisette gave her that usual sweet smile and sighed. It was a stressful situation to her that such a childish argument could have lasted such a miserable, long time. It seemed to Lisette that Carlos Mateo must be a very petty, greedy man to have resented from the very first that a young French couple dared to invade his California valley. From the beginning, they'd sensed this in Carlos, but it was not the case where Theresa Mateo was concerned. She was ready to greet them with open arms but Carlos forbade it.

Being a proud man, Paul never forced the issue again nor would he allow Lisette to try, even though she would have liked to have formed a friendship with Theresa. It would have been nice for both the two young women. Like Senora Melita, Lisette had been stunned by the sudden death of Carlos Mateo's lovely young wife, and she was saddened to think that two young sons were not to have a loving mother's arms to comfort them.

How did she answer Aimee? she pondered as all these thoughts raced through her mind. It was never Lisette's way to fault her husband, but often she'd yearn to speak her thoughts that differed from his. Something spurred her to do just that now as she told her daughter, "Aimee, when you have two very proud young men as your father and Carlos Mateo were back many years ago, and they were both unrelenting to bend to one another, it is an impossible situation. The bulls of the Mateo ranch ruined your father's vineyards that year, trampling our beautiful vines ladened with grapes ready to be picked. Your father was a man on the edge of madness, and when he encountered Mateo, he laughed at your father as though it were nothing."

"How horrible! He must be a despicable person."

"He could not appreciate our grapes any more than your father could put any value on his bulls. I can tell you that your father tried to shoot the bull but missed. He would have loved to kill that rampaging bull without blinking an eye."

"I don't blame him for that."

"Nor do I, *cherie;* our vineyards and what they mean to us make them most precious. *N'est ce pas?*"

"Yes, Mama, it is so!" Her pretty head went high with pride and arrogance as she sat quietly for a moment. "I would not wish to attend the fiesta given by Mateo. I am glad you told me all this."

"So am I, Aimee." It was nice to be able to talk to her daughter so freely, Lisette suddenly realized, and she decided she would do it more often. It had been a wonderful afternoon, one she would cherish for a long time. She and Aimee had a lot of time to make up. Those years she was away from home had left a void deeper than Lisette had realized until now.

That was going to all change, Lisette Aragon decided as they sat out on the terrace.

The morning ride to search for the bull had whetted Mano's appetite, so he stopped long enough in Minerva's kitchen to help himself to a full bowl of the beans she had sitting in the black kettle on the back of the stove. He knew that the plate covered with a white napkin contained her delicious cakes of pan bread, so he helped himself to a couple of them. After he'd

109

filled a glass with milk, he sat there at her squared work table to enjoy a late lunch all by himself in the quiet kitchen.

Having a few hours to call her own now that lunch was over, Minerva had departed to go to her own quarters in the sprawling ranch house to rest or do as she wished until the late afternoon. The two young Mexican girls who helped her in the kitchen had also gone their ways.

It was the siesta time at La Casa Grande. All activity seemed to become very quiet and there was almost a ghostly silence around the huge house for the next three or four hours. As Mano sat there finishing up the last spoonful of the brown beans in their spicy brown broth, he pondered if they all took naps. He'd never been able to do it even when he was a small tot, but his brother had.

Mario had gone to his room like the obedient lad and taken his rest, but not Mano. He smiled, recalling how he'd climbed down the trailing thick vines snaking around the trellis reaching up to his bedroom window. While the others slept, Mano had romped and played in the garden courtyard. There he'd found things to do with all that boyish energy of his. There were butterflies to chase or squirrels to watch. The flitting little hummingbirds were there to enjoy as he lay on the thick carpet of grass.

He felt the same way now that he was grown and he saw no reason to waste a glorious afternoon by sleeping. He could sleep at night, and even then, he did not need eight hours. From what Minerva had told him, this had also been his mother's way, which was a source of irritation to his father. She would not conform to the tradition of the typical Latin lady and what was expected of her as the wife of the patron of the ranchero. The older Mano got, the more he realized that Theresa Mateo did not enjoy her role as patrona of La Casa Grande.

Somehow, he knew that she found it as dull and boring as he did. She yearned so desperately for more but knew that she would never find it with Carlos. He was too demanding and so blind to her needs as a woman. Sometimes, Mano swore that her spirit was with him, for he felt so very close to her even though he had never really known her because he was so young when she died.

How did two such people even fall in love and get married? Mano pondered. He'd probably never know, he realized, for his father would never talk so intimately with him. Yet, he was most curious for the answer.

He must ask old Phil Cabrillo about this the next time he went to Half Moon Bay, he told himself.

After his hunger was sated, he found himself in need of a stroll in the garden. He had no intentions now of chasing the butterflies or lying on his stomach to watch them. He only intended to walk along the flagstone paths and enjoy a cheroot.

As he moved through the arbor of wisteria entwined with bountiful blossoms of purple and lavender, he spotted the familiar figure of the mestizo-Mexican woman sitting on the bench tossing bread crumbs to the gathering birds. He smiled as he watched Minerva enjoying this quiet moment while she was free of chores. He should have known she would spend it bringing pleasure and joy to someone or something.

Like the devious boy he had been some ten or fifteen years ago, he slipped up quietly behind her with that grin of mischief on his tanned face. When he stood directly in back of her, he snaked his hands around her eyes, daring her to guess who it was.

"You rascal! Do you think I am getting that old? It is you, Mano. Mario would never think of such a thing! Let me tell you something, young man, and hear me good. You will not outsmart Minerva—not as long as you live. As smart as you are, Mano, you will always have thirty years to catch up with me. I have lived thirty years longer," she told him, chuckling as she turned around to see the handsome young devil standing behind her.

111

"You old *bruja!* How come you are so smart?" he cajoled her.

"I just told you, *nino,* I have lived some thirty-odd years longer than you. Come, Mano, sit by me awhile."

He did as she requested, because he found this old woman a most comforting balm to his soul. Today he was troubled.

She surveyed his face, each expression carefully. She knew him well and she knew he was troubled about something. "Are you going to be here for the fiesta this year, Mano? I sincerely hope you will. You know that it was a very special occasion started to mark the anniversary of your parents when your father brought your mother here after they were married. You were away last year."

Once again, the old Mexican had stunned him with a new revelation. He'd never known that the event marked such a special time. He could imagine his mother on such a gala night. He wondered how he could share this night with Aimee Aragon and pose as Mark Perez. It was challenging enough to whet his interest.

Sitting beside Minerva, his thoughts were about Aimee, and he envisioned the magnificent gardens of the hacienda with the strolling musicians strumming their guitars.

It had been two years now since he'd been at La Casa Grande when the lavish occasion had taken place, but he still recalled the grandeur and the flamboyant setting. It was a fantastic celebration and Carlos Mateo spared no expense to entertain his guests, who came from miles around the California valley. Flaming torches lit the drive up to the hacienda and mountains of delectable foods were served, along with wines and champagnes. At the end of the night, the music enticed the guests to dance until dawn. It was a romantic evening if one shared it with the right woman. Mano knew who he yearned to share it with, so he had to think of a way to do just that.

How could he possibly manage to share the evening with Aimee without revealing to her that he was Mano Mateo? It was enough to stir his mind crazily. But to satisfy his curious nature, he asked Minerva, "Was the Aragon family invited, Minerva?"

"No, Mano, never would they be invited to La Casa Grande. Never would they be welcomed here."

Mano gave her a slow, easy grin as he retorted, "Ah, Minerva, never is a long, long time. Nothing is impossible and who knows what the future holds. There might come the day when an Aragon would be most welcomed here at La Casa Grande."

In that private part of Mano's world, he was thinking of the fair-haired French senorita who'd stolen his heart. He rather doubted that Carlos Mateo could resist her beguiling charm— if only he would meet her.

"Oh, Mano, you must be mad to think that!" Minerva protested.

He gave forth a deep, throaty chuckle, "No, Minerva, it's just that crazy Portuguese blood in me."

She reached up to give him a loving pinch on the cheek as she teased him, "We are both half-breeds, aren't we, Mano? That is why we understand one another."

He reached over to give her an affectionate kiss on the cheek. His dark eyes were filled with such warmth, while his deep voice spoke with such emotion, "Ah, Minerva, it goes much deeper than that."

The old mestizo-Mexican woman swelled with over-whelming joy. Forever she would remember this special afternoon.

Chapter 14

Carlos Mateo was in one of his pleasant moods during the evening meal he shared with his two sons. In fact, he was downright jolly, talking gaily about the fiesta they would be having shortly. Mano found himself actually enjoying the dinner hour and his father. It was rare to see this side of the usually stern, sober Carlos, but Mano found he liked *this* man very much. With *this* man there could have been a closeness and a warmth of feeling.

Mano detected its effect upon Mario as well as him. Whatever it was that was spurring such a lighthearted manner in his father, he wished it would last but knew that would not be.

Carlos was cordial to Minerva, singing her praises about the delicious pie she'd baked for their dessert. Not once did he bark out his requests for some extra service from her and she welcomed the sudden change in Senor Mateo as much as his sons did. Like Mano, she knew it was wishful thinking to hope it would last.

By the time the three had retired to the parlor and Minerva

had finished clearing away the dishes from the long dining table and blowing out the tapers of the candelabra, she realized how many steps she'd been spared tonight just because of Senor Mateo's happy mood. She turned the duty of dishwashing and cleaning up the kitchen to her young helper, Rachel, so she could go to her quarters to enjoy her own pleasures.

As Carlos poured a glass of brandy to offer each of his sons, he remarked, "It was a grand sight for me to watch you two riding together down the drive as you returned from the search this morning. That is how it should be with us Mateos. Together! That is what made this family a fine, honorable one down through the generations. My father insisted upon it, as did his father before him. I can still recall the formidable figure of my great-grandfather. Oh, he was a magnificent gentleman!"

Mano took a small sip of the brandy as he speculated what his father was leading up to. There was a reason for this speech, he felt sure. He found himself most curious to hear what Carlos was about to say.

Mario did not have the inquiring mind or inquisitive nature of Mano. He was just glad to see his father's good mood continuing and a friendly smile on his face.

"To have Pillo back at the ranch where he belongs and that he came to no harm as he could have in this valley makes me grateful to both of you," Carlos told them.

Mano sauntered over to take a seat in one of the overstuffed chairs. He sat there, giving the glass a lazy caress back and forth as his dark eyes measured his father standing by the stone fireplace with his hand resting on the top of the marble mantel.

"The thanks should go to Mario, Father. I just went along for the trip. He led the men to the spot where the bull was found," Mano pointed out to him in that usual candid way of his.

Mario appreciated Mano giving him the credit, but then Mano had always been a generous person. Mario offered a protest for Mano's sake. It had been so nice for him to witness such a serene time when his father and Mano weren't at odds about something.

"My statement stands, Mano. You were there along with your brother and that is what is important to me." That particular tone of authority and arrogance was there in his voice and the expression on his face as he directed his words to Mano.

Mano made no attempt to reply to him, for he knew it would do no good. Neither did he seek to point out to him that accompanying Mario this afternoon certainly did not mean he was now ready to involve himself in the breeding of the Mateo bulls. He had proven to himself over four years ago that he could make his own way in the world if he desired it, without the backing of his wealthy father or the allowance he gave.

Contrary to his father's opinion that he was a reckless, wasteful young rascal, Mano had acquired a fair amount of money on his various ventures away from La Casa Grande. Wisely, he'd put his money in a bank in San Francisco. There it had stayed. It took few worldly goods to make Mano a happy man.

Often he'd thought about this, and he'd finally come up with the answer. Being the son of a wealthy man had provided him with a lavish way of life since he'd lived in the spacious ranch house with its grand courtyard gardens. How many young boys had such a magnificent playground as he'd had there at La Casa Grande? By the time he was six, he'd had his own pony to ride.

The finest of leather was demanded by Carlos Mateo for his and his sons' boots. Because he'd worn the expensive frosty white linen shirts and fine-tailored pants and coats done by the same expert tailor, he'd taken them as no special privilege or favor.

It was only after he was fifteen that he found himself questioning so many things. He knew then that La Casa Grande could not be his whole life as his older brother, Mario, seemed to be able to accept.

Mano knew he had to seek out the world and go to strange places. He wanted to meet people other than the ones he'd known all his boyhood and youth. This "itch" within him grew from that point on until the day he announced to his father that he intended to explore the world outside La Casa Grande.

Forever, he would remember that day and the irate, raging father he'd faced, but he didn't waver as he stood before the fierce-looking Carlos. Never had he regretted that decision of his youth. His wanderlust had opened new vistas and worlds he'd never have known had he remained here at La Casa Grande.

All these private musings were interrupted by Mario's speaking to him, but he was so engrossed with his own thoughts about the past that he had not heard his brother's words.

"I'm sorry, Mario, what did you say?"

Mario, still being in a lighthearted mood, gave out an amused chuckle, "Thinking of some pretty senorita, eh Mano? Would you not agree with me, Father?" Poor Mario had not yet sensed that Carlos's mood was changing. Indignation brewed in Carlos that a father's praise did not impress Mano. How different the times were when he was a young man of Mano's age. He had been so intimidated by his own father's imposing presence. But not Mano! Never would he be able to bend this son to his will and his way. Mano would always be that reckless renegade who would do as he pleased, caring not if it pleased the father who had sired him.

There was no denying it anymore, and tonight was just one more time that convinced him of a secret worry he'd harbored for more than ten years. The Cabrillo blood overpowered the Mateo blood in Mano. He would always be more Theresa's son than his. He could almost hear her wicked little laugh as she rebuked him, "I told you so, Carlos."

He was as preoccupied with his private thoughts as Mano had been, so he had to apologize to Mario. "What did you say

117

about a senorita, Mario? I am sorry."

When Mario repeated his remark, Carlos gave him a halfhearted grunt as he turned aside to help himself to another glass of brandy. As his back turned on the two of them, Mario gave an uncertain glance in Mano's direction.

Mano shook his head in a gesture that told Mario he had no idea what was suddenly bothering their father. But he knew. Only Mario was the one not feeling a swelling undercurrent mounting in the parlor now, so Mano thought he'd best excuse himself from the gathering.

He rose up from the comfortable chair to stretch his long legs, giving a lazy sigh as he declared, "I think I will leave it with the two of you. I feel the need to move around some before turning in. Good night, Father, and you, too, Mario." He made a swift exit, fearing Mario might suggest that he join him. He didn't want his older brother's company just now.

Mario was about to suggest just that, but Mano's long striding steps took him out of the parlor before he could say anything. He might have just followed after Mano, but Carlos sought to speak to him about a matter pertaining to a bull they were selling to the Ortega ranch in Mexico. So Mario sat back down.

As obediently as he behaved as a child, Mario did as his father requested. Carlos came over to sit in the chair where Mano had been sitting a moment ago. His warmth had faded, and in its place was that tone of authority and his armor of cool aloofness. "I would have hoped that Mano could have shared this responsibility with you, Mario, but I guess that it is hopeless on that score. It will be on your shoulders, Mario, the trip to Mexico."

"When will I have to go, Father?" Mario asked.

"Right after the fiesta, I think," Carlos told him. "I would not wish you to break your promise to escort Reyes's daughter, you understand?"

"Of course, Father, I—I understand," Mario stammered in a hesitating voice. To be escorting Camilla Reyes for the whole evening did not thrill him, but the trip to Mexico could be pleasant if Mano would come along with him, he thought.

Perhaps he could persuade Mano to go along. It was unlike Mario to be distracted by his own thoughts when his father was talking, but tonight was different.

As Carlos continued his discussion, Mario's thoughts rambled elsewhere. A short time later, as the two of them left the parlor and Carlos went on his way down the long, darkened hallway to spend an hour or so in his study, Mario went into the gardens in hopes of finding Mano there strolling in the darkness.

But a half hour later, when he'd walked down each and every pathway to make the full circle, he saw no signs of him. He turned to go back into the house. Knowing the impulsive urges Mano gave way to regardless of the hour, he might be riding at this late night hour across the valley.

Tomorrow he would approach him and maybe he'd have more influence than his father did this evening.

Wild and free as the master astride him, Demonio broke into a fast gallop as soon as Mano reined him out of the gate onto the dirt road leading away from the ranch. He welcomed the opportunity to kick up his hooves and be freed from his stall.

Mano was feeling the same exhilaration as the cool night breeze whipped at his face as they raced up the hillside and down into the next valley.

A glorious night like this when his spirit could roam free meant much more to Mano than all the luxury his father could give him. A night like this was something he could remember forever. Wealth could buy only material goods, which could be swept away in the blink of an eye.

There was one thing that he prized most highly, and that was the fine thoroughbred he rode. Demonio was a most cherished possession. Mano considered him as he would a dear, devoted friend. When he was happy Demonio knew it, and when he was in a foul mood the animal seemed to instinctively sense it and understand. Right or wrong, Mano thought more highly of Demonio than a lot of people he knew.

As if the thoroughbred understood him now, he seemed to take the lead as they climbed the next hillside leading them toward the Chateau L'Aragon. An amused smile broke out on Mano's face as he decided to allow Demonio to lead him for a brief spell. When there was no doubt in Mano's mind as to where he was headed, his hands tightened up on the reins. The high-spirited thoroughbred obeyed his master's command, but it intrigued Mano how the animal's instinct had been his wish to come here.

Ah, yes, they did understand one another very well! As he sat there perched in the saddle, he was close enough to see the lights of the chateau, and in the second landing the flickering lamplight still gleamed. This, he decided, must be Aimee's room. He was so sure of it.

Never did he expect to be rewarded with such a glorious sight a few moments later as this figure emerged through the double doors leading out onto a railed balcony and confirmed his instincts. There was no doubt now as he sat there astride Demonio, his black eyes ogling the magnificent feminine figure moving out to the balcony to stand by the railing, her silver-blond hair flowing around her shoulders.

Being that far away he could not tell the color of the diaphanous gown draping the sensuous curves of her lovely body, but he knew it was a pale pastel. He was entranced by the sight of her, he admitted to that. No woman had ever bewitched him as this one had and he doubted that one ever would.

What was it, he asked himself, that made her so different? God, he could not actually put it into words! He'd known many beautiful ladies the last four or five years. God knows, he'd bedded many vivacious, promiscuous women experienced in the ways of exciting a man's sexual desires! All these women paled when he compared them to Aimee Aragon.

Recalling that special interlude under the old oak tree, when his fingers had teased the curls at her temples and he'd let them roam through the silky softness of her silvery blond hair, he'd have sworn she was a goddess. Those eyes of hers could have been exquisite amethysts as they gazed up at him. At times, her look was that of sweet innocence, and then there were times when he saw the most provocative creature flirting and boldly daring him to possess her. He had to confess that he wondered if he'd conquered her or she'd conquered him.

Was it possible for a sweet, innocent virgin to conquer an experienced, worldly man like him? Mano wondered. A few weeks ago he would have had no doubts. Now he was not so sure.

Aimee Aragon had done strange things to him. As much as the violet-eyed lady intrigued him, he rebelled against the power she held over him. Yet, he knew that she was so young she did not realize this. After all, he knew he was the first man who had ever loved her as he had.

This thought was enough to make Mano's ego swell with masculine pride!

Chapter 15

She had to admit that nothing was more glorious than these dark California skies, with the twinkling stars sparkling like exquisite diamonds and the cool night breezes wafting across the balcony as she stood there holding the iron railing. Aimee felt the softness of her sheer nightgown teasing her breasts and the supple curves of her body as she stood there, and she was reminded of Mark Perez caressing her body when they'd made love under that live oak tree. Dear God, she felt herself titillating by just thinking about it!

She could feel his strong hands making her yield to his powerful force and she could feel herself flaming with the fires of passion when his sensuous lips had kissed her. There was the forceful strength of his muscled thighs engulfing her, and she could not deny she was overwhelmed by all this. But all this masterful force was not as impressive to Aimee as the tender gentleness Mark had shown her with the sweet persuasion of his deep voice murmuring words of endearment, which had made her want to yield to him. He had not forced her. She would never be able to say that he had forced her to surrender herself to him, because she'd willingly given herself to him.

Wanton or not, she did not regret it! It had seemed right at that moment. Tonight, as she stood looking into the night, she still didn't regret it. Oh, she knew that she was supposed to save her virginity for her wedding night and the man she married, but what if it was not Mark Perez she married? She could not imagine feeling this way about another man, and she especially could not imagine feeling this way about Fred Bigler, who seemed to be her father's choice of the man she was to marry. *Mon Dieu*, never could she feel about him as she did Mark Perez!

Where was he tonight? she wondered. Where did he live in this California valley? She'd never heard of nor did she remember a family with that name. When would they next meet? She did not know now but she knew they would, just as sure as she breathed the night air. It had to be, she told herself.

Reluctantly, she turned to go back inside her bedroom but she doubted that sleep would come. She was too aroused with thoughts of the tall dark, handsome Perez.

Was this the way it was when a woman was so helplessly in love with a man? Was it like this with her mother when she'd fallen in love with her father? Did she dare quiz her mother about this and her feelings about Mark Perez?

There would not have been any hesitation about asking her aunt. She'd seen her *Tante* Denise in love affairs with her various men, soaring to the heights of ecstasy and joy. Never were her spirits so low as those times when she and her current lover had quarreled.

She found it hard to conceive of any man being as dashing and handsome as the magical Mark Perez, but as she moved into her bedroom and crawled into her bed, she recalled the very vivid picture Gabriella Melita had painted of this Mano Mateo, youngest son of Carlos Mateo. Strange, it seemed to her now that she'd never known of him or seen him when they had lived just down the hillside in the lush green valley below. Perhaps the explanation for that was the feud existing for almost two decades now.

As she lay between the soft white sheets and gazed out into the night, her feminine curiosity was whetted by this mysterious Mano Mateo who she'd never met. Did she have a fickle heart to be feeling this way? she asked herself.

As crazy as it would have seemed to her a brief moment ago, she fell asleep with her thoughts on this man named Mano, instead of on Mark Perez.

The twinkling dark eyes of Jolie were sparking with excitement as she shook her mistress and declared, "Mademoiselle, mademoiselle! Wake up, please. I saw him. I saw him and he is everything you said he was!"

Aimee slowly propped herself up in bed and stared up at the alive face of her maid. Fluttering her long lashes and trying to grasp what Jolie excitedly chattered about, she sleepily mumbled, "What . . . who . . . I didn't hear what you said, Jolie."

Urging her maid to slowly tell her once again what she was announcing, Aimee tried to make herself alert. Once again, Jolie declared that a most handsome gentleman had come to the Chateau L'Aragon to call on her. Jolie knew this must be the one Aimee had told her about. She had seen him when Madame Aragon had summoned her and told her to come upstairs to inform Aimee about her visitor.

Jolie had let her eyes survey the black-haired, good-looking young man sitting there on the terrace with Aimee's mother. She felt her own knees go weak as his dancing dark eyes glanced for a moment in her direction with a pleasant grin on his tanned face.

He was dressed in a black shirt opened at the neck, a scarlet-colored silk scarf tied around his throat. His pants were black like his shirt.

Jolie quickly turned away to do the madame's bidding, but she felt the overwhelming force of the man's black eyes still with her. How penetrating they were!

"Who is it, Jolie?"

"Madame gave me no name, mademoiselle," Jolie told her, but described the gentleman with her mother. Aimee knew it was certainly not Fred Bigler as she began to scramble out of the bed.

"That can only be Mark—Mark Perez! Remember I told you about him, Jolie."

"Oh, *oui*, I remember, mademoiselle! It can only be him."

In the next few minutes, it would have been difficult to judge who was the more excited as they stumbled over one another in their rush to get Aimee dressed. Because it was a much simpler procedure, she picked her brilliant blue riding skirt with a soft blue blouse instead of one of her frocks with all the petticoats to worry about stepping into.

There was no time to style her hair, so Jolie brushed the long tresses away from her face to hang loosely down her back like glowing, pale gold satin. Aimee gave her cheek a couple of pinches to bring out a hint of color and dabbed some of her toilet water behind her ears.

Breathlessly, she rushed toward the door, turning back to give out a soft little giggle as she remarked to Jolie, "What a marvelous way to start out the day!"

Jolie laughed and winked her eye at the lovely young lady she served. What a joy it was now that the mademoiselle was here at Chateau L'Aragon! The spacious stone house seemed to breathe with more life and spirit. It was a delight and pleasure to serve her, as it had been with Madame Lisette Aragon. Yet they were so utterly different in temperaments.

Aimee rushed down the long carpeted hallway, slowing her pace only as she descended the stairway. She took each step in an unhurried motion, knowing that the stairway could be seen from the opened double doors leading out onto the terrace. The expression on her lovely face and her casual manner gave forth no hint of the frenzy she'd been in only a short time ago as she had fumbled with her clothing, struggling to get dressed.

She was being observed, as she'd hoped, because **Mano** saw the lovely vision in blue coming down the steps, that glowing mass of silvery gold hair swaying on her back and shoulders as she took each step. She was truly a goddess.

Lisette knew before she turned around that Aimee must be approaching them, for she had only to look at the young man's eyes fired with adoration. He heard not a word she was saying but she smiled with amusement. He was absolutely entranced by her beautiful daughter, so how could she fault him for that?

She had spoken with this young man for over a half hour now and was very much impressed by his good manners and gracious way. She felt he was a very intelligent young man, too. But she could not recall a family by the name of Perez living nearby in the valley and she felt it would be rude to prod him about this.

Aimee wore a sweet glowing smile as she came through the doorway to greet the two of them. "A nice surprise, Mark, to see you here," she told him as she came to the table and accepted the chair he'd pulled out for her to sit on.

"A pleasure to see you again, Aimee, and waiting for you has given me the chance to have a nice chat with your mother," he told her as his eyes devoured her loveliness. As he assisted her into the chair, her closeness to him intoxicated Mano with that sweet fragrance and aroma of jasmine.

A servant brought Aimee a steaming cup of black coffee and refilled Lisette's and Mano's cups. Lisette insisted that Aimee eat a croissant and some cherry jelly when her daughter had tried to dismiss the servant and tell her she wished no breakfast.

"Now, *ma petite,* this charming young man has asked my permission to allow you to go riding with him this morning and I have given him permission, so you must eat a little something," Lisette gently urged her.

Aimee exchanged smiles with Mark Perez and she was delightfully pleased by the fact that he had bewitched her mother during the brief interlude they'd shared. Indeed, this was to be a glorious day, as she'd told Jolie!

"All right, Mother, I will have a croissant then, just to please you," she teased playfully. Now she knew she was not the only one Mark Perez's winning ways affected. She could not help wondering how her father would react when he found out that his wife had allowed this liberty.

It was not until the two young people had bid her farewell and walked down the steps of the terrace that Lisette began to wonder what Paul's reaction would be when he found out she'd given her permission for Aimee to go riding with Mark Perez. It startled her now as she sat there by herself to finish the cup of coffee. What had made her give way to this sudden impulse? she pondered. The more she thought about it the more amazing it was to her that she had not told Aimee she must ask her father's permission. Normally, this was what she would have done.

Again, she gave way to a sudden impulse as she placed the cup on the table and stood up. She decided to take a leisurely stroll through her gardens instead of the usual routine she followed every morning of the week.

Lisette felt the need of the quiet and serenity of her cherished gardens this morning, for she found herself slightly puzzled by the strange phenomenon evolving around her. For as long as she'd been Paul's wife, he had been the lord and the master and never were his rules challenged. For some unknown reason, she cared not that he might disagree with her decision this morning. Aimee was her daughter as much as she was his, so why should she not have a right to lay down some of the rules at this chateau?

Looking at the loveliness of this garden and knowing the many hours she had labored here, bending down on her knees and digging in the dirt to plant all these flowers, made her realize that she'd put much of herself into this magnificent place. Paul had not done it all.

By the time she reached the far spot in the garden where Mano Mateo had slipped over the wall to have a moonlight rendezvous with Aimee a couple of nights ago, she was ready to sit down on the same bench to rest. It was a reflective mood Lisette was in this morning and she could not explain that either. All she did know for certain was that from this day on she did not intend to sit back and be ordered around. Why she should have ever done it she did not know as she sat now at this moment in time. Did she not run her house with the same skill and expertise as Paul tended his vineyards? Of course she did and always had!

Her blue eyes gleamed with devious anticipation as she secretly wondered what Paul would think when he was faced with this new side of her. Someone observing her would have seen a hint of the capricious spirit of Aimee there in that expression.

The soft-spoken, submissive lady Lisette Aragon now surged with a gusto of self-assurance and arrogance she'd never known before in her life since she'd married Paul Aragon. She loved the feeling!

Yet it took nothing away from her complete devotion and love for her husband. No woman could have loved a man more than she had always loved him. Had she not gambled on death when she'd allowed herself to get pregnant with his babes? He could never deny that. If the truth were known, she doubted that he would have willingly sought to tempt fate as severely as she'd dared to do.

As she rose up from the bench to walk back to the house, Lisette Aragon appeared to be the same outwardly. Only she was aware of the mysterious change within her. However, by the time she arrived back at the terrace and jauntily walked up the steps, a certain air was emerging, the expression on her rather plain face gleaming with a new radiance.

Chapter 16

They made a most striking couple as they strolled along side by side. As soon as they'd moved far enough away from the house, Mano had reached out to take her dainty hand in his. There was that certain romantic glow on both their faces, and had they been moving down a crowded street or a grand ballroom, heads would have surely turned to admire the tall dark, handsome Latin and the breathtakingly blond loveliness of Aimee Aragon.

But the grounds around the winery and the estate were deserted this morning, it seemed to Mano, as they went toward the stables so Aimee could have her palomino saddled.

Her twinkling sapphire eyes darted up to Mano as she insisted upon knowing, "What did you do to her, Mark? I'll swear I could not believe my ears when she said I might go riding with you. I think I'm still in a daze."

"She is a charming lady and I am not bragging when I say I think she liked me, too," he smugly declared.

"I'm thinking you find yourself irresistible, and I'll grant you that you've more than your share of good looks, Mark

Perez. But I must warn you that I met many men in Paris who were very handsome and charming," she playfully taunted him.

His strong hand snaked around her tiny waist and drew her closer, so that she felt the heat of his muscled male body. "Ah, *chiquita,* but they were not me!" he arrogantly boasted. His head was bent down to look at her as they continued to walk along slowly. He would have had to move a short distance for his sensuous mouth to have touched her half-parted lips.

Something about him left her breathless, but she did not want this overly conceited Latin to know just how much he overwhelmed her. That slight accent to his words intrigued her and whetted her curiosity. "And who are you really, Mark? I must know. My parents know of no Perez family in this valley."

His black eyes were like black coals smoldering with torrid heat, penetrating her to the very core of her being. "I am a man who worships you, my little *violeta.* I am your admiring, devoted slave."

"You possess a silken tongue and a winning way. Time will tell if you are my devoted slave, Mark. I am a demanding lady, as my two older brothers could tell you," she gaily laughed.

A husky laugh broke out as Mano declared, "I'm sure they spoiled you, as I would have too if I'd had a younger sister like you. But I must warn you, Aimee, I am a most demanding man, so as you've said, time will tell many things. I am also curious."

She studied his tanned face as he spoke, realizing she'd never known any young man who held her interest as this one did. All the many months in Paris when her aunt always had a parade of guests coming to her townhouse, she'd met many young, dashing Frenchmen and she could not deny that some were very handsome. Always, they were all impeccably dressed and debonair. But none of them excited her as this mysterious Latin gentleman.

"That is interesting, because you see I am a very curious person, too," she pointed out to him.

There was a wicked twinkle in his black eyes but he said nothing. She wondered what he was thinking, and his silence made her curious. Perhaps this was exactly as he hoped to affect her. Mark Perez possessed some strange qualities, she'd already found out. They set him apart from other men she'd known.

As they rode down the dirt road away from the Chateau L'Aragon, Mano could not resist voicing his admiration for the fine palomino she rode. "You cut a fine figure riding her, too," he told her, his eyes moving slowly over her, from the top of her golden head to the magnificent curves of her hips as she sat in the saddle.

"Ah, my Lady is my most cherished gift Father and Mother ever gave me. She is a beautiful beast and we are the best of friends."

He smiled, realizing their thinking was a lot alike. Her sentiments about Lady were those he felt for Demonio. Mano knew that as time went by he was going to learn many other things they would share. Maybe that was the reason he'd allowed his heart to rule him instead of his head ever since the first night he'd met Aimee Aragon. No other woman had ever inspired him to give so generously of himself.

"So are Demonio and I," he told her.

Once again, they rode along and drifted along in a brief period of silence, moving now into the green valley and away from the hillside where the Aragon chateau was situated. By now, they were riding over Mateo property, but Aimee did not realize this. However, Mano was well aware of it and he wished not to run into any of the hired hands from his father's ranch. He knew it was possible, for there was always a stray roaming away from the rest of the herd of cattle.

Along with the prized bulls bred and raised at La Casa Grande, Carlos Mateo owned a vast herd of cattle. There was a spot he felt safe to take her, where he was sure they would not be seen. It was a secluded area he'd discovered a long time ago. There were only two other places he'd been where he'd found such serene splendor. Half Moon Bay was one of them, and the other was a place near Santa Rosa known as Valley of the Moon, where they grew the most magnificent grapes in the state. In fact, Mano had chanced to meet an old vintner there in Santa Rosa, who'd convinced him he should think about having a vineyard some day. Because Mano was in one of his wandering ventures at the time, he'd ended up staying over a month in the Valley of the Moon district.

Without questioning him as Mano veered off the main dirt road, Aimee reined Lady to follow him. The narrow lane was lined with many weeping willow trees, and she was forced to dip her head to keep the long, flowing branches from tangling into her hair.

"Where are we going, Mark? I don't recognize this area. I confess I'm lost," she gave out a soft laugh.

"I hope you are, *chiquita*, I truly hope so. It is my own secret spot, so I'm glad to hear you say that. You will see what I mean when we get there, and it won't be too much longer now. Trust me, Aimee, you'll love it as I do."

As they moved around a sharp bend in the narrow dirt lane, the fragrant aroma of the exotic blossoms wafted to her nose. Wild ferns seemed to flourish here in this dense cover of trees and a variety of wildflowers dotted the area. A most glorious array of colors splattered the verdant thick carpet of grass. Nothing soothed Aimee's restless nature more, when she was at the chateau, than taking a stroll through the nearby woods and gathering a bouquet of little purple, pink, and yellow wildflowers. The only things smelling sweeter were the many herbs her mother grew for use in their kitchen.

"I see already what you mean, Mark. It is a lovely place. How is it you call it your secret spot, may I ask? If this isn't my father's property, then it has to be that despicable Carlos Mateo's land."

Mano braced himself not to give way to the stunning reaction her words had fired. Such venom was obvious in that usually soft, sweet voice. *Madre de Dios*, she surely detested his father!

He turned in his saddle to look back at her as they rode slowly along the path. "You don't like this Senor Carlos Mateo, *chiquita?* I hear it in your voice."

"I have never met him nor do I care to from some of the things I've heard about him," she declared firmly.

"I see. Am I to assume that the valley is gossiping about this Senor Mateo and his surly disposition? Is he some kind of awful monster?" he quizzed, trying to sound sincere. Actually, he found it all very amusing. It would have mortified the aristocratic Carlos Mateo that anyone in the California valley would have voiced any contempt for him.

"I would not call it gossip. I would just like to know who these snobs think they are. So what if their family has lived here for two or three generations and my family came here from France?"

"Why did you come to that conclusion, Aimee? What makes you dislike this Carlos Mateo so much? Is it because you are French and he is of Spanish descent?"

There was an air of indignation about her as she retorted, "That has nothing to do with it. I resent that the Aragon family was not considered worthy enough to be invited to the grand fiesta Gabriella Melita told me about yesterday. By the way, the Melita family is Latin and they are very nice people."

Mano almost forgot himself for a minute and had to bite his tongue to keep from saying he had known them all his life. The feisty Gabriella was a born flirt and Señor Melita would do well to keep a watchful eye on that vivacious senorita.

"And that has hurt you, *si?*"

"Absolutely not! It has made me very mad at this man I do not know!" she told him. He saw the purple-blue fire in those eyes. She was a hot-tempered little minx as well as a lady of passion, he now realized. Her emotions ran deep and intense whether it be love or hate.

Suddenly, he was seized with a devious, delightful idea about this night of fiesta at La Casa Grande. It appealed to his reckless

133

nature but he wondered if it would be too daring for her. He'd approach her later about that.

By now, they'd reached the spot he wanted to show her. He reined up on Demonio and leaped off the thoroughbred. By now Aimee had led Lady up to where he stood.

His arms came up to help her down from Lady and she accepted them. As their bodies touched and the dynamic heat of him seared her, she felt herself tremble with uncertainty. What if this was only a folly for him? What if he was just a handsome scoundrel who used innocent young ladies like her for their playthings? *Tante* Denise had told her about such men. She recalled her aunt's warning that such men would break your heart and walk away to go into another woman's willing arms.

"What is it, *chiquita?* Do you not wish to stay here?" Mano asked her, noticing the apprehensive look on her lovely face. "If not, we shall leave." His dark eyes slowly searched her face. Such concern was reflected on his face that she felt guilty about the thoughts she was having.

She stammered, "Oh, no, Mark, I want to see this special place you're so impressed with. I think I know now why you find it so beautiful." The expression on her face, as his black brow was raised with skepticism, told her she had not convinced him of her sincerity. This man was not one she could play her womanly wiles on as she had with the romantic young Frenchmen in Paris, Aimee realized. He was too sharp and most sensitive to her thinking, it seemed.

"It is what I hoped you would share with me, but I would not be shattered if you do not find it so, my *violeta.* What is it they say about beauty being in the eye of the beholder? To me, it is a beautiful spot in this California countryside." He took her hand to lead her to the crystal-clear brook that weaved in and out of the dense covering of greenery.

More than ever, she was realizing that Mark Perez was an amazing young man. Perhaps this was one of the qualities that had made such an impression on her. He was a man who felt such depths of emotion about the simple things of life. She felt the warmth of his strong hand holding hers and it was a good feeling. As long as she was with him, she knew she would be safe and secure. Had he not protected her that night when that horrible man had tried to ravage her there in that darkness of the valley? He had been her knight in shining armor. Whatever the future held for her, Aimee knew she'd never forget the man walking by her side now.

She knew one thing, though, and that was if she could not have Mark, then she would never settle for the likes of a Fred Bigler. He was the most obnoxious man she'd ever known!

As he led her to a particular spot and urged her to sit down on the thick carpeted grass, she found all doubts and fears were now swept away. Her eyes absorbed the beauty of the place, with the crystal-clear waters of the brook a few feet away. As she glanced toward the sky, Aimee noticed the tree, with its yellowish-green flowers in huge clusters, which was towering over them.

"Oh look, Mark, a tree of Heaven!"

His black eyes gazed upward to observe the sight that had taken and held her interest. "The Tree of Heaven? Interesting, indeed! It seems right to me that one should grow here. It is a heavenly place." He sunk down to sit beside her. "Any time I'm with you, Aimee, it is heavenly! Do you not know that by now?"

For a brief moment, she said not a word but her eyes surveyed his face carefully. In a faltering voice, she answered him with that usual candor of hers, "I want to believe you. I want to think so, but you are a man who frightens me at times."

"Me, *chiquita?* I frighten you?" His arms were now enfolding her and urging her closer to him. His overwhelming heat was now smothering her as his lips were about to capture hers with a kiss. "I want only to love you, *querida.* Never would I want to frighten you."

As he huskily murmured his tender words of love, his hand had moved to cover one breast. She flamed with a surge of desire as it stirred such a wild, wonderful sensation with her.

"Then love me, Mark, just love me so I will not be frightened!" she pleaded with him breathlessly.

It was all Mano needed to hear and he was more than willing to oblige her. "Oh, *querida, querida,* I shall do that with all my heart and soul!"

His lips, hands, and body sought to fulfill her plea by making love to her.

Chapter 17

Tender was his touch as he moved his hands over the supple curves of her body. She arched her body to press closer to him, his torrid, heated lips capturing hers, persuading her to yield to him. Such sweet persuasion she could not refuse. She felt the strong muscled thighs encasing her and she snuggled to get closer to him.

Right now, it mattered not to Aimee who he was or where he came from. All that mattered to her was this moment of ecstasy they were sharing.

His long, slender fingers played with the wisps of her hair, moving it away from her face, and his lips caressed her cheek with gentle, tender kisses. Sweet moans of pleasure escaped her lips as she responded to the magic of his making love to her.

Perhaps he was a rascal, but he thrilled her beyond her wildest expectations of what love was all about. Maybe there was a lot of her *Tante* Denise's personality in her? Maybe there was a little of the demimonde in her? If so, she could not help it.

What would not make her happy would be to find out he was

playing her false. That she could never forgive! Whether she realized it or not, there was that fierce aristocratic Aragon pride bred in her.

Now, as she listened to his sweet, persuasive words of love being whispered in her ear, there was no way she could have stopped the surrender of herself to him. This she knew! Already, she sensed his nimble fingers unfastening her blue blouse, and the flame of his touch made her passion mount higher and higher.

She gave a soft moan of pleasure, lovingly calling out to him. He answered her by bending his black head lower so his lips could take the tip of her throbbing breast. His tongue teased and taunted her soft flesh, causing her to soar to a new plateau of ecstasy.

"Oh, *querida, querida!*" he moaned huskily. She gave him such sweet anguish that he could wait no longer to bury himself deep within her. No woman had ever carried him to these lofty peaks of rapture as Aimee Aragon did. She was the woman his dreams had always dwelled on and his imagination had envisioned all his life.

Her arms encircled his neck tightly, as if she were telling him to stay there close to her forever, and his firm muscled thighs encased hers as their bodies moved in a perfect tempo with one another.

He knew the excited pleasure she must be feeling as she gasped, "Oh, Mark! Mark! *Mon Dieu!*"

Sharing that same golden splendor of passion as she was feeling, he gave way to the rushing force breaking loose in him he could no longer control. The verdant thick carpet of grass could have been their magic carpet, as the overwhelming sensations they were both feeling in that moment made them feel as though they were soaring up the high hillside and dipping down into the deep valleys of the California countryside.

Theirs was a world known only to them at that spellbinding moment in time, but the two lovers had to descend from that pinnacle of pleasure. However, both of them were too breathless to speak, so they exchanged a smile, clinging to one another.

When Mano spoke, his voice was intense with feeling and passion. "This spot under the tree of Heaven will always be called *Paraiso*."

Softly, she murmured the word, "*Paraiso*. What does that mean, Mark?"

"Paradise, *querida!* Paradise!" He smiled as his lips sought to claim hers again in a long, lingering kiss.

When his lips released hers, she confessed to him, "Perhaps most would not expect it of you, Mark Perez, but I think you are a very sentimental man. But you would not give one that impression when they were observing you. They would think you to be the happy-go-lucky fellow without a care in the world. I think you fool a lot of people." Her deep blue eyes sought the depth of his black eyes and she knew she was right.

A smart little minx she was, Mano suddenly realized. Breathtaking beauty was not her only asset by any means. She was a most sensitive, perceptive lady for one so very young.

"*Querida mia,* you amaze me!" he gave out a husky laugh, pulling her close to him.

"And you intrigue me, Mark Perez," she admitted honestly to him. He admired this straightforward candor he'd never known before with any woman.

"Ah, that is my desire, Aimee. I want nothing more than to arouse your interest and your passion. If I do that, then I am more than pleased," he admitted boldly.

"Oh, you are truly conceited, so sure of yourself," she declared, freeing herself from the tight clasp of his arms.

He sought to playfully taunt her, for there was no doubt in his mind that he'd aroused her passion only a few moments ago. "Ah, I might point out to you, little *violeta*, that I think you are a little conceited yourself, *si?*"

A slow, hesitating smile came to her face as she admitted, "Perhaps a little."

"There is nothing wrong with having some conceit, some worth of oneself. How else will anyone think us worthy of their respect, do you think?"

Once again, she found this strange young man she'd known for only a brief time amazingly interesting. Already she'd discovered, during the few times they'd been together, that he had very firm convictions about life. But the way he spoke and his manners denoted an educated man, one with a certain worldly sophistication. Could he be the son of some wealthy man here in the valley? But how could that be, because her father would have surely recognized the name that first night he'd brought her to the chateau?

She gave him a warm smile as she remarked, "I like your thinking, Mark. Now, tell me the truth about yourself. Who are you . . . really? Where do you come from and does your family live nearby?"

Her eyes pleaded with him for an honest answer, and Mano wanted more than anything to give her just that. He detested this silly child's game, which wasn't his way. However, he was more afraid of losing her after what she'd said today about his father. She detested the man so much that he wondered if she would despise him, too, for being Carlos Mateo's son.

"I have some family here in the county, *chiquita*, and up to the north around Half Moon Bay." He considered this was not a lie. More than ever, he knew he could not continue to live this lie, because after today, Mano realized he loved her far too much to go on this way. Should she find out the truth, he knew she could end up hating him for the deception.

He was grateful that his answer seemed to satisfy her for the time being, because two playful squirrels caught her attention and she began to giggle as she pointed to them romping and rolling in the grass, almost tumbling into the pond.

He laughed with her as they watched the two little creatures of the forest. He thought to himself that it did not take wealth to enjoy the greatest pleasures of life. This glorious day spent in the company of Aimee Aragon and times spent enjoying the simple life up at Half Moon Bay delighted Mano far more than the luxuries of La Casa Grande. The elaborate fiesta his father would be having could not give him the joy or pleasure of this day.

Two such fine horses as the golden palomino belonging to Aimee Aragon and the magnificent stallion with its gray coat and black tail and mane belonging to Mano were bound to draw attention as they were tethered to the trunks of saplings near the pond on Mateo land. The dense grove of trees did not conceal the sight of those two fine animals from a passerby riding along the narrow trail of the countryside.

Sitting straight and tall in his saddle, the arrogant figure of Carlos Mateo froze, jerking hard on the reins when his dark eyes observed Mano's stallion standing close beside the palomino he knew belonged to the daughter of Paul Aragon. Every fiber in his body tensed at the sight his eyes beheld. Insatiable curiosity demanded that he must see for himself if his son were keeping a romantic rendezvous with the likes of the Frenchman's daughter. He could not return to La Casa Grande without finding out if it were true. Never would he have believed that Mano would betray the Mateo family like this. That wild streak of Theresa's background was once again blamed by Carlos.

After he'd secured his horse, he walked cautiously over the covering of thick grass to the spot he suspected the young couple might be. He had the answer to his question a few moments later, and it was as he'd suspected as he saw his son's black head lying next to the fair-haired senorita. As he should have expected from the daughter of that Frenchman, she was undoubtedly a slut. Paul Aragon might be a rich vintner, but his daughter was no better than the *puta* in San Jose's lowly cantina.

With a smirk on his face, he turned sharply on his booted heels to walk away. His younger son was a disgrace to him. But should he not have suspected something this shocking out of Mano?

A blind rage mounted in Carlos Mateo as he rode on to his sprawling ranch house. The stable boy, Paco, felt the sting of this rage when he sought to help the senor and take charge of the horse as he dismounted. Poor Paco took the reins and led the animal hastily into the stable. The fire he saw in Senor Mateo's fierce eyes was enough to urge Paco to get away from him as soon as possible, because he wished not to be struck by one of his clenched fists.

The only time Paco glanced back over his shoulder was when he was leading the horse through the stable door and he heard the firm footsteps of Carlos Mateo marching across the grounds. Who had stirred up this much fury in the senor? Paco wondered. Whoever it was, he pitied the person. Paco did not wish to be in his shoes.

When he'd attended to the senor's horse and there were no other chores he needed to do, he sunk down on the comfortable haystack to enjoy the two meat pies Minerva had slipped out to him this morning. That sweet old woman was always giving him some of the tasty foods from her kitchen. There was no better cook in the whole world than Minerva, he would have sworn.

By the time he had finished the second one, he was feeling pleasantly lazy and tempted to just lie back on the haystack to enjoy a nice siesta. He convinced himself that he was concealed in a cozy, secluded corner and would not be discovered should someone come into the stable.

His lean body gave way to the urge and his eyes closed immediately. So good the soft hay felt to his body. A pleasant languor washed over him and he felt himself sinking swiftly to sleep.

However, the sound of someone whistling a lively tune brought Paco quickly alert, but he heaved a sigh of relief when he saw Mano jauntily moving down the rows of stalls leading Demonio.

"Senor! Senor Mano!" he greeted Mano with one of those broad, eager smiles on his dark, swarthy face. He rushed up to greet Mano, brushing the loose hay from his faded blue pants as well as his tousled black hair.

"Taking your daily siesta, Paco?" Mano asked him as he watched Paco sweep away the long stray hair falling over one side of his forehead.

Sheepishly, the youth grinned and nodded his head to confess to Mano that he was doing just that. Mano gave him a comradely hug around his small shoulders and offered Paco one of his thin cigarillos, which the stable boy considered a rare luxury.

No one had ever been so kind to him as Mano Mateo, Paco considered.

"What made you seem so jumpy when I came in, Paco?" Mano inquired of the boy, for he'd noted the anxiety reflecting on his face as well as the release when he'd seen it was only Mano.

"Oh, Senor Mano, your father returned about an hour or so ago and something had made him very angry, I think," the boy told him.

"Ah, I see. Was Mario with him, Paco?"

"No, senor, he—he was alone. He left alone to ride out to view one of the bulls the foreman had spoken to him about. He was not angry when he left here but he certainly was when he returned. He—he frightens me when he is like that, senor. I cannot help it."

Mano felt sorry for the young boy because he knew the force and power Carlos Mateo presented. He'd witnessed his brother trembling with the same kind of trepidation when Mario was Paco's age. Mano's headstrong stubbornness would not allow his father to intimidate him in such a way. Paco, being a hired hand, had every right to tremble.

"He was not unkind to you, was he, Paco?" Mano's dark eyes searched the boy's face.

"No, senor, but he wanted to hurt someone. I feel very sorry

143

for that poor soul. He reminded me of one of those bad, mean bulls in the corral over there. I mean no disrespect to your father, senor."

Mano gave him a reassuring pat on the shoulder and told him, "I know you don't, Paco. You see, I know my father."

He knew the fury Paco had described!

Part Two

The Lovers' Curse

A love with such fervor,
she never had known;
the rapture of passion,
a sweet honeycomb.

Sheila Northcott

Chapter 18

Mano was a young man riding the crest of blissful happiness each time his thoughts recalled the rare summit of ecstasy he'd shared with his beautiful Aimee just a few hours ago. He never imagined that the "poor soul" Paco had spoken about and pitied was actually him.

As he'd parted company with Paco to go to the house, he walked jauntily toward the courtyard grounds, whistling a happy tune, for he was in the highest of spirits.

In the upstairs bedroom, a pair of sad eyes observed the cocky figure of Mano approaching the iron gate that opened into the stone-walled courtyard. Mario was crestfallen to think about what this evening's dinner hour would bring. Already, he'd had to endure the ranting and raving of their father while Mano looked so happy, completely unaware that he'd been observed in the company of Aimee Aragon.

That Mano was some kind of miracle man, Mario thought to himself. He'd not been back at La Casa Grande a month, but somehow he'd managed to meet and obviously woo Aimee Aragon, from what his father had told him in his shouting rage earlier. Dear God, how he envied him and wished he possessed that magic charm of his younger brother!

What he did not envy was the tongue-lashing he'd get from Carlos Mateo this evening, but then Mano could just shrug his broad shoulders and walk away as he usually did. Mario also admired that trait in his brash, bold brother.

Mario was already prepared to find Mano leaving the ranch by tomorrow after the encounter those two would have tonight, and he hated to see that happen. It had been nice to have him around lately and he'd hoped to persuade his brother to go with him to Mexico. But that was most unlikely now that this had happened.

He turned from the window to walk over to the chair. There was some time before the dinner hour and he sought not to leave his room until then. So he picked up a book and read to pass the time. For one fleeting moment, the thought crossed his mind to alert Mano about their father's black mood. But he could not be sure how Mano would react if he told him. The quiet, easygoing Mario decided to forget the notion.

He heard the clicking heels of Mano's boots as he walked down the long hallway and entered his own room. What was going to make this a more harrowing, highly tensed time was the exclusive coterie gathering at La Casa Grande this evening. A few close friends of Carlos Mateo always gathered at the ranch the night before the grand gala occurred. Mario would wager that Mano had forgotten about this little custom his father always observed before the fiesta.

Mario would have won that wager because Mano dressed in the same casual attire he would have picked for the usual evening meal shared only with Mario and his father. Nevertheless, he looked quite handsome and dashing in his deep blue fine-tailored pants and one of his white linen shirts. When he tied one of his fine silk scarves of deep rich blue, he was reminded of Aimee's exquisite sapphire eyes. But he saw no reason to wear one of his vests or a coat, because the night was too warm.

Because he was so high in spirits and in such a good mood, he bounced down the steps to join his brother and father much earlier than he normally did in the evening.

Much to his surprise, he found the lavish parlor empty. However, he did take note of the array of flowers placed around the room in silver and crystal urns. He figured Minerva was just preparing early for the fiesta guests who would be arriving tomorrow night. He knew the special attention she gave to the house for the occasion. Her kitchen was a beehive of activity for three or four days before the night of the fiesta.

Finding himself all alone in the spacious parlor, he ambled across the hallway and through the carved oak double doors. The magnificent dining room was like a fairyland aglow with twinkling candlelight. It looked wonderful, and the long table was draped with a snowy white cloth. In the center of the table was a huge floral arrangement of pink, white, and purple blossoms, giving off a heady fragrance.

Mano's keen eyes noticed the place settings of fine china and their best silver laid out for fourteen people. What was this? he pondered. Was he confused as to the date of the fiesta? He knew he was a man beguiled by romance, but he didn't think he was all that distracted.

As he stood there deep in thought, Minerva came through the door. Chiding him gently, she told him, "You'll not find anything to nibble on yet, picaro! You'll just have to wait until the others arrive for dinner."

"Others? Who are the others?" he asked her.

"Oh, Mano, Mano! For one so young, your memory is terrible. It is your father's close circle of friends he is entertaining tonight. Do you not remember that?"

"Oh God! I had forgotten, Minerva," he moaned.

The look in his black eyes and the arch of his brow reminded the old Mexican housekeeper so much of the expressions of his mother, Theresa. How often she'd seen her look exactly that same way.

Something about his manner made her want to soothe him

now, instead of tease him as she'd done earlier. "So it is not the end of the world, Mano. At least, you are here at La Casa Grande to share this fiesta with your father and brother. That is the most wonderful thing of all!" A warm, affectionate smile etched her swarthy face.

He returned her smile with one of his own. Thoughtfully, he replied to her, "Well, at least I know you feel that way, Minerva. That means a lot to me."

The aroma of the delectable cuisine teased his nose and his mood lightened. "I don't think I can stand it, Minerva, not if I have to wait much longer."

"Be off with you, young man! You'll not use that silver tongue of yours tonight and get your way. I mean it!" She turned her chubby back to him and waddled out of the dining room.

Mano watched her go and laughed at the lovable old housekeeper who was so dear to him. As he stood there alone in the dining room, he tried to recall that list of very elite guests his father always invited to this dinner on the eve of his fiesta. He knew the Reyes family would be here, as well as Senor Ramon Solado and his wife. There would be the Melita family, of course. After all, it had been the chatterbox Gabriella Melita who'd told Aimee about the fiesta and stirred up ire about the Aragon family being snubbed. But he could not recall the other six guests.

Shrugging his shoulders and dismissing the issue, which really did not concern him anyway, he ambled back toward the parlor. Seeing no reason to deny himself a drink while he waited for Mario and his father to come downstairs, he moved toward the carved teakwood liquor chest to pour himself one. Somehow, he felt the need for a shot of whiskey tonight instead of the wine his father usually served. This was what he poured for himself.

As he took a generous gulp of the whiskey, his father's deep, stern voice addressed him, "Well, Mano, I see you are here to grace us with your presence tonight."

Obviously, Paco had sized his father's mood up right this afternoon and it seemed to be lingering with him still, Mano thought to himself as he slowly turned around to look in his direction, the glass of whiskey still in his hand.

"I thought I might, if that is all right with you, sir?" his voice was as sharp and tart as the arrogant gentleman striding toward him. Mano took notice immediately of the tight lines of his mouth and the flashing fire in those fierce eyes.

The only thing bridling Carlos's tongue was the commotion at the front entrance, alerting him that his guests were arriving. At the same moment, Mario finally left his room, as he'd observed the two carriages pulling up the long, winding drive leading up to the hacienda. Now, his father could not shout and rave at Mano as he would have otherwise done, Mario thought as he made for the stairway.

Impeccably attired, Carlos left the parlor to greet his arriving guests in that lordly manner of his. Senor Reyes and his wife came through the door first, followed by their daughters, Juanita and Camilla, in their exquisite pastel silk gowns. Mario just happened to reach the base of the stairway at that moment, and Carlos requested that he escort the family into the parlor while he greeted the Melita family, whose buggy had just pulled up.

Juan Melita would do well to keep a tighter rein on his daughter, Gabriella, Carlos mused to himself as he watched her feisty sway as she walked up the cobblestone walk. That one was too bold and he'd not like it if Mario's eyes went to her during the evening or at the fiesta.

But he greeted them in the same gracious air as he had his old friends, the Reyeses. Juan Melita and his good wife were fine people. It was just that daughter of theirs he could not tolerate.

He guided them into his elegant parlor, brilliantly luminous with candlelight and gloriously colorful with the silver and crystal urns filled with flowers. He reminded himself that he must praise Minerva for her effort, because it was obvious she had tediously worked very hard the last few days.

An enormous pride swelled in Carlos as he observed Mario chatting with the Reyes family and Mano instructing the servant girl to serve the wine to the guests. They were both representing him proudly.

Oh, Mano could be the most charming fellow when he wished to be, Carlos realized. His younger son came over to greet the Melita family as they arrived in the parlor with Carlos.

"You look most beautiful tonight, Gabriella," he gallantly remarked to the Melitas' daughter. She was delighted by his remark and attention, noticing that the two silly, giggling Reyes girls were already there with their dark eyes busily darting back and forth from Mario to Mano.

"Thank you, Mano. It's nice to see you back at La Casa Grande. You were missed last year," Gabriella cooed.

Before Mano could have replied to her, he heard the voices of some new guests arriving and offered to greet them so his father might see to the Melita family having some refreshments.

"Yes, Mano, why don't you see to the new arrivals while I see to Juan and his family having a glass of wine." He supposed he'd never cease being amazed at Mano. Tonight he was behaving as the son he yearned to have.

All Carlos could ponder was just how long this behavior would last. The image Mano was projecting this evening had mellowed Carlos's ire, though. The unrelenting Carlos Mateo was as swayed by those winning charms as others usually were when Mano chose to employ them.

Excusing himself, Mano moved hastily into the hallway to be at the door when the guests entered. As he left his father and the Melita family, Juan was praising Carlos's handsome younger son. "He is a fine young man, Carlos. How blessed you are to have not one, but two wonderful sons."

"*Si*, Juan, I'm—I'm a most fortunate man," Carlos mumbled, slightly shaken by the surprising good conduct of his younger son and the excellent impression he seemed to be making on all his very aristocratic friends like the Reyes and Melita families.

It happened to be Ramon Solado and his shy little wife, Lena, who arrived and were greeted by Mano, instead of his father. It was a very friendly, warm greeting Ramon Solado gave Mano, which included a comradely embrace. "I did not know you'd returned to La Casa Grande, young man! Good to have you back home." Ramon was a very striking, good-looking Latin gentleman, with his black hair now streaked with silver. His black eyes always seemed to twinkle with a bit of devilment, Mano thought. He liked him better than most of his father's friends because he did not seem as stiff and serious as Senor Reyes and Senor Melita.

"It is good to be back home, Senor Solado," Mano told him before turning to address the little senora, his wife. He made a point of telling her how lovely she looked, even though she was a very plain-looking lady and he secretly wondered how she'd ever attracted a gentleman like Ramon Solado.

She instantly blushed when the charming young man complimented her and she thanked him gratefully. Lena Solado knew she was not pretty and she never had been. She could not blame age for making her ugly. Nevertheless, she still enjoyed hearing a handsome young man like Mano say she looked pretty. If only she could have given Ramon a son like Mano, their lives would have been happier. If only she could have given him a lovely daughter, she would have been more fulfilled as a woman. She'd been denied the joy of any babies and it had pained her throughout the years of their marriage. It had never been Ramon who'd made her feel guilty. She had put the guilt on herself, she realized.

As the evening proceeded and Carlos's guests gathered at his dining table to enjoy the delectable foods and wines, he marveled with amazement as he watched Mano entertaining his friend Ramon Soladao. The young man surely was gifted, Carlos had to privately confess. He had not done one thing all evening that Carlos could fault him about. Not one thing! It was clear to Mateo that Ramon was utterly charmed by his younger son.

Never could he remember seeing the shy, mousy Lena Solado being as talkative and vivacious as she was tonight. She was laughing and talking so gaily with Mano that she was the envy of the two Reyes girls and the pouting Gabriella.

That truly amused Carlos Mateo! There was no denying his younger son possessed a certain charm neither he nor his older son possessed. Whether he wanted to admit it or not, he filled with pride as he watched Mano in his parlor tonight.

It was that bewitching charm and warmth of Theresa that Mano had inherited, which drew people to him.

Chapter 19

Knowing the impetuous ways of his son Mano, Carlos should have known that the entire evening would not have gone without some incident happening. He faulted himself for allowing his guard to be down. At least, the dinner hour was very pleasant. After dinner, the daughters of Senor Reyes entertained the guests by Camilla singing and Juanita playing the guitar.

The first incident that put Carlos in a disgruntled mood was the sight of Gabriella Melita moving over to join Mario as he stood alone. This did not please Carlos at all. Why could she not have picked Mano to work her wiles on, for he could have handled the little minx? A young lady like her could completely bewitch his oldest son, Mario.

However, Mano was dividing his time between the Madrona family and Ramon Solado, Carlos observed.

Reviewing the evening, Carlos had to confess it had been a tremendous success and it was obvious his guests were all thoroughly enjoying themselves. He had Mano to thank for a fair share of that.

It had to be the loose-tongued, flirtatious daughter of Juan Melita who spoiled the marvelous evening for Carlos Mateo. Everyone seemed to be in a most lighthearted, gay mood by the time the Reyes girls finished their performance. The parlor resounded with applause from the guests gathered there enjoying Carlos's fine wines. Some of the gentlemen excused themselves to walk out in the gardens so they might enjoy smoking their cheroots.

This was Mano's intention as he ambled along with Ramon Solado and Senor Madrona, when the vivacious Gabriella swayed up to his side. There was no denying she was a fetching female in her crimson gown and sultry Latin loveliness.

"And who are you bringing to the fiesta tomorrow night, Mano?" she asked him. Mano considered she was due a shock, and that devious streak in him urged him to give her a stunning blow. He had not noticed that his father stood nearby when he impulsively replied, "I am bringing Aimee Aragon, Gabriella."

Gabriella flinched as though he had slapped her pretty face. But she was not the only one to have a violent reaction to his comment. Carlos Mateo could not believe the audacity of his son to invite an Aragon to attend the fiesta.

One guest hearing Mano's remark was sent into an almost uncontrollable, turbulent rage. All he could think about was how that little French bitch had turned her snobbish nose up at him every time he was around her. It had galled him to the core of his being to be so nice to her father and stay in his good graces. Fred Bigler could not believe that Paul Aragon had given his permission for his daughter to attend the fiesta with Mano Mateo. That he could not believe.

Since he had accompanied Jim and Katy Harrington here as their guest at the elegant dinner given by Senor Mateo, he willed himself not to give way to his feelings. It didn't come easy, though, to the man he really was—Ross Maynard. God, this character he had been playing was fraying his nerves! He could not honestly say that he liked this Fred Bigler, who was too genteel for Ross Maynard's ways.

His old buddies, Joe and Bear, had deserted him and were riding back to Texas. Damned, he could not blame them, because California had not been the "paradise" he'd expected to find. His scheme had seemed so perfect in the beginning but now he was starting to have grave doubts. Nothing had gone right since the moment he'd arrived in California and presented himself as the governor's nephew.

Ross thought he'd find the governor a very generous individual toward a nephew he'd not seen in twenty years. This had not been the case. The gentleman was a discerning, frugal person, so Ross had not been lavished with the luxurious lifestyle he'd presumed he'd be living as the nephew of the governor of the state of California.

So Ross Maynard posing as Fred Bigler was a man as frenzied as Senor Carlos Mateo, standing there in the elegant parlor of La Casa Grande listening to the remarks of Mano Mateo. Ross had a score to settle with Mano, anyway.

The night the giant Bear had attacked Aimee Aragon, Ross was supposed to have been the knight in shining armor, coming to Aimee's rescue. Instead, Mano had happened upon the scene to assume the role. Much to his chagrin, Ross did not get to carry out his plot for that evening.

In a strange way, he and Carlos Mateo shared some mutual feelings at this particular moment, as the self-assured, arrogant Mano boasted about who he would be escorting to the fiesta.

While Ross managed to keep his feelings under control, Carlos did not handle his emotions so well. In the presence of his guests, Ramon Solado and Senor Madrona, Carlos's piercing black eyes locked with his son's as he quietly hissed, "No Aragon is welcome under this roof, Mano. You are well aware of this!" That tall, towering figure of his turned sharply to go away from the three gentlemen ready to go out on the veranda.

As he turned his back to walk away, Carlos knew he had not ingratiated himself with either of his old friends, Madrona or Solado. Mano had been the cause of a painful wound tonight,

157

which would not heal soon. He knew he must appear the overbearing monster to both of these two fine gentlemen. He must remember this in the future and never forget just how shrewd and cunning his younger son was.

Where Mano was concerned, Carlos had always sworn he heard that soft, lilting laughter of Theresa's echoing in his ear. Tonight he heard it again. She was surely applauding her son.

What was more insulting to Carlos was Mano seeking not to respond to him. A slow, easy smile etched his face, but he said nothing. As Carlos turned to walk away, Mano urged his father's guests on toward the veranda and the refreshing night breeze flowing gently there in the darkness.

Ramon Solada was the first one to light up his cheroot and comment, "I did not realize Carlos still felt so strong about the Aragons."

Senor Madrona echoed his sentiments. Mano offered him a light for his cheroot before lighting his own. He gave out a deep, throaty gale of laughter as he declared, "Ah, my father never forgets, but I can tell you, gentlemen, I can tell you Paul Aragon does not forget either."

Ramon Solado laughed as he patted Mano's broad shoulder, "Then, young man, I tell you quite frankly you have a mountain to climb. It would seem to me that the son of a Mateo and the daughter of the Aragon family would be a difficult courtship. However, I suspect this lady must be a most exceptional one."

"Ah, she is that, Senor Solado!" Mano laughed.

There was a spark of interest in Ramon's dark eyes, as well as in Madrona's eyes. Both of them knew the reputation of Mano Mateo where the ladies were concerned. Few young men possessed the impressive impact on the fair senoritas that Mano had had since he was sixteen.

Ramon confessed to Mano, "I may be an old man, but I must confess you've whetted my interest to see this charming young lady, Mano. But then I must confess to you that I am a true Latin—a most romantic gentleman."

"I can believe that of you, Senor Solado, after tonight. I am sorry I have not had the opportunity to talk to you or Senor Madrona more in the past."

Both the older gentlemen were impressed with this younger son of Carlos Mateo. Somehow, they were both feeling that the tales they'd heard about him were not true.

They stood by the fountain in the gardens of the beautiful courtyard, enjoying the pleasure of their cheroots. It was Ramon Solado who spoke the words that would forever endear him to Mano, tender sentiments about his mother, Theresa. His deep accented voice was soft with emotion as he declared, "I remember her, Mano. She stood here by this fountain on a night like this. She was the most beautiful woman, Mano, and her heart was the kindest. The simple things of life were her most cherished treasures. She was a most fascinating lady."

Mano listened intently to Ramon Solado's glowing praise of his mother, and he thought to himself that he'd never heard his own father speak with such depth of emotion as this gentleman. It seemed to Mano that this man had more understanding of the woman Theresa than his father, who had been her husband. No one would ever say that about him, he vowed. No one would know his woman more intimately than he would!

"I was so young when she died that I have only few memories of her, but those are most precious to me." He did not add that he felt her presence with him quite often, as he had all his life.

Ramon's dark eyes surveyed his face slowly before he remarked, "You are very much like your mother, Mano. You remind me of her very much in so many ways. I do not see her in Mario but you—ah, yes!"

"I've heard that before many times, sir," Mano laughed, recalling how often over the years his father had made a point of telling him this.

Senor Madrona began to chuckle as he reminded Ramon, "Remember, Ramon, remember the night of a fiesta such as

159

the one tomorrow night, when Carlos discovered Theresa in her fancy emerald-green gown sitting here where we are now and dangling her bare feet in the waters of the fountain. Remember how angry he got and poor Theresa looked up at him as innocent as a newborn babe, so shocked by his wrath. She had no idea that she'd done something so wrong."

Ramon laughed, nodding his head, for he also recalled the incident. "That was what made Theresa so wonderful. This is what I was talking about, Mano."

Mano smiled, nodding his head, for he did understand exactly what both of the men were saying. For a long time now, Mano had suspected that his mother would not yield to the demanding Carlos Mateo any more than he would. The more he'd spent time up at Half Moon Bay and talked with old Phil Cabrillo, who seemed to know his mother better than anyone, the more Mano understood the restless nature of her. He could not fault her for leaving La Casa Grande from time to time.

Sweet reminiscing about Theresa Mateo was the topic of conversation when Carlos Mateo walked out on his veranda to join his friends, Madrona and Solado, there with his son. Mano noticed that his father's presence halted any more discussion about his mother and he wondered why. He also noted that the gay, lighthearted air was now gone. For some reason, the manner and mood of both the gentlemen became stiff and restrained. Mano decided that it was a proper time for him to excuse himself.

He did not wish to return to the parlor to be cornered by one of the Reyes girls or Gabriella Melita. So after he left the three older gentlemen there on the veranda, he decided to take a walk around the courtyard.

As he walked along the flagstone path, he looked toward the hillside where he knew the chateau was situated and where the young lady who had stolen his heart was sleeping this night. Was she thinking of him as he was of her at this moment? So rare she was with that face of an angel and the soft curvaceous body of a seductress. He could forever lose himself in those amethyst eyes of hers.

A glowing mellow moon was shining down tonight on the California valley and La Casa Grande. How perfect it would be to have Aimee standing here by his side, Mano thought as he stood there alone. To claim some woman as his wife had never entered his mind until he'd met her, but now he had to admit to himself that he wanted her so much he would be willing to marry her.

Madre de Dios, he had to confess that she had thrown him into a state of utter confusion, denting the armor of the elusive bachelor. He'd always taken his pleasure with the ladies, then turned his back on them to walk away.

It was not that way with Aimee Aragon when she had surrendered herself so completely that day under that old oak tree. God, his interest was whetted to know more and more about this lady, who fascinated him with her irresistible charm and her dynamic powers to bewitch him.

What amazed Mano and made Aimee such a special lady was she did not know the power she held over him.

Chapter 20

It was not a pleasant evening around the Aragon dining table, Lisette concluded. Everyone sitting at the table knew Paul Aragon was in a gruff, unpleasant mood. He could not believe that Lisette had allowed Aimee to go off riding alone with that Mark Perez, and he'd exploded with a raging temper when she'd quite casually mentioned it before they'd come downstairs to dine that night.

"Are you addled in the head, woman?" he'd yelled at her.

"Not at all, Paul. I saw nothing wrong with it and I saw no reason to deprive the young couple of spending a pleasant afternoon. I consider Monsieur Perez to be a nice gentleman. We had a most enjoyable visit as he waited for Aimee to come downstairs this morning."

"And of course he would be the gallant gentleman around you, Lisette. He sought to win you over so he might have the company of our daughter. God, Lisette, you are a naive woman!"

Rarely had Paul witnessed Lisette acting so haughtily as she did now and shrugging her shoulders to walk away. "I may not be as naive as you think, Paul. I might add that you might not be as smart as you think you are." Without waiting to hear his reply, she marched out of their bedroom to go downstairs without him. Paul was momentarily stunned by this strange behavior of his sweet wife.

Mumbling to the emptiness of the room, he stammered, "What on earth is happening in this house tonight? I can not believe my ears!" He finished dressing in a slight state of shock.

Emile and Armand were in the parlor when their mother entered, and the two Aragon sons immediately questioned her appearance without their father by her side. Yet, they were both thinking to themselves how grand she looked tonight.

Emile commented about his mother's appearance as she joined them. She gave him a warm, motherly smile and patted his broad shoulder, so firm and muscled from the hard work he did daily in his father's vineyards. Her sons were such good boys, asking so little in return for the long hours of labor they did for their family.

There were times when Lisette felt sorry for Emile and Armand. They were so devoted to their father and she thought that Paul usually asked too much of them. Aimee would never yield to her father's will as they had, and he was a fool to think so.

She thanked Emile for his words of praise and inquired of him about the grapes on the vines. She knew the buds appeared about March and by the early summer the tiny little grapes were formed there on the branches. But it was the hot summer sun that brought forth the fine clusters of grapes that they began to harvest in the months of September and the first weeks of October.

"Ah, Mama, they are looking especially good this year. I think we could have a very fine zinfandel or cabernet sauvignon this year."

"Wonderful, Emile! Ah, that is wonderful," she enthusiastically declared. Nothing pleased Lisette more than to

163

hear the news from Emile that it could be a fine vintage year for Aragon wines. She had taken great pride throughout the years in that achievement and in their efforts since they'd come to this new country from France.

She recalled herself as a young woman coming here with her new husband from her beloved country of France, with their cherished vines from their homeland and a dream for their future of the life they would carve for themselves in this glorious land of opportunity. Oh, they had surely done that since the time they'd arrived here in America and settled in California. They had accomplished so much more than she'd ever imagined when they set out on their odyssey so many, many years ago.

She was very proud of Paul and his accomplishments, but it had only been lately that she had experienced this new pride in herself. It had all come about after Aimee had returned from France. She admired this independent spirit of her daughter and it had given her a new value for her own self-respect and self-worth.

Lisette liked this feeling of self-assurance she was experiencing tonight, causing her to stand up and talk to Paul as she had earlier. She had Aimee to thank for that!

She accepted the glass of sherry her son Armand offered her now and graciously thanked him. It was at this moment that her husband and her daughter arrived in the parlor.

Aimee looked her usual radiant self but Paul seemed distressed and tensed. Her daughter joined her brothers and her as Armand immediately rushed to serve his sister a glass of sherry as he had his mother. When he had handed the cut-crystal glass to her, she had thanked him and welcomed his warm, friendly smile as he looked down at her.

Paul had approached his family, which was gathered there in the parlor, with discontent. His wife of many years had openly defied him and he had a most rebellious daughter who would not obey his wishes. He was not a happy man because he felt he had lost control. For a man like Paul Aragon, he could not accept this.

He walked over to pour himself a glass of wine of his choice, which was certainly not the sherry his wife and daughter were enjoying. He'd greeted no one as he entered the room. Emile and Armand exchanged glances with one another, noticing that their sister and their mother seemed to be ignoring their father's moody disposition tonight.

This was strange to the two Aragon sons, who'd always considered their mother to be most solicitous toward their father. Tonight she didn't seem to care that he was not too pleased. Instead, she sat on the brocade settee talking with Aimee as they both sipped their sherry, and Paul was left to talk with his sons.

Emile and Armand welcomed the sight of Hetty standing there in the parlor doorway to announce that dinner was ready. Only then did Paul turn to Lisette and address her as he offered his arm, "My dear."

She rose to join him and take his arm. Aimee got up to be escorted into the dining room by her two older brothers, where the most delicious aroma of food permeated the air. Aimee knew they were going to enjoy a delicious roast duck tonight, with that special orange marmalade sauce she loved so much.

The sumptuous meal was delectable, but it still did nothing to change Paul's quiet, serious mood. After the dessert was served and the three men had retired to the parlor to leave Lisette and Aimee alone, the young girl inquired of her mother, "Father is in a foul mood tonight because you let me go riding with Mark today, isn't he? Why does he disapprove of him, Mother?"

"Yes, he is angry with me for giving my permission for you to go riding. I can't answer your other question, Aimee. I can't tell you why he disapproves of Monsieur Perez, but I have informed him that I like the young man." Lisette spoke with a cool, calm air, which Aimee admired very much. Naturally, it delighted her to hear that her mother liked Mark. It was comforting to know that her mother would be on her side if it ever came to trying to convince her father that Mark Perez was the man she loved.

"I find it hard to believe that he would not feel a debt of gratitude to Mark after what he did for me. It seemed to me that he looked at him with disapproval even that first night Mark rescued me and brought me back to the chateau. Is it because he is a Latin, Mother?"

Lisette did not know how to answer Aimee. It was quite possible, though. Now that Aimee had asked about this, Lisette realized that Paul had never hired any Mexican hands for his vineyards. Shaking her head, she replied, "Once again, *ma petite*, I can't say for sure. The hate for the Mateo family is still very real to Paul and I suppose it will be for the rest of his life. He can't forgive the way we were snubbed by the aristocratic Carlos Mateo, who seemed to look down his nose at us from the moment we moved into this valley. Paul felt and still does that Carlos Mateo considered himself some kind of emperor to rule this region. The only people deserving to live in the valley or hillsides around here were those of Spanish descent. The rest of us were outsiders."

"I can understand his feeling, Mother. I would feel the same way, but Mark is not responsible for the way this Carlos Mateo acts or feels," she pointed out to Lisette.

"What you say is very true, but it is his background and being of Spanish heritage that leaves the foul taste in your father's mouth. He has such grand plans and dreams for you, *cherie*. You are his only daughter, you know."

Aimee smiled as she told her mother, "But he can't live my life for me, Mother. I must do that. The man I marry will share the rest of my life with me, not my father! He must be the man I choose."

All she said was true and Lisette could not possibly argue with her. Nothing would sway Aimee's thinking. There was such a firm, determined tone to her voice as she spoke that Lisette knew that nothing Paul said or did would bend that will and determination if it did not suit Aimee.

All Lisette could say was, "I understand, Aimee. I truly do."

Rarely did Lisette see Aimee look so solemn as she did now, so she realized how adamant her daughter felt about her own life and her future.

"I'm glad to hear you say that, Mother. I might need to have that understanding on my side in the future. But I would not wish to cause any trouble between you and Father. You see, I don't wish to disappoint him. I wish to be the kind of daughter he can admire and be proud of."

Lisette reached over to pat her daughter's hand. "Don't worry about that, Aimee. Don't you fret about that for a minute. Just because I love your father and always have does not mean that I have to always agree with him. Will you not feel the same about the man you love? I suspect you will!" Lisette gave her a sly wink of the eye. Aimee had never felt so close to her mother as she did tonight. Lisette could have been her *Tante* Denise, and Aimee liked this lighthearted, intimate moment of time they were sharing. She hoped it would continue to be this way.

Both of them finally decided it was now time they joined the Aragon men in the parlor.

Jim Harrington had been a friend, as well as an adviser, to the governor of the state of California, and there was no one he admired more than John Bigler. Something about this young pup of a relative of his raised his bristles as well as those of his perceptive wife, Katy. Katy had been the first one to mention some things about the young man she didn't find too admirable. At first he'd excused Fred's coarse, crass manner as just his youth. Now he knew it was more than that. It was the young man himself.

That shrewd little wife of his had excused herself when they'd returned to their own home after the dinner and evening spent at La Casa Grande. An elegant dinner it had been! Jim Harrington had expressed his regrets to Carlos that he and Katy would not be able to attend the fiesta the next night because of some pressing business he had to attend to for the governor.

Fred was spending the night at the Harringtons' ranch and would be traveling to the governor's mansion with Jim Harrington. This very impressive lawyer with his snow-white hair made Fred very nervous and tense anytime he was around him. Those bright blue eyes seemed to pierce him and he felt like he was stripped bare with all his secrets revealed when he was around Harrington. He was a huge man with a pot belly. His torso was tremendous, when you considered the short, stubby legs supporting it.

There was always a jovial air about Harrington, and Fred suspected he was giving you a warm, friendly smile at times when he was condemning you with utter disgust. Fred swore that those blue eyes of his were making a most severe judgment.

He almost regretted to see Jim's wife, Katy, exiting the room, leaving them alone. Somehow, he felt that Harrington had something on his mind, and it could be that his wife had cleverly made her exit so that they could have a man-to-man talk. She was one of the sharpest ladies he'd ever met. Being exposed to the expertise of the astute, shrewd Jim Harrington all the years of their marriage had certainly rubbed off on her, Fred figured.

As soon as his wife had left the room and closed the doors of his study, Jim ambled over to his liquor chest, pouring a glass of his fine French brandy for Fred and himself. Very abruptly and without an embroidered conversation, he came directly to the point, "I was given to understand that you had very serious intentions toward Mademoiselle Aragon. At least, this is what the governor told me. I understood that you had invited her to the ball. I was rather surprised to hear Mano Mateo say that he was escorting her to the fiesta tomorrow night."

"So was I, sir," Fred stammered, trying to keep his voice from cracking with irritation and resentment that Aimee

Aragon was making him look like a stupid fool.

"I tell you quite frankly, young man, I know Paul Aragon and I can't believe he gave his daughter permission to go with a Mateo anywhere."

Fred knew he must give this imposing gentleman the right answer. He hesitated for a moment before he sought to make his next remark. "Then one can only assume that Mano lied tonight, would you not say?"

A twinkle came into Jim Harrington's blue eyes as he declared to Fred Bigler, "That, or he is a most conceited, self-assured young gentleman. Tomorrow night will give us the answer to that, won't it?"

"Tomorrow night she will not be at La Casa Grande, sir. I could swear to that," Bigler told him, but he was not so sure of that himself.

Aimee Aragon was an unpredictable, headstrong young woman, he'd discovered in the last few weeks.

Chapter 21

Ross Maynard was weary of this role he'd assumed as Fred Bigler. He abhorred the character of this man he was trying to portray. It went totally against his nature, and that explained why he'd continually failed to make his scheme work. He was a rough, rugged Texan and he had never coddled his women. He was damned well tired of pampering this spoiled little French mademoiselle, Aimee.

After he'd left Jim Harrington's study to retire to his room, he thought about what he must do. He decided that he could not accompany the attorney to the governor's mansion tomorrow morning as they'd originally planned. Instead, he would remain here in San Mateo County and make a call at the Chateau L'Aragon. Already, he'd thought about what he would say to Jim Harrington in the morning about his change of plans.

Ross was firmly convinced that a gentleman's ways were not for him. Best that he go back to his old ways of doing things, as he had in Texas. He realized now that had he worked this whole thing with the cunning method of fraud and trickery of his past, he could have been back in Texas with Joe and Bear, with a nice little fortune in his coffer by now.

Just the thought of returning to himself and his old ways made Ross Maynard sleep soundly and deeply. Come the dawn, he knew exactly what he was going to do. No longer was he going to float aimlessly in this limbo he'd been floundering in for too many weeks now. Ah, how he was going to make Aimee Aragon pay for turning her snobbish nose up at him, he vowed. Oh, yes, he was going to enjoy humbling her! He would take great delight in the act.

Some six hours later, when the bright California sun came streaming through the guest bedroom of the Harringtons' ranch house and the brilliant rays urged Ross to open his eyes, he was ready to leap out of bed to get started on his day and his new plan of action. The Aragon family was going to pay, and pay dearly, for all the inconveniences they'd caused him, he said to himself as he scurried around the room to get dressed.

He bounced jauntily down the steps, wondering if he would even find the Harringtons up. But, to his amazement, they were already enjoying steaming hot cups of coffee in their informal little breakfast room, furnished in white wicker furniture. Such a lovely view greeted them from the windows of the room, because they could gaze out to see the glorious gardens that were Katy's pride and joy. In two corners of the room stood two huge palms, which almost touched the ceiling. Along the windowsills, numerous cacti lined the double windows.

The image of Katy and Jim Harrington represented the perfect married couple, whose marriage had been a wonderful, happy union. Each complemented the other, it seemed to Ross Maynard. That was enough for him to admire the pair.

Jim Harrington was a man everyone admired, and it was easy for Ross to see why he had been so close to John Bigler throughout the years. He was a fastidious man—a perfectionist. It would have been hard to fault Harrington on anything. Jim's vivacious wife, Katy, was a perfect match for such a man. It was obvious to Ross that Jim utterly adored her, and more importantly, he respected her intelligence. What Ross found most delightful about Katy Harrington was her casual informality, which made him relax when she was around.

"Ah, Fred, I trust you slept well," she greeted him.

"I certainly did, Mrs. Harrington," he told her as he took the seat she indicated and joined them at the table. "This is a most cheerful room, may I tell you."

"Why, thank you, Fred. It's nice to hear you say that, because Jim and I have always found it to be a cozy setting to start off our days sitting here."

Trying to be the gallant gentleman, like her husband, Fred gave her a warm, friendly smile as he replied, "I can't think of a nicer way to start off any day, Mrs. Harrington. That's a magnificent view out the window. Such a picturesque countryside. I have to admit I always thought Texas was beautiful country, but California is beautiful country, too."

Katy Harrington gave out a soft little gusto of laughter as she confessed, "Oh, I'll agree with you about your state of Texas. Jim and I were there a few years ago and I found the country absolutely wonderful, as well as the people."

Ross Maynard playing his role as Fred Bigler considered that he'd ingratiated himself to Jim Harrington's wife long enough now to approach her husband about his change of plans.

"Yes, ma'am, Texas has a lot of good folks and I can figure that you and Mr. Harrington would be well received by the people of Texas." He gave her his nicest smile before turning to direct his conversation to Jim Harrington.

"Sir, I trust you will understand if I tell you I need to stay on here today in San Mateo County instead of returning to the capitol with you. I've thought about the matter we discussed last night and I feel I should look into it more thoroughly, if you know what I mean," Ross Maynard said, his face etched with concern.

Jim Harrington was very impressed by this serious side of

172

Fred Bigler, which he'd not witnessed in the past. He found himself admiring the young man for the first time since the governor had introduced them. "Of course, Fred. I think you've made a very wise decision. Katy will be staying here at the ranch, so if you wish to remain another day or two, you know you are welcome, young man."

Everything had gone as perfectly as Ross had hoped it would. An hour later, Harrington had departed alone from his ranch, while Ross had remained. Two hours later, he galloped out of the corral, on one of the fine thoroughbred horses belonging to the Harringtons, to ride to the Chateau L'Aragon and pay Paul Aragon a visit.

When he arrived on the grounds of the Aragon estate, the first sight to catch his eyes was Aimee strolling in the gardens with the man he'd met last night. The man was Mano Mateo. There was no doubt in his mind as he viewed the tall, towering figure of the young Latin, his Spanish-style black felt wide-brimmed, flat-crowned hat hanging on his back and his black hair gleaming as the sunlight reflected on it.

He could not believe what he saw—a Mateo strolling leisurely in Aragon's gardens. But he had to believe it.

Assuming that role expected of him as Fred Bigler, Ross Maynard spent only a few brief moments with Lisette Aragon. She'd informed him that Paul was up in the vineyards with his sons this morning, inspecting the vines. She gave him that soft, warm smile of hers as she remarked, "No one can appraise those grapes like Paul. Our sons are very good, but they are not Paul."

"Then it would be all right if I rode up there?"

"Oh, of course, Monsieur Bigler. Of course! Paul will be delighted to see you."

"Very well, I—I think I shall. It was nice to see you again, Madame Aragon." He gave her a most gracious bow, preparing to make his exit.

As she left the doorway and he turned to go back down the front steps, his eyes glanced toward the garden area to see the couple strolling there, their backs turned toward his prying eyes. The little bitch, he swore under his breath. She swayed those sensuous hips in a most suggestive way as she walked by Mano Mateo. Yet, she could treat him so chillingly cold when he'd been around her, acting like it was such an effort to carry on a conversation with him. An evil smile broke on his face as he anticipated how he'd make that fair-haired maiden pay for every insult she'd dealt him.

When he mounted up on the fine Harrington thoroughbred, he spurred the horse into action with a ruthless thrust. Jim Harrington would not have approved of such treatment of any of his horses. But the intimate closeness of Aimee strolling with Mano Mateo brought forth such a venom in Ross Maynard that he had to strike out at something. The poor horse just happened to be the innocent victim.

The vineyards were a short distance from the two-story stone house he'd left after bidding Lisette Aragon good-bye. As he approached the vast fields of the Aragon vineyards, he was forced to admire the magnificent sight of the endless long, straight lines of grapevines, so rich and green with the flourishing, cascading branches of grapes.

Ross had to admit, as he galloped up the lane leading into the vineyard, that there must be admiration and respect for a man like Paul Aragon, whose wealth did not keep him from roaming down the rows of his vines in an old straw hat and simple attire like the rest of his hired hands. Ross thought about the sons of the wealthy Texas ranchers and he knew they did not dirty their hands or work up a sweat on their brows like Emile and Armand Aragon did almost daily on their father's land.

Ross Maynard had never kidded himself about the type of man he was. That was the way it was, and he had no great degree of esteem for himself and what he'd done with his life. But he knew he was too old to change now. Perhaps this was why the Aragon family had fascinated him since the moment he'd first met them. They were a most unusual bunch.

He called out to Paul as he came within a hundred feet of the

Frenchman. "Monsieur Aragon—hello!"

Paul turned to see Fred Bigler coming in the opened gateway of the vineyards. A warm, friendly smile broke on his tanned, weathered face as he threw his hand up to wave to Bigler.

As Fred dismounted from the horse and offered his hand in a friendly gesture, Paul declared, "Well, this is an unexpected pleasure, Fred. I have to say I am delighted to have this opportunity to show you our grapes, which produce our fine wines." He proudly announced to Bigler, "Look at these grapes. I must say I think it will be a wonderful year. The vines are heavy with the finest grapes I've ever seen."

"Well, I congratulate you, sir."

"Ah, I look up at the sky and tell that sun to keep shining. It is the torrid heat of that sun which brings forth the magnificent berries that we will crush in the autumn. Now, I must tell you that the true potential of these beautiful grapes and their juices will not be known for two or three years. You see how patient we must be?"

Fred gave him a slow, easy smile as he remarked, in that Texas drawl of his, "Sir, it would take a very special breed of man to do what you do with such success."

The young man's declaration greatly pleased Paul Aragon and he graciously thanked Bigler. Aragon confessed to him, "I love it, Fred, and that is the truth. To watch the grapes grow and mature gives me pleasure. They are the joy of my life. Well, I must correct myself about that. I do find great joy in my devoted family, but it is most gratifying to produce a wine to delight the palates of people all over this whole world. Can you imagine the excitement of knowing that?"

"No sir, I—I can't imagine that!"

Paul took off his straw hat and ran his fingers through his grey-streaked hair, damp with sweat. "I know it, and I can tell you it is a most wonderful feeling."

"Your family must be very proud of you, sir. Perhaps you would understand what I am about to say to you after what we've just talked about. The proud Aragon name as well as the

175

family should never be played false."

Aragon's heavy brow arched with skepticism as he inquired, in a faltering voice, "Are you hinting that my family is being played falsely, Fred? And by whom, may I ask?"

"There is a young man walking with your daughter at this very moment in the gardens surrounding your home. Do you know him, Monsieur Aragon?"

A smile broke on Paul's face and he quickly responded to Fred Bigler, "You are speaking of Mark Perez, Fred. He is the only one I can think of who might be walking with Aimee. I am sorry but I must confess that I see no reason why this should be such a disturbing factor, Fred. This young man did save our daughter from a brutal attack some weeks ago, and as my good wife, Lisette, pointed out to me just last night, we are beholden to him."

Fred Bigler's next words were like a branding iron being pressed against his broad chest. "The man walking with your daughter is not Mark Perez, sir. The man is the son of Carlos Mateo. The man is Mano Mateo!"

Paul had heard the tales and gossip flowing through the California valley about this Mano Mateo. He was a reckless, irresponsible renegade that Carlos Mateo did not approve of.

To think this man was with his daughter, Aimee, filled Aragon with repulsion! To think that he had lied to him as well as all of the family, this Paul found despicable. But then what could he expect from a member of the Mateo family? He was the son of Carlos!

Chapter 22

Paul Aragon was stunned by Fred Bigler's shocking revelation and he could not have recalled the rest of their conversation if his life had depended upon it. He did remember bidding Fred a hasty farewell and immediately walking over to tell his son Emile that he was going back to the house. Already, he was planning his action once he arrived and found the son of Carlos Mateo there with Aimee. Mounting his horse, he rehearsed the dismissal he would give the young man, warning him to stay away from the Chateau L'Aragon and his daughter.

But when he arrived back at his home, there was no high-spirited stallion hitched to his post. The fine grey stallion with its black mane and tail was not in sight. When he entered the cool hallway of the spacious stone house, he was greeted by Lisette descending down the stairway.

In an abrupt, sharp voice, he inquired of his wife, "Where is Aimee?"

What was the matter with him now? Lisette questioned. Her soft voice reflected her own feelings as she gave her husband the answer to his query. "She is in her room, Paul. She was

177

complaining of a headache, if you must know."

"I—I see. A headache she has?"

"That is what I said, Paul," she indignantly assured him. What in the world was bothering him so much this early afternoon?

Suddenly, Paul felt awkwardly ill at ease. He had no intentions of confessing to Lisette that the son of Carlos Mateo had outsmarted him.

"Did Fred come on down the vineyards to talk to you, Paul?"

"He did," he mumbled as he was turning to leave.

But Lisette was not about to allow him to leave with only that brief comment. "And what was on Fred's mind, may I ask?"

"Oh, nothing in particular. I think he had come to call on Aimee but found her occupied with another young man. Mark Perez was here again from what Fred said. He saw them walking in the gardens."

"He was. Should I have not allowed that, Paul? It seems you enjoy blaming me for everything Aimee does which doesn't meet with your approval." Never had he heard such an arrogant tone in the voice of his sweet little wife. But Lisette stabbed him with another cutting blow as she added, "You should have thought of a lot of things, Paul, when you allowed Aimee to live all those months with your high-stepping sister in Paris. You know her to be a frivolous libertine. Age has not changed Denise."

He made no effort to argue with her, for she spoke the truth and he knew it. He knew now that his reasons for allowing his daughter to stay with his sister had been the wrong ones. He should have been smart enough to know that the certain style of sophistication Denise could impart to Aimee would also bring forth certain traits in his lovely daughter he would not desire. Paul privately chided himself for ever allowing her that freedom she obviously enjoyed in Paris with Denise. That was the source of some of his problems with his beautiful daughter right now, he had convinced himself.

A strange look was on his face, Lisette noticed, and he said not a word to her as he turned to walk away. She watched him go out the front door of the house and knew just how painful it was for Paul to admit that he had made a mistake. That manly pride of his would never allow it. She suddenly felt sorry for him, watching him go. There were times in life that a man should be able to shed tears just like a woman.

Lisette had never seen Paul shed a tear about anything and she wished she could say she had. She'd love to have seen such a depth of emotion pour forth from him because she knew he'd felt that way many times.

If she could have read his mind at that moment, she would have known that Paul Aragon was a very angry man and mainly at himself. He could not tolerate being outsmarted by that young pup who'd fooled him. Mano Mateo was a clever young man—maybe too clever for his own good!

How he must have laughed at the Aragon family the night he'd brought Aimee home safely after the attack on her and in that very straight-faced manner had lied to all of them. All of his family had believed him, even Aimee.

Well, that was going to be corrected, but he'd do it his way, Paul thought as he rode along the trail back to the vineyards. He was not about to confess to Lisette what he'd just learned from Fred Bigler a few moments ago. He would play his own little game like this Mano had for the last several weeks.

He knew one thing for certain and that was that no daughter of his would be leaving his home tonight to attend any fiesta given over at La Casa Grande. He'd see to that! But he had to question how this Mano intended to take Aimee to the fiesta, as he'd boasted about last night to his father's guests, if she thought he was a young man named Mark Perez.

That boggled Paul's mind, he had to confess to himself. It would be interesting to observe his beautiful daughter this evening at dinner. Observe her, he would most carefully.

Her sense of adventure and daring was whetted by Mark's proposal, Aimee had to admit, as they'd walked in the gardens surrounding the Aragon house this morning. She knew that they both possessed a certain devious streak in their natures when his black eyes twinkled with mischief as he boldly dared her to join him in his scheme for that evening.

"I think you have a right to feel as you do, *chiquita*. I think this Carlos Mateo deserves to be taught a lesson for obviously snubbing such a fine family as the Aragons. I have shared that snobbery in my own life. Shall we seek a little sweet revenge, *violeta?*"

She gave out a gale of laughter and her fine-arched brow lifted with speculation as to what he was talking about. What— how could you and I enjoy any sweet revenge, Mark? I can't imagine how that could be done. Perhaps you should enlighten me."

A broad grin broke across his face as he told her, "Ah, I shall. There is always a group of flamenco dancers who perform during the fiesta. I just happen to know one of the men and his lady. For one of the dances, we could slip in." His dark eyes searched her lovely face to see how she was going to react. He saw with delight the slow, devilish smile come and he knew he was right about her. There was a touch of the vixen in her. She was going to agree to go along with him on his plans.

Giving out an impish giggle, her deep blue eyes sparkling like a couple of magnificent gems, she declared, "But I won't know how to dance like that, Mark. I saw some flamenco dancers when I was in Paris and they were so divine, so graceful. I could never do that. But I'd love to do as you suggested."

"Then there is nothing else to concern yourself about, *chiquita*. I will lead you and you will follow me, as if we'd danced together all our lives. I swear to you! Shall we do it? Say yes! It would be fun, I assure you."

She gave him a weak protest, "But my fair hair, Mark, how could I possibly look like a Spanish lady."

He gave her a reassuring kiss on her rosy lips as he murmured softly in her ear, "Ah, Aimee, leave that up to me. I will take care of everything. To be loved by a Latin must make you a little Latin, eh? My adorable one, there is always a colorful silk scarf to cover those lovely golden curls of yours."

"You make it all seem so simple, Mark. You amaze me. You give me the impression that you live a most carefree, happy-go-lucky life, never sad or lonely."

"Oh, no—no, Aimee, that is not the case. I have my times of moodiness and my times of sadness," he openly admitted to her.

"You, Mark? I would have never believed that."

"I do, but never when I'm around you. Never! You give me happiness, *querida*. A happiness I've never known before in my whole life." His black eyes fired with the deep emotion pounding within him. She found herself convinced of his sincerity.

His words of love so overwhelmed her she could not speak. All she could manage was a lovely smile. His dark head bent down to let his lips take hers in a kiss that flamed both of them, but a commotion coming from the direction of the house made them break apart. They glanced over in the direction of the front gardens to see Fred Bigler marching up the flagstone path.

Aimee insisted that Mark should take his leave and she promised to meet him in the gardens that evening.

"I will be waiting here in the garden at this spot at nine for you, all right?"

"I will be here, Mark. I promise," Aimee said as he lifted her dainty hands to press them to his sensuous, searing lips for one last kiss before he departed.

She found it hard to break away from him, too. But there was the night to anticipate, when she would meet him again. As Mano departed through the thick growth of shrubbery to climb over the stone wall, Aimee fled from the spot of their rendezvous to go into the house. If she expected to avoid an encounter with Fred Bigler, she knew she must go through the back entrance and up the back stairs. So this was what she did, gently admonishing Hetty to dare not let her mother know she was in the house yet.

The little imp, Hetty thought to herself as she watched the pretty young lady with her bouncing golden curls sneaking up the back stairs to go to her room. Monsieur Aragon would never control this one as he did those two big, husky sons of his. Madame Aragon was certainly no match for the likes of her.

Hetty had seen her strolling in the gardens outside her kitchen windows. She'd watched the pair as they'd walked to the far end of the stone wall enclosing the grounds before she'd gone outside to collect some of the herbs she grew just outside the back entrance of the house.

The rosy-cheeked Hetty considered they made a most striking couple. This Mark Perez was a handsome black-haired devil if she were any judge of men. What a contrast they were, with the little mademoiselle being so fair and delicate-looking as she strolled by the side of the tall, powerful-looking Latin gentleman.

Ah, how wonderful it would be to be that young again, she lamented!

Aimee knew she would never be able to join Mark in the gardens by nine that evening if she joined her family in the dining room for dinner. There was only one way she could possibly manage to slip out of the house to be with the man she loved and go with him on the daring little adventure he'd proposed tonight. Somehow, she felt that he was also seeking a little revenge against Carlos Mateo.

She knew she must play a game of deception by pretending to be sick. Nothing too serious, she decided. A headache and an

182

upset stomach would be enough to convince Lisette Aragon that she should just stay in bed and have a tray brought to her room by Jolie. Aimee was not concerned about trusting Jolie to go along with her to carry out her plans.

An hour later, when Jolie came to her room, Aimee told her what she was planning tonight and that she would need her help. The maid helped her change into her batiste nightgown, so she could play the role of an ailing young lady.

"It all sounds so exciting, mademoiselle. Ah, you have brought such life to this house I used to find so very quiet," Jolie declared.

Aimee giggled, "Are you telling me I'm a disturbing force to all this quiet and peace, Jolie?"

Jolie knew she was merely teasing her, and she, too, gave out a gay little laugh. "I would call it a disruptive delight you bring here to the Chateau L'Aragon, mademoiselle. It is never dull now that you are here."

"Oh, Jolie, you are a jewel and a very nice friend to have."

Such a warm look was on the tiny Jolie's face. She swelled with gratitude for the kind words spoken by her young mistress. Fortune had smiled on her when she found herself employed by the Aragon family. To have her own quarters in this fine house and delicious food to eat each and every day was enough to make her content. Besides, she received a generous wage for her services to such a fair maiden as Aimee Aragon. To be considered as a friend was the grandest tribute Jolie could have received.

There was a mist of a tear in her dark eyes and a slight crack to her soft voice as she responded to Aimee's remark, "I will always be your friend, mademoiselle, until the day I die. You have always been so very good to me."

"And why should I not be when you are so good to me, Jolie?" She gave her a friendly pat on the shoulders.

"I have worked for others who were not as good and kind as you, mademoiselle. Some ladies of quality are very hard to please. Some can be very cruel." Her dark eyes looked up to meet those of her young mistress, and Aimee saw a reflection of pain and sorrow there. Compassion swept over her for Jolie and her unpleasant past.

"Life will be kinder to you from now on, Jolie. I'll see to that," Aimee vowed to her. Jolie gave her an understanding nod of her head, for she had the utmost faith and trust in Aimee.

Jolie had no doubts about Aimee's promise to her. She knew she spoke the truth.

Chapter 23

A glorious golden sunset gleamed across the hills and the valleys of the California countryside. As the sun sank lower in the western sky, the heat of the summer day seemed to cool. The Aragon men left their vineyards to go home for a relaxing evening and a pleasant meal, their reward for a long, hard day's labor.

This was the way of life for Emile and Armand Aragon. It was the only way of life they'd ever known. They'd had no time or inclination to go carousing and drinking all night like a lot of young men their age. By the time they had washed away the dirt and soil from the vineyards and their hearty appetites were satisfied with delicious foods and fine wines, they did not seek the company of young ladies too often. To court young ladies consumed a tremendous amount of time, they'd discovered by the time they were nineteen.

Emile had given his heart and his love to only one girl and had ended up being hurt because she was not willing to compete with the Aragon vineyards. Another young man came along with more time to woo and win her.

Armand was not the outgoing person like his brother, so he had never became serious about any young lady in the valley. He romanced the grapes, instead of the girls. His quiet nature was more like Paul's and his passion for the vineyards was very real and serious.

Both young Aragon men had been made aware of themselves as a very different breed of man since Mark Perez had come into their presence and lives. Perez was just a likeable fellow that they'd both found pleasant and interesting. He had certainly caught Aimee's interest and held it, and that was enough to tell Emile and Armand he had to be a most unusual man, no ordinary fellow.

They both shared the same feelings about Fred Bigler and sympathized with Aimee's protest about being courted by him. Neither of them understood why their father had pushed her toward this man with the shifty eyes. Both felt he was a tricky little weasel even if he was a relative of the governor of the state of California.

Neither of them were prepared for the startling news Paul Aragon told them as the three of them rode down the lane at sunset on their way home. It absolutely stunned both of them when Paul said, "The man we've known all these weeks as Mark Perez is actually Mano Mateo. The scoundrel has been having his fun with us all these weeks and most likely laughing his fool head off."

It took Emile a moment to get his voice to speak. "How do you know this, Father? How did you find this out?"

"From Fred Bigler. He just happened to be at La Casa Grande for a dinner given by Carlos Mateo and his little elite circle of friends on the eve of his grand fiesta."

"But . . . I . . . how is Bigler a friend of Mateo? He has not been in California all that long. Was he representing the governor?" Armand inquired of his father.

"No, he accompanied the Harrington family, and before the evening was over, this Mano Mateo was boasting that he was escorting Aimee to the fiesta. Can you imagine such brashness

186

in the man? I don't know what devious plans this man has in that head of his, but Aimee will not leave the house tonight. I call on you two to see that this does not happen."

Emile was quick to point out to his father, "Perhaps she will not wish to leave when she knows who he is. Have you told her yet? Does she still think he is Mark Perez?"

"I am assuming she does not know. I would find it very hard to forgive her if she did know he was Mano Mateo and still sought his company. I would find that deplorable of any daughter of mine."

Rarely had Emile voiced a resolute opinion to his father as to what source of action should be taken on matters they discussed. This was about to be one of those few times. But he adored his younger sister and knew she was no addled-brain miss like most young girls her age.

"Aimee should be told, Father, and I think she is wise enough to make the right decision if she's allowed that privilege," Emile declared to his father.

"Never doubt that she will be told, Emile. I will give her the opportunity to make the right choice, but should she not do that, then I will make it for her," Paul declared bluntly to his son.

By this time they had reached the grounds of the estate and they dismounted from their horses, allowing the two young stable boys to take charge of the animals as they proceeded into the house.

A ghostly silence engulfed the trio as they entered the door to go their separate ways. That same silence remained with Emile and Armand as they left their father, because each of them was lost in his own private thoughts about this startling turn of events.

There had been this genuine feeling of liking Mark Perez, and to be so disillusioned that he had played them both for fools had hit the two young men with a mighty blow. What was it going to do to Aimee? they both wondered.

Both had already decided that they had better not lay eyes on

187

him again on this land or in the company of their sister. If Mano were so bold as to try to see her, he'd rue the day.

Just as they were about to enter their separate rooms across the carpeted hallway, it was Emile who broke the awesome silence they'd lingered in, shaking his dark head in disbelief to say to Armand, *"Mon Dieu,* I really liked the man! I still find it hard to believe what father told us."

Armand agreed. "I liked him, too, and I know our sister is going to be hurt. She liked this man, Emile. I saw it in her eyes, on her face. I don't look forward to this evening, Emile. I don't think you do, either."

"It won't be pleasant, but I will see you later and we will try to comfort her as best as brothers can under the circumstances, *oui?"*

"Oui, we will do that," Armand said, giving Emile a weak smile. He moved to enter his room.

Emile went on through his bedroom door. In the adjoining room, with only a wall dividing them, Aimee sat on her bed enjoying a lighthearted chat with Jolie, having no idea of the drama evolving around her where her family was concerned. Her heart was light and gay as she anticipated the night ahead of her. The wild side of her nature was excited about the episode she was to share with Mark.

But this lively bliss was soon to be shattered, because Paul was now having a very serious discussion with his wife in her sitting room. Like her sons, Lisette was finding the bright, cheery serenity of this small room she always enjoyed being clouded with gloom as she listened to the disturbing news Paul was telling her.

A short time ago, she'd been sitting in her green and pink chintz floral chair and looking out the windows draped with little ruffled curtains made of the same chintz pattern. The room was truly Lisette's, with all the things she loved. Her baskets of yarn were here, as well as her display of numerous blooming flowers like the lovely pink amaryllis, violets, and the deep pink budding fuchsia with its exotic blossoms.

There was always a most refreshing aroma permeating this room from Lisette's little containers of dried flower petals and herbs. Her most precious possessions were the small miniatures of each of her children sitting on her lady's desk. This room was her haven and she spent many hours here. This was where she usually waited for her husband to return from his vineyards before going upstairs to refresh herself and attend to her toilette, then joining the family for the evening meal.

This late afternoon she was not finding it a pleasant occasion to spend this brief moment with Paul. His news devastated her. She could not tell Paul what she was truly thinking as he told her that this Mark Perez was really Mano Mateo, because he would have gone into a rage. She did not care what the young man's name happened to be; she had liked him and she still did. For this reason, she insisted that she be the one to go talk to Aimee.

"I think it would be terribly cruel to inform her during the meal or before we dine. Let me go to her and talk to her, Paul. I suspect that I will be sending a tray up to her tonight, for she was still not feeling well a short time ago when I checked with Jolie."

"Of course, Lisette. I understand that a mother can talk to a daughter easier than a father. I ask only one thing of you and that is that you let this young lady know that no son of Carlos Mateo will be allowed to ever come to Chateau L'Aragon again."

"I will tell her, Paul," she told him, laying aside her needlepoint to rise up out of her overstuffed chair. "I will go to her now, Paul."

She left him there in her sitting room, and Paul was amazed that she had not shown more repulsion over his revelation about Mark Perez. Lisette had perplexed him completely lately and he had to confess that it was beginning to bother him very much.

Lisette was not the same woman and yet he had to confess that he was ignited with a strange interest and curiosity about the changes he'd seen in her. He'd watched her leave the room, and the swaying of her petite figure had aroused him as it hadn't for a long time.

Paul's secret yearnings would have surprised Lisette. At this particular moment, however, her husband was not her concern. Her daughter and her reaction to what she was about to tell her was what concerned Lisette.

At the sound of her gentle rapping on Aimee's door, Jolie opened it and greeted her. Lisette returned her greeting as she glided into the room. "Feeling about the same, *ma petite?*" she inquired of Aimee.

"Yes, Mama. I feel no better," Aimee told her.

Lisette moved to sit on the edge of her bed. Her hand reached for Aimee's forehead and she found it free of a fever. Her experienced eyes saw no flush of fever on her daughter's face, either. "Shall I send up a tray for your dinner and you just rest tonight, eh?"

Aimee gave her mother a nod of the head, agreeing that it would be best. Secretly, she was thinking to herself that it was all going so perfectly, almost effortlessly on her part.

However, her mother tossed her a slight surprise when she requested Jolie to leave the room for a while. She had something to speak to her daughter about in privacy.

Jolie and Aimee exchanged questioning glances with one another for a brief second before the maid did as the madame requested. Once the door was closed and the privacy was theirs alone, Lisette wasted no time in getting directly to the subject of what she wished to discuss with her daughter.

"I do not enjoy what I must tell you, Aimee. I thought it better it come from me instead of your father. The young man you have been seeing—the young man I have come to like very much—is not Mark Perez. There is no simple way to say it but just to say it as it is. Mark Perez is actually the son—the youngest son—of Carlos Mateo. His name is Manuelo Mateo. Everyone here in the valley knows him as Mano. I will add that he has not had a very admirable reputation. They usually refer

190

to him as Carlos's renegade son."

Aimee's lovely face gave no hint of her feelings to her mother; it was expressionless. The shock and the pain was too deep within her. The stabbing pain was in her stomach and she trembled as though she had been struck by a mighty blow. Her head whirled with a giddiness, as though she had drank too much of her father's fine wines.

But when she spoke in that soft voice of hers, she maintained a calm that amazed her. God forbid, she was hardly calm!

"Well, now I know why Gabriella Melita was raving so about this Mano Mateo. He is a magnificent man, isn't he, Mama?" Her deep sapphire eyes demanded the truth from Lisette and her mother could not deny that he was that.

"Oh, I am sorry, Aimee! So sorry to be the one to ruin something for you. I found the young man so charming and I know you did, too."

Aimee gave her mother's hand an affectionate pat as she assured her, "There is nothing to feel sorry about, Mama. You've spoiled nothing for me. Whatever his name might be, we both knew the man he was—the man he is. *Oui?*"

"*Oui, ma petite!*" Lisette agreed in a hesitating voice.

Aimee smiled and she reached out to embrace her mother. They clung together, understanding one another. Aimee softly whispered in her ear that it was all going to be all right.

"His name matters not to me, Mama. It is the man I measure," Aimee told her.

Lisette wasn't certain about her daughter's feelings as she left the room. At least, Aimee now knew who the young man was. What she did about it now was her own decision.

She knew one thing, and that was that the handsome Mano would be a hard man to turn one's back on and walk away from. He had a certain charm so powerful and compelling that few women could resist him. Lisette felt it, so how could she fault her own daughter?

Aimee was glad for that period of solitude before Jolie

returned to her room. At first she was tempted to not meet that handsome devil she'd known and loved as Mark Perez. Ah, yes, it would serve him right to wait for her in the gardens and have her never appear. He certainly deserved that, being the arrogant, conceited man.

But then she thought about another scheme that would pain him more deeply, and this was her desire.

She wished to wound Mano Mateo with the same stabbing pain he had caused her!

Chapter 24

By the time Jolie had returned to the bedroom, Aimee was sitting up in her bed with her golden tresses fanned out over the pillows. There was a smug look on her lovely face and Jolie was happy to see her looking so pleased with herself.

"Mademoiselle, may I still bring you a tray for dinner and do you still wish me to carry out your plans?" Jolie asked her young mistress.

"Yes, Jolie, I still wish you to bring my dinner tray to the room. Nothing has changed. I will still be slipping out of the house at nine as I'd told you." She gave her little maid a sly smile and a wink of her eye.

Jolie smiled, delighted that the exciting escapade was still planned. Perhaps she was just a silly romantic fool, she told herself. If she could not enjoy such folly herself, she felt she shared a part of it with Mademoiselle Aimee.

As her young mistress had instructed her to do, she marched down the steps at the appointed hour to get her dinner tray. All the time Jolie was gone, Aimee spent plotting exactly how she was going to carry out her charade, which was not going to be easy. She knew she was going to have to pull all the strength and willpower from herself to resist this man's powerful, masterful force. He could render her utterly helpless very swiftly and she knew this so well.

She would resist that force, she vowed. Whatever it took, she would do it and leave him wanting at the end of the evening. Only then would she enlighten him about what she knew. Only then would she tell him that she'd known all evening he was Mano Mateo.

She had to confess privately to herself that Gabriella Melita had spoken the truth about him. He was a most charming devil with a silken tongue. Now, as she sat up in her bed, she thought about the last several weeks since he'd come into her life. His sweet, sensuous lips, so persuasive, had made her so willing to surrender to his magic charm.

Damn him to hell! she muttered to herself. She'd make him pay in the worst way. Oh, by the time this evening was over, he'd know he should have never played her so false. Until the moment she picked to tell him, though, he'd never suspect a thing.

Never would she look more fetching, she promised herself as she walked over to her ornate armoire and opened the door. She knew the sort of costume the flamenco dancers wore, since she had seen them perform in Paris.

She lifted the vivid purple batiste tunic from her chest, with its full flowing sleeves gathered at the wrist. The drawstring neckline allowed it to be gathered as tight or as loose as she desired. She had already decided she would allow it to reveal the alluring cleavage of her breasts. Not too much but just enough to tease and tantalize the eyes of the lusting man she figured Mano Mateo was.

The skirt she would wear was the one with the ruffled flounce, and its colors of lavender, purple, and white would blend perfectly with the tunic. In her hair, she would have Jolie put some of the lovely gardenia blossoms flourishing from the potted plant on her balcony.

When Jolie returned with the tray of food, she ate with a ravenous appetite. It never ceased to amaze Jolie how heartily the little mademoiselle could eat and never put on any excess weight.

Aimee churned with a mixture of emotions as she ate the food off her plate. There was the spark of excitement as to how she would play this rascal, whose sensuous mouth and hypnotic eyes could lie so easily and convincingly. There was the feeling of hating him for fooling her and playing her for an idiot. No woman enjoys that sort of abuse from a man.

She had never set out to seduce a man before in her life, but this evening she was going to dare to be the most beguiling seductress she could possibly be. When she had him weak from wanting her, she intended to tell him that she knew who he really was. This night he would not have his way with her, as he'd managed to do before, by just holding her in his strong arms, his magnificent lips claiming hers. Oh, no, not tonight!

It was all these musings that whetted her appetite and she finished every morsel on the plate Jolie had generously filled. Hetty had fixed her delicious fish baked in that special sauce and seasoned with a hint of lemon juice. Garnished with those fresh herbs from her garden, Hetty had done herself proud once again. Jolie had brought her a silver carafe of one of her father's best white wines, which enhanced Hetty's delectable fish.

Completely sated, she gave out a pleased sigh as she told Jolie, "Ah, you must get down to the kitchen and get yourself a plate of this fish before it is all gone, Jolie. It is wonderful!"

"I shall, mademoiselle. It smelled wonderful. I'd say that Hetty must know how much it is enjoyed by your family from the size of the huge pan she fixed tonight."

Lifting the tray from her lap to give it to Jolie, Aimee insisted, "Go on down the back stairs, Jolie. Go on down to the kitchen and enjoy yourself as I have just done. I can slip into the simple little frock I intend to wear. By the time I am ready to make my departure, you will be back. Then I will need you."

"*Oui,* mademoiselle, I will be back. Won't you need me to style your hair though?"

"No, Jolie. I shall wear it loose. From what Mark told me, it will be tied and concealed in a scarf anyway," she told her maid. It suddenly was difficult to utter the name Mark now that she knew it was not his name at all. Mano—Mano—Mano! She silently kept repeating it over and over again, and it seemed strange to her. She did not know this man, Mano, but she knew most intimately the man, Mark Perez.

"Oh, a shame, mademoiselle! A shame it is your gorgeous hair must be hidden in a scarf. But I suppose it is necessary, for all that golden hair could never belong to a Spanish lady," she giggled.

"Never!" Aimee declared. She could still not convince herself that the plan could be carried off as Mark—or Mano—had assured her, by changing places with one of the dancing couples who would perform in his father's courtyard gardens this evening during the fiesta.

The petite little Jolie did not have to be urged to do her mistress's bidding by helping herself to some of the tasty good food in Hetty's kitchen. The aroma had teased her nose as she'd brought the tray to Aimee. She played anxiously with the sides of her frosty white apron as she asked Aimee if she was sure she could do nothing for her before taking her leave.

"Go, Jolie, right now!" Aimee laughed, motioning her to be on her way.

Jolie smiled and nodded her head as she moved to go out the door. As the little maid went out the door, Aimee moved to fling her shapely legs over the side of the bed, and in her bare feet, she padded over to the mirrored armoire to take out the outfit she planned to wear. She had no intentions of wearing the cumbersome petticoats under the flowing, billowing floral skirt.

196

After she'd dressed herself in the brightly colored tunic and tucked it tightly inside the waistband of the skirt, she surveyed her image in the full-length mirror. Pleased with the effect, she sat down on the velvet-cushioned stool at her dressing table to brush her long, flowing silver-gold hair. She brushed it until it gleamed like an exquisite, glossy silk fabric.

Aimee liked the reflection she saw in the mirror. Like a thunderbolt had hit her, she pulled out the drawer of her dressing table to see if she could find a particular little item. How perfect those huge golden rings earrings would be for this ensemble and this evening's occasion. She also recalled that wonderful, carefree evening in Paris when she and her *Tante* Denise had strolled through the marketplace where the vendors sold their goods. The passersby could buy anything from fresh flowers, spices, wicker baskets, and foodstuffs. There were also lovely displays of laces and handiworks of embroidered articles in those endless rows of booths lining the cobblestone street. Her *Tante* Denise thoroughly enjoyed the quaint little shops and bazaars with their fancy, unique wares. This was where Aimee had purchased her golden gypsy hooped earrings, because they'd caught her eye. They'd lay dormant in the little leather pouch and she'd never worn them. But tonight she was going to put them on her dainty ears.

As she looked at her image in the mirror and placed the golden earrings on each of her earlobes, she could not help questioning if this were the reason for her buying them. Did she know that there would come a night such as this when those simple gold earrings would serve her well?

She stood before her mirror with her hands placed on her hips, giving them a sensuous sway as she'd seen the flamenco dancers do in Paris. She smiled smugly because she knew she looked just as entrancing as the ladies she'd seen in Paris doing their stimulating flamenco dances. As much as it galled her to admit it, the man she'd known as Mark Perez had made her aware of the sensations her curvaceous body could feel. There was a certain feminine pride as she observed herself in the full-length mirror.

She also knew that this sensuous body of hers had a certain power and force over that handsome Latin scoundrel she knew now was Mano Mateo, and that was a weapon she intended to use this evening. Before tonight was over this Mano Mateo was going to feel the sting of her venom and her disgust.

Oh, yes, she was going to make him hurt as he had made her hurt when her mother had told her the startling revelation a few hours ago. But she knew one thing, and that was that she was going to have to exert a powerful will to endure the tremendous force of his magnetic charm, which always rendered her so weak she so willingly surrendered to his amorous charms and caresses.

By the time Jolie returned to her boudoir, she felt she had done a magnificent job of convincing herself that she could handle anything Mark Perez or Mano Mateo tossed her way. When Jolie came through the door and saw how exotically alluring the little mademoiselle looked, she gasped with amazement, "I have never seen you look so beautiful, mademoiselle. You—you look so different!"

Aimee gave out a soft little gale of laughter. "I feel different tonight, Jolie. So strangely different that it frightens me, Jolie."

"Are you all right, mademoiselle?" Jolie asked with an air of discernment on her face.

Jolie's genuine concern was cherished by Aimee Aragon and she assured her devoted little maid that she was just fine. Forcing herself to exhibit a flare of lighthearted gaiety she was not feeling, she invited Jolie to join her in a glass of the white wine remaining in the silver carafe.

"Then I must be on my way to the gardens to meet Mark," she told her maid. The hands of the clock told her there were some twenty minutes before the appointed hour she was to be at that spot in the far corner of the walled garden.

As each of them took the last sip of the fine white wine, Jolie

198

remarked in a more serious tone, "I'll hope that the night will be all that you hoped for, Mademoiselle Aimee." Somehow, the anticipated excitement she was feeling was no longer there. It seemed to Jolie that the mood of her mistress had changed since she'd left the room to go downstairs to eat and no longer was Aimee feeling as she had earlier.

Aimee did not make a reply to her remarks. Instead, she requested that she check out the hallway. "It is time for me to leave, Jolie." She went over to the chair to gather up the white lace shawl to drape around her shoulders.

Jolie did as she was ordered. Seeing that the hallway was deserted and no one was there, she moved back through the doorway to motion to Aimee to follow her.

The two young women quietly slipped down the back stairs together, and when they reached the door at the back of the house, Jolie bid her mistress good-bye as Aimee rushed out into the darkness of the night to meet her lover.

As she scampered across the thick carpet of green grass, her dainty feet shod in the leather sandals, Aimee questioned whether it would have been smarter to have not met him there in the appointed spot, allowing him to wonder why she hadn't showed up.

No, she told herself, the hurt she planned for him would be far more harsh to a man like Mano Mateo with his overwhelming conceit and ego. There was no shadow of doubt that she'd made the right choice to carry out this plan of action.

Ah, yes, before this night was over, Mano Mateo would know well the wrath of this French woman! She recalled a similar circumstance with one of her *Tante* Denise's friends, which had wounded the arrogant gentleman's ego so tremendously that his friends pondered his morose mood in the weeks to come.

All of them had decided that it had to be a woman. This was what Aimee hoped to do to Mano Mateo. She hoped to devastate him with such total rejection tonight that everyone would wonder why he was so crestfallen.

As the French would say, *"Cher chez la femme."* Aimee wanted to be that woman to ruin this arrogant man who'd played her wrong! She hoped that all his friends would say that it must have been a woman.

She wanted all of them to know that the woman was Aimee Aragon!

Chapter 25

Anyone seeing the dashing petite figure of Aimee Aragon, with her silvery blonde hair flowing back over her shoulders as she rushed across the dark gardens with the bright moonlight guiding her way, could have thought she was a capricious little wood nymph.

She could not imagine the fascinating sight she made, but Jolie watched her go to meet her lover and sighed with admiration. How absolutely breathtakingly beautiful she was! the little French maid thought to herself.

As she turned her back on the night outside the rambling two-story stone house, Jolie could not help envying her little mistress and wishing it were her going to meet a handsome young lover like Mark Perez. Who was to say it would not happen someday for her? she asked herself. She had to hold on to her dreams, for it was all she had right now.

It was not as if she were old and wrinkled with age, Jolie reminded herself. Her figure had a fair curve to it, even though she could hardly claim it to be voluptuous. She certainly did not possess a beguiling, luscious loveliness like the mademoiselle, but she did possess delicate features, with a thick lovely mane of jet-black hair and a soft, smooth light tawny complexion.

While there was not a conceited bone in her body, Jolie's mirror told her that she was certainly not ugly.

Before she sought to enter the back door to go into the kitchen, she lingered for a moment by Hetty's herb garden, enjoying the sweet fragrance of the blooms on the herbs. Knowing that Hetty would not mind, she bent down to pluck a few of the blossoms, which she found to be as delightfully pleasing to smell as any of the flowers growing in Madame Lisette's garden.

A deep accented voice made her quiver as she stood there smelling the pale lavender flower of the chives and a wee blue-purple flower of the thyme.

She turned to sigh in relief at the sight of Emile Aragon. "God, you gave me a fright, monsieur!"

"Forgive me, Jolie, I certainly did not intend to do that," he chuckled lightly.

"To turn around in the dark and see such a huge figure standing behind you is a little frightening, monsieur."

Emile smiled at her, wondering why he had never taken notice before of this very attractive young lady living right here under his roof. Too much work and too little time to play had obviously made him a very dull person, he realized suddenly. He was not exactly dead with old age. The truth was he was in his prime, and perhaps it was time he began to live a little as most young men at his age did.

"For one as tiny as you, I can see why a big ox like me could frighten you, Jolie." They stood there for a brief moment just gazing at one another. It was Emile who finally broke the silence when he asked Jolie, "Where was she going, Jolie? Was she meeting Mark Perez?"

There was no way Jolie could have lied to the young man standing so close to her, with his piercing eyes demanding an honest answer. "*Oui*, she was going to meet him, Monsieur Aragon."

He nodded his head in a gesture that told Jolie he understood and sympathized with his sister. He also appreciated Jolie being honest with him.

For a moment, Emile searched her face, wondering if he dared to give way to the impulse stabbing at him. Finally, he obeyed an impestuous desire to ask her to go for a stroll through the gardens with him.

Jolie was absolutely stunned to be asked to join Emile in a stroll through the gardens. Knowing him to be a shy man, she was overwhelmingly impressed by the invitation.

She gave him a lovely smile as she accepted his offer, "I'd be most honored, Monsieur Aragon."

"Then shall we go, Jolie?" he said, moving to her side. "Please just call me Emile, Jolie. I appreciate very much the respect you are paying me but you can reserve that for my father. We are both young, *n'est ce pas?* I—I just wish to enjoy your company and I am not thinking of you right now as a servant in the Aragon household. Do you know what I am trying to tell you in my awkward way, Jolie?"

She looked up at him and a slow, easy smile came to her face. "I—I think I do, Mon—Emile." They both broke into a light, gay gusto of laughter. He slowed his gait to match hers as they walked side by side in the moonlit gardens, and Emile suddenly realized just how much he had missed the last few years working so hard in his father's vineyards. It was nice just to be taking a pleasant stroll in the evening with an attractive young lady like Jolie. It might just be a simple pleasure but he had not felt so gay and lighthearted in many, many months.

A night bird called to its mate and a light, cooling breeze rustled through the tall trees as the two of them walked along the flagstone pathway. The sweet fragrance of the numerous blossoms growing there in Lisette's garden wafted to their nostrils. "It is wonderful, this garden your mother has created

203

over the years. Such devotion she has given to it! She is one of the most gentle, good-hearted ladies I've ever known in my life."

Emile readily agreed with her about that. "She could have been no other way and been married to such a volatile man as my father," Emile laughed.

Jolie grinned, daring not to agree with him about Monsieur Paul Aragon. He could not be the easiest man to live with, she had concluded. Instead, she said to Emile, "Your sister has the kind, gentle heart of your mother."

"Ah, I will agree with you about that, Jolie. However, Aimee is a very different lady than my mother and I think you would agree with me about that."

"*Oui*, Monsieur—I mean Emile. I would surely agree with you about that."

They walked and talked as they made the complete circle of the garden. As they neared the back entrance of the kitchen door, Jolie was standing by Hetty's aromatic herb garden when Emile approached her. She was sure that Emile Aragon yearned to kiss her and she knew not what she should do. Being a mere servant, she found herself in a dilemma. Oh, she did not object to his kissing her, for she found Emile a most handsome man. She knew him to be a hard-working, devoted son. Tonight, she was impressed by his sincerity and honesty. He'd seemed to enjoy her company as much as she had enjoyed his.

Emile took notice of a sudden shyness coming over the tiny little maid and he suspected what she was thinking. A warm, friendly smile creased his tanned face as he addressed her, "I appreciate the nice hour we've spent together, Jolie. I hope you did too. I—I don't usually get to enjoy such a pleasant evening as this. After dinner, I'm usually off to bed to get up at the crack of dawn and go to the vineyards."

An effusive splendor rushed over her and she felt herself blushing as she stammered, "I—I enjoyed the stroll with you, Emile, I enjoyed it very much!"

With an eager grin on his face, he suggested to her, "Let's do it again sometime. Would you like that, Jolie? I—I know I would!"

"Oh, yes! I would like that very much, Emile. Whenever you wish that I walk with you and I am not attending to the mademoiselle's needs, I shall be most happy to accompany you."

Emile gave her an eager nod of his head and bid her good night, awkwardly backing away as she entered the doorway. He, too, was feeling shy and ill-at-ease around the little French maid because he was suddenly consumed with the overwhelming desire to take her in his strong muscled arms and kiss her rosy red lips. This was a strange emotion Emile had not experienced too often in his life.

The thought of her sweet revenge on this Mano Mateo made Aimee titillate with a strange excitement as she rushed across the thick carpet of grass toward the appointed spot in the garden.

Silvery moonbeams dramatically played across the area. Possessed with a most vivid imagination, Aimee envisioned herself in a magical fairyland there in her mother's wonderful gardens. Ah, what a glorious fragrance swept across the manicured lawns and gardens as she breezed along the path, her long hair flowing back from her face.

The low scooped-necked blouse, exposing the soft silken flesh of her cleavage, caused the same sensations she felt in her face with her hair blowing back. The billowing folds of her full gathered skirt swelled like a long crestless wave in the ocean. There was a certain magic tonight, she realized.

A few feet away from the spot where she was to have met her lover, as her dainty sandaled feet were taking their fast-paced steps, she found herself suddenly swept up in the viselike grasp of two strong arms.

Her deep amethyst eyes were gazing into the intoxicating jet-black ones of the man she'd known and loved as Mark Perez. Dear God, she knew how difficult it was going to be to carry out her well-laid plan for this night!

Mano pressed her close to his broad chest, allowing his nose to deeply inhale the sweet jasmine fragrance she wore as his lips caressed her cheek.

Breathlessly, she gasped, "God, Mark! You scared me to death!" He held her there in his arms and her feet no longer touched the ground.

A deep, throaty laugh broke forth in Mano as he murmured softly, with the warm emotions surging within him, "Ah, *chiquita,* you are no longer scared, are you? My arms are holding you and nothing will ever happen to you when these arms are holding you. Do you not know that by now?"

Oh, what a lying silver tongue this Mano Mateo possessed! How very sincere and convincing he could sound, she reminded herself. She must turn a deaf ear to all this sweet talk tonight and not allow herself to weaken for even one unguarded moment. If she did, she would surrender to his sweet persuasion as she had in the past. No more would that happen! she silently vowed.

"Oh, you are impossible, Mark Perez," she declared. She loathed having to address him as Mark Perez tonight now that she knew he was Mano Mateo.

"Oh, no, I am not impossible at all. You are the most fetching female these eyes have ever seen. You have never looked more beautiful than you do tonight. Ah, Aimee, you do something to me that I can't even explain to myself!" His strong arms held her slightly tighter as his warm lips whispered against her cheek, "I'm not impossible, Aimee. I am a man insane with love for you."

He had such an overwhelming talent for bewitching a woman that she found herself beginning to fall under the spell he was casting. Knowing she must be freed from those powerful arms, she began to wiggle and push away from the searing heat of his fine male body.

"Put me down, Mark. If you don't, I won't make a very presentable sight at the fiesta," she insisted.

Giving out a lighthearted chuckle, he lowered her back to the thick-carpeted grass. Playing the role of a gallant, he gave her a low bow as he responded, "Yes, ma'am. Your wishes are my command." A wicked, teasing twinkle sparked in his dark eyes.

He watched her with amusement as she fussed with her skirt, twisting it back in place and tucking the sheer tunic inside the waistband.

"Now, little *violeta*, are you ready to be on our way, eh?"

Her attention to her skirt and blouse had given Aimee a chance to regain control of her emotions, which were quickly getting out of control. Now she could gaze up at him boldly, as she wanted to do, and she let a slow, easy smile crease her lips. "I am ready if you are."

Like thieves in the night, they moved along the enclosed garden wall until they came to the iron gate. Once outside the gate, Mano led her to where he had tethered Demonio. In a fast sweeping motion, she felt herself lifted up to rest on the fine animal's back. Hastily, he moved to mount the animal behind her. Instantly, he spurred the thoroughbred into action.

His arms enclosed her snugly as he held the reins and guided the high-spirited horse in the direction of the Mateo ranch. There was something in the air of the night that promised wild excitement as the magnificent animal galloped across the countryside.

Her senses were titillated, as were Mano's. Both sensed this, even though neither of them mentioned it to the other. There was an acute awareness of everything around them as they rode along. Her eyes observed the magnificent bright full moon above them in the dark California sky. The odor of the numerous wildflowers blooming there in the valley and in the hillside they'd just left behind had an intoxicating effect on her. Her ears heard the calling of a nightbird, lonely for its mate.

Already, she was feeling regret that she must do what she knew she must do tonight. This was a night made for lovers, but tonight she could not allow him to be her lover as he had been in the past. She must not!

Never would Mano Mateo have imagined the devious plot hatching there in that pretty head of hers. Never in a million years!

By now, his eyes had caught sight of the numerous twinkling lights invading the night's darkness. He recognized the sight as the many torches lighting up the courtyard of his father's garden. He knew that the guests were already mingling there in the spacious gardens as they were being entertained by the strolling musicians hired by his father for the fiesta.

Minerva's delectable food was probably being tasted and enjoyed. He knew that she and her helpers always prepared enough for the one night of festivities to feed a small army.

"There is it—La Casa Grande!" he announced to her.

Mano had made his arrangements with the pair of dancers whose places they would step into for one dance. Lorenzo Romano and his wife, Lita, were more than willing to go along with Mano's request. Both of them had found him the most likeable of the Mateo family. He shared a certain earthy quality with the two of them. Their troupe of dancers had been coming to the fiesta put on by Carlos Mateo for many years now. Mano was a mere youth of seventeen the first year they'd performed at La Casa Grande.

Aimee saw the sparkling lights over in the distance and she noted the certain tone of pride in his voice as he spoke about his home, La Casa Grande.

In an air of facetiousness, she declared, "Well, Carlos Mateo's grand house will be invaded tonight by an Aragon whose family is every bit as grand as his. His audacity to snub them is rather ludicrous."

Mano watched her lovely face, her head held high with pride. He admired this beautiful young woman for defending her family so devotedly.

Someday, he hoped to have that degree of devotion from her. Someday, he hoped she would look at him with those lovely deep blue eyes, adoring him as she could never adore any other man on the face of the earth.

Mano knew that there was no other woman he'd ever feel such depth of emotion for as he felt for Aimee.

Chapter 26

Gay lighthearted laughter resounded within the stone-wall courtyard gardens of La Casa Grande. A glorious array of colorful gowned ladies strolled on the arms of their gentlemen, finely attired. The musicians strummed lively tunes on their guitars as Aimee arrived with Mano. She had no knowledge of his carefully laid-out plans with the Romanos as they approached the far side of the courtyard gardens where the caravan of wagons were stationed.

As Demonio paced up to the four wagons, Aimee was fascinated by the colorfully costumed couples coming forth to greet them with smiles on their swarthy faces. One couple stood out from the others. Aimee found the dark-complexioned lady standing by the man with the colorful kerchief tied around his head absolutely gorgeous. Her long black hair flowed around her shoulders, and her sheer white peasant-styled blouse barely covered her shoulders. The blouse barely concealed the woman's voluptuous full-blooming breasts. Her dark eyes sparkled with warmth and her lovely sensuous mouth creased in a friendly smile as she waved to them. Aimee had no doubt about the camaraderie existing between these people and this man she now knew as Mano Mateo.

She could not deny that she found it intriguing that the son of the wealthy Carlos Mateo could be so friendly with this traveling troupe of dancers. But it was obvious, even before he had lifted her off Demonio, that they adored him.

The man and the woman both embraced him warmly as they came up to them. The man she knew as Mark Perez urged her forward as he spoke and she moved to take the friendly hands they extended. "May I present Mademoiselle Aimee Aragon. Aimee, this is Lorenzo and Lita Romano. They are my very dear friends."

It was the lovely Lita who first spoke her words of praise about Aimee's beauty. In a slow, lazy drawl, she sighed, "Ah, *bonita!* You are most beautiful, but I am sure you are told that all the time."

"It is always nice to be told that, Madame Romano," Aimee replied.

Lita smiled, noticing her flawless gardenia-white skin, and her dark eyes darted over to Mano as she pointed out to him, "The hair can be concealed but this lovely, delicate complexion will be another thing. But we shall try if Aimee is willing."

"Oh, I am willing," she quickly assured the sultry-looking Lita.

"Then shall we leave these two and get busy trying to make you look a little more Spanish, eh?" Lita suggested, extending her hand out to Aimee. Aimee took it and found herself hastily led away by the fiesty flamenco dancer.

Aimee noticed the carefree sway of her round hips as she walked at her fast pace and she admired the alluring figure of the older lady. The constant dancing must contribute something to her maintaining such a fine figure, she decided.

She followed Lita as she mounted the step of a covered wagon, accepting her hand as she was hoisted inside. The interior was like nothing Aimee had ever viewed before. Colorful bright cushions and blankets lined one side of the wagon. Shining brass lanterns hung from the supports of the canvas covering enclosing the wagon. A crude-looking pole was installed to hang their brilliant, colorful costumes and clothing. But the thing that captured and held Aimee's interest in these meager living quarters was a magnificent gold gilt little dressing table with its scarlet velvet cushioned stool.

"Ah, I see you appreciate my pride and joy. My Lorenzo bought me this in France a few years ago, when we were touring Europe. It is beautiful, isn't it?" Her eyes twinkled with such a glowing pride for the gift from her husband. "He said I must have it to sit there and make myself beautiful so when we dance together I would inspire him with my beauty. Is that not the sweetest thing a husband could say to a wife?"

Aimee agreed, declaring, "You are a very lucky lady, Lita, to have a man love you so much."

Lita's dancing black eyes sparkled and she smiled, "So, little one, you are a silly romantic like I am, eh? I am a very lucky lady to have my man, Lorenzo." Her fine arched brow raised as she gave forth a dramatic gesture by pointing her finger in Aimee's direction. "I think maybe you are a lucky lady, too, to have such a man as—uh, such a man as you have." She had almost had a slip of the tongue and said Mano. She chided herself to be more careful.

Aimee sought to make no reply, merely giving the lovely, vivacious lady standing there a warm, friendly smile.

Lita invited her to have a seat there in front of the cherished little dressing table. A gale of lilting laughter broke forth from Lita. "Lucky for you that I have a gorgeous purple silk scarf, because it will match perfectly with your blouse and skirt. Ah, but it seems a shame to cover such a magnificent crown of hair as yours. If we are to make this little escapade work as your man wishes, it must be done."

"Then let's do it!" Aimee told her.

Lita gave her a nod of her head. From one of the numerous boxes stacked one on stop of the other, she lifted the lid to take out the particular scarf she was talking about. From a teakwood box situated there on the dressing table, she lifted a pair of gold hooped earrings very light in weight.

"These you must wear."

As Lita placed them on her ears, Aimee was amazed that they were not as heavy as she would have thought from the looks of them. Quite skillfully, Lita's hands worked at the scarf, tying it at the back of Aimee's head. By the time the scarf was in place with none of her silver-blond locks showing and the dangling gold earrings were on her ears, Aimee was amazed and fascinated by the image of herself in the mirror. She looked different and she even felt different sitting there in Lita's wagon.

"*Mon Dieu!*" Aimee gasped.

"*Si*, senorita, you do look different from the girl who entered my wagon. Right now, I could not tell you which one I find the most enchanting," she giggled.

Now Lita faced the real challenge of checking her various little jars of makeup to find something that would darken that fair, flawless complexion.

While the two women were away and Lorenzo and Mano had this time alone, Lorenzo's curiosity could not restrain itself any longer. He was compelled to ask Mano, "How do you ever hope to pull this off, amigo? You surely know that you will be recognized by the senor's guests."

"I will wear a kerchief tied around my head like Aimee and I will use your Lita's kohl to make myself a mustache. I think it will work, since the platform is the distance it is from where the guests are seated to watch your troupe perform." Mano was so sure it was going to work that even Lorenzo could not have discouraged him from trying it.

Tonight he was so happy and he had already decided that

before this evening ended he was going to gamble on Aimee's love for him. He was going to tell her the truth. There was a boyish eagerness on his face as he prodded Lorenzo, "Is she not as lovely as I said?"

"Ah, amigo, that one is lovelier than you described. Now, I would be the first to say that you are a connoiseur of ladies. I have seen your selection of ladies over the years. All of them were very gorgeous women but this one has that extra special something which sets her apart from all the others. This is why she fascinates you so, *si?*"

"This is why, Lorenzo." Mano gave him a sly grin.

"I know the feeling, amigo. It was the same when my eyes first gazed on my Lita. Never has it changed."

Mano suddenly noticed that Lorenzo's dark eyes were not focused on him nor was he listening to anything he had to say. He was gazing at the two women who were coming from the direction of his covered wagon. The one who entranced him was Aimee, but she hardly looked like the lovely French maiden who'd left them a short time ago.

Now she looked like the very provocative, sultry dancer Lita's magic had created. She was utterly breathtaking! Like Lorenzo, Mano watched the sensuous sway of her hips as she walked beside Lita. Her head was high and arrogant, as though she were proud of this new person she'd become. The two ladies exchanged a few words before they broke into a lighthearted laughter. Mano assumed that they both knew the devastating effect it was having on them.

It was true that Lita had shown Aimee some very exotic, sensual body movements, which never failed to excite any hot-blooded gentleman. Giggling, she had told Aimee, "If a man is not aroused when a lady moves like that, then he is dead anyway, so you forget him."

Aimee had copied the motions of Lita's curvaceous body and inquired, "Like this, Lita?"

Lita had given out a pleased moan of praise, "Ah, exactly like that! You are a born dancer, *nina*. Did you know that? You have such a natural grace and I must say something to you, Aimee. I hope you will not think I am being bold, since we have not known one another but a brief time. But I know—I know right now that you are a lady of deep, deep emotions. You love with your heart and your soul. The reason I can speak so bluntly is because I, too, am such a woman."

A smug expression was on Aimee's lovely face. She had instantly liked this lovely lady and she'd sensed that the feeling was mutual with Lita Romano. "You are a most perceptive lady, Lita Romano. I am a lady who loves completely. I am a lady who hates with as much consuming passion," she declared to the flamenco dancer.

Her words were enough to make the experienced older lady wonder just what she meant. Was it just a mere expression of her straightforward honesty or did something heavy weigh on this lovely senorita tonight? the earthy Lita wondered.

After a brief moment of silence, Lita asked her, "Well, shall we join our men?"

Aimee agreed with her, but all the while the earthy Lita was wondering if Mano had figured this lady right. Mateo had given them the impression that she was his woman. But Lita was not convinced that he had conquered this lovely lady. She was a different breed of woman than any of the others Lita had seen Mateo escort to these fiestas given by his father in the past years.

More than ever, Aimee was intrigued with Mano. From the first moment they'd met, she'd sensed he was a man of mystery and perhaps that had been the thing that had intrigued her in the beginning. Never was she more inquisitive about this tall, dark Latin than she was tonight. If he were Mano Mateo, as Fred Bigler had informed her father he was, then how did he hope to fool all his father's guests? Such a strikingly handsome man as Mano would be instantly recognized by all the people at the fiesta.

Her curious nature was whetted to a fine point. Oh, how she would have liked to be able to read what that cunning brain of his was plotting! Was he that clever?

What she could not know was that Mano had made a very brief appearance, roaming amid the gathered guests there in his father's gardens, and then like a phantom, he had swiftly disappeared from the courtyard to go upstairs and change out of the elegant attire he had on.

At the planned time, young Paco had Demonio saddled and ready to go to the Chateau L'Aragon. Mano had felt very smug about everything going off without a hitch. Now, he was watching the lovely lady he loved coming to him. She looked exactly the way he'd hoped Lita could disguise her when he'd schemed with the Romano couple. Never had she looked more provocative!

His tanned hands reached out to her as the two women approached him and Lorenzo. "Ah, *chiquita,* you—you are enough to take my breath away. You look like the most beautiful flamenco dancer I have ever seen." He took her hands in his before turning his attention to Lita to thank her for the magnificent job she'd performed.

"Ah, it was my pleasure, Ma—Mark!" Lita had once again almost had a slip of the tongue and her husband, standing back slightly, could afford the privilege of an amused grin. He knew that she had almost said Mano instead of Mark.

Mano had sensed it too and hastily drew Aimee's attention to him by telling her they would observe the first dance from a concealed place in the shadows by the side of the platform.

A soft little laugh came from Lita as she told Mano, "I can tell you that our Aimee here is a born dancer. I showed her a couple of steps and body movements, and I can tell you she did them with much feeling, eh Aimee?"

Aimee laughed lightheartedly, "I think you are being most generous with your praise, Lita."

"Oh, no, *nina.* To move as you did, one must feel the spirit and fire. Our dance pulls from the very essence of our being. Is it not so, Lorenzo?"

Lorenzo looked at his wife and there was an intense warmth

as his dark eyes danced over her lovingly. Aimee saw the same look of passion in them that she'd seen in the black eyes of Mark Perez when he'd made love to her.

"*Si, querida,* it is so," he told her.

Mano listened to Lita's raving comments about Aimee. He knew in the most intimate way the fire and passion of that lovely body. He knew how sensuously she'd moved with him as he'd guided her in the art of making love. Ah, such ecstasy was theirs!

His eyes devoured her as his deep voice remarked, "Aimee is a woman of fire and passion, and that is why she took to the dance so easily. I knew she would!"

He thought he had paid her the greatest degree of praise until he chanced to see the purple fire sparking in her lovely eyes.

She was devastatingly gorgeous when she was enraged as he knew she was at this moment. He was enraptured by the sight his eyes beheld.

Desire swelled within him to crush her in his arms and kiss those sweet-honey lips! But he also saw the fury he had provoked by his remarks. Dear God, how he'd riled that spitfire temper of hers! He tried to soothe himself by hoping that they would do the most fantastic dance Carlos Mateo's guests had ever witnessed—or the worst. Somehow, he felt that all that fury and fire would prove to be the talk of the whole evening's entertainment.

Looking at those eyes piercing him now, Mano realized that he had met his match. She was as impetuous as he was!

Chapter 27

The minute the music signaled for Lorenzo and Lita to join the rest of their troupe of dancers up on the platform, Mano sought to move close to Aimee's side as they stood there in the shadows of the festive courtyard gardens. Aimee had stolen a couple of fast glances at the young man standing beside her now. He was just as handsome, but he appeared to be a stranger after Lita's skilled hand had transformed his face with some quick motions of her kohl eye makeup.

It was truly remarkable, Aimee realized, and she found herself admiring tremendously the talents of the Romanos. She pondered if Mano was feeling the strange effects of this most unusual evening as she was. It seemed like she'd suddenly stepped into another world.

She was so entranced by the grace and charm of Lita and Lorenzo as they danced that she did not hear Mano telling her that the impressive figure dressed in black, strolling along the walkway to chat with his guests, was Senor Carlos Mateo.

Her chilling aloofness wounded his masculine pride, as she seemed to be ignoring him. "Did you not hear me, Aimee, and why are you acting so cold and indifferent to me suddenly?" There was a harshness and sting to his deep voice that she'd never heard before.

She turned slowly around to face him, looking deeply and intensely at his perplexed face. "I don't like that you announced to your friends that you obviously knew me so intimately, Mark Perez! I did not like that at all! It—it embarrassed me."

"Dear God, I was paying you a grand tribute, I thought. *Madre de Dios,* I will never understand women!" he declared dejectedly as he threw up his hands in a hopeless gesture.

"It is obvious you don't understand this woman, Mark."

He looked at her now, wondering how they would ever perform the dance due to begin in a short time. She was as cold as the ice maiden. He knew not how to reach her.

"I meant no disrespect, Aimee. If you choose not to believe me, then I can do nothing to change that. Lorenzo and Lita are my very dear friends and we feel very close to one another. We do not stand on ceremony with one another. I have few people I feel so close to." There was such sincerity in his words that she found it hard to believe he was lying. She shared his feelings for Lita and Lorenzo Romano. Even though she'd known them only a couple of hours, she felt a very warm, friendly feeling toward both of them.

But she could not allow sentiment to get in her way, because if she did, she was lost and she certainly knew that. But he was having an overwhelming impact on her, standing there so close to her side, and she was finding it very hard to feel cold toward him.

His strong hand clasped hers, pressing it as he said to her, "We will dance as good as Lorenzo and Lita. You will see, *chiquita!* Our bodies understand one another as we do. We are both driven by a primitive instinct as old as the ages and we allow our spirited natures to give way to the feeling. Is it not so?"

She felt his penetrating black eyes searing her flesh and she could not deny that what he said was true. Dear God, he held the strangest powers over her! She wondered if she would have the strength to endure this night, because she knew the most trying time was yet to come.

"What you say is true, Mark. We will dance our dance and look very good together. As you say, our bodies do respond to one another." Her eyes searched his handsome face and she watched a pleased smile emerge there. As quickly, she saw it fade as she added, "But I wonder about our hearts."

When he would have sought to inquire about her remarks, he heard the cue that meant Lorenzo and Lita would be exiting the platform stage and he and Aimee would be moving out of the shadows to take their place, as the rest of the troupe kept the steady beat of the flamenco music going.

There was a vigorous rhythmic beat to the music of the flamenco dance, which had originated with the Andalusian gypsies, and there was a sensuous, earthy quality about it. It had fascinated Mano ever since the first time his father had hired the Romano troupe to perform here at La Casa Grande. Aimee was stirred by the sensations it ignited far more than she cared to admit. There was something wild and wonderful in the music. When he urged her to come with him and join him there on the platform, she suddenly began to tremble with fright and uncertainty. But he quickly soothed all those fears by assuring her, "*Querida*, I will lead you and you will follow me, *si?* You will see."

Strange as it might seem from the plans she had conjured in her mind for him this evening, she believed him. She followed him out to the platform. As they passed the departing Romano couple, Lita gave her a quick peck on the cheek and assured her that she would be great.

Mano's magnificent male body had the agility of a matador as he moved slowly with her across the platform. She imitated his graceful motions, which she found easy to do. As the tempo became faster, Aimee realized this was a dance of passion, with the most alluring, erotic gestures. Yet, she found herself stamping her feet and clapping her hands to the sounds of the other members of the troupe in the background.

Lita had told her about the origin of the dance, which differed very much from the traditional Spanish style of dancing. Flamenco dancing was the more sensuous gypsy style rather than the Spanish style expressing the more delicate suggestion of passion and love. There were chanting sounds with the flamenco performers, which originated with the Sephardic Jews.

Mano was entranced by the beauty of her face as she followed him in the dance. He knew that she was completely caught up by the magic of the music, allowing her free spirit to move her. God, she was utterly magnificent! Never had he known such a woman as his enchanting Aimee and never did he expect to meet anyone who could compare to her.

He pulsed with the wildest desire as he watched the alluring movements of her body. It was as if she were trying to seduce him there as they moved around the platform. She teased and tantalized him unmercifully and he wondered if she realized just how wicked she could be.

When she had stood still with that inviting look in those deep amethyst eyes, before coaxing him to move toward her as they danced, he wondered if she knew the provocative look of the seductress she displayed. How could she when she was so young? he asked himself.

By the time they had finished the dance, Mano was weak from just wanting her as he'd never yearned for her before. The only thing bringing him alive and alert was the sight of his brother, Mario, rushing toward the stage.

Aimee was like the actress wishing to take a second bow, spurred by the uproar of applause from her appreciative audience. She was elated and Mano saw it in her flushed, radiant face.

Try as he might, he saw that he was not going to drag her

away fast enough to evade Mario. When Mario came within some thirty or forty feet of them, he was calling out for them to wait. Mano had never seen his older brother so unrestrained and exuberant.

"Senorita, Senor! Please wait!"

Under his breath, Mano was muttering a flow of cusswords. Already, Aimee had stopped to give an audience to the finely attired young man approaching her. She recognized Mario Mateo as he approached them. She knew few words in Spanish, but she knew enough to reply, "*Si*, senor, you are addressing us?"

"*Si*. I—I just had to say that I've never in all my life seen a more wonderful pair dancing," Mario told her as he came to stand in front of her. Aimee could not know the fascination engulfing Mario Mateo as he gazed at her with complete adoration. Now, as he looked at her, he was more beguiled by the breathtaking loveliness of her face. She could have been the Latin version of the fair-haired Aimee Aragon with her delicate, ethereal beauty.

All the time he'd watched her dance, he kept telling himself that this lovely dancer could not be Aimee, yet he could not convince himself it was not her. Now he stood before her and he was more befuddled than he'd been before.

When he found his tongue, he stammered, "You were magnificent, senorita. So were you, senor." His dark eyes took a more scrutinizing look at the man standing by her side. Damned, if he didn't envy this man!

"We thank you for your generous praise, Senor," Aimee told him, letting her eyes dart over to Mano. She found it hard to believe that this man, his brother, did not recognize him. But she, too, found his disguise a most remarkable change of character.

There in the shadows of the garden courtyard, with the moonlight playing back and forth through the tall, towering trees, Aimee decided that it was possible one brother would not recognize the other. She had to admit that both Mateo men were very handsome devils. Somehow, she decided that they were complete opposites in personality and temperament. They were as different as day is to night.

Mario was searching the face of this flamenco dancer. He did not recognize this member of the Romano troupe and the woman surely had to be new, for he could have never forgotten that glorious face had he seen it before.

It was not only the beguiling beauty of the woman's face and figure that fascinated Mario Mateo. The man held a strange effect over him that he could not explain. At first glance, the man was a stranger, and yet when he looked into those piercing black eyes, he would have sworn he'd seen this man before.

"I am Senor Mario Mateo. May I ask your names? I can't believe I've ever seen you dance before with Senor Romano's troupe. I fear I shall be terribly embarrassed if you tell me otherwise," Mario admitted with a smile on his face.

His request for a name caught Aimee completely unprepared and her deep blue eyes darted swiftly over to Mano. As he usually did, he quickly gave his brother an answer. She realized that he was an amazing liar. It was no wonder she was so gullible to his silver tongue, she thought to herself. Without a moment's hesitation, Mano replied to Mario, "We are Luis and Linda Delgardo, senor, and it has been our great pleasure to dance for the very respected Mateo family." There was such dramatic gusto and charm to his voice that Aimee decided then and there he could have charmed a rattlesnake. All she had to do was look at Mario Mateo's face to know that he believed every word Mano had just told him.

How could two blood brothers stand so close to one another and fool each other? she questioned. Never would Emile and Armand have been able to do this, she knew. But then Emile and Armand knew one another so well. She decided that Mario and his younger brother, Mano, did not share such a closeness. Somehow, Gabriella's words came back to haunt her, that

Mano was considered a renegade by the rest of the Mateo family.

She felt a little sick with disgust that she had been as weak as she had been to allow such a renegade scoundrel to have his way with her. All the young men she'd known in Paris and the California countryside had never had more than a little kiss from her. None of them could ever go off and brag that they had had their way with her. No one, but Mano Mateo could boast of that!

Damn him! Oh, she'd make him pay for using her so sorely while he pretended to be someone other than Mano Mateo. Oh, he must have thought himself so clever and smart! He had to have known that he would never have been welcomed inside the portals of Chateau L'Aragon that first night if her father had truly known who he was.

He chanced upon the scene of her being ravaged and decided to take advantage of the Aragon family as well as of her. Now that the clouds of deception had been removed and she was thinking more clearly, she was repulsed by his sly trickery. He'd had more than enough time to confess the truth to her if he'd wished to do so. How long did he intend to keep up this farce? Perhaps he intended to continue it until he could make the Aragon family the laughing stock of the county and this California valley.

Well, tonight it would come to an end! she vowed. But Aimee did not try to fool herself for one minute that the hurt and pain in her heart and soul wouldn't go on for a long, long time.

Perhaps, she sadly thought to herself, it might go on forever. A man like Mano would not be so easily forgotten just because she told herself she must do so.

If she had to be truthful, Aimee knew Mano and his flaming, searing lovemaking would burn within her as long as she lived. Forever would her dreams be haunted by his strong arms holding her close to him and his sensuous lips urging her to yield to him.

Whoever the man might be that she would share her future with, Aimee knew it would be Mano she was surrendering to—giving her love and her passion!

When she closed her eyes it would be Mano she pretended was holding her in his arms and kissing her lips, because no man could ever make her feel as he had. Of this, she was convinced!

Chapter 28

It was a night holding bittersweet memories for Aimee as Mano took her home after the fiesta. Had she not known who he really was, it could have been the most exciting night of her life. It had been a wonderful experience meeting the Romanos and pretending to be a flamenco dancer for one brief moment in time.

When she had said her farewells to the Romanos, Lita had presented her with a tiny gold cross, fastening it around her throat as she declared, "It is for good luck, *nina*. We shall meet again, I know, and I have come to love you very much in a very short time. This is good, *si?*"

"This is wonderful, Lita." Aimee had laughed softly as she kissed the lovely lady on the cheek. "I shall never forget you and Lorenzo."

"Nor shall we forget you, Aimee Aragon," Lita declared.

After a warm embrace from both Lita and Lorenzo, Aimee took Mano's hand and allowed him to lead her to where Demonio was tethered. He hoisted her atop the huge animal and leaped up behind her, spurring the spirited thoroughbred into action. After a few brief moments of silence, Mano could not resist asking her, "Well, *chiquita*, what did you think about La Casa Grande? Was it what you had imagined?"

"It was a very elegant place, Mark. The garden courtyard was most magnificent. I am sure I would have found the spacious house as elegant and very luxurious. But I did not feel the love and warmth of my own home there. It was missing." She searched his face for a clue or a reaction to her words. "I found Mario Mateo a very nice man, kind and gentle, and your friends the Romanos were wonderful, and for that encounter with them I will forever be grateful. I thank you, Mark, for that."

"There is no need to thank me, for it was my pleasure."

Another brief period of silence engulfed them before Mano dared to quiz her about her very brief encounter with his father, Carlos Mateo. It had been a very fleeting moment, as Carlos had graciously thanked the troupe for performing for his fiesta. He had moved swiftly along the lined group of the performers, shaking each of their hands. A smug smile had creased Mano's face as his father had shaken his hand in a perfunctory air, as he had all the other performers in the troupe. Carlos's eyes did not meet with any of the performers. Aimee was the rare exception. When he shook her dainty hand, he lingered for one brief moment.

Mano had seen the look in those fierce black eyes of Carlos Mateo and he knew exactly the thoughts running through his father's mind. There was a sense of resentment swelling within Mano, as it had been when Mario's eyes were adoring Aimee earlier.

As they rode through the night at an hour past midnight, a multitude of twinkling stars shining down on them like diamonds, Mano knew he could not wait any longer to confess the truth to the lady he loved. To delay it any further was gambling too much to suit him. He could not chance losing her and he knew he would if she ever found out that he'd lied to her.

When they arrived on the grounds of the Aragon estate, he hitched Demonio's reins to the post just outside the walled gardens. After he'd helped Aimee off Demonio's back, the two of them slipped through the gate leading into the gardens. He had intended to guide her to the secluded spot of the gardens where they'd kept their little rendezvous earlier. He'd hoped to confess the truth to her and kiss those honey-sweet lips.

She allowed him to lead her to that particular spot and she allowed him to enclose her with his arms as she gazed up at him with the look of love on her face. His head had bent down as his lips had searched to capture hers. She allowed him this pleasure for one very fleeting second.

Aimee was a determined lady tonight and she was not about to allow him to carry her beyond the point where she would be out of control. Suddenly, she pushed herself away from him so she could not feel the overwhelming heat of his powerful male body and she could not be weakened by the effect of his persuasive sensual lips as they pressed against hers, urging her to give in to his demands. Tonight, she would not do it! But she could not deny that she did not wish to. God knows, she wanted to more than ever!

How strong was her will? She knew this had to be the ultimate test! Crazy as it might seem, she thought of her *Tante* Denise, and in her secret thoughts she called on her to help her cope with this moment of hellish torment.

As Mano was bending his head and his lips were hungry to capture the sweet nectar of Aimee's lips, he felt her push away from him.

He was not prepared for the harsh, stinging blow of her dainty hand assaulting his face nor the sparking hate in her lovely eyes as she hissed at him, "Oh, no, Mano Mateo, you'll never kiss me again or have me as you have in the past. No longer will you play me for the fool! I hate you!" She turned to rush away into the night's darkness, leaving Mano in a state of utter shock.

How did she find out that he was Mano Mateo, instead of

Mark Perez? He knew he had gambled and lost, so it really didn't matter now. She knew!

Now that she knew who he was, she hated him and he doubted that anything he could do or say was going to change that. Damned, if he could blame her for feeling as she did, for it had been a cheap, cruel deception he'd played on her.

That first night they had met and he'd rescued her from the clutches of that brute of a man, he could excuse himself for that lie. But he should never have carried it as far and as long as he had. Before he had shared that glorious afternoon under the oak tree making love to her, he should have been honest with her.

Selfishly, he had not wanted to lose her and Mano feared he might if he'd made his confession. But the path he'd taken had been the wrong one, obviously, because he had lost her tonight. He saw it in those eyes blazing with their dark blue fire as she'd slapped him to rush into the night's darkness.

The ghostly quiet of the Aragon gardens held no enchantment for him now, he decided dejectedly. So he turned to leave. He was a man walking in a daze as he went to fetch Demonio and ride to La Casa Grande. A night that had been filled with such happiness had turned into a tormenting hell for Mano. Never had he felt such a stabbing pain of hurt in his gut.

He rode through the night, conjuring up a dozen ways he would try to win her back. By all that was holy, he promised himself that whatever it took he would get her to return to his arms and love him as she had before.

There was nothing he couldn't do if he set his mind to it. Old Phil Cabrillo had told him that and he agreed with that old Portuguese. Tomorrow he would think more clearly. To sleep tonight, he wished only to numb the hurt and the pain, so he planned to drink generously from his best whiskey once he arrived back at the ranch.

Once Demonio was secured in his stall and Mano had gone into the house, he went directly to the liquor chest, helping himself to a bottle of whiskey before he mounted the stairs to his bedroom.

The occupants of the house were all in a deep, exhausted sleep after the gala fiesta which had ended about two hours ago. Whether they had been asleep or not had not mattered to Mano as he entered his room and closed the door. He'd flopped into the chair and removed his leather boots, flinging them to the floor carelessly. He removed his shirt and tossed it to the floor, along with his pants. Dimming the lamplight, he sat on his bed, drank the whiskey, and looked at the night's blackness sparkling with multitudes of twinkling stars. Soon the dawn would be breaking and this miserable night would be over. A new day would be born.

Sleep was going to come hard to him, he suspected as he lay his dark head down on the pillow. He was hoping Aimee was enduring as restless a night as he was.

It would have comforted Mano to know that Aimee was as restless as he was as she lay on her bed looking up at the same starlit night.

As she'd rushed away from him through the gardens, she'd dared not look back until she had reached the safety of the door. Neither would she have confessed that she had secretly expected the handsome devil to rush after her. He was not a man to be denied his way with a lady, she was certain. He was certainly not a man discouraged by any gentle protest when he wished to kiss or caress a lady. But he had not done it, she reminded herself.

After all, he had accomplished what he'd set out to do from the very beginning, so he had no desire to run after her now that he knew his little game was over, she had to conclude. He'd made the fool of her. He could brag all he wished that he'd lain with Aimee Aragon, the French vintner's daughter. Most likely if he were the arrogant, conceited man like his father, she would be the topic of conversation among his Latin friends.

How they would probably laugh about the easy conquest she'd been, surrendering to his irresitible Latin charms.

The thought of all this made her flame with a furious anger as she'd lain there in the bed.

The dawn was breaking by the time her eyes grew heavy with sleep from sheer exhaustion. But when sleep did come, it was a deep one and free of any dreams about Mano Mateo.

When Jolie gently roused her the next morning, inquiring if she wished a breakfast tray or if she was going down to join her parents, she sleepily mumbled that she would like a tray brought up.

Excusing herself to do her mistress's bidding, the curious little maid had to admit that she was wondering how her evening had gone. She was most eager to hear Aimee's comments about the fiesta over at La Casa Grande. She was also eager to tell Aimee about the pleasant stroll she'd shared with Emile Aragon. If it was not for the close feeling they shared with one another, Jolie would never have dreamed about mentioning the nice evening she had enjoyed.

When her maid returned with the breakfast tray, placing it on the bed while Aimee adjusted her pillows behind her back, she suddenly sensed Jolie's anxious expression. But she sought to ignore it as she began to eat from the tray. Right now, she wished not to discuss Mano Mateo with anyone. This included the lovely little Jolie.

Jolie sat down to await her orders about what Aimee wished her to do after she'd finished her breakfast.

Finally, Jolie could not remain silent any longer. In a soft, hesitating voice, she ventured to say to her little mistress, "I had a lovely evening after you left, mademoiselle. I—I strolled the garden with your brother Emile."

There was a quiet moment of silence as Aimee absorbed what she'd said. She glanced up from her breakfast tray to look upon Jolie's excited, lovely face. The fact that Emile had invited Jolie to walk around the gardens did surprise her for a few fleeting seconds.

"Emile asked you to walk with him, Jolie? He is a rather shy person, so I guess I'm surprised," Aimee said, smiling sweetly.

"Ah, mademoiselle, you are surprised? I was the one surprised. I was there by the herb garden, watching you go to meet Monsieur Perez, and your brother came upon me there. I—I felt very honored by his request. He is a very nice man, so kind and gentle."

Aimee nodded her head, agreeing with Jolie. "Emile is the kindest person I know and I don't say that just because he is my older brother. He does have a gentle soul, and even though most people looking at his huge build might expect him to be fierce, he isn't at all."

Aimee wondered privately if her brother Emile were attracted to her pretty little maid. How wonderful for them both if he were! It was long past time for Emile to find himself a nice young lady, and Jolie was certainly that. What did it matter that she happened to be a servant at the Chateau L'Aragon? The truth was that Emile was a simple man, even though he was the son of a wealthy man. She could see how someone like Jolie could give Emile that great and wonderful happiness he would not find with some of the young women he'd courted through the years. Perhaps that was why none of those courtships had lasted too long for Emile.

What was Aimee really thinking? Jolie wondered. "Mademoiselle, I—I did nothing wrong by walking with your brother, did I? I would not want you to disapprove of me in any way." Her dark eyes searched Aimee's face.

A tender warmth sparked in Aimee's eyes and her hand reached out to give Jolie an assuring pat on her shoulder as she told her, "You did absolutely nothing wrong, Jolie. You merely took an innocent walk with my brother. Obviously, he wished you to join him or he would not have asked you. Knowing him as well as I do, I would say he wanted to walk with you and share your company very much. Emile is not a bold one where the ladies are concerned. Neither is Armand. As you know, they work too many hours in the vineyards for anything else in their lives."

"*Oui*, I've never known such a hardworking pair as those two," Jolie agreed.

Quite thoughtfully, Aimee confessed to her maid, "Sometimes I think Papa has demanded too much from both of them!"

As though she were thinking out loud, Jolie muttered almost in a whisper, "I fear Monsieur Paul Aragon would not be as understanding as you have been if he knew I walked with Emile last night. I fear he would highly disappove, mademoiselle."

Aimee gave forth a halfhearted laugh as she confessed, "Well, I fear, my dear little Jolie, he would not have approved of me last night in the company of Mano Mateo."

"Ma'am? I fear I don't understand you?"

"The man I met in the garden and the man I've thought for weeks was Mark Perez was none other than Mano Mateo, son of my father's bitter enemy, Carlos Mateo."

"Oh, mercy, mademoiselle. I hear a bitterness in your voice. Your evening was not a gay one, I suspect."

"It will always hold a bittersweet memory for me. Someday I can tell you about it, but not now, Jolie," Aimee told her with a look of sadness on her lovely face.

"I understand, mademoiselle. When you wish to talk to me, I will be here to listen," Jolie said with a wave of melancholy sweeping over her.

Mademoiselle Aimee was suffering from a broken heart!

Chapter 29

No one would have suspected the lovely Aimee suffered from a broken heart as she saucily bounced down the stairway the next morning to join her parents and her brothers for breakfast in the bright, sunny little room adjoining their main dining room. One wall of the room, with its double windows facing the east, allowed the bright sun to flow into the small casual area.

Lisette's blue and white checked ruffled curtains were draped back to allow the lovely view of her gardens to be observed as they sat at the table enjoying their morning meal. Her table was draped in a matching blue and white checked cloth. Always, there were crisp white napkins on the table and a small vase holding the white and blue flowers of her garden, depending on which ones were in bloom.

Like everything else in her home, that very special touch of hers was seen in this simple little room. Aimee had always appreciated and admired those special little effects of her mother's that brightened their home. No one could question how much Lisette Aragon loved her family and her home.

Aimee's appearance in the doorway seemed to give her family a surprised but pleased delight. Lisette was the first to speak, "Oh, *ma petite*, come join us for coffee at least. I know you have already had a tray, since I saw Jolie taking it up to you. I feared you might not be feeling well this morning. Seeing you now though I know I was surely wrong."

She rewarded her mother's kind remarks with a loving smile. "You are such a caring mother. You worry about all of us too much, I think, Mother."

"Ah, that is what it is like to be a mother, Aimee. Someday you will probably be the same." Lisette could not possibly know how her innocent remark would hit a nerve so sharply within Aimee. The thought of being a mother had never entered her thoughts before. But she suddenly realized when a woman and a man had made such passionate love as she and Mano had, it was certainly possible she could be carrying his child at this very moment. Oh, what a horrible catastrophe that could be!

"I—I would never be as perfect as you, Mother." She tried to sound more casual and frivolous than she was feeling right now.

But she managed to sit with her family and have a cup of coffee with them, sharing this pleasant time together. In unison, her father, Emile, and Armand rose from the table, and in turn, each of them bent down to place a kiss on Lisette's cheek as they bid her farewell. It was only Emile who bent over to kiss Aimee.

She knew he must be curious if Jolie had told her about his invitation to stroll with him in the gardens last night. She had given him one of those sly little smiles of hers and a wink of her eye. A broad grin had broken out on Emile's rugged face, because she reminded him of the impish brat of a sister she'd been some eight or nine years ago.

He found it hard to believe she was such a stunning young

235

lady now, for he still looked upon her as that adorable little pest who liked to tease and annoy him as he was in his teens. He suspected Armand had never been as enchanted with a younger sister coming along and interrupting his life. Aimee's arrival had made Armand the middle child. For Emile, it had been exciting to have a baby sister.

When the men were gone and it was only Aimee and her mother left at the table, Lisette announced to her daughter, "Our gowns are to be delivered today, Aimee."

"Our gowns, Mother?"

"Yes, *ma cherie,* for the ball. You have forgotten?"

"No, Mother, I had not forgotten," she lied convincingly.

In fact, the Governor's Ball appealed to her now. She would go to it and she would have herself a grand time, she suddenly decided. She would prove to Mano Mateo that he'd made no fool of her. Every man there would know Aimee Aragon was in her gorgeous lavender gown that her father had paid a small fortune to drape her in.

Oh, she'd allow Fred Bigler to escort her, but that did not mean she would be tied to his side the whole evening!

Lisette's conversation was not absorbed by Aimee because her mind was whirling right now with many thoughts about how she planned to even the score with the despicable, deceitful Mano.

Fred Bigler could not have chosen a more perfect time to pay a visit to the Chateau L'Aragon, and he was delightfully surprised to find the lovely daughter of Paul Aragon so receptive to his charms. He'd come to the Aragon estates to deliver a message from the governor. The state of California and Governor Bigler had placed in Fred's hands the papers and documents Paul Aragon would need to make his tour of France, Italy, and Germany, at the request of the governor, to inspect the vineyards. It was a very grand honor offered to Aragon, as well as a tribute to him, to be given such a task. The governor was convinced that the vines of Europe could thrive and grow in this California valley. It would bring a prosperity that could sustain and last longer than the gold fever now invading the area.

The governor considered Paul Aragon to be the man for this mission because he had brought his vines from France and made them thrive here in the valley. Aragon had proved that it could be a most lucrative business.

The mission of Fred Bigler today, representing the governor of the state of California, was official. Paul Aragon was to leave immediately for Europe and all the arrangements had already been made for him.

But never had he expected the bountiful blessing he'd received when he'd arrived at the Chateau L'Aragon and been treated so graciously by the beautiful Aimee Aragon. He was momentarily befuddled by her warm, friendly attitude toward him as he encountered her in the gardens on the estate. There was an almost bold air about her as she invited him to join her for a stroll in the gardens. A soft, lilting laugh broke from her as she told him, "I love taking these breadcrumbs from Hetty's kitchen to feed the birds. It is a wonderful sight to watch them gather here to eat."

Now, Ross Maynard did not give a holy damn about any birds, but this woman was something to excite any red-blooded man. She possessed certain qualities that instantly set a man's heart to pounding faster and his wildest desires to sparking. Having had a fair share of women, Ross appreciated the sensuous sway of a woman's hips when they seemed to invite a man to grow bold. He had only to look at her lovely face and grow weak with an ache in his groin. Those eyes were the loveliest he'd ever seen and her lips were so luscious, pleading with you to kiss them. God knows, he yearned to do just that!

Playing the role of the coquette, Aimee purred softly, "I am looking forward to attending the ball. It sounds like a marvelous evening, Fred."

"I am looking forward to it too, Aimee, especially if I have the honor to escort you."

"Oh, you do, Fred. I thought you knew that."

"Well, I had thought so, but there have been some times I felt that you were not exactly eager to attend the ball with me."

"Oh, did I give you that impression, Fred? I surely did not mean to. I fear I must give many people the wrong impression since I've returned to this country after living abroad with my aunt in Paris for a year. You see, over there I was used to doing as I wished. I—I am not adjusted to life back here at Chateau L'Aragon yet, I guess. I must appear to you, as well as my parents, as being very rebellious. But life in Paris is very different than it is here."

"In other words, you are telling me that you lived in a more worldly, sophisticated surrounding and I gather you enjoyed it. Am I right, Aimee?" Ross Maynard asked her. He'd always suspected, from the first moment they'd met, that her sweet face and all that pure innocence displayed there was not the case. Within that curvaceous body of hers was the heat and passion of a woman who could hardly be called the shy, bashful maiden.

"I did love the world my *Tante* Denise lives in, and Paris is a city always alive and exciting whether it was day or night. There was always somewhere to go and things to see. I never got bored there," she admitted to him.

His hand took a more possessive hold of hers as they strolled in the gardens, and he tried to display his most charming qualities as he told her, "Perhaps the ball will give you the chance to enjoy yourself as you did in Paris. If you will give me the chance, I will try to make it a delightful evening for you, I promise."

"Now, that is very sweet of you, Fred. It truly is, and I am sure it will be a wonderful night." She tried to respond to him and smile. But as her eyes surveyed his face, she found it hard to imagine having a gay time with this man. She was still remembering the handsome devil, Mano Mateo. When she felt the pressure of his hand on her arm, she felt the urge to draw away but she didn't.

She had already reminded herself not to measure Fred or

any other man by the irresistible, tall dark Latin's effect on her from the mere touch of his hand on her flesh. God, she doubted that any man would ever have that overwhelming effect on her again as long as she lived!

Maybe the magic of that moment and his love only happened once. Maybe, she told herself, some women go through a whole lifetime and never know such a wild and wonderful ecstasy. If that be so, then she was glad it had happened, even though she despised him for his trickery. She could never forget those lofty heights of rapture he'd shown her. So if she never soared that high again, she had known those moments with Mano. A part of her would always love Mano and she knew it. But she hated him for spoiling her for any other man who might enter her life.

Ross Maynard turned to gaze on her lovely face. Christ, she took his breath away and he swelled with such desire for her!

He had to fight the wild desire of his nature, because if he was back in Texas and he was with a pretty girl like this one, he would have pulled her down on the grass and had his way with her.

These California people were a different breed, Ross had concluded. There was a stiff formality here that Ross Maynard could not relate to, even though he was playing the role of Fred Bigler, relative of the governor of the state.

"I'm going to be the proudest man at the ball, Aimee. I will have the most beautiful lady in the whole state of California by my side. I have no doubt about that," he told her.

"Now, aren't you nice, Fred Bigler. I have to confess I did not realize just how gallant and charming you were."

Fred chuckled as a wave of cocky conceit took over. For the first time, he was encouraged that he was finally making some mark on this snobbish little bitch. Even when she addressed him as Fred, he resented that he could not tell her he was Ross Maynard, a rugged Texan and damned proud of it.

"You're a hard young lady to convince, Aimee. You've

really not given me a chance to prove anything to you." This soft, mellow tone of his voice was not and would not have been his way in Texas. Damned, if he could wait to get back there!

She broke into a soft, lighthearted giggle as she looked at him. Obviously, she had given him a very hard time when he had wished only to court her.

"I'll try to be nicer in the future, Fred. I promise I will. But now I must get back to the house. Our gowns for the ball are to be delivered today. I'm sure you understand." The urgent need to leave this spot in the garden had nothing to do with the gowns being delivered. Aimee was suddenly possessed by the need to leave this spot and be rid of Fred Bigler as well. She could not have explained it to herself. She did not understand it but she felt a most strange feeling engulfing her. Her heart was pounding with an erratic beat and a trembling feeling took charge of her hands. She had the urge to run just as fast as her feet would carry her from the gardens.

Perhaps it was a pair of fierce, angry black eyes looking at Aimee that made her feel so uneasy. She did not know this. She did not know that Mano had been watching her and Fred Bigler take their leisurely stroll through the gardens. She could not know that when he saw her give Fred her sweet smiles, it took all his strong willpower to keep from leaping down that stone wall to punch that dandy little dude with his forceful fists.

Actually, Mano was so filled with rage that he would have liked to have slapped the lovely face of Aimee, who he worshipped so much and so utterly.

God, he would have never imagined that a woman could do this to him!

He knew the moment his piercing black eyes must have been having an effect on her. As crazy as it might seem at this particular moment, old Phil Cabrillo up at Half Moon Bay came to his thoughts. Phil would have told him that he was putting a hex on the lovely Aimee. Mano sat there praying he was doing just that.

He watched the couple as they made their hasty retreat and

he especially ogled the sensuous swaying of Aimee's hips as she moved back up the flagstone path.

As Mano sat there atop the stone wall of the Aragon gardens, he muttered to himself, "You can't belong to anyone else but me. Don't you know that, Aimee Aragon? I will put my hex on you. I will drive you crazy if need be. I will drive you as crazy as you are doing to me!"

His forceful presence had made its mark on Aimee, even though she did not understand it. A strange madness lingered with her the rest of the day. As much as she trusted Jolie, she could not discuss this with her.

While she didn't understand it, she knew it was the fever for Mano Mateo in her blood!

Chapter 30

Aimee had forgotten how exquisite the lavender gown was that Madame Corrine was making her for the ball. But now that it lay across her bed, along with the luxurious cape, she admired it and praised the expertise of the seamstress. It was absolutely beautiful. She had to admit she was completely unprepared for the surprise her father had handed her during the evening meal.

He'd offered her a small case and told her, "These were my mother's, Aimee. How she knew I would ever have a daughter whose lovely eyes would match these gems so perfectly, I'll never know."

She took the case and opened it. There, resting on the deep blue velvet-lined case, was the most magnificent pair of amethyst earrings, lined in small, exquisite pearls.

She gasped, completely awestruck by their rare beauty. "Oh, Papa, they are the most beautiful things I've ever laid my eyes on. Your mother must have had very exquisite taste in her jewelry if she picked these out. I am sorry that I never knew her."

"So am I, *ma petite*. She and you would have gotten along very well together. She was a wee one, like you, but very much the little hellcat! When she was angry and hissed at us, we knew we better obey her. I can admit I certainly did!" he lightheartedly chuckled.

Aimee let her fingers slowly stroll over the lovely cut gems and she already knew that she would cherish them as long as she lived.

Her long-lashed blue-amethyst eyes fluttered and there was a mist in them as they looked into those of her father. "She must have been a wonderful lady, Papa. It is obvious you admired and respected her very much. I—I would like to think that I was a little bit like her."

"Ah, you are, I assure you of that, Aimee. You have always reminded me of her since you were a small child, with that iron will of yours."

When the evening meal was over and she had gone upstairs to her room, the first thing Aimee did was take the lovely earrings from the case to lay them against the lavender gown delivered late in the afternoon. They were sheer perfection!

As Aimee was pleased with her jewelry and her lovely gown, Lisette was as pleased with her gown of hyacinth blue silk. The lovely color reminded her of the flowers that bloomed in the spring in the French countryside where she'd lived.

Now, as she sat at her dressing table, brushing her long hair, Paul was already in bed propped up on pillows, looking over the missive sent to him from the governor.

"Aimee was overcome with your gift, Paul. It was the perfect time to have presented them to her."

"You think so, my darling?"

"I know so, *mon cher*."

"Then you make me very happy. I can leave feeling very good. I sometimes feel I have done something very wrong along the way. I have been a very hard man in a lot of ways, but I never meant to be, Lisette. I was just wanting to be so good. Do you know what I am trying to say?"

"Oh, I think I do, Paul. I understood the many hours you put in the fields were not just for yourself but to give your family a bountiful harvest, *oui?*"

A broad smile came to his face as he replied, "*Oui*, that was it! But do Emile, Armand, and Aimee understand this?"

She turned around on the velvet-cushioned stool, her glossy hair flowing over her shoulders. Paul found her a most attractive sight to behold. She soothed him by saying, "Ah, Paul, if they don't understand now, they will someday when they have their own children. Only when they have walked in your shoes will they appreciate you, *mon cher.*"

Never had he loved her more or appreciated her more. He had been a man most blessed to have had such a woman as Lisette. She had been the miracle that had spurred him to be the man he'd been. She had been the spark that had fired him to prove to himself that he could make his vines grow here in this new world. This California earth had not rejected the grape vines he'd brought from France some three decades ago. He owed it all to Lisette. But for her it would never have happened, and he knew that.

His voice was warm with passion as he told her, "I shall be very lonely, Lisette, on this tour in Europe. I want you to know that."

She ambled over to the bed. "I know this, Paul. I have never doubted your love for me. I shall miss you, too. You have been paid a very high honor, Paul, and I am so very proud of you. That will keep me from being too lonely."

He smiled, pleased by her sweet words. "Come, Lisette, come lay in my arms. I have a great need to hold you tonight."

She moved toward the bed, and as she slipped between the fresh white sheets, she softly murmured to her husband, "I, too, have a great need for you to hold me tonight, Paul."

His arms enfolded her and she felt the strength and power in them. It was a divine, comforting feeling to experience that marvelous warmth. So loving and tender was the sweet sensation of his caress that Lisette felt the most serene rapture.

It was a rapture to equal their most exciting sexual moments in a very different way. Yet, there was a wondrous feeling to share there in his strong arms, as she felt so secure and protected.

"I have not told you often enough, Lisette, just how much I love you. But I do, and I shall miss you very much while I am touring Europe," Paul confessed to his wife.

"And I shall miss you, too, Paul. I must tell you that even though you did not tell me you loved me, I knew you did because you showed me your devotion in so many other ways. There are many ways a man speaks to a woman of his love, *mon cher*."

Paul gave her a tender kiss on the cheek and declared, with deep affection in his voice, "Lisette, you are the wisest woman I've ever known. Do you know that? I—I guess I've never told you that before but I've always thought it."

She turned to kiss him. A lovely smile glowed on her face as she thanked him. "I value your praise very much, Paul. It's wonderful to have your husband think so highly of you."

A sublime serenity suddenly enfolded the couple as they lay quietly in one another's arms and a peaceful sleep fell upon them.

There was a beehive of activity going on around the Chateau L'Aragon the next day. It began at dawn, when Paul departed to go on his tour for the governor. Lisette could have felt the void of his absence that day and during the evening but for her own busy schedule, with preparations for their departure to the Governor's Ball.

Emile was appointed to be his mother's escort since Paul could not be there to accompany his wife. So it would be the three of them journeying to Sacramento the next morning. They would be the guests of their old friends, the Huntingtons, during their stay at the capitol.

Armand had insisted that he remain at home and not attend the ball because he didn't care in the least for such an occasion as this. Eagerly, he accepted his brother's suggestion that he go with their mother. In fact, he heaved a deep sigh of relief that the obligation did not fall on his shoulders. He declared to Emile, with a broad grin on his tanned face, "You would be much better at this than me, Emile. I would not want to embarrass our mother by acting the clumsy ox at this fancy ball."

Emile did not try to argue with him because Armand had spoken the truth about himself. He was a huge man who moved awkwardly and would have felt very ill-at-ease in an elegant ballroom.

"Then I shall go with our mother and you carry the load here, eh Armand?" Emile offered. Armand quickly agreed to that, eager to be rid of the responsibility.

The next morning as the sun was rising, the Aragon carriage moved down the long, winding drive carrying Emile, Lisette, and Aimee. They had some fifty miles to travel to get to Sacramento and their destination on the outskirts of the capitol city. The estate of the Huntington family was situated five miles out of the city. The palatial mansion was set on a high slope of ground overlooking a most picturesque landscape an.. a magnificent view of Folsum Lake.

Some two hours behind the Aragon carriage, leaving San Mateo County, was the carriage bearing Carlos Mateo and his oldest son, Mario. His younger son was not with them.

Like Armand Aragon, Mano had sought not to accompany his father and his brother to the gala festivities at the capitol. He did not wish to punish himself by watching his beautiful Aimee dancing in the arms of other gentlemen, especially the likes of one Fred Bigler. He'd known his breed of man before and it did not matter that he might be a relative of the esteemed governor of the state of California.

No, he didn't need that form of brutal punishment, he convinced himself. By the time his father and Mario had left the ranch, Mano knew it was once again time for him to take his leave from La Casa Grande. He felt the overwhelming urge to go to Half Moon Bay and seek the sage counsel of old Phil Cabrillo. He did not wish to leave here or Aimee Aragon, but he was feeling so desperate he knew not what course to pursue to win her back. Somehow, he knew old Phil would provide the answers as he had so often in the past. Mano knew he did not have them and all he could do was cuss himself for being so stupid. Once he had made his decision, he did not tarry. Immediately, he began throwing a few things, which he would need for his stay at Phil's, in a bag. With the bag in his hand, he marched down the stairs in that fast-paced step of his. He wanted to be away from this place as soon as possible. He sought Minerva, as he usually did when he was about to make one of his hasty departures. As he rushed through the kitchen door, she saw that old familiar bag, instinctively knowing what he was about before he uttered a word to her.

A frown came to her dark face and her voice was harsh as she demanded to know, "What are you up to, picaro?"

He gave out one of those deep, throaty laughs of his, "Now, come on, Minerva, I am not such a rascal and you damned well know it!"

"I know nothing of the sort. You are up to one of those mysterious little trips of yours. This I know, nino."

"Now, there you go again. I can hardly be called a boy anymore."

Slowly, she moved from her stove to walk toward him. A great love glowed in her dark eyes for the young man standing there in her kitchen. Always, Mano had pulled at her heartstrings and she could not explain it.

"I will call you nino, Mano, all the days of my life, I guess. I think you are a young boy running away once again. This time I think you are running, not because you are angry, but because you are scared." She watched as a deep frown creased his handsome face and she knew he resented her remarks very much. But that didn't faze her.

He just stared at her for a moment with those piercing black eyes of his. She saw the mixed emotions reflected there on his face. When he finally spoke, his words were slow and thoughtful, "Minerva, I don't like admitting this and I probably wouldn't to anyone but you. I guess, for the first damned time in my life, I am a little scared."

Compassion flowed through her for this young man she'd known all his life. "Then go to your Half Moon Bay, Mano, and let old Phil help you find the answers."

Her words startled him. How did she know that he always found his solace up there with Phil Cabrillo?

She saw the stunned look on his young face and a slow, easy smile came to her face as she inquired of him, "You think I haven't known where you take off for when you are upset, Mano? I have always known you weren't too far away."

"How did you know this, Minerva? How could you possibly know where I went?"

Her dark, wrinkled hands caressed his cheeks and her eyes searched his face as she told him, "You are your mother's son, Mano. It was where Theresa always went when she had the need to find her peace. Half Moon Bay—she always murmured it so softly and lovingly. It was her haven, Mano, and I think it must surely be yours, too. So go there and find your answers, Mano, to whatever it is that is troubling you so much."

Mano embraced the old mestizo woman because he loved her dearly. "I am, Minerva. I am going right now, and when I return, I will have the answer."

She believed him. When he released her and turned to leave the kitchen, a mist of tears came to her eyes. As she had so often with the lovely Theresa, she prayed he would find the answers he was searching for. Poor Theresa never did!

This must not happen with Mano!

Part Three

A Faded Love

Though another's love was there,
it can't begin to compare,
to the splendor of his touch,
the man she loved so much.

Sheila Northcott

Chapter 31

As the Aragon carriage approached the fine country estate of
Lawson and Beth Huntington, Lisette realized just how long it
had been since she was last there. It had been two years ago.
Paul had made two or three trips to Sacramento on business
and enjoyed a visit with their friends, the Huntingtons.
Whatever her reasons had been at the time—and right now she
couldn't recall them—Lisette had remained back at the
Chateau L'Aragon.

It was going to be wonderful to see Beth and Lawson again.
She knew they would be surprised to see her lovely daughter
and how grown-up she'd become in the last couple of years.
Lisette smiled with amusement, anticipating the look on Beth's
face when she saw Aimee. However, the sight of Emile would
be no different than that of the same young man he'd been for
the last five or six years.

How lonely Beth must be with her only son so far away in the
East, Lisette mused. How lucky she was to have all her three
children still with her. How very blessed she'd been to have
raised three instead of just one, she thought to herself as the

carriage rolled along the dirt road.

The landscape they traveled along now gave forth to familiar sights that she remembered from her past visits to Huntington's Haven. Lisette knew that everything would be exactly the same in Beth's luxurious home, reflecting her friend's taste as well as her personality, having come from the deep South. As she was a lady with great dignity and charm, Beth insisted that her home reflect a peaceful, serene atmosphere.

Soon she knew they would be turning down a road lined on either side with tall, slender trees, which would lead them to the front of the huge two-story white house. The structure and design was like the impressive plantation houses she'd seen when she and Paul had traveled through the South on their journey to California.

In less than an hour, they were doing exactly what Lisette had anticipated they would be doing shortly after they arrived at Beth's home. She, Beth, Aimee, and Emile were sitting out on the cool veranda enjoying Beth's special chilled mint tea. As she'd recalled, it was a delightful, refreshing beverage.

Beth was chattering away in that soft, southern drawl of hers, "I do declare, it is a wonderful day to see you sitting here on my veranda, Lisette. Lordy, it's been a long time. I can't wait for Lawson to get himself home." Throwing her hands up in an excited gesture, she declared, "Oh, I haven't told you yet, Lisette, about our Brad coming home, and he thinks he's going with a law firm right here in Sacramento. Isn't that wonderful! Lawson and I are simply thrilled to death."

"Oh, yes, Beth. I know you must be very happy that he'll be returning home. I—I hadn't expected to get to see Brad. Oh, I wish Paul could have been here, too," Lisette told Beth.

"Oh, so do I." She turned her attention to Emile to inquire of him, "Am I right, dear, are you three years older than Brad?"

"That's right, ma'am. I believe that's right."

"That was what I thought." Beth's appraising eyes were then focused on Aimee. She gave out a soft little gale of laughter as she remarked, "You, my dear, are going to strike my son blind when he sees just how beautiful you are now. Sweet Jesus, you are more lovely than the roses in my garden—and your mama knows how I feel about them."

"Why, that's so sweet of you, Mrs. Huntington," Aimee replied as she tried to recall what Brad Huntington looked like. She only vaguely remembered him.

The image she recalled was of a tall young man who looked like his father, with a head of thick sandy-colored hair and sparkling bright blue eyes.

Aimee did not have to rely on memory too long because that image she recalled came striding out on the veranda, accompanied by his father.

"Dear God Almighty, Lisette, is it really you?" Lawson exclaimed with a big, broad smile on his face. He gave her a friendly kiss on the cheek and gave Emile a warm embrace as he greeted him. Then his blue eyes turned to survey Aimee sitting there with a lovely smile on her face. He shook his head in disbelief as he muttered, "Can this be—no, it hasn't been all that long since I last saw you, young lady. All this can't have taken place in that short time. That young miss we last saw has become a gorgeous lady, Beth, I do believe." He chuckled and stood there shaking his head, as though he could not believe what his eyes were beholding. "God Almighty, Paul Aragon must strut around the county being the proudest father of a daughter like you, Aimee. By the way, where is he?"

Lisette informed him about Paul's mission for the governor and explained to Lawson that Emile would be taking his place as her escort for the ball.

"Shame it could not be delayed for a few more days so Paul could have attended the ball," Lawson said as he moved over to sit down on one of the wicker rockers.

"The truth is, Lawson, the excitement of this tour holds far more enjoyment for Paul than any ball. The grand social scenes were never for him, as you will recall."

While Lawson and Lisette were engrossed in their conversa-

253

tion, Bradford Huntington moved forward to greet the Aragon family there on the veranda. His eyes were devouring the lovely sight of Aimee Aragon. What a divine creature she was! This had to be his lucky day, coming back home and finding such an enchantress right here under his own roof.

He gave Emile a warm, friendly greeting, but it was Aimee he was eager to welcome to the Huntington home. When he moved on around the gathered circle and came to stand directly in front of Aimee, he gave her a gallant bow and his most charming smile as he remarked, "My father's sentiments are mine, Aimee. I can't believe you are so grown-up since the last time we saw one another. I doubt that you even remember. I must say that there has to be some truth that Paris is a city of magic and wonder. I am completely convinced of that now." He gave out a lighthearted laugh and she joined him. She was confessing to herself that she had not remembered him as possessing such an impressive charm as he seemed to now.

"There is a certain magic about the city and I will certainly agree to that, Brad. I did enjoy my stay there with my *Tante* Denise."

"How long were you actually there?" Brad inquired as he allowed himself the freedom of letting his eyes roam leisurely over her. There was a certain air of sophistication he did not find in most young ladies her age and those a few years older. Maybe a more worldly, sophisticated city did have such an effect on one.

"Almost a year, but I went to school back in the East before I sailed for Europe, so I was actually away from California two years," she told him.

"Well, California is happy to have you back home. It seems we have both been leading a similar life. I just recently came back here and I, too, have been back East with a law firm there. I am planning to stay out here now. I trust you are not going to run away from us again." He left no doubt in Aimee's mind that he was attracted to her. The way he smiled at her and the way his eyes were adoring her made her know that he found her

254

attractive. Mano Mateo had educated her about such things where men were concerned. Now she would always recognize that certain twinkle in a man's eyes when he desired a woman. Brad Huntington had that look right now.

With a shrug of her dainty shoulders and a casual tone to her voice, she declared to him, "I have no plans to leave the Chateau L'Aragon again for a while, Brad. It's nice to be with my parents and brothers again."

Seeing that her husband was engaged in conversation with Lisette and her son, and that Brad was utterly hypnotized by the lovely Aimee, Beth Huntington moved over to talk with Emile.

While Beth Huntington was one of the nicest, sweetest ladies he'd ever met, Emile was suddenly kicking himself for being so generous toward Armand. If he were back at his home, he could have been enjoying nightly walks in the gardens with his sister's maid, Jolie. Here, he found himself bored. Now, Emile knew that his happiness waited for him back at the Chateau L'Aragon. To be here wasting his time talking to Beth Huntington, as nice as she was, convinced Emile that he must pursue his own life and his own happiness.

He welcomed the moment when they finally left the veranda to go to their individual rooms to rest or relax before the appointed dinner hour. Like his father, Emile was not the least bit impressed or excited about attending the elegant ball and mingling and talking with the finely attired guests. By the time he was finally sequestered behind the closed door of his room, he pondered how he'd ever manage to make it through the next couple of days.

The Chateau L'Aragon was already beckoning him and he was already yearning for the glorious sight of it. Suddenly, he realized why certain things didn't interest him as they did most young men his age. His roots were there in those vineyards of the Chateau L'Aragon, and his passion was, too. At least, it was until he'd shared those few brief moments with the pretty Jolie. Now he also realized she had aroused a passion within him he had not known existed. But that tiny little mite of a black-haired miss had ignited a wild passion and it was the most wonderful feeling he had ever experienced. He hungered for more!

If Emile Aragon was a virile young man hungry with his yearning for the pretty little maid of his sister's, then it could be said that Brad Huntington was a randy young man determined to woo and win Emile's beautiful sister. Never had a woman fired him with such a searing, burning flame of desire as Aimee had this afternoon. Dear God, she was a glorious goddess with that silvery blond hair of hers and those devastating deep blue eyes! He cussed himself that he was already committed to escort Sally Martindale. He knew there was no getting out of it now because the time was too short. If only he'd known that such a treasure as Aimee would have been here, he'd never have agreed to take Sally.

Brad would have been thrilled and delighted if he'd have been privy to the private musings of the lovely Aimee as she relaxed in her bedroom. They were sharing very similar thoughts about their respective escorts. Brad Huntington appealed much more to her than Fred Bigler did but she, too, was committed.

She liked his lighthearted, happy-go-lucky manner and his good looks. Oh, he didn't possess that overwhelming Latin charm of Mano Mateo nor did he have that certain magic of Mano, which took her breath away when he was near her, but she found him fun to be around and that was far more than she could say about Fred Bigler.

Sitting in the middle of her bed clad only in her chemise, she stared out the window. Her thoughts were about Mano, even though many miles separated them. She could feel his forceful presence there with her now.

In a soft, hissing voice, she muttered, "Damn you, Mano! Damn you for spoiling me for any other man! You—you devil!"

Get a Free
Zebra
Historical
Romance
*a $3.95
value*

Affix
stamp
here

ACCEPT YOUR **FREE GIFT** AND EXPERIENCE MORE OF THE PASSION AND ADVENTURE YOU LIKE IN A HISTORICAL ROMANCE

Zebra Romances are the finest novels of their kind and are written with the adult woman in mind. All of our books are written by authors who really know how to weave tales of romantic adventure in the historical settings you love.

Because our readers tell us these books sell out very fast in the stores, Zebra has made arrangements for you to receive at home the four newest titles published each month. You'll never miss a title and home delivery is so convenient. With your first shipment we'll even send you a **FREE** Zebra Historical Romance as our gift just for trying our home subscription service. No obligation.

BIG SAVINGS AND **FREE** HOME DELIVERY

Each month, the Zebra Home Subscription Service will send you the four newest titles as soon as they are published. (We ship these books to our subscribers even before we send them to the stores.) You may preview them *Free* for 10 days. If you like them as much as we think you will, you'll pay just $3.50 each and *save $1.80 each month* off the cover price. *AND you'll also get FREE HOME DELIVERY.* There is never a charge for shipping, handling or postage and there is no minimum you must buy. If you decide not to keep any shipment, simply return it within 10 days, no questions asked, and owe nothing.

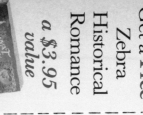

Chapter 32

Most people would have never imagined the iron will of that dainty, soft-spoken lady Beth Huntington. She ruled her palatial mansion like an empress. All the houseservants were well aware that her orders were to be carried out unless they wanted to be relieved of their services at Huntington's Haven.

Lisette could only praise her and admire her greatly after the enjoyable evening and delicious dinner she'd enjoyed her first evening there. Beth had to be the perfect, gracious hostess and it was no wonder Lawson was so proud of her, as reflected in his blue eyes when they roamed her way.

She observed them during the evening and had to confess she envied that earthy, outgoing quality about Lawson that Paul had always lacked. Oh, she knew he loved her but he found it so hard to express his love and devotion.

But in that moment, as she was feeling a wave of envy wash over her, she quickly chided herself for such thoughts, reminding herself what a hardworking husband she had. So hard had he labored for her and their family that it had to surely have been his desire to show all of them how much he loved them.

Sitting now in Beth's opulent, luxurious parlor, with her favorite colors of Wedgwood blue and white, enhanced with shades of lavender and purple, she swore she'd never seen a more beautiful setting. She knew that all the pretty little lavender, purple, and blue velvet pillows resting on the blue velvet settees were lovingly stitched by Beth.

She knew, too, that no housekeeper had arranged the lovely floral pieces. That was the expert touch of Beth Huntington. It had always seemed to Lisette that her friend had that special talent to make something beautiful by the mere skill of her dainty hands.

There were the four of them occupying the parlor after the dinner hour. Lisette, Emile, Beth, and Lawson chatted as they sipped Lawson's imported French brandy. Brad had wasted no time inviting Aimee to take a stroll in the gardens. This didn't surprise Lisette at all.

Lisette had watched the young people leave the parlor together and had to confess they made a most striking couple. She could not resist doing a little secret matchmaking, thinking how nice it would be if her daughter and the son of her dear friend, Beth, would marry. Such lovely grandchildren those two would have, bringing joy to the winter years in the lives of the Aragon and Huntington families. She would have had to have been blind not to recognize Brad's intense interest in Aimee all during the evening meal. He could not keep his eyes off her for a minute.

She wondered if Beth and Lawson had been aware of it. She knew Emile had noticed it, for she saw the look on his face, and she was proud of his very protective attitude toward his younger-sister.

Beth's busy eyes had most assuredly observed her son's worshipping eyes ogling Aimee and she could certainly not find fault with him. In fact, she was thinking to herself what a divine match it would be. Dear God, he would be the envy of every man around! To think that he had been the one to woo and win such a breathtakingly beautiful woman as Aimee was always an asset to any man.

In the part of the country where she had been reared, Beth knew that a lady of quality, with such exquisite beauty as Aimee Aragon's, was most impressive. What a feather in Brad's cap it would be if he could win her, she thought to herself. She enthusiastically approved of Aimee!

Lawson's thoughts were in a similar vein, with the touches of a more earthy, male attitude. It made him want to be a young rooster again, like his son, Brad. Privately, he thought to himself that if his son let this alluring lady slip through his fingers, he had to be an absolute fool. Lawson knew he'd move heaven or hell to get her if he were in Brad's shoes.

Funny now that he recalled how he'd wooed and won his beautiful Beth, he privately mused. He had connived and schemed to entice her away from the man she was engaged to be married to in a couple of months. As it had turned out, he was the man she married just one month later. He knew that she'd never regretted that he'd swept her off her feet and they'd eloped to another county in Georgia to be married.

Bradford Huntington was just as conniving and sly as his father. He had already made up his mind that Aimee Aragon was going to be his. He worshipped her, and he could not deny it. It was as if she were some divine goddess who had cast her beguiling spell over him. His eyes could not leave her lovely face when he was near her. Never had he felt such intense feelings about any woman. He had had many women in his lifetime, but none challenged him like Aimee.

Now he managed to get her all alone in the moonlight, which shone down on the lovely manicured gardens his mother had patterned after the gardens of England. The magnificent shrubs were sculptured into perfect molds his mother had ordered. He was the first to admit that the gardens were a masterpiece of his mother's planning.

Aimee admired them, too, and told him so as they leisurely strolled down the narrow flagstone pathway. "It seems our mothers share a common interest in their gardens, Brad," she remarked.

"They are both very special ladies, Aimee. They both live by the traditions of their past; yours with her French heritage, and my mother with her English background. They seem to share a bond of closeness, don't they?"

She gave out a soft little giggle. "Ah, there is no doubt about that. I never knew my mother to be such a talkative lady as she has been here at Huntington's Haven."

They came to the area in the gardens where a fountain was situated and along the sides of the bubbling little pond were wrought iron benches. There was a secluded aura about the spot, with the sago palms and tropical plants thriving there. It would seem that this countryside did not accept that the summer was fading and autumn was approaching when the gardens flourished with blossoming flowers everywhere. Their fragrance permeated the air with the most wonderful aroma. She was reminded of the gardens at the Chateau L'Aragon.

The only sounds in the gardens were the soothing flow of the fountain and the echo of the light spray cascading down into the pond where huge goldfish swam around. Brad told her that his mother had had those fish sent from San Francisco.

Aimee gazed down on them and pointed to one particular goldfish, doing a very feisty wiggle. It brought a gale of laughter as she remarked, "That one is something else. Look at her, Brad. Isn't she cute?"

"Now, how do you know that it is a female, Aimee?" he gave out a throaty laugh.

"Ah, I just know it. She wiggles so cute. She must be a female," she teased him.

"You are right, you know. We call her Goldie and she can shimmy in a style all her own. She is Mother's favorite."

Aimee watched as Goldie put on her little show and could understand why Beth Huntington would consider her the star of the pond.

Instinctively, she knew that sooner or later Brad was going

to guide her toward one of the benches situated around the pond. When his strong hands guided her in that direction, she allowed herself to follow him.

As they sunk into the seat, he gave out a dejected sigh, "God, Aimee, I wish I had known you were coming here. I wish to hell I was not going with someone else tomorrow night. I would give anything to be escorting you to that ball."

"Brad, I guess we are both in the same dilemma. I care not for the man who is escorting me. In fact, I can't abide him. He was my father's choice, not mine!"

He gave out one of his easygoing laughs, "Now, isn't that one hell of a note—if you'll pardon me being so blunt. My services were also arranged by my parents and I was willing to oblige them, shall we say. Christ, Aimee, what can we do about this? Why should we be doomed to a miserable night when the two of us could enjoy ourselves so much?"

She could not resist a gale of laughter pouring forth. "I don't know, Brad. Perhaps we could slip away from our two companions during the evening and enjoy a dance or two. What do you think?"

His bright blue eyes seared her with the depth of his desire as they moved slowly over her lovely face. "Ah, Aimee, I want more than a couple of dances with you. I want to spend the whole evening with you and I shall be miserable being with this other lady, knowing that we could have been spending precious moments together."

She wore a most provocative smile on her face as she pointed out to him, "Well, it might not have to be just a couple of dances, Brad. Fred Bigler is not the brightest gentleman in the world, from my encounters with him. I have a very devious streak in me which I'm sure I inherited from my *Tante* Denise, so I think we could pull this little escapade off with ease."

Such a twinkle was sparkling in those sapphire eyes of hers and he saw a bit of the devil in her. He liked it! He made the hasty conclusion that Aimee Aragon was a most remarkable young lady and a very exciting one, too. Coupled with all that was her striking, breathtaking beauty, which made her the most desirable woman he'd ever met. He could not let her get away from him, he told himself.

He dared to become a little bolder, and his hand clasped hers as he grinned, "I think you and I could do just about anything we set our minds to. I have the opinion that you are as determined as I am. I—I would also venture to say that we are both a little stubborn, wanting our own way about things."

She gave him a nod of her head as she admitted, "I have to confess you are right, Brad. I am very stubborn and most determined to have my own way. I always have been, and my two older brothers could certainly attest to that. I guess since you were the only child in your family you usually had your own way."

"I did, and I have to confess that I loved every minute of it. Since I never had a sister or a brother, I can't say in all honesty that I missed them."

"I can understand that, Brad. I am sure I would have felt the same way."

He looked at her for one brief moment before he spoke. He was taking into consideration how much younger she was when he compared their ages. She seemed so much more mature than a lot of the ladies he'd squired back East, who were only a few years younger than he was or his own age. But none of them were as sensible or as interesting to talk to as Aimee. He'd found most of them empty-headed idiots or silly, giggling little flips. If they didn't fit into those two categories, they were ladies playing their little games of wiles on him because they knew or had found out from his friends that he was the son of a very wealthy man back in California.

With Aimee, he found he could be himself, with no armor to protect him. He felt free and relaxed. It was so wonderful, and he could not recall a time he'd so thoroughly enjoyed himself as he had this evening. It was Aimee he had to thank for it.

She had a magnificent quality of warmth and he pondered if she were really aware of this genuine, rare gift she possessed.

262

She drew people to her with such ease. Brad had seen it this afternoon around his father and his mother. It was there tonight around their elegant dining room table, as the servants waited on her. All of them adored her.

While he would be the first to say that Lisette Aragon was a sweet, gentle lady and Paul was a fine, upstanding gentleman, neither of them had this particular gift of their daughter. Now, Emile was very much like his father and his mother, with similar traits, Brad could see. Aimee stood apart from the rest of her family and that was what made her so unique.

Brad was a cool, calculating young man, just like his successful businessman father. While he could have given way to the overwhelming urge surging within him to try to kiss those tempting rosy red lips, he decided to wait until tomorrow night at the gala ball. But he damned well intended to enjoy that golden splendor before the night ended tomorrow. By the time the midnight hour came he would taste the sweet nectar there on those luscious lips of hers, he promised himself.

Tonight he played his role as the gallant, debonair gentleman, trying to favorably impress her, and he was satisfied that he had done just that by the time he walked her back toward the house.

Oh, it galled him to deny himself, for it was something the spoiled Brad Huntington had never done. It had never been necessary during his whole life to do so. Never had he wanted for anything. But never had he wanted anything or anyone as much as he wanted Aimee Aragon.

This was something his father's money could not buy for him and he knew it!

Chapter 33

Never had Ross Maynard seen a more gorgeous vision as Aimee was in her exquisite lavender gown, swishing to and fro as she entered the reception room of the governor's mansion accompanied by her mother, Emile, and the Huntington family.

Every sensuous sway of her hips had an effect on him as he strolled across the room to greet them and take his place as Aimee's escort for the ball. There would be no lady at the ball tonight who would hold a candle to her. Her gown was not daring but there was just enough of her gardenia-white flesh exposed at the neckline and off the shoulders to seduce and drive a man crazy with wanting.

The expensive amethyst teardrop earrings encircled with tiny pearls hung from her ears and matched the necklace draped around her throat. Ross figured that had cost Paul a handsome sum of money. Perhaps the Frenchman did not live in an ostentatious style or dress up in fine attire as most men would have with his wealth, but Ross knew he was a very rich man from what John Bigler had told him when he first came to the mansion.

The truth was he'd rarely seen Paul in anything but the work clothes he wore to toil in his vineyards alongside his sons. Tonight was the first time he'd seen Emile in anything other than his old faded blue shirts and dark cotton pants. He was a damned handsome gent all dressed up as he was now.

Beth and Lawson Huntington had seemed like nice friendly people but then he'd only met them once before. He was curious about their son, who was also attending the function with them. Obviously, he was escorting some local young lady since he was not with the rest of the gathering now.

After Ross had cordially greeted each of the members of the group, he moved to Aimee's side, wasting no time in telling her how lovely she looked. "I have never seen anyone so lovely as you, Aimee," he declared.

She thanked him graciously but already her repulsion for this man was washing over her. Just his closeness by her side was irritating and she could not exactly explain why.

Ross Maynard playing his role as Fred Bigler sensed her cool manner. He might not have the genteel manners of the men always gathered around the governor and his close friends, but he knew women and their ways. All that sweetness she had showed him just the other day, when he'd gone to the Chateau L'Aragon, was missing this evening. Ross had to wonder why.

By this time, one of the servants had approached the group, carrying glasses of champagne on a highly polished silver tray. The room was beginning to rapidly fill with the guests arriving.

As Aimee strolled along with Fred at her side, she had to confess she was rather surprised that the old mansion had an air of simplicity. It certainly did not possess the elaborate interior decor of some places in Paris where she'd attended soirées with her *Tante* Denise.

Ross noticed her scrutinizing appraisal and remarked to her, "The governor is a most conservative man, adhering to very traditional ways. He lives very simply. I can tell you were expecting something more flamboyant."

She felt slightly embarrassed that she'd been so obvious to a man like Fred Bigler, who hardly knew her at all. "I—I guess I was," she found herself stammering honestly.

But she did not have time to worry about her embarrassment too long because Fred had led her around one of the small alcoves, away from her mother and Emile. This section had as many milling guests as the other one. Ladies in their colorful gowns and gentlemen in their elegant attire were enjoying the champagne as they chatted and greeted one another.

Suddenly, Aimee caught the sight of a tall black-haired gentleman standing with a lovely black-haired Latin lady. She felt like her heart had stopped beating. She noted how his black hair teased the back of his white collar not covered by his black frock coat. It had never dawned on her that she would encounter Mano Mateo here at the Governor's Ball, a rather foolish slipup on her part. After all, the Mateo family was prominent and most distinguished in the state of California.

A flurry of trembling broke loose within her and she felt like a cornered animal, not knowing how to escape. Because of her rattled nerve, she greedily gulped the champagne in her glass. Ross took an instant notice and an amused grin broke on his face.

He thought to himself that this young lady was no little innocent country girl, even though she'd been raised out on her father's country estate. Not this one! After all, if she'd traipsed around Paris with this aunt of hers and she could gulp champagne the way she was doing just now, she'd lived more than most people would think as they looked at that angel face of hers.

So Ross said nothing as he sat there watching her take the generous sips of the champagne.

She could give him all the signals she wished for him to keep his hands off her, but before this night was over he intended to have his way, by God! No longer would she play him for some damned fool!

Aimee sat entranced by the sight of the tall dark, handsome

266

Latin and she felt she could hardly breathe as he slowly turned around. A slow, easy smile broke on his dark face as he gave her a slight nod of his head to say he saw her, and Aimee heaved a deep sigh of relief when she discovered it was Mario Mateo, instead of Mano.

After a few brief moments, her heart quit pounding so erratically and the trembling subsided. She was grateful that Mario stayed there by the lady's side and made no effort to come her way.

Mario instantly detected her apprehension. He had no desire to make her uncomfortable or spoil her evening by an encounter with a Mateo. But he had to admit that she was a thing of splendor. If Mano were here to see her, nothing would have stopped him from sweeping her into his arms and running away with her.

The one time in his life that Mario had felt pity for Mano was when his brother had told him about what had happened between him and Aimee. Never would Mano have told him if he'd not been so drunk that night. For sure, Mario was convinced that when he and his father returned to La Casa Grande Mano would be gone.

Grateful as Aimee was that the man she'd thought was Mano was his older brother, Mario, she was cast into a new turmoil. The sight of Mario ignited bittersweet thoughts of Mano. His haunting, disturbing vision was there with her now and that was enough to torment her.

But the sight of the good-looking Brad Huntington strolling toward them with the lady he had brought to the ball was a welcoming sight. She saw that look of mischief in his twinkling blue eyes and knew his secret thoughts. As he gazed into the deep amethyst pools of her eyes, he detected the same message.

After all the proper introductions were made, and Brad and Sally accepted a glass of champagne, they sought to linger there with Aimee and Fred Bigler. Now Fred knew why Aimee had given him such a cold shoulder tonight. He had seen the glances exchanged between the two of them. Sally Martindale might be naive and not have noticed it, but he had. There was something going on between Aimee and Brad Huntington, and he planned to have his eye on both of them during the evening.

Brad Huntington formed an instant dislike for this upstart relative of the governor's. He was a swaggering, cocky little bastard, as far as Brad was concerned. He had the gnawing desire to double up his fist and give him a mighty blow on that smirking face of his. There was nothing about this fellow that slightly hinted of him being any relative of the refined Governor Bigler. Brad, being a lawyer, began to question and analyze the facts he knew about this stranger who'd happened upon the scene out of the blue a few months ago. All he knew was what his father had told him. But it was enough to put his sharp mind to work.

He was secretly telling himself that he was going to keep an eye on this character tonight for Aimee's sake. He'd watch those shifting eyes of Fred Bigler's and he wouldn't trust him any further than he could throw him. Another thing Brad noticed, which made him more the skeptic, was that this gent seemed out of character here in a fancy ballroom. Brad envisioned him more at home in a brawling tavern.

The way the two men's eyes bored into each other, it was as if both were trying to remove the masks they were wearing. However, the only mask Brad Huntington was wearing was that he would have preferred to be squiring Aimee, instead of Sally Martindale.

By the time the first sounds of the music began to echo throughout the huge ballroom and Aimee had been led onto the dance floor, she was so miserable she was ready to scream. After the first dance with Fred, she found him awkward and clumsy when compared to the graceful Mano, with whom she'd moved together as one. Dear God, he had forever spoiled her for any other man! His masterful body and hands had guided her to follow him as he led her, and it had been a delight to be in the circle of his arms. Fred's arms enfolding her were sheer hell! Brad glanced across the room as he was dancing with Sally and saw that helpless look on her lovely face. He yearned to rescue her from that oaf she was dancing with.

But when the music stopped and before it began again, Brad was unable to get across the room. However, he was happy to see that she was in the arms of another man instead of Fred Bigler. He was still compelled to dance again with Sally.

Brad noticed that his own mother was being asked to dance more often than his own lady, Sally Martindale. He was more than glad to see his own father coming over toward them, and when Lawson Huntington asked for the privilege of dancing with Sally, Brad eagerly placed her hand in his father's. He was very grateful that his father had rescued him.

Now his busy blue eyes searched the vast area for some sign of Aimee. Such a sea of couples were surrounding him and he knew it was not going to be easy, so he looked for a lovely lavender gown. She was so very petite that such a crowd would swallow her up.

He moved into a particular corner so he could look from one end of the room to the other. After he'd done this for several minutes without seeing her, he moved on the other side of the little alcove. He stood there surveying this area but nowhere could he see her. But his ears did pick up the silence from the music having stopped. He did not wish to have Sally back on his hands, so he moved swiftly out the double doors leading to the terrace just outside the ballroom.

He gave way to the urge to light up one of his cheroots, which his mother detested. It was nice to be there alone in the refreshing night air, listening to the mellow music inside. He puffed on his cheroot and watched the various couples strolling through the garden area. There, in the privacy of the darkness, Brad unbuttoned the fine-tailored frock coat he was wearing, for it was a very warm night even though autumn had come to the California countryside.

Where was she? he wondered. Where was that lovely goddess in the lavender gown? He let his eyes roam over the dappled moonlit gardens and thought of her lovely hair, which looked like silver moonbeams. God, she was the most beautiful thing he had ever seen! If anything would urge him to stay on here in California, it would be Aimee Aragon!

Needless to say, the law firm in Sacramento had offered him a most challenging offer and a generous lucrative salary. But none of this inspired him like the exciting challenge to win the love of the beautiful Aimee. To win her would have been to own the world, Brad considered. He could be the happiest man alive.

Brad would never be able to explain it to himself later, but as he stood there taking his leisurely puffs on the cheroot, something urged him to leave the terrace and roam down the garden pathway.

He was not a superstitious person but there was a strange force that some might call a premonition urging Brad to roam through the gardens.

For once, Brad had to listen to his heart, instead of his cool, calculating head. Logic and facts did not matter to him. He was a man guided by the deep feelings of love for a lady he hardly knew.

Somehow, he knew instinctively she was calling to him and so he went to find her!

Chapter 34

Aimee had welcomed the reprieve she'd had by being claimed by one gentleman after another. This parade had gone on for the next four dances. There was a lighthearted giddiness making her head whirl by the time she had finished the fourth dance with a very nice grey-haired gentleman by the name of Robert Carson. He had invited her to join him and his wife for a glass of champagne.

He was so nice she could hardly refuse him. When they joined his wife, seated at the table awaiting her husband's return from the dance floor, Aimee noticed that the woman was unable to dance. There by her chair was a gold gilt-handled cane.

"I told Robert I must meet you, my dear," his wife addressed Aimee. "I have been admiring you all evening, and when I found out that you were the daughter of Paul Aragon, I told Robert he must bring you over here so I could tell you how beautiful you are and tell your father how much we enjoy his magnificent wines."

Robert Carson wore a broad smile on his face as he told

Aimee, "This is my darling wife, Aimee. My Michelle." Aimee saw the loving glow of admiration in his eyes as he took her hand.

Michelle Carson motioned for Aimee to take a seat by her and the elderly Robert Carson moved to take the seat next to his wife.

"I thank you, Madame Carson, for your kind remarks about both me and my father. I have to tell you I enjoyed the pleasure of dancing with your husband. He is a divine dancer," she said with a twinkle in her eyes and a charming smile on her face. What a treat it was to dance with an older gentleman like Monsieur Carson, who was far more skilled in the art of dancing than the awkward Bigler.

"It was my pleasure, mademoiselle," Robert Carson declared.

"He is a fantastic dancer, madame," Aimee gaily told his wife.

This young lady was not only beautiful but she was a warm, lovely person, Michelle Carson decided after a few brief moments with her. "Oh, I hope to tell you he is. Why do you think I put my claim on him years ago?" she laughed.

"I don't blame you. I would have done the same thing," Aimee lightheartedly laughed.

The trio sat there enjoying themselves and sipping the champagne. Aimee found the couple utterly delightful to be with, even though they were much older than she was. She was more than ready to remain there with the Carsons if it meant being rid of Fred Bigler.

She was sorry when the elderly Monsieur Carson inquired of her, "Is it not the governor's kin who is escorting you tonight?"

"Yes, Monsieur Carson, it is."

"Well, I thought so, and I spy him coming to reclaim you, my dear. I can't fault him for that, but selfishly I wish we could have enjoyed your company longer. Is it not so, Michelle?"

His charming wife agreed with him. "But I shall not be

greedy. May I just tell you that it is not often these days that I meet and see a young lady so outstanding as you, Aimee Aragon. I will look forward to our next meeting." She reached over to pat Aimee's hand and added, "I just wanted you to know that before your young man whisked you away."

Aimee wanted to scream out that he was not her young man nor would he ever be that. But she merely gave her a warm smile, for she was such a lovely, gentle lady and she could not know how her remarks pricked her like a thorn.

Aimee didn't have to turn around to sense Bigler's obnoxious presence as he came to stand behind her chair. She knew the minute he was there and she resented the way his hand came to rest on her shoulders, as if he possessed or owned her. She flinched, turning her eyes upward with a purple-blue fire sparking in them.

Ross Maynard felt the flinching of her satin flesh and he saw the displeasure in those devastating eyes of her. But he went through the perfunctory motions and conversation he knew he must in front of the Carsons.

He waited for Aimee to take the last sip of her champagne before suggesting that they take their leave. Giving a courteous bow to Michelle Carson and a warm smile in Robert Carson's direction, he told them, "I thank you for taking such special care of my lady here."

There was a coarseness in his manner, which Michelle Carson noted, and his efforts to portray the refined young gentleman were a struggle, she felt. She watched Aimee Aragon reluctantly rise from her chair to accompany him, and she yearned to call out to her not to leave them if she did not wish to do so. Of course, she didn't utter a word, but oh how she wanted to.

It was only after the couple had left their table that she leaned over to her husband to declare, "I don't care for that man, Robert. I don't care for him at all!"

Robert Carson understood her feelings, for he felt the same way. He patted her hand as he replied, "Nor do I, my dear.

Guess there is some truth in that old saying that there is a black sheep in every family. If he be kin to John Bigler, then he must surely be the black sheep of that family."

Under protest, Aimee finally agreed to take a stroll in the gardens of the mansion. She came to the conclusion that a walk through the gardens was better than being held in his arms while they danced. Besides, she'd found it impossible to follow his clumsy footsteps. When they'd returned from their stroll, Aimee was praying that Brad Huntington would rescue her as they'd plotted the day before.

She could not know the evil intentions this man was harboring nor how fiercely his rage had been goaded by her aloofness. Right now, he was sick and tired of this stupid role he'd been playing for weeks as Fred Bigler. Right now, he was himself—Ross Maynard. This was a man who could be cruel and heartless, as he'd been the night he'd murdered the nice young Fred Bigler, who'd never suspected that he was about to be killed.

Ross Maynard had not had one minute of remorse nor nagging of his conscience when he'd killed the trusting young man who was on his way to visit his relative in California. In fact, the real Fred Bigler had told Ross all his plans when he'd met up with him and his cohorts along the trail. Believing that all men thought as he did, poor Fred had left himself vulnerable for the tragic fate that befell him.

That night, Ross was just a cold, calculating man, seeing that the young Bigler was an easy prey. Besides, he and his partners were in need of a little money and some supplies. Fred Bigler was certainly easy pickings.

Tonight, Ross was just as cold and calculating, but he was a man filled with a blazing rage. His male ego had been sorely wounded by this little French snob. It seemed she could warm up to everyone but him. That galled him to the core of his being. He damned sure was going to make her pay for causing him to feel less than a man.

He was at a point now of not caring if he had to hightail it out of Sacramento this very night after he had what he wanted from this saucy little bitch. There was no shrewd, clever logic going on in that head of his now. That wild, crazy side of his nature had completely taken over as he led her down a path in the gardens, which he knew was the most secluded area and far enough away so that her screams would not be heard when he took her as he intended to.

Aimee had no inkling of the ominous threat hovering over her as she walked in the moonlit gardens. If she had, she would have yanked up the folds of her lavender gown and run as fast as her dainty feet would carry her.

"My goodness, Fred, it seems we've strayed a far way down this garden. I feel I have walked a mile on these satin slippers. Can we not find a bench to sit down for a minute to rest?"

It had suddenly dawned on her, as she'd glanced back over her shoulder, that all the glittering lights of the mansion looked far away. Her mother's gardens were less than half the size of this one.

Fred Bigler had hardly spoken a word to her since they'd left the Carsons. She was not disturbed about that, for he was not the greatest conversationalist. She could not help thinking about the times she'd spent with Mano and how easily they could talk an hour away.

"I think there is a place over there where we can sit down to rest, Aimee," he told her, guiding her even farther back into the gardens.

The satin slippers were pinching her feet and she was ready to sit down, so she followed as he led her. It was not until she sank down on the bench that she became aware of the strange tone of his voice. A certain instinct came alive within her. Her eyes darted over to observe the face of the man sitting down beside her.

There was an eerie quiet in this area of the garden. No longer were there strolling couples nearby. She was helplessly alone with this man she utterly disliked and certainly did not trust with his beady eyes devouring her. Something about him made her quiver with a fear she found disconcerting, as well as a little frightening.

"Do you feel better now, Aimee?" he asked her. But there was no genuine concern in his voice, and as she darted a glance in his direction, she saw that his face was expressionless.

"Yes, thank you. I feel much better."

"Good. I would not want you to be uncomfortable. I would not want that at all." He let his arm snake around her shoulders and he moved closer to press his body next to hers. He sat so close to her that she could feel his hot, oppressive breath against her face. No longer did Ross Maynard try to play the role of Fred Bigler as he muttered in her ear, "What's the matter honey, eh? Ain't I got the Latin charm of Mano Mateo or that dapper dandy, Brad Huntington?"

She felt the powerful force of his arms suddenly making her his prisoner and his mouth coming closer and closer. "You liked that Mex, didn't you? And I saw tonight that you liked that fancy dude, Huntington, while all the time you turned your fancy nose up at me. Well, let me tell you something, you little bitch. I've had better women than you in taverns in Texas and Mexico. But just to be fair, I'm going to be sure and satisfy my curiosity tonight. I'm going to taste your fine wares. Oh, yes, you snotty bitch, I'm going to take my fill of you. I'll see just how much woman you are, I assure you." Already, he was fondling her breasts roughly and Aimee was trying to free herself from his clutches. Dear God, he was strong! She felt herself fighting a losing battle.

A sickening feeling engulfed her as she felt his heated breath on her throat and neck. She was repulsed by his panting, which reminded her of some animal instead of a man. She wiggled frantically to be rid of his pressing body against hers. There was no doubt in Aimee's mind about what he intended to do to her. God forbid, she could not allow that and be degraded by such a man as Fred Bigler. Never would she allow that! she vowed to herself.

Frenzied by the wild passion pulsing in his veins and his desire heightened by the sensuous little wiggles of her body, Ross Maynard was a man driven by the insatiable desire to quench the lusty needs of his male body.

His hands reached out to grab each side of her lovely face in a firm, viselike grip. Holding it just so, his mouth sought to capture her lips with his. He kissed those lips he'd yearned to kiss for such a long, long time. But they refused his prodding tongue from entering as he sought to do. As forceful as he was, he could not urge her to allow the entry he sought. His hand left one side of her face to move down to the low scooped neckline of her gown. With no gentle touch, his hand prodded the satiny flesh of her breasts.

A new panic struck her when she felt his wet lips licking at the nipple of one of her breasts. Dear Lord, she wanted to die! She felt soiled as she endured the touches of his tongue. It gave her a sudden surge of strength she did not know she possessed to move her petite body just so to free one of her encased arms.

With her arm free, she swung it back as far as it would go to gather the force and power necessary to slap his stupid-looking face. The blow to his face was enough to create an explosive reaction in Ross and he released her, rubbing his cheek as he cussed her.

But it was the moment and the opportunity Aimee needed to leap up from the bench and run like a frightened gazelle down the dark pathway.

She heard his coarse, angry voice back in the distance, but she just kept on running, never turning back to see if he was running after her or not. As long as his arms didn't restrain her, she knew she was free of him and that was all she wanted.

Brad saw this magnificent sight rushing in his direction and he could not believe what his eyes beheld. One luscious lovely breast was exposed for his eyes to see and her lovely silver-blond curls were flowing down over her bare shoulders. Her hands were holding the silk folds of her gown high over her knees so she could run faster and be unhampered by the flowing skirt of her gown. The sight of her rushing down that path was something he knew he'd never forget. She was absolutely glorious!

His arms were there to gather her up in them as she eagerly came to him. As he embraced her, he felt the pounding of her heart as she gasped for breath. For one divine moment, he held her there in his arms, feeling the sweet heat of her pressed against his broad chest.

His lips soothed her as they caressed her cheek and he inhaled deeply of the sweet fragrance of her. He comforted her as his lips murmured softly, "You are safe now, Aimee. Nothing or no one will hurt you now. I'll kill that bastard if he should dare to come near you again." His hand went slowly down to the bodice of her gown, and with a most tender touch, he yanked it up to conceal the exposed flesh of her bosom.

All she could manage was a deep, exhausted sigh, "Oh God, Brad, take me away from here. I can't face anyone here tonight. Will you just take me away from here?" Her pleading eyes were looking up at him in a way he would have found hard to refuse.

"You won't have to, Aimee. I shall get you to my carriage and in the safekeeping of my driver. You and I are going immediately back to Huntington's Haven, if you would like."

"I would like that very much, Brad," she stammered in almost a whisper. The thought of facing her mother or her brother did not appeal to her. The taint of Fred Bigler was upon her right now and she wanted a cleansing bath to remove his touch from her.

"Your wish is my command, my darling," Brad told her as he took her by the arm to lead her out of the gardens. Taking full charge of the situation, he told her that he would inform his parents and her mother and brother that he was taking her to Huntington's Haven.

Aimee reminded him that there was Sally Martindale to think about. He gave her a sly grin as he replied, "I'm going to

278

give your brother the privilege of escorting her home."

That was enough to bring forth a gale of laughter from Aimee—and a laugh was certainly what she needed right now. She was more than willing for him to take full charge and he seemed to have a masterful quality to do just that.

She willingly put herself in his capable hands!

Chapter 35

Ross Maynard was not prepared for the little hellcat whose claws had stung his face with such a vicious blow. It had stunned him so, for a brief moment, that he stood there in the darkness, frozen like a statue.

He watched her flee through the gardens with that silvery hair of hers flying back wildly in the night breeze, the silken folds of her gown billowing as she ran away from him. A sardonic smirk creased his face as he watched her. At least, he'd enjoyed scaring the hell out of her and she deserved that. Maynard reasoned that she'd dare not tell anyone, for that pride of hers would not allow it.

He sat back down on the bench for a moment to gather his thoughts about his next move. Oh, he knew there was no way she would ever agree to him coming to court her. He knew that he'd never set foot on the property of the Chateau L'Aragon again. But he could not leave California and return to Texas without settling the score with the Aragon family, especially Aimee. No woman had ever wounded his pride as she had. He was determined to make her pay, and pay dearly, for wounding his male vanity. This was the worst sort of insult for a man like Maynard.

To make both her and her old man pay would be the gratification Ross wanted now that he had not satisfied himself with her sensuous body and luscious lips. He was pacified by assuring himself that he could have a woman any time he wanted one, as he'd always had in the past. But what he had in mind would yield him a handsome bounty to take back to Texas and say farewell to this state once and for all.

With his plan of action firmly plotted, Maynard moved from the bench in the garden to go back toward the mansion. However, he had no intentions of going inside the mansion or the ballroom. He was going to the stable to saddle up his horse and ride to a nearby tavern he'd often frequented since being here in Sacramento. He had some business to attend to before this night was over.

He swaggered down the pathway, going over all his plans for the Aragon family. So engrossed in those devious thoughts was Ross that he was not prepared when two strong hands grabbed his shoulders, swinging him around. Before he knew who his assailant was, he felt the mighty blow of two fists against his face. It was only when he lay there on the grounds that he looked up in a dazed state and heard the familiar voice angrily declare, "You ever come near Aimee again, you bastard, and I'll kill you next time. You hear what I'm telling you, you scum?"

Maynard had no chance to answer the man standing there towering over him. Ross watched him turn sharply on his booted heels to march down the flagstone pathway and he realized he had certainly underestimated Brad Huntington. He was far more than just some dapper dandy in his fine attire. The man could be vicious!

This ferocious side of Brad Huntington was not showing when he joined Aimee and his driver, Matt. He was as cool and calm as he'd been when he'd placed Aimee in the care of Matt while he'd gone to inform his parents and her mother that they

281

were returning to Huntington's Haven. Emile had agreed to see Sally Martindale to her home when Brad had confided in him about Aimee's misfortunate and upsetting experience in the garden.

Brad had to calm Emile's hot temper by telling him he had already taken care of everything and that Aimee was in his carriage, in the safekeeping of his dependable driver.

He'd also informed Emile, "I've bloody well warned Bigler to never come near her again. So now if you could just see that Sally gets home, I'll forever be beholden to you, Emile."

"You take care of my sister, Brad, and I promise you I will see that Mademoiselle Martindale gets home safely," Emile assured him.

"We have a deal, Emile. I'll bid you good night so I can go to Aimee," Brad Huntington said, patting the husky Frenchman on the shoulder.

Without further ado, he turned to leave the crowded ballroom.

Brad Huntington might have been the victor tonight but Ross Maynard swore to even that score before he left the state of California. As he gathered himself up off the carpeted grounds of the garden and found the strength to make his way to the stables, he suddenly realized that blood was oozing from the side of his mouth and he took out his handkerchief to swipe that side of his face.

Ah, yes, there were some scores to settle before he left to return to Texas. He would settle them as he always had back in Texas, and all of them would know before he left that it was Ross Maynard dealing out their punishment.

He managed to get to the stables and saddle up his own mount, removing the expensive tailored coat he'd worn and rolling up the sleeves of his expensive linen shirt.

Without the coat and his sleeves rolled to his elbow, he was feeling much more like the man he knew so well. This was his style. This was his breed of man.

He wasted no time mounting the feisty little mare and departing for the tavern a few miles away. In less than a half hour, he was entering the boisterous tavern, where he hoped to make a deal with a pair of dudes he'd shared enough drinks with to know they were void of any morals or scruples. A pair of this sort were exactly what he wanted now that his old buddies from Texas had deserted him to return to their old haunts.

He took a table back in an obscure corner to enjoy the shot of whiskey he'd ordered. He felt a hell of a lot more at home here in these surroundings than he had at the fancy Governor's Ball tonight. The dirty floor and the liquor-stained tabletop were not new to him. He liked the sounds of raucous laughter echoing throughout the small area.

He was not to be disappointed about seeing the two men he'd hoped to meet here tonight. They arrived together, as they had before on nights when he'd been there. They were a mean-looking pair, with their jet-black beards and thick manes of hair always looking like they were in need of a haircut. Both of them were tall and husky. There was a swagger to their walk, as if they were openly inviting anyone there to challenge them.

Ross knew that they were exactly the type of men he wished to hire for the job he wanted done to the Aragon family. He also knew, before he approached them, that they were the sort who would do anything if enough gold was laid in their palms.

He allowed them to enjoy their first drink before sending his message to them via his waitress. He waited, watching as they turned to the secluded corner where he sat. Without any hesitation, they readily accepted the drinks Ross had bought for them. Ross had no doubt that they would accept his offer for a drink as he watched them move away from the bar to join him at his table.

"You buy us this drink, mister? Why?" one of the men inquired.

"I did. Would you join me here? I've a matter of business to discuss with the two of you," Ross told him.

"Business?" one man roared with laughter. "You've got business to discuss with us? Hell, we don't even know you, fellow! You hear that, Cody?"

"I heard, Buck," the other man chimed in.

Ross motioned the two to sit down. "I know you don't know me and I don't know you either. But I've seen the two of you in here before and you look like a couple of dudes who would not object to a deal to make some easy money."

This got their attention and they exchanged glances as they slowly sunk into the seats.

"Before we waste too much of our time or yours, fellow, just what kind of gold are you talking about?" the man called Cody asked Ross.

"I'm talking about enough to whet a lot of men's appetites," Ross told him, looking him straight in the eyes. It was obvious to Ross that this Cody was the leader and the one called Buck was the follower.

If Ross had had any doubts about the two, he didn't after Cody sought to ask him, "You got someone you want taken care of. Is that what's on your mind, fellow?"

"Not exactly that. But I'm glad to know that you aren't squeamish. I figured I'd pegged you two right, so now I know I did."

Once again, the two men exchanged glances. Buck was the next one to speak. "So just what is it you want of us that you are willing to pay for our services then?"

Ross knew that they were willing to listen to his proposition now and so he slowly went over the details of his scheme. He also told them what he was willing to generously offer them for their three days of service. "Is that not a fair wage for just three days of your time?"

"Hell, yes," Cody declared, giving Buck no time to consider it one way or the other. "We're on. You set the time and the day and we'll be ready."

"I'll meet you here at this same time two nights from now and give you the final instructions. Is that a deal?"

"You've got yourself a deal. Don't even know your name, mister?" Cody remarked.

"Nor do I know yours. We'll just leave it that way for the time being. But to assure you that I'm serious, I'll give you something to make you think about all the others you'll collect after you've done the job for me that I'm hiring you to do," Ross smiled, laying two gold coins on the table in front of Buck and Cody.

There was no mistaking the instant eager reaction in both of the men's eyes as they ogled the shining gold coins. He certainly had impressed the pair! He watched as their anxious hands reached out for the coins. He allowed the men to enjoy the feel of them and anticipate the numerous coins they'd receive just like those two when they did the job he'd proposed.

As the two pocketed the gold coins and rose up out of their chairs, Cody assured Ross that they would be there on Monday night.

Ross Maynard gave them a nod of his head and watched the pair saunter out the door of the tavern. He suspected that they were heading for the nearest bordello to enjoy themselves for the rest of the night. The gold coin would buy them a night of pleasure.

There was a smirk on his face as he watched them go out the door. They were the perfect choice to do his dirty work.

Ross was ready to leave this place and seek the comfort and softness of his bed. It had been a night to make a man weary, and God knows, he was weary!

As he moved away from the table to amble out the front door of the tavern, he realized that he had the right to be bone-weary tired. Aimee Aragon had slapped his face with a mighty blow, raking her long fingernails across his cheek. Brad Huntington had pounded his face with a fierce, cruel blow, stunning him so that he'd fallen to the ground.

That was enough for one night, Ross decided. That was enough punishment to urge him to seek the comfort of his bed, and now that he'd had two generous glasses of whiskey to ease his pain, he was ready for sleep.

As he had watched Cody and Buck take their leave, a pair of piercing black eyes had watched him take his leave. The dimly lit room of the tavern had not alerted Mano to the trio huddled there in the corner. But as he'd sat at the table alone, he'd recognized Fred Bigler with the two unsavory characters. Bigler was so engrossed in his conversation with the two men that he'd not noticed Mano.

What could he possibly have in common with such characters as those two? Mano wondered.

His curiosity was whetted enough that he strained to try to hear their conversation. But all he heard was that the trio was to meet there in two nights. If he had known that their meeting in two nights was to plan the evil plot against Aimee and her family, Mano would have never gone on to Half Moon Bay. But he had not heard anything about Aimee in their conversation.

Nevertheless, when he left the tavern to travel to his destination, Half Moon Bay, he left with a heavy heart. Something was bothering him, but he knew not what it was. Tomorrow, he hoped he would find the answer when he arrived at Phil Cabrillo's cottage and that peaceful serenity he always found there. Mano needed the answer to many things prodding his heart and soul, and he knew of no other place to find them except Half Moon Bay.

What was it about that little fishing village that soothed his troubled being? There had to be an answer and he knew someday he would know it.

Tonight, he knew Aimee was calling out to him. He felt it! God knows, he would have gone to her! His whole being ached for her.

He and Demonio rode through the night and a rushing breeze whistled through the trees. He swore that the sound he heard was the name of the woman he loved with all his heart. Aimee . . . Aimee . . . Aimee! That was the sweet melody of the tender, gentle breeze rustling through the tall trees of the trail he traveled.

Chapter 36

The drive back to Huntington's Haven was relaxing and peaceful for Aimee. It was a welcomed comfort to be sitting there beside Brad as the carriage rolled along the dirt road. She appreciated him engaging in a lighthearted chatter, not bringing up the subject of what had transpired back there in the gardens of the governor's mansion. He was acting as if nothing like that had taken place and she was very grateful for his kind consideration. She was finding herself admiring Brad more and more as she was spending time with him.

In fact, she'd already told herself that Brad Huntington could be the tonic she needed right now to help her forget that handsome devil Mano. Brad was a very striking-looking young man, and in his own way, he was as good-looking as Mano Mateo and also possessed a certain charm.

Feeling this way, she urged herself to give him a chance to at least woo her if he wished, and she was certain that he did want to make love to her. She recognized that particular look in his eyes, exactly as it had been in Mano's black eyes. She had already decided that if he tried to kiss her, she would allow him to do it. Besides, she was curious to find out if another man could fire her with such a flaming blaze as Mano had. There was surely more than one man who could create such wild, wonderful sensations in her, she reasoned.

If Brad's kisses could ease the pain in her heart for Mano, then she would welcome them. With this in mind, when they arrived back at his family's estate and entered the quiet hallway, she accepted his offer that they go out on the side veranda and enjoy a drink.

"Champagne, my lady?" he asked her with a crooked grin on his face.

"That sounds wonderful, Brad."

He led her in that direction, and when he had her sitting comfortably in one of the white wicker chairs there on the veranda, he excused himself to go for their champagne instead of summoning a servant at this late hour.

When she waited there alone in the night, Aimee wondered just what Brad had told her mother and his parents. There was also Sally Martindale, and she was curious about what he'd possibly conjured up to excuse himself, since he was her escort for the ball.

However, tonight had convinced her that Brad Huntington had a definite charm and finesse, which would impress women. He had certainly won her admiration this night.

These were her private musings when he returned to her with their glasses of champagne. "Ah, this is the way I would have wished it to be tonight anyway, Aimee. Just you and I sitting here under the stars, sipping a fine champagne and enjoying one another's company. Fate seemed to work it all out for us, I think. I think it's a good omen."

"I guess you are right, now that I think about it. But I must know—being the curious person I am—what you told everyone," she said with a quizzical grin on her face.

"Well, I told Emile the truth and asked him a favor. He is to see Sally home for me. I was not so truthful with my parents or your mother, because I did not wish to upset them. I have to say that I handled it all quite cleverly and they accepted my little white lie."

She raised a fine-arched brow as she declared to him, "I think I am beginning to like you, Brad Huntington, more all the time." She gave out a gale of lighthearted laughter.

"Well, now, I think I like that very much, Aimee Aragon. Need I say to you that I want you to like me. I've made no effort to hide the fact that I'm very attracted to you, as you must surely know. I think we are two of a kind, Aimee. I don't play stupid games nor do you, I suspect."

"No, I don't, Brad. It's not my nature—whether it's right or wrong."

"Good. I'm glad to hear that and I'm just a little pleased to know that I was right about you."

With those remarks exchanged between the two of them, they both sat back in the wicker chairs to sip their champagne and enjoy themselves in a gay, casual banter of conversation.

However, after she'd drank the second glass of champagne Brad had offered her, Aimee felt a giddy feeling that told her she needed no more. She rose from her chair to announce that she must excuse herself. "It has been a very busy evening and I must tell you I enjoyed the later half more than the first half, Brad. I have you to thank for that."

He quickly noticed the slight sway of her petite figure and he went to her side, placing his strong arm around her tiny wasp-thin waist.

"I'd say that you've had a big-enough evening and it is time I see you to your room so you can get some rest, young lady," he chuckled. She allowed him to guide her off the veranda and through the long hallway. His arm supported her as they climbed the winding stairs and walked down the thick carpet of the hall.

As they reached her door, Aimee turned to smile at him. She raised up on her tiptoes to plant a gentle kiss on his cheek. Then she swiftly turned through the door, only to be stopped by his forceful arms urging her back toward him. Once he felt her tightly against him, his blue eyes pierced her. His head bent slowly and determinedly as he sought to capture her lips with his mouth.

There was a firm, assured tone to his voice as he murmured in her ear, "Ah, no, Aimee, I'll not settle for a half measure. I will want you completely or not at all. Right now, I want no little sister's kiss. I want a woman's kiss."

He proceeded to kiss her as a man would kiss a woman he desired. When his lips finally released hers, Aimee had no doubt that he desired her as she stood there looking up into his bright, sparking eyes.

In the coolest, calmest voice, he told her good night, allowing her to move from his arms to go through the door, closing it after she had entered.

She moved slowly toward the dressing table to remove her jewelry. There was a thoughtful look on her face as she measured what had transpired between her and Brad Huntington this evening. He'd meant what he'd said that he didn't play games where love and romance were concerned.

His romantic overture had startled her, she had to admit, and she admired that masterful force in him. The disappointment for Aimee was that when his lips had taken hers in a most passionate kiss, she had not felt that same exhilarating magic Mano had stirred. God, she hoped she would have but she didn't!

Dejectedly, she took off the earrings and the necklace and sunk down on the velvet-cushioned stool to look into the mirror. She studied her reflection, asking that image what she was to do to ever rid herself of the haunting vision of that tall, dark, handsome devil who'd captured her heart so completely.

She didn't know where or when she would find the answer. The only person she could have turned to for that advice was so many miles away across a vast ocean. She knew of no one with more knowledge about the ways of life and men than *Tante* Denise. Oh, if only she could curl up in a chair and talk to her right now, how happy she would be! After their talk, Aimee knew she would have the answer to the tormenting thoughts driving her crazy.

But her aunt was in Paris and she was here in California, so that was out of the question. Aimee knew that she had to find the answer for herself but her restless heart did not want to accept what her head was saying to her.

As attractive as Brad Huntington was, Aimee knew now that he could never fill the void left by Mano Mateo and she was absolutely determined not to settle for less now that she'd known the rapture of his arms and his love.

She knew she could never be happy with any man who could not offer her the wild, wonderful joy and ecstasy she'd known for that brief moment of golden splendor with Mano.

Mano swore that there was some kind of strange magic about this area he knew as Half Moon Bay. He was definitely convinced of this tonight, for he was deeply troubled when he'd left the tavern to ride to the bay area. But the minute he'd reined Demonio down that winding lane, which would lead him to the cottage of Phil Cabrillo, his spirits lifted. The moon was shining down on him, and over in the distance, perched on the branches of one of the many trees, he heard the screeching of an owl.

A short distance away he heard the howling of a dog and knew it could be the two old hounds of Phil's—Red and Rosie. It certainly sounded like the duet those two could put on as Mano recalled from his last visit.

He realized that he was going to be arriving at Phil's at an ungodly hour, but that wouldn't bother Cabrillo because he lived an unconventional lifestyle. For sure, when he got to the hitching post just outside the picket fence, those two hounds would rouse Phil from his night's sleep.

It was not the hounds' howling that had prevented the burly, shaggy-haired Portuguese from drifting off to sleep this evening. It was that primitive instinct of his working actively with Mano on his mind. He knew the young man was soon to arrive on his doorstep. So he sat on his small porch and puffed on his clay pipe, sipping and savoring a glass of the Portuguese wine his friend Vester had bought for him.

Phil had stored six bottles in his cupboard, which Vester had bartered from the crew of a ship coming into port for several baskets filled with fresh vegetables and fruit from his orchard. But Phil wouldn't let Vester leave his cottage this afternoon without a share of his catch of the day from the bay. Phil figured Vester was enjoying his fish tonight at his evening meal, as he was now enjoying the fine taste of the wine from Portugal.

Cabrillo's keen ears heard the sound of Demonio's galloping hooves long before his eyes caught sight of the grey coat of the thoroughbred, with its thick black tail and mane. A sly, smug grin broke out on his tanned, weathered face. It was Mano riding down the lane!

Old Red and Rosie erupted into a siege of barking now as the intruder came closer to Phil's property. They continued this gale of barking until Mano reined up on Demonio and leaped down to the ground. He called out to the two hounds, "Shut up, you two. It's just your buddy, Mano. Don't you know me? Stayed away too long, I guess."

He had not noticed the shadowy figure sitting there on the porch yet, as he proceeded through the gate. He had no fear of the two big dogs because by now they were already wagging their tails.

He sauntered up the dirt path, bending down to give Red and Rosie a pat on the head as they followed at his side. "You two guarding the place while old Phil sleeps, eh?" Mano asked them as though they could surely answer him.

Suddenly the darkness resounded with that deep, gruff-sounding voice of Cabrillo as he declared to Mano, "Old Phil is not asleep, Mano. He sits here waiting for you to arrive this night."

At the same moment, the two of them broke into a gusto of

laughter. By this time, Mano was moving up the two steps onto the porch to see the robust figure sitting there in one of the two chairs situated at the side.

"Knew I was coming, did you?" Mano grinned.

"Told you I did, son. Got the feeling when I was eating supper. I knew I would see you before dawn of the next day."

Mano went up to the elderly man, a warm smile on his face, and gave him a friendly embrace. "Good to see you, Phil. How have you been since we last saw one another?"

"I have no complaints. How about you, eh?"

For a moment, Mano hesitated before he replied to the old man sitting there. It was senseless to try to lie to him, Mano knew. "I guess I need some answers, Phil, and you and Half Moon Bay have never failed me yet. I suppose I needed to see you and talk."

"I see. Then we shall talk, Mano. As you know, I am one hell of a talker. Sit down, young man." He motioned to Mano to take the other chair beside his.

Phil Cabrillo sat there thinking about how many problems he and Mano had discussed in recent years since the young man had been coming up here to his cottage. Before him, it had been his mother, Theresa, who had sat out here on the porch of this little cottage. When her heart was heavy and her shoulders were burdened by the woes of her life back at La Casa Grande, she would also seek Phil's advice.

"How are things back at the ranch, Mano? How is your father and your brother, Mario?" Phil asked him as he sunk down into the weathered old chair.

"They are well, sir."

"Then may I suggest that you go in the house and get yourself a glass to join me in some fine Portuguese wine. You seem to need some and then we shall talk, yes?"

Mano gave him a nod of his head and did as he suggested. Never would he know what made this old man so easy to talk to.

When he returned to the porch and Phil poured him a generous glass of his prized wine, the old man wasted no more time, coming straight to the point by insisting on knowing what was troubling Mano.

Readily, Mano confessed to him, "A beautiful lady! The most beautiful lady I've ever set eyes on."

Phil gave a nod of his thick grey head as he let out a slow drawl, "Ah, yes, a woman! I should have known. What heavenly bliss those divine females can give us, but they can also give us a hellish torment as well. Obviously, this lady is tormenting your soul, Mano. I am eager to hear about her."

Mano drank deep of the wine as he declared, "Aimee Aragon has done exactly that to me and I must confess that no woman has ever affected me like this. *Madre de Dios*, I've known all kinds of women and had a fair share of them!"

Phil Cabrillo gave out an amused smile as he told the young man sitting there with him, "Ah, but there is always that one woman in a man's life who is like no other. This Aimee Aragon is the one in your life, maybe?"

"Aimee is most assuredly that woman, Phil!"

Chapter 37

Phil Cabrillo was a good listener as Mano told him about his meeting with the beautiful daughter of his father's bitter enemy, Paul Aragon. He admitted to Phil how he'd lied about his identity, knowing that he would have been refused entry to the Chateau L'Aragon if he had not done so.

"I never intended that it go on so long, and that is the truth, Phil. I merely meant to let her think that I was Mark Perez until I felt she cared for me as much as I did for her. Time just went by so fast that the right time never seemed to come."

"How often one could say that about so many things," Phil remarked.

Mano threw his hands up in a helpless gsture as he commented, "I gambled too long and I lost."

"Who is to say that you have lost? I rather doubt you have lost, Mano, unless you don't care enough to fight for this lovely lady you've so vividly described to me. I doubt that!"

"Tonight I feel I have but maybe tomorrow I will feel different about a lot of things. It has happened before, as you well know, once I get to your cabin and think more clearly."

Phil Cabrillo smiled and his eyes were now heavy with the need to sleep. "Tomorrow is already here, my young friend. Look!" He pointed to the skies, with a new dawn breaking. A creeping fog was moving in through the trees from the bay a short distance away. Long ago, old Red and Rosie had curled up on the other side of the porch to sleep cozily.

Phil moved his brawny body out of the chair to announce, "I think it is time this old man got himself to bed, Mano."

Mano stood up to stretch his firm muscled body, giving a lazy laugh, "I can tell you that this young man is ready to lay his tired body down, too, and get some sleep."

The two men went inside the cottage together. Mano knew by now that he was to sleep on the narrow cot in a small cubicle off the kitchen. There was only one bedroom in the house. Both of them were so pleasantly relaxed by the fine Portuguese wine that they barely mumbled a hasty good night before going their separate ways.

Now Phil had no problem going to sleep, because Mano had arrived as he'd felt he would. His sleep was a deep one, but the old man was one of those people who required only a few hours to wake up feeling refreshed and stimulated to meet the new day.

So the next morning Mano still slept long after old Phil was up, starting his day. He had had his breakfast and the hounds had been fed. By the time the tousle-haired Mano had stumbled out on the porch, he found Phil enjoying a steaming cup of black coffee and thinking about all the things Mano had told him a few hours ago. He had to help the young man who was dear to his heart, so he was searching for the sage advice he should give him.

Always, he'd regretted that all his advice and experience from living had not been enough to help the lovely Theresa. Perhaps no one could have helped her, he had to admit. But dear God, he wished he could have! Forever, it would pain him that in some way he had failed her.

As many traits as he saw in Mano that reminded Cabrillo of

Theresa, there was a vast difference in those two and for that he was glad.

When Phil turned to see Mano standing there in the doorway, he grinned, suggesting, "A strong cup of coffee is what you need, lad. Go get yourself some, eh?"

Mano gave him a nod of his head and turned to go back inside the cottage.

He joined Phil out on the porch and they shared their cups of black coffee. Later they roamed through the woods with the two hounds trailing along beside them. They talked of many things, but the subject of Aimee Aragon was not brought up by either of them.

This was not to say that both of them did not have the lovely lady on their minds. But a strange silence prevailed as they spoke of other things.

Mano followed as Phil guided them along the trail, knowing not that they were making a full circle around the dense forest surrounding the cottage. Suddenly, they emerged into the clearing and Mano saw the little cottage directly ahead of them. A surprised look came to his face as he declared to Phil, "I—I had no idea we were so near your place."

"No, you didn't, but I did. One has only to know where he is going to find his destination. I knew where I was going."

Mano exploded with laughter. "You smart old scoundrel! I know exactly what you are trying to tell me in your own way. Well, I've got news for you, and I decided it as we were walking all this time."

"Ah, you do, do you? Then you tell me, lad?"

"I've had a dream for a while now and I am going in search of it, Phil. I hope that someday Aimee will want to share that dream with me. But with or without her, this is something I intend to do."

"Sorry, son, but I don't follow you," Phil declared with a confused look on his face.

"I am leaving here in the morning to go up to the region known as Valley of the Moon. There is a place up in the mountains, just outside Santa Rose. Surrounded by a forest of redwoods stands a magnificent old manion of a house. I fell in love with this place the first time I saw it. That colonnaded old mansion needs a lot of work done on it but that would not bother me. I would enjoy it."

There was an understanding look in Cabrillo's dark eyes as he asked of Mano, "So the bulls of La Casa Grande will never interest you, will they, Mano?"

"Never!"

Phil Cabrillo, of all people, understood why the bull or the grand ranchero did not interest Mano as it did Mario. So he listened as Mano told him about the winery there, with the buildings made of redwood that the owners had built and constructed from the lumbers of the nearby forest.

"The soil seems to produce a very delicate and delicious cabernat sauvignon. The family produces a very small crop of grapes compared to the vineyards of Aimee's father. But it excites me, Phil, and it challenges me as nothing I've ever known before. Do you understand what I'm trying to say?" His dark eyes pleaded with Phil to try to understand this wonderful dream he had.

"Ah, yes, I do understand, Mano. You go to your Valley of the Moon and capture your dream. Everything else will fall into place, I assure you."

"Oh, thank you, Phil, for saying that," Mano gave out a lighthearted little laugh. "That is why I stopped off in Sacramento yesterday to draw out the money I'd need to buy the property I've just told you about."

A sly grin came on Phil's face and he was very proud of the young man there by his side. Mano had not needed his advice to guide him—not really! He was a man of strength and determination, Cabrillo was now convinced. But it was nice to know he enjoyed sharing his time here with him at Half Moon Bay.

"So you will leave for your Valley of the Moon in the morning?"

"Yes, but I shall return here in a couple of days if that is all right?"

"Of course it is. Me, Red, and Rosie will be here waiting for you," Cabrillo chuckled.

"Then tonight we should have a grand feast and drink much wine, eh amigo?"

Cabrillo agreed with his young friend that they would surely do just that, as they went through the picket fence gate and into his small yard.

A nearby neighbor and an old friend of Phil's had stopped by his cottage earlier that morning, before Mano had woken up, to leave him a fine-cured ham butt and a dozen eggs. In turn, Phil had filled a basket to the brim with the various vegetables in his garden. This was the way it was with the settlers here on Half Moon Bay. It was the same when one neighbor traded his skills for another when something needed fixing or repairing.

This was the friendly camaraderie that endeared this little village to Phil Cabrillo, where he planned to live the rest of his life. Nowhere could possibly be as peacefully serene as this little secluded area.

It was as if Mano had been reading Phil's thoughts as he spoke to the old man when he stepped up on the plank porch. His hand clasped the wooden post support, swinging around in a lighthearted manner as he declared, "Ah, Phil, this is a wonderful little piece of paradise you have here. You and those hounds can go into your woods and get yourself a squirrel or a rabbit any time you like. That stream over there is ripe with fish for the catching. All those juicy wild berries are out there in the lanes by the side of the road."

Phil grinned, "So you've taken notice of all the good things my life here provides, eh?"

"Yes, sir, I certainly have."

"Well, my cupboards are always supplied with plenty of food and I've never known a hungry day in my life, I'm proud to say. As a matter of fact, my good friend, Grover Marshall, brought me the finest ham you'll ever taste and that will be our supper tonight. His good wife, Madge, sent me a dozen of her good fresh eggs. Think we aren't going to have ourselves a feast tonight, young man?" he chuckled, giving Mano a robust pat on his shoulders.

"You got my appetite whetted already, you old rascal," Mano playfully teased Cabrillo. The two of them laughed as they entered the cottage, a feeling of good spirits engulfing them.

A few hours later, after the sun had set and twilight had settled over the region, the two men sat at Phil's square oak table, indulging themselves in the feast he'd promised they would have that night. Never had Mano tasted anything as good as Phil's light biscuits with the delicious ham gravy. He'd fried potatoes in the cast-iron skillet and had also fried some of the fresh eggs the Marshalls had sent over.

"Dear God, Phil, I feel like I'll never want to eat again. I'm so full I don't think I can get up out of this chair," Mano moaned, rubbing his stomach.

Phil laughed and leaned back in his own chair. Right now, he had to admit he was feeling the same way, but he knew that feeling would pass. By morning, his hearty appetite would have to be satisfied once again.

When the two of them retired, sleep came swiftly to both. Even his thoughts about Aimee did not keep Mano from quickly drifting off. A contentment flooded him tonight, and as much as he worshipped her and wanted her, there was something else Mano wanted. He was firmly convinced of what he wanted for his future, and tomorrow he planned to go to the Valley of the Moon country. If it was not too late, he was going to purchase that land and the little winery.

To share this dream of his with Aimee Aragon was what he yearned to do. But with or without her, he had to do as his heart was dictating about this land he could not quit thinking about. It was like the first time he'd set eyes on Aimee and then he could not forget about her. It was a different sort of passion, but it was a passion all the same.

301

When the bright California sunshine came streaming through the narrow little window and across the small cot where Mano was sleeping, he woke up instantly. So eager he was to get started, he brewed a pot of coffee and got dressed without waking up Phil. He felt no need for any food, just two cups of the strong black coffee.

As soon as he'd taken the time to scribble Phil a short note, telling him he should be back in four or five days, he went immediately to get Demonio saddled up so he could be on his way to Santa Rosa and the Valley of the Moon.

The force was so strong and powerful that Mano could not shrug it aside. Intuitively, he knew he had to obey. That hillside in Santa Rosa called out to him.

His restless heart would not allow him to ignore that calling.

Chapter 38

Aimee was filled with mixed emotions when she found out that her mother had been persuaded by the lovely Beth Huntington to stay on at Huntington's Haven for two extra days after the night of the ball. She sensed immediately that Emile was displeased by his mother's decision and Beth Huntington's influencing them to remain longer than they'd planned. But Emile realized that she'd not been away from the Chateau L'Aragon for a long time. Her husband was due to be away from their home for weeks. She deserved a little pleasure with her friend Madame Huntington.

Aimee's feelings were torn two ways. It was not so much the urge to return to their home as it was with her older brother, Emile, but the presence of Brad Huntington was very disconcerting and she found herself very confused.

He was a strikingly good-looking man and he had a charming personality. She had to admit that she found him a most interesting individual. During the times they took walks together and sat around talking, he kept her entertained. It was only when he sought to kiss her that Aimee wished she were not with Brad.

A small voice within her kept urging Aimee to give him a chance. She was not being fair to this young man, it chided her. She also knew why, and she secretly cussed the handsome devil responsible for it. Her beautiful eyes could appreciate a handsome man when she saw one, and Brad Huntington would be considered that by any lady. He had a certain style and charm few men possessed. In fact, if she was to be quite honest, he had all the traits and talents to make him a prime choice for any young lady. He was the ideal gentleman for a suitor or a husband.

She enjoyed the touch of his hand when it held hers, and she was not repulsed by the heat of his arm encircling her waist as they took their leisurely strolls in the twilight around the grounds of Huntington's Haven. She even loved his infectious laughter as they'd cantered their horses over the countryside the last two mornings.

Why was it then she could not make herself respond as she yearned to do when his lips met hers in a kiss? Dear God, she'd truly tried to give herself up to his lips as he'd embraced her!

She'd seen the quizzical, skeptical look in his blue eyes as his arms released her, and she knew this man was certainly no fool. But the frown always quickly dissolved and a slow smile came to his face. He was clever enough to never make an issue about it. It seemed he simply shrugged it aside quite casually. But it was hardly casual or simple to the arrogant Brad Huntington. It was taking all his strong willpower to restrain his impatience. She was surely the most complex, moody young lady he'd ever met, but she was also the most entrancing one, too.

By now, Brad knew he was completely beguiled by this silver haired maiden. His mother had made it very clear to him that she would eagerly invite this young woman into their family. He found this most unusual for his scrutinizing mother. Until Aimee Aragon had appeared a few days ago, most young ladies he'd squired seemed to have some faults according to Beth Huntington, Brad had concluded.

But his mother was not the only one singing Aimee's praises. His father was obviously taken by her spellbinding charms, he'd also found out. In a husky voice, he'd declared to his son, "Hell, son, there's no man on the face of the earth who'd not be proud to have that lovely lady hanging on his arm and be the envy of all. She's the kind of woman who makes an old man like me wish he were young again, if you know what I mean?" He'd given Brad a playful nudge and a wink of his eye.

Brad had always known that his father had an admiring eye where pretty ladies were concerned. After all, he'd wooed and won the beautiful Beth Howard, who had been the belle of Atlanta, Georgia.

After the grand ball, when the entourage had returned here to Huntington's Haven, there was no doubt in Brad's mind that both of his parents were in agreement that he should try to win the favor of Aimee. He knew that was probably the main reason she'd urged her friend Lisette Aragon to linger there for a couple of days.

While Brad had always appreciated his father as the shrewd businessman, he also admired his lovely mother as very cunning, using her charming wiles to get her own way. Often he had watched that southern grace and charm of hers work its magic.

After today, he realized that he had some magic to work if he was to gain any ground with the elusive Aimee. He was absolutely confused after spending this afternoon with her. One minute, she seemed to be warming to his charms and he was encouraged to take the liberty of enfolding her in his arms and gently kissing her. But then that mercurial air of hers suddenly changed and he felt her draw away from him. Her half-parted lips were so soft and sweet when first his lips had captured them. She had seemed to cry out to him to kiss her, but when he did she flinched, like a frightened little doe. He dared not force her.

He was a prideful man and he'd decided that no longer would he be so gentle with her. As much as he wanted her, he would

305

not be played the fool by her.

This evening, if she joined him in one of those evening strolls through his mother's gardens, Brad knew the approach he was going to use on her. Being a young lawyer, there was that practical side of him, and he had to deal with truth and reality. If some other man had already won her heart, then he might as well know it right now. He knew for certain that Fred Bigler did not have her favor, so who might it be? he wondered.

Aimee chose the azure-blue organdy gown of stiff muslin, with its ruffles around the low scooped neckline. Dainty puffed sleeves gave it a soft feminine look and the smooth fitted bodice made her waistline look so tiny as the full gathered skirt billowed generously to her ankles.

Around her neck she wore a lavaliere with the brilliant blue topaz stone that was her birthstone. The necklace was treasured by Aimee because it had belonged to her grandmother, the mother of her father and her *Tante* Denise.

As she put the final touches to her toilette, by dabbing her favorite fragrance behind her ears and at her throat, she muttered to her reflection in the mirror and to the emptiness of the room, "Now, damn you, Mano Mateo, stay out of my life tonight! I don't want that face of yours disturbing me!"

She did not expect an answer as she rose from the cushioned seat and turned away from the mirror. All she wanted was the freedom to give Brad the chance that little voice within her kept urging her to. Tonight she intended to do just that! Dear God, she hoped she could be free of that haunting face of Mano's tonight when she was with Brad!

She moved away from the dressing table and went toward the door. As the door closed behind her and she swayed down the long carpeted hallway, her head was held high, as if she were defying Mano Mateo to leave her alone. She wanted to be free of him. As she was moving down the winding stairway, she had convinced herself that Mano would not intrude, for she would not allow it. By the time she had reached the base of the stairs, she was confident he would not spoil this evening for her.

When she was greeted by the sight of the handsome Brad Huntington there in the archway, looking so devastatingly handsome in his rich deep blue coat and blue striped pants, she realized she would be a fool not to give this man a chance to woo her. Tonight, she would!

The two mothers stood back in the parlor, observing the two young people, and they exchanged smug, glowing smiles as they watched Brad take Aimee's hand in his to greet her. They were an absolutely marvelous couple and Lisette shared the same feelings as her old friend Beth that it would be the ideal match. Had Paul been here by her side, she was certain he would have approved of the union.

Lisette knew that she had to be prejudiced, but Aimee had never looked more beautiful than she did tonight. The lovely organdy gown was most flattering to her. She presented a captivating sight for a man or a woman. She noticed Beth's eyes as she viewed Aimee, observing her friend's fluttering eyelashes as she appraised her gorgeous daughter.

Lisette had to secretly confess that the year spent in Paris with Denise had given her daughter a certain air of sophistication one would hardly expect in a young lady Aimee's age. She'd taken notice of that more than ever tonight. Observing Aimee here in Sacramento, she felt a great deal of pride in her. She was a most outstanding young lady!

There was no doubt in Lisette's mind that Beth's son was in love with her daughter, but she was not so certain about Aimee's feelings. After all, Lisette had witnessed the special warmth she'd seen between Aimee and Mano Mateo, and she could not convince herself that her daughter's eyes reflected those same feelings toward Brad Huntington.

"Mercy, I don't think I've ever seen anyone more beautiful than you tonight, Aimee!" Beth Huntington sighed as the two came up to where their mothers were sitting in the parlor.

"Oh, thank you, Madame Huntington. You are most kind," Aimee responded.

"Mom, you didn't give me a chance to tell Aimee that. I was about to say exactly what you've just said," Brad playfully teased his mother, whose doting eyes kept darting from Aimee to her son.

She gave him a grin of mischief. Forever, there would be a part of her remaining that frivolous southern belle, even though her fiftieth birthday was approaching. "Son, I'll not apologize for that. Next time maybe you'll speak up faster."

It was at this moment that Lawson Huntington and Emile entered the parlor to witness the gay atmosphere of the gathering there. Emile was glad to see that his mother and sister were enjoying themselves so much. As for him, he was ready to return to the Chateau L'Aragon. He was not faulting Lawson Huntington, for he was a very warm, friendly gentleman, but Emile was not the least bit interested in the fine breeding horses he'd viewed for the last hour or in Lawson's endless ramblings about the thoroughbred. Emile yearned to return to his vineyards and he was also aching to see that pretty little Jolie.

Like everyone else in the room, Emile had never seen his sister look more beautiful than she did tonight. He pondered if this radiant glow was because she was falling in love with the handsome Brad Huntington. He could certainly understand why any young lady would fall in love with a man like Brad, who looked like a Greek god. Maybe he had had it all wrong when he had seen her with Mano Mateo, who they'd thought was a man named Mark Perez, but he could have sworn the dashing Latin had surely won Aimee's reckless heart. Oh, he knew all about the devious game of deception this man had played on his sister, but he also understood why he might have done it.

Emile could not lie about the fact that he'd genuinely liked the man he'd known as Mark Perez, and it was obvious he'd won the favor of his sister from the moment they'd first met.

But Mano Mateo had to have known, when he'd brought Aimee home that night, that he would not be welcome at the Chateau L'Aragon if he told Paul Aragon he was the son of Carlos Mateo. No, he could not fault Mano for lying that night! Mano's failing was in continuing to lie to Aimee after he'd surely known she was strongly attracted to him.

The evening at Huntington's Haven followed the usual elegant routine of the previous nights since the Aragon family's arrival. There were the finest wines and a most delectable dinner. After dinner, the gentlemen excused themselves to enjoy their cheroots out on the terrace as the ladies retired to the parlor.

But it was obvious to Emile that Brad was more interested in making a hasty departure from him and his father, so that he could be with Aimee. He could certainly understand that. Right now, he would have much preferred being with his sweet little Jolie, strolling in the gardens of Chateau L'Aragon, to standing here on the terrace with Brad and his father.

When his patience could stand it no longer, Brad asked the men to excuse him. "I think I'll see if Aimee would enjoy a walk in the gardens," he announced to the two of them.

"A lovely night for a walk," Lawson commented.

Emile gazed upward at the dark sky to see the big full moon shining down on the grounds and he mumbled, "A wonderful night for a stroll." He was thinking about the gardens of Chateau L'Aragon. That same moon was shining brightly back there, he knew.

He wondered if Jolie had missed him as much as he had missed her since he'd been away these last few days. *Mon Dieu*, he prayed she had! These few days apart had made Emile very aware of his need for her and he had decided to do something about it when he returned to his home.

When his father returned from his trip abroad, he also intended to talk with him about some things on his mind. After all, he was no youngster anymore. He was a man who should have a life of his own and a family of his own. He'd never given any thought to these things until he'd spent that marvelous time with Jolie. After that night, many things had begun igniting in Emile's mind.

After that night, everything had changed for him. He liked the feelings flooding his huge body. Now he knew there was a void in his life that needed fulfilling.

Jolie could fill that void!

Chapter 39

Emile was probably the only person at Huntington's Haven who was not thoroughly convinced that there was going to be a commitment made between Brad Huntington and his sister before their family left to return to Chateau L'Aragon. But there was not that same radiant gleam in the lovely Aimee's sapphire eyes when she gazed up at Brad as there had been when she was in the company of Mateo.

Lisette and her friend Beth were more than pleased when Brad had returned to the parlor and invited Aimee to take a stroll in the gardens with him, after having excused himself from the company of his father and Emile. The women exchanged pleased glances and nods of their heads as the two young people left the parlor to go out on the veranda and walk along the garden pathway in the moonlit night.

Emile observed his sister as she walked across the veranda, holding Brad's arm, and he felt that she was forcing the lovely smile on her face. Her older brother was far wiser than Aimee would have imagined had she known his private musings. He was also more sensitive about her feelings and reactions than

311

she would have thought. But then, Aimee had never really known how special and precious she had been to this older brother. Always, he had adored her! Each year of her life she had become more dear to him. Maybe that was why he held Mano in such high esteem since the night he'd brought Aimee home safely after she'd been attacked. He'd rescued her from this brute who sought to do her harm, and that was all Emile had to know about Mano to win his respect.

The next hour Emile could not get Aimee off his thoughts nor could he forget the man he knew was the right one for his sister.

The moment Aimee and Brad went out the front door, onto the veranda and into the starlit night, she looked up at the dark sky and thought she saw a lovers' moon shining down on them as they walked onto the thick carpet of grass.

Was there a special magic about such a moon as this? Folklore declared there was. Aimee prayed it was so because she needed that rare hope for this faded love she'd known with Mano.

She walked by Brad's side and felt the warmth of his hand holding hers. It was a good, comforting feeling. Their conversation was light and casual as they walked along the flagstone path. She was very much aware that he was leading her to the far corner of the gardens. She knew exactly his reasons for taking her to the certain spot in the garden that would give them the most privacy. A smug smile came to her face as they walked along.

Long before Brad Huntington led her to the little gazebo, Aimee knew exactly what he had on his mind. If she'd been made a fool of by Mano, at least she'd learned a few things about men and their ways. She was not the naive, young innocent she'd been when Mano had played his wiles on her. Tonight, she was prepared when Brad graciously seated her in the gazebo and poured forth his generous dose of charm. In turn, she responded with her own bewitching charms. Privately, she thought to herself she should be grateful to Mano because he had made her far wiser than she would have been had she not met him. Maybe she could be grateful to him for that, even though she resented the pain he had caused her.

Brad looked at Aimee when he had her seated on the little bench inside the gazebo and he observed this unfathomable expression on her face. What was she thinking? he wondered. What was going on inside that pretty head of hers?

In a low, deep voice, he called her attention to him as he told her, "Aimee, you are the most beautiful woman I've ever seen." His expert hands were now guiding her to look at him and gaze into his searching eyes. Tonight, Brad was determined to have the answers to some of the questions troubling him about this complex young lady he was falling in love with.

When those devastating deep blue eyes were upon him, he was helpless and weak with desire. Her half-parted lips were hesitant to speak and he knew it, but dear God, she was enough to drive a man crazy with the wildest desire to crush her into his arms. This is what he yearned to do.

"Tell me, Aimee, tell me right now if I have a chance to win your love? If I don't, then I'll waste no more of my time or yours. It is as simple as that."

She searched his face and she knew he spoke sincerely and honestly. She respected his straightforward manner. Being the type of person she was, she had only one answer for him. "I—I don't know what to say to you, Brad. I truly do not. Believe me, I don't wish you to waste your time. I enjoy your company very much and I've had a wonderful time here at your home."

A weak grin creased Brad's face. "Come now, Aimee, we both know I'm talking about much more than that." His arms became more forceful as he pulled her closer to him and his head bent lower so that his mouth could meet her luscious lips in a kiss.

He allowed his lips to caress the satiny flesh of her cheek as he huskily whispered in her ear, "I'm going to let your lips give

313

me the answer, Aimee. If another man is standing in my way, then I think I will know it."

His abrupt declaration startled her for a moment. But she had no time to ponder it as his hot, sensuous lips came down to claim her and she felt the heat of his male body pressing against her. His hands were not idle, either. She felt the slow, determined movement of them as they left her tiny waistline. One of them went to her back to move her closer to him and the other moved upward to cup one of her breasts.

She gasped as she felt his hand encircling her flesh. "Oh, God, Brad!" she muttered softly. He cared not whether it was a protest or moan of delight at this point. He was tired of her moody air. Tonight, he was going to find out one way or the other if she was truly attracted to him as a man.

"Yes, Aimee, yes, I am a man burning with desire for you and I must know how you really feel, my darling. I love you—and very much. If you don't feel this way, you'd better let me know right now," he warned her. The emotions reflected in his voice told her that this was no time to play any coquettish games as she had in Paris. Strange as it might seem at this time and place, she realized that Brad Huntington and Mano Mateo were a lot alike.

A lady did not toy with the affections of men like Brad or Mano, Aimee concluded. Both of them were strong personalities, very sure of themselves.

So when she saw his fine-chiseled face moving closer to hers and she knew he was going to kiss her, she decided to surrender to his caress. As their lips met and joined, Aimee closed her long-lashed eyes, pretending that there had never been a Mano Mateo in her life. Brad Huntington was the one there with her now. It was his sensuous lips teasing and tantalizing her.

She felt his strong arms pressing her closer and closer to his broad chest, until she could barely breathe, and she did not try to pull away. She felt the heat of him permeating her own body and she felt the raging pulsation of his heart. She also heard the deep intakes of his breath telling her that his desire was mounting.

She wanted to submit to his amorous touches. Oh, how she wanted to! If giving herself to Brad would remove the haunting face of Mano from her thoughts, she would have welcomed it. If her reckless heart could have been conquered by Brad Huntington, she knew she would have been a far smarter young lady. It was clear that he wished to win her love and she was sure he would not play her falsely as Mateo had. Brad would have no reason to gloat over his conquest of her as she was certain Mano had done.

But when she felt Brad's nimble fingers teasing the neckline of her gown, she knew he was about to free one of her breasts. She also knew he would then seek to take the nipple with his heated lips. The very idea offended her and she suddenly pushed him away with all her might.

In a faltering, embarrassed voice, she stammered, "I—oh, Brad, I—I can't. We should not be doing this. It is not right!"

He glared down at her lovely face for a brief moment before he dared to speak. His whole body was tense with the strong emotions flooding him. He had certainly reached the end of his limit.

When he did speak, his blue eyes sparked with indignation and a wounded ego. "Is it not right, Aimee, because it is with me instead of someone else? Pardon me if I say that I know you've been kissed before with as much fervor as I was just kissing you. I don't think anything I've done tonight has been a shock or surprise." She heard the sarcasm and contempt in his voice as he spit out the words.

She moved back on the bench as she yanked at the bodice of her lovely gown. "I don't think I ever tried to give you any false impressions about me, Brad. Yes, I have been kissed before and more than once as you just now kissed me. Why should I deny it?" Her lovely head rose up in defiance and Brad thought to himself that she'd never looked lovelier.

"I am pleased to know you aren't going to lie to me. Your honesty I can admire, Aimee. I will just have to conclude that I

315

had it all figured wrong, and maybe I'm not as great a lawyer as I thought," he gave out a weak laugh.

"I think you are a little harsh on yourself, Brad. It was just not the right time for me, Brad, and I admire you too much to fake it. I'm no good at playing games and pretending," she firmly declared.

"Nor am I, honey. Perhaps the right time would have never come for us, Aimee. I confess I envy the scoundrel who owns your heart, for he surely does. That, my pet, is why tonight was not the right time for you."

He was acting so sure of himself that she felt a rage of anger erupt within her. "No man owns me, Brad, and no man will ever do that!" She rose from the bench.

"I apologize for my poor choice of words. Nevertheless, there is some man who occupies your thoughts right now, so that no other man has a chance with you. I don't think you'll deny that."

She made a most desirable silhouette there in the dappled moonlight, looking so proud and bold. Those lovely amethyst eyes of hers glared at him. "I see no reason why I have to deny anything to you, Brad. Our relationship has been a very brief one, wouldn't you say?"

"Yes, a very brief one, Aimee."

Swishing her organdy skirt in a most dramatic gesture, she turned away from him to start down the long garden pathway toward the house. In a cool, calm voice, she declared to him, "I think I will go to the house now, Brad. There is no call for you to escort me, for I shall find my way."

He did not hesitate in rising from the bench and catching up to her with his long striding steps. His hand reached to take her arm. His voice was deep and husky as he told her, with a broad grin on his good-looking face, "I'll treasure this brief interlude we shared, Aimee, even though it did not turn out exactly as I'd planned it, hoped it would. With a woman as rare as you, I was the fool to think it would have been the ordinary courtship."

Seeing the grin on his face, she could not help mellowing

toward him. She gave him an amused smile, allowing her eyes to survey his face for a second. With that charming candor of hers, she said, "I'll confess to you that I truly wished it would have happened for us, Brad. I wanted it to! But I respect you too much and I could not be so cruel to you. Happiness would never have been ours. I don't know about you, but as for me, I'll not settle for less."

Such wisdom she spoke for one so young that Brad was amazed by this young lady walking along with him. Romantically, it had not worked out for them, but somehow he knew that they would forever be friends. A friendship with such a wise, gracious lady as Aimee Aragon was something he'd always cherish. She was special!

As if she were reading his thoughts, she suggested to him, "I hope, Brad, that we can still be friends. I'd like that very much."

He bent over to kiss her lightly on the cheek. A warm sincerity laced his words as he told her, "Forever, we'll be friends, Aimee Aragon."

Now that she had touched his life, Brad Huntington knew his world had changed. As she had declared to him that she would not settle for anything less than the happiness she sought, he was determined now that neither would he.

This tiny French miss had inspired him to seek a loftier height as his goal in life. Forever, he would be grateful their paths had crossed!

Chapter 40

Emile was not ready to retire, even though that was the excuse he'd used when he'd bid his mother, Beth, and Lawson good night almost an hour ago. Instead, he'd moved quietly through the double doors leading out onto the veranda to roam the gardens.

He was standing in the seclusion of the shrubs and trees when he spotted Aimee and Brad returning from their stroll, and his brotherly curiosity was whetted. Had she allowed Brad Huntington to embrace and kiss her? Was he winning her heart as Emile knew he wished to do?

He could not convince himself that Brad had already made her forget Mano Mateo. After all, Aimee was not a fickle female, flying from one man's arms into another's. Granted, he was prejudiced, for she was his sister.

It was obvious to him that their moods were light and gay as he heard the soft echoes of their laughter. But Brad was not holding her hand, Emile noticed.

After Emile watched them move inside the house, he continued to roam the gardens. It was ridiculous to him that the Aragons linger here any longer. He'd hoped to have had a chance to talk to his sister this evening in private and persuade her that they should be getting back to the Chateau L'Aragon.

With his father gone and him being away, Emile knew the added responsibiity Armand had on his shoulders. By now, he was feeling his time was being wasted here at Huntington's Haven. He rationalized that his mother and Aimee had gotten to attend the grand ball, which was very exciting for the two of them. Lisette had enjoyed a few days with her old friend, Beth. It was now time for them to return to Chateau L'Aragon. Emile knew those lush berries from their vines were due to be picked, and then their labors would go from the fields to the winery.

When Aimee told Brad good night and departed from him to go her own way, she was sharing her older brother's feeling, but not for the same reasons. She was more determined than Emile that she would have a talk with her mother before she retired tonight.

As she moved down the dark hallway, she paused at her mother's bedroom door to rap softly. "Mama, may I talk to you?" she called out softly.

The door opened and Lisette stood there in her wrapper, with her hair flowing down over her shoulders. She was preparing to dim the lamp on the nightstand and crawl into bed when she'd heard Aimee's rapping on her door.

"*Ma cherie*, come in." Lisette invited her daughter to enter her room. The first thing entering her mind was that Aimee might have an announcement to make concerning Brad Huntington. If ever she'd seen a couple who looked like the perfect lovers, it was the two of them tonight as they'd left the parlor together to go on a moonlight stroll in the gardens.

She and Beth had talked about the two young people later, both of them speaking with pride about their children. Lisette had to confess to herself that Brad had all the qualities a mother would seek in her daughter's future husband.

"I—I know it is late, Mama, and I apologize for that. But I wanted to talk to you."

319

A warm smile brightened Lisette's face as she cupped Aimee's two cheeks. "Aimee, it does not matter what the hour is if you have a need to talk to me. You know that. Come, my dear, and sit down so we can talk."

"Oh, I know that, Mama," Aimee told her.

Aimee took one of the velvet chairs by the window and her mother sat down in the other one. Lisette noted Aimee's hesitation to speak and she observed her lovely face. She knew there was no happy announcement about to be made.

In that straightforward way of hers, Aimee came right to the point. "I think we should go home, Mama. I think we should leave in the morning."

"If this is what you wish, Aimee, then we shall," Lisette replied thoughtfully. Her eyes searched her daughter's face for the urgency as she wondered what had gone wrong between her and Brad in the last couple of hours.

"It is, and I am sure that Emile is bored by now. I'm sure that it would be the best thing for everyone concerned. You see, I know that Madame Huntington has had her heart set on me and Brad becoming romantically involved, but it is not going to happen. But he and I have parted this evening as good friends and I would like for it to continue that way."

"I see," Lisette slowly drawled. In a stammering voice, she admitted to her daughter, "I guess we were both a little guilty of that, *ma cherie*. But mothers can be so very foolish sometimes, where their children are concerned. I guess they are forever trying to pair them with the ones they think are the best matches. It rarely works out that way."

"Any mother would think that about Brad Huntington, Mama. But he is not the man for me any more than Papa's ideas about Fred Bigler. Neither of them could ever have my love."

Lisette nodded her head to let her daughter know she understood. Oh, she did understand so well what she was telling her. Sitting there at this moment with her daughter, Lisette knew the man who had already won Aimee's love. Two young people should not have to suffer for the sins of their stubborn fathers, Lisette decided then and there.

She did not say this to Aimee but she knew what she was going to do to help her daughter have the man she loved and wanted. Instead, all she said to her was, "We shall start for home the first thing in the morning, *ma petite*. Now, you go to bed and sleep well, *oui?*"

"*Oui*, Mama, I shall." She embraced her mother and turned to leave the room. At the door, she paused for a moment to tell Lisette, "Thank you, Mama. I appreciate your understanding."

Once the door was closed, Lisette moved back to one of the velvet chairs and sank down on it. She stared out into the night's darkness and her thoughts reached back to the years past. As much as she loved her two husky sons, nothing had given her the joy Aimee had. All mothers must think that their lovely daughters are the most gorgeous, but Lisette remembered the first moment her eyes looked down on that tiny fair-haired angel and she swore there was no babe as beautiful. It had delighted her when she saw the babe's eyes were blue like hers. There had been a feeling of smugness overflowing in Lisette about that.

But Lisette had to admit that as the baby grew older, she took on the traits of the Aragon family. She had a gardenia-white complexion and her eyes were no longer the bright blue of Lisette's. They were becoming the deep sapphire blue of her paternal grandmother.

By the time Lisette finally moved from the chair to go to her bed, she was eager for morning to come so she could be traveling back to the Chateau L'Aragon.

She felt the need to get back home!

The day after Lisette, Emile, and Aimee had departed for Sacramento, Armand and the housekeeper, Hetty, were surprised by the sight of Paul Aragon appearing through the dining room door with his valise in his hand. Flinging it carelessly down on the carpeted floor, he announced, "Well, I hope you have enough food for a devilishly hungry, weary man."

"Oh, yes, Monsieur Aragon. I—I always fix extra around this household," she stammered, wondering why he was back here instead of out on the ocean as he was supposed to be by now.

Paul took his usual seat at the head of the table and Armand could see the tiredness on his father's face. The tight lines around his mouth also told Armand that he was disgusted and displeased with whatever it was that had changed his plans.

"Three days of absolute waste, Armand, and you know how I can't stand wasted time. This Captain Madison's packet developed a problem and now there are repairs which could take a couple of weeks—maybe three to be exact."

"So you won't be leaving for a few more weeks then, is that right?" Armand inquired, hating to hear that because, as capable as he and Emile were in both the vineyards and the winery, they still sought Paul's expert counsel on the processes of making their fine wines. As devoted as he and Emile were, Armand knew that the experience and knowledge of their father had taken years to develop.

"No, that is not right, son. I had a lot of time to think as I traveled back to the Chateau L'Aragon. I wasted three good days and I don't know that I wish to be away for as many weeks as this trip would take, as this is the most important time here. If Governor Bigler wishes me to go on this mission to Europe, I've decided to tell him I can't make it until the springtime, when my vines are growing the grapes."

Armand gave him an agreeing nod of his head, for it would be a far more practical time of the year. "Well, surely there is nothing so pressing about this trip that a few months would hurt, and after all, the winter is not a good time for crossing the ocean."

"This is another aspect that has crossed my mind. The autumn is almost upon us now, and I'd want no delays when my mission was completed over there and I was ready to leave."

By now, Hetty had placed the platters of good-smelling foods in front of the two men. The aroma was enough to make Paul eager to fill his plate, for he was starved.

The two of them ate like a pair of hungry wolves and enjoyed glasses of their finest red wine. Paul could not believe his good fortune when Hetty brought out a generous helping of a fresh baked peach pie.

In such a good humor, he teased her, "Now, Hetty, don't tell me you knew I was coming back home tonight?"

"Oh, no, Monsieur Aragon. Joshua brought the peaches over yesterday from his orchard and they were beauties. I was thinking how I wished Emile was here to enjoy this pie tonight. Like you, it is his favorite."

As Paul and Armand stuffed themselves with the flaky-crusted pie, with the sweet juicy peaches sliced into the syrupy sweetness, Paul asked his son, "Are they not due back by now, Armand?"

"If they had departed right after the ball, but Mother said they might decide to stay on there with the Huntingtons for a couple of days, so I guess that is what they decided to do."

"Then they'll probably return tomorrow," Paul remarked.

However, they did not return that next day or the day after that. It was on the third day after Paul had arrived back at the house that the carriage bearing his wife, son, and daughter appeared through the gateway of the stoned wall enclosing the grounds of the house.

The view of it was a welcome sight to Aragon. To know that his dear family was back home safe and sound lifted a heavy load off Paul's shoulders. The day before, his eyes had caught sight of a strange rider near the edge of the woods near his estate. When he'd seen that Paul had observed him, he quickly reined his horse around to move back into the dense thickness of the woods.

This morning he'd seen that same rider again in almost the same location. Paul didn't like it at all and he had fully intended to talk to Armand about it. He'd planned for Armand and a couple of his hired hands to search around the area to see if they'd find the stranger who seemed so curious about the goings-on at the Chateau L'Aragon. After all, those woods were Aragon property.

But the arrival of his wife, daughter, and son distracted Paul. They had so very much to talk about. He was most eager to hear about his old friends, the Huntingtons, and it came as a surprise to him that Brad had returned to California. Of course, he was interested in hearing the two women discuss the fancy ball given by the governor of the state of California. After all, he'd spent a small fortune on those two lovely ladies' gowns for the occasion.

His very perceptive eyes were quick to note that Lisette was chattering far more enthusiastically about their trip to Sacramento than was his pretty daughter. He made no point of it, but he promised himself to ask Lisette about that later when they were alone.

"Well, I am sure of one thing, and that is that the two Aragon women were the loveliest there," he declared proudly.

Lisette and Aimee broke into a soft gale of laughter, swearing he had to be a little prejudiced. His wife pridefully told her husband, "There was no question about the most beautiful young lady at that ball, Paul. I wish you could have been there, *mon cher*, for you would have beamed with pride as I did. She turned every head in the room or wherever she went that night. Beth and Lawson could not quit raving about her."

Paul gave out a smug chuckle. "And their son, Brad, how about him? I can imagine he was smitten by her, eh?"

Lisette was now wishing she had not gotten so carried away with her talking about the Huntingtons, as she noticed the look on Aimee's face. But she did answer her husband's question, "Yes, I think Brad was smitten by her charms."

"Please, you two, you are embarrassing me," Aimee gently chided them, forcing a smile to her face.

A short time later, she excused herself to go upstairs and freshen up after the long trip from Sacramento. She was in no mood to be bombarded with questions about Brad Huntington by her father.

She'd let her mother tell him about that, she decided.

Chapter 41

Lisette was utterly delighted, as well as surprised, to see her husband when she and her family had disembarked from the family carriage. It was only natural that she was as perplexed as she was pleased. After he'd had a chance to explain the dilemma he'd faced once he'd arrived at the port and met with the captain of the ship he was due to have sailed away from the shores of California, Lisette pondered if it was a strange turn of fate stepping in to change Paul's plans. Somehow, she felt it was.

Perhaps, she was being silly. God knows, she'd always been the worrying kind. After all, she had two strong sons to look after her while Paul would have been gone those several weeks in Europe, but when he confessed to her that he had decided to tell the governor he would wait until spring to make such a venture, it was sweet music to Lisette's ears.

It was glorious to be back at her home and she was happy Aimee had urged her to return sooner than she'd planned. Lisette sensed that her beloved Paul could not wait to get upstairs to the privacy of their bedroom, so he could quiz her about the very eligible bachelor son of Lawson and Beth Huntington. All she'd had to do was look at his face down in the parlor, where the family had gathered after dinner and the subject of Brad had been brought up, to know what Paul was thinking. He was considering that Lawson's son and his lovely daughter Aimee would make the perfect match. She and Beth had been just as guilty in trying to matchmake the young people, but it had not worked.

This is exactly what she'd told him the minute they were alone in their bedroom and the door was closed. Paul paced the floor with a disgruntled look on his face as he grumbled, "What in the hell is it this girl wants in a suitor, Lisette? Brad Huntington would be a fine choice for Aimee. Now, I have to admit that I wasn't all that impressed by the man Fred Bigler was, but he did come from a good family. John Bigler is a fine gentleman. Regardless of all the other things Aimee might be thinking as young as she is, the family background is most important."

"Everything you say is true, *mon cher*. I will not argue with you about that. Aimee and Brad parted as friends, she told me. She just did not feel romantically drawn to him and she would not lie to him about that. I have to admire her for that, and obviously Brad did, too."

Paul took off his coat and flung it angrily on the chair. "Maybe you read her too many fairytales, Lisette. Maybe she's expecting some knight in his shining armor to ride into the Chateau L'Aragon and carry her off in the sunset. We both know that such is not true in real life. Aimee will surely be disappointed in life and love, I fear."

By now, Lisette had changed out of her frock and slipped into her gown and robe. Going over to her dressing table to let down the long twisted coil of her hair, she sat down on the stool and reached for the brush. "Perhaps she will be disappointed, Paul, but I can assure you right now that your daughter will settle for no less. Whether you like it or not, that is the way it will be."

"We'll see, Lisette. We'll see."

Right now, Lisette was having a number of private thoughts as she stroked her long hair that fell all the way to her waistline. In a very assured tone of voice, she told her husband, "I can tell you this, Paul, and that is that the man Aimee chooses will be a strong, forceful man, as stubborn and determined as she is. She would never pick one who could not conquer her. Brad Huntington could not!"

"*Mon Dieu*, what man could possibly fill that bill?" he gave out a low moan.

Lisette smiled but said nothing. She suspected Aimee had already encountered such a man. But she'd dare not mention that name to her darling Paul.

"I'm sure such a man exists, Paul."

Shaking his head in disbelief, Paul declared, "Then I guess you are more optimistic than I am, my dear wife. Maybe that is because you are more the romantic than I am. Being a woman, I guess that explains it."

Lisette laid the brush aside and rose from her dainty little stool. There was a feeling of smugness about her as she moved over to her side of the bed. Taking off her robe and laying it down at the foot of the bed, she slipped in between the sheets and fluffed up the two pillows before lying her head down on them.

Silently, she thought to herself how blind her husband was or he would have seen it as she had when Aimee was with the man they'd known as Mark Perez. That marvelous glow in her deep blue eyes as she looked at him and that same sparking fire in his black eyes as he devoured her. That was the wonderful magic of love Aimee desired and that was what she intended to have.

Lisette was convinced that if she could not have that, then she would have no other.

Tonight was not the night to speak of this, though, the wise French lady decided.

*   *   *

Emile's nerves were slightly frayed from the impatience of going through the family routine of the dinner hour and the endless after-dinner time spent in the parlor. He was very grateful when Aimee excused herself to go to her room to retire because now he felt free to do so.

He wondered if Jolie would sense his need to see her after his period of absence from the house. He knew that she would be attending to his sister's needs for a while after she went upstairs to her bedroom.

But once Aimee had entered her bedroom, she noticed the hasty movements of her little maid as she flew around the room like a butterfly, laying out Aimee's gown and robe. She could hardly suppress the grin coming to her face as she watched Jolie. She knew the young maid was most anxious to be through with her duties so she could be dismissed for the evening. Aimee was certain that as soon as she left her bedroom, she would be slipping quietly down the back stairs to meet her brother in the gardens. There, they would take their little stroll and possibly hold hands. She wondered if Emile had been so bold as to kiss her yet.

She tried to sound very casual as she told her maid, "Why don't you run along, Jolie. As you can see, I have no fancy hairstyle to take down tonight. Besides, I am very tired after the trip from Sacramento. I'll see you in the morning, eh?"

An eager smile broke out on Jolie's face and she gave Aimee a nod of her black head. "In the morning, mademoiselle." She turned to rush out of the room, and as soon as she had shut the door, Aimee let out a breezy little giggle. Jolie would have normally asked a million questions about the grand ball and all the excitement of the evening. But tonight Jolie had only one thing on her mind, and that was rushing into the gardens in hopes of encountering Emile.

After she had changed into her sheer gown and brushed out her hair, Aimee strolled over to look out her bedroom window. She hoped that out there in the moonlit gardens Jolie had found Emile waiting for her.

It was about time Emile shared his life with a woman. The

vineyards could not warm his bed at night nor give him companionship. He needed something more to look forward to each day.

Privately, she stood there playing the matchmaker, just as her mother and Beth Huntington had tried to do back in Sacramento. Recalling a magic moment she had experienced down there in that same garden not too long ago, she knew the overwhelming barrier that prevented any romantic ties binding her and Brad together. The barrier was the tall dark, handsome Mano Mateo!

She recalled every magnificent feature of his tanned face as she stood there now. Oh, she could envision those devastating black eyes as they danced over her with that devious glint in them and how she felt weak all over. When his strong arms went around her, pulling her close to his broad chest, how helpless she was to resist his overwhelming Latin charm. His hot-blooded nature had mesmerized her, and before she had realized it, she was surrendering to his will.

Dejectedly, she turned away from the window. Why did she wish to punish herself by all these painful musings? she prodded herself. Thoughts of him brought nothing but pain.

When she lay down on her bed and stared at the darkness outside her windows, she wondered what the solution would be for her to rid herself of this pain. The only answer coming to her mind was that she leave California and the Chateau L'Aragon. This countryside would forever remind her of Mano Mateo. The answer was clear to Aimee. It would be best if she returned to Paris and her *Tante* Denise.

His mission in Santa Rosa had been successful and he had acquired the property he had wanted to buy. Almost two hundred acres of ground in the folds and valleys of the hills were all his now. He could also lay claim to the redwood forest surrounding the one border and a crystal-clear stream of water that wove its way along the south of the property.

As Mano rode back toward Phil's cottage, he was a man with his spirits soaring to the loftiest heights of joy. He was like a young boy, so anxious to tell Phil his good news. Demonio sensed his master's exhilaration and he galloped along the countryside with his head high and his tail swishing to and fro, giving vent to his high-spirited nature.

As the two of them swiftly covered the picturesque countryside, Mano could not take his mind off the beauty of the place he was soon going to call home. The lovely little cottage occupied by the present owner was not as elegantly or luxuriously furnished as the home owned by his father. But every corner and nook of the house beamed with a cozy warmth that appealed to Mano.

After all, Mano reasoned, a house could always be enlarged if desired. But he liked the quaint fireplaces in the parlor, kitchen, and main bedroom. The main bedroom had a small little balcony enclosed with a wood railing, where one could enjoy the magnificent view of the verdant hillside nearby.

A short distance from the house stood the lofty board and batten structure that was the winery. To the back of the winery were the laid-out long rows of the vineyard. Never had Mano seen such lush, large grapes as this owner was gathering in huge baskets now that they were ready for crushing. The elderly vintner had told him that the red wines were fermented with their skins left on.

"Those grapes are the ones that make the finest cabernet sauvignon or the zinfandel wines, Monsieur Mateo," the elderly Frenchman told him.

Mano listened to every word Bertrand Dupree told him, for there was no doubt in his mind that the man was a fountain of knowledge, with his years of experience here in this vineyard where he'd spent his whole lifetime. But now his age was demanding that he sell it, for he had no sons to carry on for him and he'd lost his dear wife the year before.

The few days Mano had spent in this region they called Valley of the Moon had been the most pleasant time he'd

331

known since the night Aimee had angrily turned her back on him and walked out of his life. Often, he and Bertrand sat and talked in the bright, colorful kitchen, which reflected the loving handiwork of his wife. Bertrand had pointed out the black pot that hung there inside the fireplace, telling Mano about the good food that iron kettle had brewed for him over the years.

On the hearth lay a colorful rug of many colors that Bertrand boasted proudly about, which his wife's hands had braided and sewed. He grumbled, "But damned if I have the green thumb that my Michelle had. See how all her lovely flowers are dying on me."

Mano grinned, noting the numerous pots on all the windowsills, with their yellowed leaves.

"Maybe my lady's touch will bring them back to life, Bertrand. Maybe that is what it takes, eh?"

The old man chuckled and agreed. Mano allowed him the joy as well as the time to talk endlessly about his wife Michelle. It seemed to please him to tell Mano about their life together and the happiness they'd shared here on this wonderful hillside.

If he were a man disappointed about no heirs to carry on for him, he didn't speak about that. Mano could only conclude his Michelle had given him such a fulfilling life that he did not feel cheated. Theirs must have been a very special, rare love.

As the time came for Mano to leave, he was filled with a wave of sadness that Dupree could not live out the rest of his life on the land he loved so dearly, which held such beautiful memories of his past. On a slope of green grass, where clusters of wildflowers grew profusely, stood a majestic live oak tree. A small walled area made of native stones outlined the grave of Michelle Dupree.

As Mano roamed the grounds on his last day there, he inspected the stable at the back of the cottage. He'd not taken the time before to climb the stairs leading to the second landing above. He was amazed to find a huge room there, with an abundant amount of light flowing through the wide double windows.

A few old pieces of furniture were stored there and an old kereosene lamp sat on a rough-hewn table. An old cot rested against one wall and an artist's easel still sat in a spot where the bright sunlight came through the windows. In one obscure corner, draped in cobwebs, were several wooden crates.

Mano stood there in the quiet of this lofty room and an idea was born. Somehow, he felt Michelle Dupree was speaking to him, urging him to insist that Bertrand remain here near her. He could envision this huge space being converted into a very comfortable, cozy place for Dupree to live. Mano decided that he would make it a pleasant place for him to stay and enjoy the winter years of his life. Besides, Dupree had much he could contribute to making this vineyard thrive and grow once Mano took charge.

That evening, as they sat and dined together, sipping the tasty cabernet sauvignon Dupree had brought out for them to enjoy with their dinner, Mano told the elderly man about exploring the room above the stable.

"Ah, that was where my Michelle spent many hours during the winter doing her paintings. A nice room, isn't it?" Such a pleasant reflection was there on the old man's face.

"A very nice room, Bertrand. It could easily be made a very nice room again with a little cleaning and repairs. I think Michelle would be most happy if you would remain here and take over this room she loved so much. I really need you here, too, Bertrand. I honestly do. It could be the answer for both of us. What do you say?"

For a brief moment, Bertrand Dupree was too overcome with emotion to speak. A lump came to his throat, making it impossible for him to utter a word. He was a proud man but he was not strong enough to stop the mist coming to his eyes. To sell this place and have to leave these grounds was killing him. But he had been impressed by this young man from the moment they'd first met.

Oh, he'd thought about asking if he might occupy that old loft room above the stable, but who'd want an old man like him around? he'd reasoned. He might be ailing, but there was still an enormous amount of pride churning in his frail body.

His white head was held high as he looked Mano straight in the eye. Oh, Mano saw the mist there and he knew the depth of the old man's feelings at that moment. He heard the cracking of his voice as he finally spoke, "Young man, I'd be most happy to accept your generous offer. You are a fine, kind-hearted young man and I'm happy you are the one to take over this place." For a moment, he hesitated before he added, "I hope you'll find what Michelle and I found here. You see, I named it for her. Her hair was so beautiful and gold, and she made my life such a magnificent splendor."

Mano reached out to pat the old man's hand and assured him, "It will be as it has been for all these many years, Bertrand. It will be known as you named it years ago—Golden Splendor. So it will be for me. I know it; I felt it the first time I set foot on the land."

Bertrand Dupree was a happy, contented man and he knew Michelle was, too! He blessed the day Mano Mateo had ridden up his hillside to inquire about the sale of his winery.

Here he'd lived the happiest days of his life and here was where he wished to die. Now Mano had made this possible. Now he had a reason for living, for he wished to impart all his vast knowledge about being a vintner to this fine young man.

God had been good to him!

Chapter 42

To meet a fine old gentleman like Bertrand Dupree, so genuine and wise, was certainly an inspiration. Mano considered himself very fortunate to have acquired his fine vineyards and persuaded him to remain there on the land. But the more he thought about it, he realized it had taken little persuasion on his part to convince Dupree to stay.

Now, as he rode toward the Half Moon Bay region, there was another very dear old man he was anxious to see. How lucky he was to have two such individuals in his life!

There was only one thing missing from his life now to make it complete. He had to have Aimee Aragon there in that circle to complete it. Whatever it took to have her back again in his arms, he was prepared to do it. Feeling this overwhelming need of her so much, he had decided that he was not going to linger long once he returned to pay a brief visit with Phil.

As it had been some days ago when Mano had arrived at Cabrillo's cottage late at night, Phil was sitting in the same spot on his porch as he did most evenings at this time. There was no bright moonlight tonight and the hounds lay there quiet and lazy. Clouds were moving in from the bay, blotting out any signs of the moon up there in the sky.

Phil was thinking that the young rascal had stayed away longer than he'd expected him to. Perhaps everything wasn't running as smoothly as Mano had hoped it might. Phil had hoped that he would accomplish the thing he'd sought out to do, because it seemed he wanted this land so much. He supposed Mano would never cease to amaze him, but then he didn't know why he should feel otherwise. After all, he was the son of Theresa—the irrepressible Theresa. Never had he known a more beautiful woman than Theresa—except for her mother. She, too, was gorgeous!

He heard the chiming of the clock in his small parlor. It reminded him that he had to get up early in the morning if he wanted to accompany his friend Tom on an all-day fishing jaunt in the bay.

He moved out of his chair and sauntered toward the door, bidding his two hounds good night. But as he was about to shut the door and call it a night, his ears heard the galloping hooves of a horse. Instinctively, he knew it had to be Mano returning. He stood there in the doorway until he assured himself that it was. There was no mistaking that magnificent animal Demonio. Such an outstanding beast he was, with that silvery coat and his jet-black mane and tail!

Phil did not have long to wait until he saw the sight of the thoroughbred galloping full speed toward his gate. He also sensed from the air of the horse and the rider that both of them were in the highest of spirits. Phil grinned, feeling a swelling of happiness well up inside him. Mano had gotten what he wanted and that made the old Portuguese very happy.

He stood there in the same spot, watching Mano leap off Demonio and call out to him, "I've wonderful news to tell you, Phil, as soon as I've tended to Demonio. I'll be in soon, eh?"

"All right, son. Which would you like—a cup of coffee or a strong drink?"

"A very strong drink, I think," Mano laughed, taking the

reins in his hands to lead Demonio toward the barn at the back of the cottage.

Phil moved on through the door, going to the kitchen to get a bottle of whiskey he kept there in his cupboard. Somehow, he knew that he was not going to get to bed as soon as he'd thought. In fact, he might not make that fishing trip with his friend in the early morning hours. Mano was going to have much to tell him, the old man suspected.

He was absolutely right, because they talked for almost two hours after Mano had come into the cottage. At that old kitchen oak table they sat and talked, drinking Phil's whiskey. It mattered not to Phil how late the hour was when he saw the gleam in Mano's eyes as he talked about his vineyards and the winery, Golden Splendor.

Phil also thought of the irony of it all. This was the son of the arrogant Carlos Mateo, breeder of the finest bulls in the state of California. His arisotcratic family had been settled here in the region for decades. Phil knew that it was the tradition of Spanish families like Mateo's for the sons to carry forth from their father, just like Carlos had done and Mario would do whether he wished to or not.

Mano was obviously not going to abide by the conventional Latin traditions, and Phil could well imagine how this was going to affect Carlos. This was the torment of Theresa when she had been his wife, that she could not conform to his strict, rigid rules.

Ah, so much of Theresa was bred in this younger son of hers! Never more did Cabrillo know it than he did this night. Phil had to admire the young man who he thought should fulfill this dream of his, even though it would not meet with Carlos Mateo's approval.

Mano could never fit the mold of Carlos nor would he be willing to try, as Mario would.

By the time they were ready to retire, Mano insisted that Phil keep his plans to fish in the bay. "I will be leaving tomorrow, Phil. I must get back to La Casa Grande. There are things I must attend to now that I am the owner of a winery," he declared with a grin on his face. He didn't add that there would still be a void in his life until he sought out Aimee and won her heart again.

As elated as he was about this prized land he'd acquired, he would not feel whole until he also had the woman he loved with all his heart to share this lovely paradise up in the Valley of the Moon. He must have her, too!

Before Cabrillo left the kitchen to retire to his bedroom, he gave the young man a warm embrace. His dark eyes searched Mano's face for a moment before he spoke, "Then I will say good night, son. Until we meet again, I wish you a safe journey and look forward to our next meeting." He was so damned tempted to say more, but that Portuguese instinct of his told him not to, so he didn't. It was not the right moment.

Phil Cabrillo was sure he would know when the time was right. He would rely on that to guide him.

Mano noticed the thoughtful look on Phil's weathered face and he figured it to be that the hour was late and he was weary. But something was prodding at the old man. Mano knew that Phil was not going to tell him what was troubling him tonight, so he did not pursue it. Besides, he had to admit that his long day's journey had left him bone-weary tired and he was ready for the sweet comfort of the cot in Phil's back room.

"If you are to go with your friend and I am to leave for La Casa Grande, I suggest that we get ourselves to bed," Mano declared.

"I would agree," Phil replied.

So the two of them moved out of the small kitchen, after Phil had dimmed the lamp, and they went to their beds to retire for the night.

Mano slept later than he had intended the next morning because clouds had moved in during the late night hours and there was no bright sunlight shining through the windows to wake him up.

But when he ambled into Phil's small kitchen, he found no

signs of the old Portuguese there in the cottage so he assumed that he had gotten up early to leave on the fishing jaunt with his friend.

While a pot of strong black coffee brewed on Phil's stove, Mano gathered up his gear and dressed. His destination before the sun set tonight was San Mateo County and La Casa Grande. He was a man with no time to waste now, and the minute he returned, he planned to seek out Aimee.

Aimee did not have to ask Jolie if she'd met her brother in the garden the night before. Her lovely face glowed with a radiance when she'd entered Aimee's bedroom the next morning, reflecting her happiness.

That devious streak in Aimee could not be controlled. She teased her little maid, "I don't have to ask if you and Emile met last night. I know you did." A smile was on her face, declaring that she was very pleased Jolie and Emile were finding such joy with one another.

Jolie gave out a lighthearted laugh, "Ah, mademoiselle, you are too smart, I think. So I shall not try to fool you or lie to you. I will just hope that it meets with your approval. I want that most desperately."

"Oh, Jolie, you have it, don't you know that? I think you could give much to Emile and I want him to be happy."

Jolie rushed to Aimee and took her hands in hers. Her pretty face had a most serious, concerned look as she declared, "Oh, mademoiselle, I would try so very hard to make him happy. But I am afraid that your father would never accept a simple servant girl like me for the wife of his son."

Aimee understood her little maid's apprehensions and fears. But Emile was no youngster anymore, and he was certainly a man ready to claim himself a bride. Aimee reached over to take Jolie's hand as she said, "I don't think Papa will influence Emile any more than he has me where my heart is concerned, Jolie. As much as Emile honors our father, he will follow the

339

dictates of his heart. So shall I."

With a feeling of great humility and gratitude, Jolie managed a weak smile as she patted her mistress's hand. How very fortunate she was to have such a kindhearted lady to serve. Destiny had surely led her here to the Chateau L'Aragon!

"Merci, mademoiselle," she murmured softly.

"Oh, Jolie, I thank you for being such a very devoted friend to me since I've returned from Paris. I don't know what I would have done without you here to talk to."

"It is nice to hear you say that, mademoiselle. It is so very nice," Jolie declared.

Aimee was not in the mood to join her family for breakfast, so she requested that Jolie bring her a tray. She considered this the best way to avoid any questions from her father about Brad Huntington.

Now that she was back in this California valley, the thoughts of Mano were with her again more than ever. She wondered if she'd ever be able to stroll through the gardens without remembering Mano Mateo. If she chose to ride through the countryside, would she ever be free of his presence as he had ridden up to her on that magnificent horse of his? God, she wondered if she'd ever be free of him!

She asked herself how one man could do this to a woman. The answer would not come. She could certainly not explain it to herself. She knew not where to turn to get that very important answer.

All she could do was try to soothe herself and cuss the fact he was Carlos Mateo's son. But for that, they might have had a chance for happiness. But in that same moment, a voice came to remind her that it had been Mano who had lied to her. For weeks, he had lied to her. There was no excuse for that.

Contrary to her father's strict orders that she not ride away from the grounds of the estate, she told Jolie to lay out her bottle-green riding ensemble. She noticed the hesitation in Jolie as she went to the armoire.

"Your riding ensemble, mademoiselle?"

"That's right, Jolie. I plan to go riding this morning. As I told you, Papa will not tell me what to do or will he tell Emile. I will not be a prisoner here, Jolie. I could not stand that."

"*Oui*, mademoiselle, I understand." Jolie did as her mistress had requested, moving to the armoire and taking the fine-tailored deep green riding skirt and jacket from the chest.

As she helped her mistress dress, Jolie could not resist a word of warning, "Please be careful, mademoiselle. Don't ride too far away from the grounds."

"Oh, I won't ride too far, Jolie. I just want to be free to ride out of these grounds when I wish. I can't be confined behind walls like my father would like to lay down for me. That is why I said to you what I did about Emile. Father may lay down the rules here at the Chateau L'Aragon, but that doesn't mean we will abide by those rules."

Jolie pulled Aimee's silvery hair free of her blouse, allowing it to flow down her back and around her shoulders. In a most sincere voice, she told her young mistress, "My only concern is that you will be safe."

"Jolie, you are a jewel! I promise you I will try to be very careful, for my sake as well as yours."

Neither of them knew what the next hours of that autumn day held for them. If they had, neither one of them would have left the serene comfort of that bedroom.

Jolie watched her go out the bedroom door, looking so beautiful. But why did she feel such a heaviness in her heart? she wondered.

Aimee Aragon was in danger! Jolie felt.

Chapter 43

The sight of such a fascinating young female like Aimee astraddle her fine palomino could stir up a blazing fever in any man's veins. The rich green riding ensemble molded her curvy body, leaving no doubts about her alluring figure. Although the two men watching her were a short distance away, they knew her face was breathtakingly beautiful, with that long, flowing fair hair billowing back wildly in the breeze.

"Ain't she something, Cody? Did you ever see any gal as pretty as that one?" Buck excitedly exclaimed as his eyes stared across the way to the hillside where Aimee rode her horse.

"I'll agree with that. Never saw any gal's rear look so good sittin' in a saddle. No sidesaddle ridin' for that one. She likes to straddle her horse and ride him like a horse is supposed to be rode," Cody remarked, indulging himself in some very lusty thoughts all his own. Those thoughts he did not confide in his buddy Buck.

Buck scratched his tousled brown hair as he quizzed his friend Cody, "Wonder why that guy wants us to snatch that pretty gal and keep her hidden up there in that cabin for him, Cody? Now, I'll tell you for sure I don't mind doing that for all the money he's promised, but I'll tell you right now, Cody, I won't harm that pretty little thing. I won't kill her for him. No siree!"

Cody's eyes darted over to Buck. Sometimes, he wondered why he'd ever hooked up with an oaf like Buck. He and his buddy were total opposites. To be quite honest, Buck was a chickenhearted coward. Cody had been filled with utter disgust at those times when he'd witnessed the lanky Buck literally shaking in his boots.

"Nobody said a damned thing about killing the woman. Christ, Buck, what's the matter with you, anyway? You're like some old nervous woman, do you know that?"

"I ain't either, Cody," Buck snapped back in defense.

"You are, too."

Buck sat in silence, figuring that there was no point in arguing with Cody, for he'd never won when they'd disagreed about any matter.

Cody turned to see the sullen face of Buck, who looked like a pouting kid. But he knew how to get him in a good humor, as he usually did when Buck got like this. "How about gettin' that flask out of my saddlebag, Buck. We can have ourselves a drink before we grab that little gal, eh?"

Without any hesitation, Buck leaped up to do Cody's bidding, as he usually did. "Yeah, Cody, that sounds like a good idea to me." He scurried through the grove of trees where the horses were tethered out of sight.

After he'd taken the flask out of the saddlebag, he rushed back to the spot where Cody sat, leaning back against a fallen tree trunk. "Here it is, Cody," Buck said, handing the flask to him like a dutiful child would do for his elder.

"Ah, this will cure what ails us, won't it, Buck?"

"Sure will, Cody," he said, watching his buddy take the first generous gulp of the whiskey. Already, his thirst was whetted for the taste of the whiskey; this is what Cody knew about his pal.

Cody's eyes watched Buck's face as he took his drink from the flask and slowly lowered it to hand it to his buddy. Once he'd had a few drinks from the flask, Buck wouldn't be so lily-livered about the job they were hired to do and that was how Cody wanted him for the next few hours.

Once they got the girl back to the cabin, Cody didn't have to concern himself about old Buck.

Cody wanted the cover of the thick woods when he grabbed the girl. He had plotted out the area for three or four days. Finally, he had decided on this particular spot. Oh, he'd known when he'd been spotted a couple of times by some man across the way at the two-story house belonging to the Aragon family.

That was exactly why he had changed his plans as well as the point where he and Buck would rush her when she rode by, just as that dude who'd hired them had assured Cody she would do.

Had Paul Aragon listened to his best instincts and carried forth with his own plans to search the area when he'd spotted a stranger lurking up there in the woods, his search party would have found Buck and Cody's campsite. They'd camped out back in the dense woods for a couple of days.

Aimee knew she was defying her father's very explicit orders when she rode past the point on the estate he'd deemed safe for her. But she was pulled by a force she could not resist. She could not will herself not to go down into that valley where the live oak stood so majestically with its long, spreading branches, which had provided the bower for the romantic interlude she'd shared with Mano.

She knew she was being foolish to torment herself so, and yet she could not make herself turn Lady around to go back toward the house. She had to go on.

When she arrived at the spot that would always hold a certain magic for her, she stood there thoughtfully for a few brief moments, tears streaming down her lovely face. It mattered not to her if his name was Perez or Mateo. What did matter was that he had lied to her for so many weeks. She could understand why he might have lied that first night when he had rescued her, knowing how their two fathers felt about one another. But the hurt and pain was in knowing that once she'd so willingly surrendered to him, he had not confessed the truth.

Dear God, he had to have known that she cared very much for him to have given herself to him as she had!

All she could surmise was that he'd taken their lovemaking so lightly and that she was merely another conquest for the handsome Mano Mateo. With that handsome face and fine physique, he could have obviously had almost any woman he wanted. Now, as she stood there in the spot where they'd first made love, she realized how easily he'd won her with those dashing, devilish charms of his. How amusing he must have found her and how easy a conquest!

As she turned away to walk back and mount Lady, she made a confession to herself. The truth was she still loved him as passionately and as furiously as she had the last time she was with him. Right or wrong, it was that way!

His arms might never hold her again and his flaming lips might never touch her flesh again, but she would forever remember that glorious rapture he gave to her. Endlessly, she would recall the ecstasy of his powerful male body masterfully conquering her, demanding that she yield to his will. Surrender was sweet and divine! That overwhelming Latin charm of his made her eagerly willing to give to him all he desired. She was helpless to cope with the magic he ignited within her, and she knew if he appeared this very moment, she would be unable to resist that power he held over her. She would go right into the circle of his arms.

But he didn't come to her, and she mounted Lady to ride back to the house and the emptiness there. Somehow, she knew she must persuade her parents to let her return to Paris and *Tante* Denise. It was the only solution to rid her of this malady that ailed her. Fred Bigler was not the answer nor was Brad Huntington. To get away from here was the only answer.

These were the thoughts occupying her mind as she reined her palomino around to take her homeward. So engrossed was she with her private thoughts, that her usually keen ears did not detect the advancing horses coming her way. When she did perceive them, Aimee realized that she was in an impossible situation as she saw the two rugged-looking characters approaching her, blocking her way and her path of escape.

Who were they and why were they trying to waylay her? she wondered.

Never had she seen those two characters before, she knew. Those two faces would have made an impression on her, she realized as she spurred Lady to go as fast as she could gallop. The palomino stretched herself to go as swiftly as her trim long legs could, but there was no way she was going to escape the two chasing her.

In the short space of a few minutes, she found herself overpowered by the two men. One of them had her placed in the saddle in front of him and Aimee watched as Lady galloped in solitude toward her home after the other man had given her a sharp tap on the rump. The reins dragged on the earth as Lady moved across the countryside.

In a few minutes she'd been subdued, completely helpless even though she'd fought like a wildcat. Her wrists were tied with a leather strap. Her struggling had been an act of futility, because there was no way she was going to win this battle.

Aimee was no fool so she gave up—for the moment, at least. Lady returning home without her would surely alert her family that she was in trouble, and she comforted herself by counting on them to come to her rescue. By now, she was feeling slightly sick by the fetid, hot breath of the man pressed against her back. She tried desperately to move as far away from him as she could, but it was not possible to move that far, she found out.

Once again, she attempted to struggle against her captive, but an overwhelming weariness flooded her as she gave out a deep sigh of exhaustion.

"Honey, you aren't gettin' away from Cody, so you might as

well quit fightin' me," the bearded man lustily whispered in her ear.

"Why are you doing this? I don't know either one of you!"

The sweet fragrance of her hair as Cody's nose nuzzled it made him heady with the wildest desire for her. His arms encircled her waist as he held the reins, feeling the warmth of her supple curves. God, she was a luscious female!

"That's right, little lady. You don't know us. Why we are doing it is my business and my pal's business. You'll just have to wonder about that."

"Then you and your pal, as you call him, must be very foolish. The whole countryside will be hunting for me. I am the daughter of Paul Aragon," she told him.

"Hey, honey, we know exactly who you are," Cody told her.

"Then, Monsieur Cody, you are more stupid than I thought. I have two brothers who would be delighted to tear you apart. I just hope that you realize what you might be facing for such a foolhardy act."

"I have no fear of your brothers or your father, miss."

She turned her lovely head so that her eyes pierced Cody, reflecting the rage of fury boiling within her. "You'll rue the day you did this, I can assure you," she hissed at him with venom in her soft, firm voice.

Damned, if she wasn't a spitfire female, and it only whetted Cody's lusty desires more as he threw back his head to give way to a roar of laughter.

"Laugh, you fool! Laugh now while you're able, 'cause very soon you won't be able to even open your ugly mouth." Aimee stiffened her body and leaned as far away from his foul body as she possibly could. Cody tensed with deep resentment that she was so bold to speak to him that way. Who in the hell did this little bitch think she was? He'd take great pleasure in humbling her before he was through with her.

Cody had no idea what this dude had planned for this high-class lady with her snobbish airs, nor did he really care. Unlike Buck, he didn't have a mellow heart, but he knew he was going to enjoy himself one time with this fair-haired lovely before he left her. That was a promise he was making to himself right now.

A wave of fright suddenly washed over Aimee as she sensed the heavy breathing of the man sitting there on the horse behind her. Instinctively, she knew he was thinking evil, salacious thoughts about her. The very thought of this man touching her was enough to make her sick.

Another thing that frightened her now was the countryside, which was suddenly unfamiliar to her. Where was she being taken? she wondered. The thought of Chateau L'Aragon lying so far back in the distance scared her. Never had she felt so desolate and all alone.

It was a horrifying feeling, which chilled her to the bone!

Chapter 44

Emile had seen his young sister ride away from the estate grounds. He hoped she would heed their father's advice for once, now that Paul Aragon had told him about seeing a strange rider lurking up there in the woods on a couple of occasions in the last four days.

"I wish you'd told me about this sooner, Father," Emile told him.

"I had intended to get Armand to take a couple of men to check out the woods, but that was when you, your mother, and Aimee arrived back home, so I forgot all about it."

But his father's revelation had stuck in his mind all morning long, and when he'd seen Aimee ride away, it disturbed him. A special protective attitude dwelled within him.

By mid-afternoon, Emile made some lame excuse to Armand so he could leave the winery, go to the house, and check on Aimee to see if she'd safely returned from her ride.

When he entered the gate to go into the grounds and through the gardens, he encountered Jolie strolling there with a wicker basket draped over one arm to hold the flowers she

349

was picking. As his dark eyes gazed upon the lovely vision of her bending down to pick one of the colorful blossoms, he allowed himself the pleasure of enjoying the sight of her and Aimee was forgotten for that brief moment.

Emile's broad chest swelled with overwhelming passion as he recalled the light, gentle kiss he'd taken from her sweet, sweet lips last night here in the gardens. Now, as he savored the sight of her in the bright sunlight, he thought to himself she was just as beautiful as she was in the moonlight.

Her glossy black hair looked like black onyx, and her dainty figure was perfectly proportioned with the supple mounds of her breasts and curvy hips, along with her wasplike waistline. Around her waist she wore a snowy white apron tied to cover her simple little frock of ecru-colored sprigged muslin with clustered blue flowers.

Slowly, he moved toward her, but Jolie did not hear the robust Emile coming up behind her. He stood directly in back of her before she turned around suddenly to see him there and greeted him with a broad, pleased smile.

For one fleeting moment, a wave of embarrassment rushed over her as she recalled his romantic gesture the night before when he'd kissed her. But that gentle, warm smile of his quickly eased away that disconcerting feeling by the time she found her tongue, exclaiming, "This is an unexpected pleasure, Emile."

"Now that's sweet of you to say, Jolie. I am glad to find you here, for I know you can tell me if Aimee has returned from her ride. I suspect that she probably hasn't."

"No, she hasn't. Are you concerned about her, too? I would have expected her back about forty-five minutes ago and that is why I decided to come on down to pick a fresh bouquet for her room. I guess I have been looking down the lane for some sight of her, too."

Emile gave her an understanding nod of his head along with an understanding grin. "Aimee is lucky to have such a devoted maid and friend as you, Jolie."

"Oh, thank you, Emile, for saying that. She is my dearest friend—that is true. So I can't help worrying about her."

It was a comfort to him to know that she, too, shared his concern. What he was wondering now was if he should voice his fears to his father. He didn't want to stir up an undue panic in his father or mother, but he felt Aimee must be in some kind of trouble.

Perhaps he should just do a little investigation on his own, he decided as he bid Jolie farewell.

But the very perceptive Jolie seemed to be reading his mind as she inquired of him, "You are going to look for her, aren't you, Emile?"

"I am, but don't say anything to my mother or father just yet."

"Oh, I won't. I'll just be praying that you find her," Jolie sighed. She sought to pick no more flowers, and as Emile started to walk away, she turned to go back into the house.

Her dark eyes gazed down at the flowers in her basket, their beauty reminding her of her lovely mistress. Oh, how she hoped this heavy feeling on her chest was just a case of being overprotective where her mistress was concerned.

She was glad she had not encountered Madame Lisette as she moved through the house to go up the stairs. Jolie did not find it easy to mask her feelings when she was worried or upset. There was no denying that she was certainly upset now after her talk with Emile. She wasn't being a silly, panicky woman! Emile had confirmed that by his concern.

Thoughtfully, she began placing her lovely multicolored blossoms in a cut-crystal vase in Aimee's bedroom, but the moment her eyes glanced over to see the hands of the clock, she became more disturbed.

Something was most assuredly wrong! she knew now.

By a strange coincidence, as the twilight hour engulfed the California countryside and Emile was reining his horse around to give up his search for any sign of his sister, Mano and Demonio were approaching La Casa Grande. That happy-go-lucky air and high spirits would not have been his to enjoy had he known the feelings of Emile Aragon as he finally decided to ride back to the house without his sister in tow. A feeling of utter helplessness flooded Emile, because he knew something was terribly wrong and Aimee was not safely at home.

Unaware of all this drama happening just a few miles away involving the woman he loved so very much, Mano could now see the red-tiled roof of the two-story house that was his home. By the time he rode through the wide archway onto the enclosed grounds of the property, there were still a few of the hired hands milling around the corrals and barnyard.

A few of them recognized the returning Mano and threw up their hands in a welcoming gesture. It was young Paco who came running across the corral when he saw it was Mano riding down the long winding drive, wildly waving his hands in the air and calling out Mano's name.

Mano gave out a deep, happy laugh, calling out, "Hello, amigo! Good to see you." Demonio seemed to know he was home as he paced faster toward the corrals.

"Senor Mano, what a pleasant surprise to see you back so soon! You didn't stay away so long this time," Paco exclaimed, delighted to see Mano back on the ranch. It was always a happier time for Paco when Mano was there to talk with and be around.

Mano, seeing the genuine warmth on the youth's face and how truly happy he was to see him, made a decision about Paco. He'd take him with him when he left to make his home up in the Valley of the Moon country.

"No, Paco, I didn't, did I?" he grinned, throwing the reins at the youth. Paco grabbed them as Mano leaped off the horse.

Together, they walked toward the stables, and Mano lingered there with the young man for a short while before he left to go into the house and announce his return to La Casa Grande.

By now, darkness fell over the grounds of the walled gardens as Mano moved up the flagstone pathway and away from the iron entrance gate. He could not help wondering what kind of response he would receive from his father when they met tonight. At this hour, he didn't expect to encounter him, knowing his father's very strict routine. The same would be true with Mario. If he met anyone along the way to the stairway, it would be that adorable Minerva.

But as it happened, he did not see her as he moved up the steps to the second landing. He thought to himself how ghostly quiet it seemed in this palatial old mansion. Now that he thought about it, it had never been a house that rang out with life and laughter. Maybe that was the thing that had smothered his mother so much at times that she had to escape to old Phil's cottage up at Half Moon Bay. Well, that made them two of a kind!

His home would not be that way, he promised himself. It would be cozy and inviting, with a feeling of love and warmth. This was always what he'd found lacking within the walls of La Casa Grande, but a comforting warmth always flourished in Phil's humble cottage. Now, his future home was much grander than Phil's little house, and Mano had a multitude of plans to improve the lovely two-story stone house. However, it could hardly be compared to the palatial luxury he'd been surrounded by here at his father's ranch. But it was exactly the type of place Mano yearned to live in, and if only he could share his dream with Aimee, he would be the happiest man alive. But with or without her, Mano was going to live there.

These were his thoughts as he walked inside his room and closed the door. As it would happen, he had successfully managed to come up the long stairway and get to his room without encountering anyone, not even Minerva.

However, he barely had time to place his bag on the floor and fling his flat-crowned, wide-brimmed hat across the room to land on the overstuffed chair when there was a knock on his door. Mano muttered, "Oh, God!" As he slowly ambled toward

353

the door, he hoped it was not his father who had spotted him coming across the grounds or seen him enter the house.

It was sweet relief to see his older brother, Mario, standing there instead of his father. Mario came into the room, telling Mano that he had chanced to be looking out his window as he had come up the drive.

"I am glad you didn't stay away so long this time, Mano," Mario told him as he walked over to the overstuffed chair, removing Mano's black felt hat to sit down.

"Pressing business required that I return, Mario," Mano explained as he sat down on the edge of the bed to yank off both of his leather boots. His long trail ride demanded that he wash the dust and grime away.

"Business, Mano?" There was a quizzical look on Mario's face, for he was certain it was Aimee Aragon and the thoughts of her that had persuaded Mano to return to the region.

By now Mano was slinging his shirt aside and standing in front of Mario bare-chested. His next move was to remove the belt around the waistline of his dark twill pants.

"I must confess that I would have thought it the beautiful senorita, Aimee, calling you back so soon, Mano," Mario declared, a teasing grin on his handsome face.

A devious grin also broke on Mano's face as he admitted, "Oh, she is a part of it, I confess. But I have some news to tell you, Mario, and you are the first to know." Mano almost strutted like a proud peacock and his broad chest swelled with pride as he paced across the room to the small teakwood chest to get a bottle of whiskey he kept there, so that he and Mario might share a drink when he told him his wonderful news.

"Then tell me, Mano," Mario urged.

"I am the owner of a winery, Mario. Can you believe that? I am the owner of the Golden Splendor Winery up at Santa Rosa. Remember when I came back home in the spring and I told you about this place they call the Valley of the Moon, which is such fine country for growing grapes? Well, I saw this place and I fell in love with it almost as fast as I did when my

354

eyes first saw Aimee. I had to have it and I got it, Mario!" Such elation was overwhelming him that he was like a young boy at Christmas or at that particular time in their youth when the two of them had been given their first horse.

"I am happy you have acquired what you wanted, Mano. It must be wonderful for a man to feel as excited as you are right now. I—I envy you, Mano. I truly do." He didn't add that he never expected to really have what he wanted in life, being the eldest son of Carlos Mateo. But he'd always known that Mano would. He'd just not expected it to come this soon.

"It is the most wonderful feeling a man can have, Mario. I would urge you to seek out your destiny as I have just done. To hell with old established traditions of the past! I never gave a damn that Father and his father before him got such joy and satisfaction out of breeding their ugly bulls. They never excited me, so why should I live the rest of my life being miserable and doing something I cared nothing about? I ask you, Mario, why should I or why should you?" Mano's black eyes were ablaze with the depth of his feelings, and Mario could think of nothing to say because the truth of the matter was what his brother had said made very good sense.

God, how he wished he was as strong-willed and bold about his own life as his younger brother was—as he'd always been! He could not be anything but honest with Mano now, as he agreed, "We should be able to live our lives as we choose, Mano, and I admire you tremendously for doing just that." Suddenly, there was a sad, forlorn expression on Mario's face as he began to speak again.

"I am not your breed of man and I wish to hell I were."

Never had Mano felt so close or so compassionate for his older brother sitting there in the chair. Being the type of man he was, Mano was affected by such praise given to him. "I'll always cherish what you just said, Mario. Whatever the future holds for the two of us, I'll always remember what you said."

Chapter 45

The two Mateo brothers parted company with a new bond of good will and depth of true feeling for each other. Although neither of them mentioned it, they both realized that Carlos Mateo would not be happy about his son's acquisition of a winery. In fact, the moment Mano announced his news there was no doubt about the raging storm that would erupt in their parlor tonight.

It was not as disturbing to Mano as it was to Mario as he returned to his own room to dress for the evening meal. Being such a serious young man, he hated to see his brother and his father tear one another apart as they so often did. There was such a great love in his heart for both of them and he felt a certain degree of loyalty for each of them. It pained him deeply.

In the privacy of his own bedroom, Mano was also dwelling on his thoughts about Mario. He was certainly not like their father, Carlos, nor was he anything like their volatile, impulsive mother, Theresa. Mario was kind and gentle. He had an understanding, tender heart, Mano realized. He would forever be Carlos's dutiful son, because he would never dare to rebuke or deny their father. But now Mano knew that he didn't exactly like the role his brother must play in life and he felt an overwelming wave of sorrow for Mario.

Mano wasted no time worrying about himself or how his father would react to his announcement that he was to become a vintner and the owner of a winery, instead of sharing the inheritance due him as the son of Carlos Mateo. He realized his father would immediately consider that he was not being the loyal son, true to the Mateo heritage, but Mano could not concern himself with that old Latin tradition. Times had changed and sons did not carry on forever with the edicts set forth two generations ago, Mano knew. Carlos had never ventured outside his own private world of La Casa Grande as Mano had over the last five or six years. His father's whole life had been spent within the confines of La Casa Grande. Mano had known quite early in his life that this was not for him, for he wanted to explore other worlds.

This was exactly what he had done when he'd reached the age of nineteen. He would never regret those days and nights he'd gone out on his own, forgetting that he was the son of the wealthy Carlos Mateo, to pursue a different lifestyle.

Exploring life and the world outside those walled gardens of La Casa Grande, he did to the fullest. He'd seen strange shores and countries when he'd shipped out on packets, leaving the state of California. He learned that there were other ways to live besides the rigid, stern rules laid down all his life by Carlos Mateo.

There were always women eager to fawn over him, women much older and more experienced than he had been when he'd first left La Casa Grande. Now Mano was the first to admit that he had been an eager and willing student to be taught the lessons of love. Greedily, he'd taken his fill of all this.

But after two or three years of this reckless wanderlust, Mano sought more out of life. He still did not know what it was he wanted to do with his life, but he was firmly convinced that ranching and raising and breeding bulls were not for him. He was not willing to commit himself to this. It was when he'd passed his twentieth birthday and had just returned from one of his jaunts on a packet that he had the impulsive urge to go up to visit old Phil Cabrillo at Half Moon Bay. It had happened very slowly, this bond of confidence and trust, along with the great respect he found in the old Portuguese. The old man spoke such words of wisdom and knowledge of life, and Mano found his whole world changing. After that first visit up at Half Moon Bay, Mano found himself going back there from time to time when he needed the old man's counsel. Phil Cabrillo filled a deep void in Mano's life that Carlos Mateo had never done. He also filled the deep need left in a young man who had never really gotten to know the love of a mother who'd died when he was so young.

Few had ever realized that the happy-go-lucky Mano, with his reckless, devil-may-care attitude, was a man who'd dwelled many times in loneliness. He knew his older brother would have found this hard to believe about him. But somehow, Mano knew that after their talk a few moments ago, they were closer as brothers than they'd ever been before.

Interestingly enough, Mario Mateo was having the exact same thoughts about his younger brother as he moved around the quiet solitude of his own bedroom. Mario had made a most important decision. He was going to stand by Mano's side when they confronted their father at dinner. More than that, Mario was determined that he was going to do everything he could to help Mano win the woman he loved.

He had seen the lovely young lady at the Governor's Ball, and no other woman was as gorgeous as she was. But there was a sadness in her lovely sapphire-blue eyes as she moved around that festive, opulent ballroom.

Mario knew that Aimee Aragon and Mano were the perfect pair. Love gleamed like a beacon in both of their eyes when they were standing close to one another.

358

These two must get back together, Mario was convinced. He made himself a promise to help them. If he could not have his dreams, maybe Mano could. As an older brother, that would be gratifying to him. There had been times in their lives that Mario had felt he had failed his younger brother. At least, he had been blessed with those extra years of the loving comfort of a mother, which Mano had never known.

He had always known why Mano was pulled like a magnet to Phil Cabrillo and Half Moon Bay. It gave him a part of their mother that nothing else could. Here Mano had learned about that particular side of Theresa's character that was inborn in her, coming from her heritage. Mario had realized a long time ago that Mano was never going to accept, as Carlos would have wished him to do, that his heritage was wholly Spanish.

Being the oldest son, Mario had known that his father had been pricked like a thorn by this Portuguese blood that flowed in the veins of his lovely wife and the mother of his two sons. He had secretly resented it, Mario recalled, when he was about sixteen and his father had made a very snide remark that told him he considered her family inferior to his.

After that, Mario had buried the hurt deep within him, but it had pained him greatly. There was nothing about his mother that was inferior as far as Mario was concerned. He knew then what a pompous, arrogant man his father was and how miserable he must have made their mother during their marriage.

As the years had passed and Mano had grown older, Mario felt that their father had turned that wrath on his younger son. Helplessly, Mario had witnessed it and been unable to do much to ease the tensions existing between the two of them.

Now the time had come that he could, and by all that was holy he would, come to Mano's aid. It wasn't too late for him to do that.

There was another very definite decision Mario had made after he had returned from Sacramento and the Governor's

Ball. He'd not given Carlos the slightest hint about his feelings, for he saw no reason to stir up a hornet's nest, but he had escorted Reyes's daughter for the last time. Whether it met with his father's approval or not, he could not care less. He was not as bold as Mano, but Mario knew he was not willing to saddle himself with an empty-brained idiot like Camilla Reyes for the rest of his life, just to appease his father and her father. Hell would freeze over first!

As he always did, Mario dressed himself with great care. Meticulously, he surveyed himself in the mirror to see that he had brushed his hair just right and that his attire was as it should be. Giving a final tuck to his white linen shirt and buttoning the last button on his black vest, he turned away from the mirror to leave his room.

He wished that he could anticipate a very pleasant night ahead, sharing the evening meal with his father and brother, but he was not foolish enough to dwell on that sort of whimsy. So he prepared himself for the tense scene he'd have to witness when Carlos and Mano met in the parlor.

As it would happen when he entered the parlor, he was eased to find Mano there alone. Obviously, he and their chubby housekeeper, Minerva, had been having one of their little chit-chat sessions, as they often did, and she was shuffling out of the parlor as he was entering. It was also obvious from the broad smile on her dark face that she was overjoyed to see Mano back home.

Mano was already enjoying a glass of wine and Mario noticed that he was munching on something—something Minerva had brought to him as a special treat.

The old mestizo woman had always had a special place in her heart for the youngest Mateo son, and Mario knew it. He had always figured that it was because Mano was so young when their mother had died, so he'd never resented her for that. Now he sought to tease Mano as he sauntered up to him, "That Minerva is still up to it, isn't she? Giving you one of her little delicacies, eh?"

Mano swallowed the last bite and grinned sheepishly as he confessed the truth. "That dear old woman enjoys spoiling me—always has. I've enjoyed every minute of it, too."

Carlos heard the duet of laughter as he descended the stairway and he knew before he marched into his parlor that Mano was back once again. A part of him was overjoyed but another part of him bristled and tensed. Why was it such strange, puzzling emotions always erupted in him where his younger son was concerned? Oh, God, he wished that he knew! For years, he'd pondered this tormenting situation but he'd never found the answer to it.

As Mario had prepared himself before leaving his room, Carlos now steeled himself before making his entrance. He would not dare admit it to himself, but his youngest son, with that indomitable will of his, could be very intimidating to a man as masterful as Carlos.

He had moved through the doorway before his two sons knew he was in their midst. Both were engaged in lighthearted laughter and thoroughly enjoying one another's company, it was obvious to see.

Carlos cautioned himself to play his hand very carefully, for he must not make himself look like the overbearing monster in the eyes of his oldest son, Mario. That he couldn't afford to do for his own best interest. No, he admonished himself privately, that he must not do so he wouldn't lose Mario's loyalty and respect at this point in his life.

In that deep, sonorous voice of his, Carlos greeted the two young men standing there by his hearth involved in conversation.

In unison, they turned to address him, "Good evening, Father."

Carlos walked slowly toward them as he directed his next remark to Mano, "So, my son, you have come home again. You were not gone too long this time. La Casa Grande called out

361

to you, perhaps?"

Mano knew he was baiting him and he did not intend to grab for it. Nor did he intend to bring up the fact that he had purchased some land and a winery until after they'd had a pleasant dinner. There was a cunning grin on Mano's tanned face as he quipped, "Many things called to me, Father, called me to return when I did." He would be damned if he were going to give him the satisfaction by agreeing that it was this ranch beckoning to him. Now he could only silently pray that Mario didn't innocently let out the news about his land purchase.

Quickly, Mario came to the rescue of the situation by suggesting that Carlos join them in a glass of wine before dinner.

"Yes, thank you, my son. That would be nice," Carlos told him as he moved to take his place in his favorite chair there in the parlor, the high-backed gold brocade upholstered, overstuffed one.

Mario immediately moved to get his father the wine, and he was glad that it seemed to have eased a conversation that could have become tense and strained.

Mario and Mano exchanged glances as Carlos took the glass and the first sip, his eyes lowered so he did not see the amused grins on his sons' faces. Mano knew then that Mario understood.

As it would happen, the dinner hour was most pleasant, with Minerva serving her usual delicious platters of tasty, good food. But the most wonderful thing Mano ate was her fresh-baked cherry pie, with its sweet, thick juices she'd topped with a thick, rich cream.

He playfully teased her as she moved around the table to remove the plates. "You knew I was coming home tonight, didn't you, Minerva? That's why you baked my favorite pie."

"I knew, Senor Mano," she said with a sly smile on her face, and there was so much conviction in her voice Mano never doubted for a minute that she'd spoken the truth. He gave her an understanding nod of his dark head and a boyish wink of his eye!

For one fleeting moment, Mano was possessed by the wicked thoughts that he should take Minerva with him to his new home, just as he planned to take Paco with him when he left La Casa Grande.

But he knew that as much as she adored him, she considered La Casa Grande her home, as it had been for so many years.

Chapter 46

Righteous wrath and raging anger churned within the tall, imposing figure of Carlos Mateo as he listened to his own son tell him that he would soon be leaving the ranch where he was born and raised to seek his fortune up in Santa Rosa as the landowner of a winery and vineyard.

When he finally found his tongue to speak, he barked out at him, "Mano, do you have no pride in your name—the name of Mateo? That should be the most important thing in your life, as it was in mine and my father's before me. It seems to have escaped you."

"That is where you are wrong, Father. I am very proud of my name and myself, but this does not mean that I can't pursue my own way of life. Surely, that is no disgrace or dishonor to the name of Mateo, Father."

For a moment, Carlos remained silent, knowing that he spoke the truth. In a stammering voice, he finally declared, "It is not a matter of dishonor or disgrace, Mano, and you know that. It is a matter of loyalty to one's family and pride—a great pride in the traditions that have been followed through the generations. That pride, Mano, is so glorifying and satisfying that it becomes the most forceful thing in your life."

He listened to his father speaking and observed the aristocratic arrogance on his expressive face, which could be most dramatic when he was making such a speech as this one. His father would have made an excellent statesman or politician. There was a certain kind of eloquence, strong and powerful, about Carlos Mateo, and Mano would never try to deny that. He could even admit that he admired the dignified gentleman standing before him now.

"I feel a great deal of pride in my name and my heritage, Father. I always have, whether you believe it or not. But I don't feel that I am being disloyal to the name of Mateo because I wish to be a vintner, instead of a breeder of bulls. I will not spend the rest of my life, Father, living a lie. That is not my way and I don't apologize for that."

In his own way, Mano was as impressive as Carlos, reflecting a masterful dignity to rival his father's. Carlos could not deny that as he listened to the words his son spoke to him. He was glad that he and Mano were alone in his study and Mario had excused himself to go to his room a short while before.

He looked into the black eyes of his son and saw the firm determination there. To speak to him any longer was a waste of his time, Carlos realized. He turned away to refill his glass of brandy, and in a sharp, curt tone of voice, he muttered, "Then I guess there is nothing else for us to discuss, is there, Mano?"

"I will let that be your decision, Father," Mano replied, watching that stiff, unbending figure of his father fill his glass. He thought about how often his mother must have been given that same cold, harsh treatment during the years of their marriage. How frustrated she must have been with him and this chilling torment he dealt out in mammoth portions.

So be it, Mano thought to himself as he silently sauntered out of the study, closing the heavy carved oak door behind him. There was a small part of Mano's heart that felt sorry for Carlos Mateo, for he surely had to be a very lonely man. He rather doubted that his father ever knew how to give of his love to anyone—not even to his wife or his sons.

For all his wealth and his so-called family tradition, Carlos Mateo was going to die a lonely old man. Mano considered that very, very sad. Having just met an elderly gentleman so full of love and warmth as Bertrand Dupree, Mano knew the type of person he'd pick to pattern his life after.

Mano only hoped that Mario would not end up the same way. He would try to make sure this never happened to his older brother, he promised himself.

By the time he'd reached the second landing and turned to walk down the dark hallway, he had decided that there was no point in him lingering too long here at La Casa Grande.

Tomorrow, he was going to the Chateau L'Aragon to seek out the woman he loved. Nothing was going to stand in his way, he vowed. He would see her!

A black cloud of gloom hung heavily over the Chateau L'Aragon this morning, as it had throughout the evening and the night before. No one had slept in the two-story stone house, and the servants moved around attending to their household chores as if they were puppets. There were no happy faces or lighthearted smiles.

From the moment Emile had returned to the house and informed his father and mother of his suspicions, the heaviness of gloom and dismay had taken over. Lisette was beside herself with concern and worry, giving way to a flood of tears. The usually calm, easygoing Armand gave way to a fury of anger that anyone would dare do something like this to his sister, and he marched out of the room to go on his own search through the countryside to see if he could find her. But like Emile, he returned to the country estate three hours later, his search having yielded no sign of his sister.

Tired and weary, he stumbled into the house to go to the kitchen. After his long day's work he'd not eaten his evening meal and he was starved. But he knew that Hetty would have something waiting there to fill his belly and satisfy his ravenous hunger.

He was not disappointed, relishing three of the meat pies and two glasses of milk. His pain began to ease. But all the time he ate, his lovely sister's face was there before him, in that ghostly quiet kitchen, as he slumped in a chair at the square oak table all alone. Was sweet little Aimee in pain or hurting? he wondered. Was she hungry and all alone with some crazy idiot? He figured it had to be some insane madman who'd dare to do such a dastardly act as abducting the daughter of Paul Aragon. This whole California countryside knew the Aragon family, and such a thing as this was just not done.

Armand had been surprised to come into a dark, lifeless house when he'd returned. He'd expected to see the two-story mansion ablaze with light. After he'd finished the third meat pie, he rose from the table to move out of the darkened room, because he'd not lit the lamp.

His appetite was now sated, but he still felt bone-weary tired as he climbed slowly up the stairway. He found himself surrounded by that same ghostlike stillness as he reached the second floor of the house. There was no beam of light there in his parents' room nor in Emile's. It was only when he walked by Aimee's room that he saw a dim light glowing, so he paused for a moment. Once he stood there in the quietness he heard the sobbing sounds, so he did not hesitate a moment before opening the door, in that rare hope it might just be Aimee. Perhaps she had returned while he had gone in search of her.

But it was not the figure of his sister he saw lying across the bed, the petite body shaking from her crying. The husky Armand filled with compassion when he saw the deep, sincere sorrow of the little maid.

He found himself feeling awkward and embarrassed that he had invaded her privacy. He knew not what to do. Should he try to comfort her or should he try to slip out of the room so she'd never know he was there? Like Emile Aragon, he was a giant of a man, with his tremendous muscled arms and broad chest. In comparison to the hugeness of his upper torso, the lower part of his firm muscled body seemed small.

Like his brother, he had the same dark hair and eyes, but Armand's features were more coarse and rugged. That fierce air about him was a total contradiction, however, because he was as gentle and kindhearted as Emile.

As he was attempting to turn and move back toward the door, Jolie was alerted to his presence in the room and her dark, tearstained eyes looked up at him. A more pathetic little miss Armand had never seen in all his life.

It was she who was embarrassed now as she looked upon the questioning face of Armand Aragon. In a faltering voice, she tried to explain her presence in the mademoiselle's room at this late hour. "I couldn't sleep, Monsieur Aragon, so I came here to feel near her wherever she might be. I am so distraught! You see, I love her so very much!"

Armand saw the mist of tears coming into her eyes again. He felt so helpless as he awkwardly ambled over to the bed where she was now sitting on the edge.

"Aimee is very lucky to have your love and devotion. I—I can understand why you would want to be here in her room. You and she spend so much time together."

"Oh, thank you, monsieur, thank you for being so kind and understanding," Jolie smiled as she wiped the tears from her cheeks.

Slowly, he sunk down into the small overstuffed chair next to the bed, which was hardly wide enough to accommodate his huge body. He had a warm smile on his face as his huge tan hand gave hers an understanding pat. "I'm happy to know Aimee has so much love flowing around her and I'm sure she would be too if she knew it. In fact, Jolie, I think you should just stay here in Aimee's room tonight. If it would give you comfort, then I am certain that is what my sister would want."

Her dark eyes looked up at him as she carefully surveyed his face. "You—you think it would be all right, monsieur?"

"I think it would not only be all right but I'm sure Aimee would want it, Jolie. There needs to be a light burning in Aimee's window and there needs to be life in this room, Jolie. We don't wish this room to be lonely and lifelessly silent, do we?"

"Oh, no, monsieur! Never that!"

"Then I say that you occupy this room, Jolie. I give you permission in Aimee's absence to do so, *oui?*"

"*Oui,* Monsieur Aragon, then I shall!" She gazed up at this rugged-looking gentleman, realizing that she'd looked upon him many times before but never really seen the true person. Perhaps it was because he was such a quiet, reserved man that she'd never taken notice of the qualities he possessed.

As he sought to rise from the cramped quarters of the dainty chair there by his sister's bed, Armand was having some very private musings about the delicate-looking little maid who had served his sister here at the Chateau L'Aragon since she'd returned from France. Until tonight, he had never taken notice of her. He had been too preoccupied with the vineyards and winery.

"I bid you good night, Jolie, and I hope you have a good night's rest. We will have our Aimee back with us and very soon. Don't you doubt that for a minute! I assure you of that."

"Oh, I believe you, Monsieur Armand. I believe you with all my heart."

That wide-eyed trust did something to Armand, igniting feelings within him he'd never experienced before in his whole life. Women had never held that much interest in his thoughts or his time, but this one he gazed upon now was different. She pulled from him emotions he was not aware he had. It was so absolutely wonderful to feel so at ease and great around her as he did now.

He stood for a moment, just savoring the sweet smile on her face and the utter trust in her big eyes. Dear God, he wanted so desperately to place his big hands around that tiny waist of hers and hold her close to him! He wanted more than anything in

369

the world to kiss those rosy red lips of hers. He could not remember ever feeling this way about any other young maiden in his life.

This encounter with Jolie tonight had awakened Armand to all the things missing in his life, and he knew as he closed the door to Aimee's room that he'd never be the same again. The funny thing about it all was he didn't want it to be the same, because now he knew what he'd been missing all these years.

Long after he'd entered his own bedroom and closed the door behind him, he was warmed by thoughts of Jolie. Such a flame of desire swept over him that sleep became impossible as he flung his tired, weary body across the bed.

It was true that a man needed a woman to be complete. It was the way things were meant to be, and for years he'd tried to deny it.

Tonight, he knew it was so. Oh, he needed Jolie most desperately!

Chapter 47

None of the Aragons enjoyed a sound sleep that night but Armand found that thinking about the pretty little Jolie acted as a soothing balm for him. But it would not have been sweet or soothing if he had known about Emile's infatuation with their sister's little maid.

However, Emile had said nothing to Armand or anyone else about his feelings for Jolie. For the moment, it was too special, so it remained his secret.

Up in Aimee's bedroom, Jolie was awake, tossing and turning restlessly. It seemed to her she should not be here in her mistress's bed, even though Armand had suggested she stay in the room. Yet, on this terrible night her own quarters would have seemed isolated and unnatural.

It was a lonely old mansion tonight, moaning with sorrow over the absence and fate of the beautiful mademoiselle. Jolie lay there across her bed now and looked out the windows. It seemed that the heavens were also dark with gloom, for there were no stars twinkling brightly nor a golden moon shining down on the gardens. Heavy ominous clouds shrouded the

California countryside and there was no cooling breeze flowing through the slightly opened window. The air permeating the room was oppressive.

For all of those occupants of the Chateau L'Aragon, that endless, long night did end with the dawning of a new day. But the bright sunlight did not appear and the gloomy cloudy skies remained from the night before. A subdued quiet dominated the table as the family gathered, none of them having a hearty appetite as they were being served.

The sheriff from San Jose was due to arrive sometime soon because Paul Aragon had realized the previous evening that he and his sons were going to need help if they were to find Aimee. He could not delay any longer, for that could jeopardize his daughter's safety. Oh, he'd thought about sending out his own searching party, but when Armand had told him about the area he'd covered, Paul's concern heightened.

Dear God, he was glad he'd not caught that ship to sail for Europe. He would have been gone and poor Lisette would have been facing this without his support!

Surely the hand of fate had guided him homeward!

This was where her thoughts were wandering now—homeward. Aimee would have given anything to have been at her home, safe and secure in the bosom of her loving family. By now, she could imagine the frenzy and panic going on back there.

She had no inkling of what time it might be, but she was certain it was now long past the hour when she would have joined her family for dinner. Her stomach was telling her that as she sat in the small, dark cubicle of a room where the man called Cody had roughly pushed her through the door.

Being free of his presence was enough to make her rejoice at the sight of the quiet room. Even though she'd stumbled in the darkness, slamming up against some crude piece of furniture, and her nose detected the musty odor surrounding her, she

372

welcomed that after the fetid smell of his body so close, pressing against her.

She took advantage of the dappled moonbeams shining through the branches of the tall trees she'd seen as they'd rode up to this godforsaken place. She had observed that they'd traveled deep into the backwoods of some region unfamiliar to her.

Now she could make out that it had been a bed she'd slammed into. There was nothing else in the room but a straight-backed old oak chair and a washstand. There were two windows, very small and narrow. Hastily, she moved toward the windows while there was still some light to see her way across the room.

Suddenly the room was again filled with darkness. But by that time she was standing there at the window, void of any curtains. She was able to make out the hitching post where Buck and Cody had tethered their horses. Of the two men, she had already decided she might be able to reason with the lanky Buck more successfully than she could with the obnoxious Cody, who turned her stomach.

During the two or three hour ride with these two unsavory characters, it was obvious to her which one was the boss. But why did these two strangers want to abduct her and bring her here to hold her a prisoner? What were their intentions? she pondered.

It took her only a few moments to realize that the small windows were securely locked and all her straining to open them was an act of futility. Satisfied about that, she now moved toward the spot where she'd seen the chair. She had accomplished that little feat with ease.

No one had to tell her she was in one hell of a mess and she sat there thinking about what she could possibly do to protect herself. She had no weapon to use against them. The only things were her wit and her wiles. It was going to take all the shy, cunning tricks she could conjure up to outsmart these two—and she knew it.

Being one petite lady, she realized she was overmatched where power and strength were concerned. It would be hopeless and she would be completely at their mercy. There was only one way she could compete and that was to make one of them her so-called protector. It would have to be Buck. But the idea of his filthy hands touching her filled her with utter distaste, too.

These were the thoughts she was mulling over when the door opened and the tall, reedlike figure of Buck entered with a lamp in one hand and a plate in the other.

"Ain't much, miss, but it's all we got up here." He set the lamp down on the stand and handed the plate over to her.

"What is it, Buck?"

"Beans and corn pone. You drink coffee?"

"Yes, I like coffee very much," she told him, smelling the aroma of what he'd been drinking. It wasn't coffee.

"Then I'll go fetch you some." He turned to survey the room, shaking his head as he muttered, "God Almighty, it's stuffy in here!"

Dejectedly, she nodded as she agreed with him, "I know!" She gave out a depressed sigh, as though she were miserable. It was her first little act in hopes of pulling forth some sympathy for herself from Buck. He was her only hope.

When Buck went out the door to go for the coffee, she had played her role very successfully. He did feel sorry for the lovely young lady he knew was not used to roughing it, having lived a very pampered existence. It riled him that Cody was so damned heartless.

By the time he'd poured a generous cup of coffee and left the small kitchen to take it to Aimee, he was already a victim of her beguiling charms. As he took the coffee into the room and handed it to her, receiving a grateful smile and a polite thank you from the sweet little lady, Buck had already declared himself her protector.

Aimee had no idea that she had made such a devastating impact on the dull-witted drunkard Buck. She made him feel good when he just looked upon her lovely face, and her soft voice entranced him. He left her there to enjoy the hot coffee, knowing he could never treat that young lady with anything but kindness.

The food was tasteless and cold, but Aimee forced herself to eat it. Otherwise, she would only allow herself to grow weak and she could not do that. If she were weak and weary, she could not think how she should act to protect herself.

The best thing of all was the steaming hot coffee, which helped her swallow the bites of food lodging in her throat. Never had she eaten such horrible food. More than ever, she appreciated Hetty's delicious food. Oh, if only she could be sitting there in that candlelit dining room right now, she would not yearn for anything else.

Nothing in life had prepared her for the horrible situation she found herself in right now. It seemed to Aimee that her return to California had been ill-fated from the moment she'd arrived, and a part of her wished that she'd remained in France with her *Tante* Denise. She could not imagine anything like this ever happening to her there.

But there was another part of her that reminded her if she'd not returned home and chanced to meet the handsome Mano Mateo, she would have never known the ultimate fulfillment of a rapture so rare and wonderful. Perhaps it was the only glorious interlude of ecstasy she'd ever know, she thoughtfully lamented there in the darkness of the musty room. At least she had that!

After she had forced herself to eat everything on the plate, she had nothing to do but sit there on the bed to dwell in wild and crazy whimsy. She knew it had to be a form of insanity taking over her but she gave way to her wild imagination. She envisioned Mano galloping up on that magnificent grey stallion of his and taking care of these two ruffians in short order. Then the two of them rode away atop Demonio, into the twilight toward San Mateo County.

She knew she was foolishly daydreaming but she did not

care, because it was a way to ease her frayed nerves and it gave her a comforting feeling. Tonight she needed that more than anything else.

So comforting it was that she stretched out on the bed, her eyes feeling heavy with sleep. A few moments later, she had drifted off to sleep.

She'd not dimmed the wick of the kerosene lamp on the nearby stand because she had not expected to sleep a wink this night. But that period of sleep and rest was not to last throughout the night. The loud sound of men's voices in a heated argument aroused her and she quickly sat up in the bed to listen.

She could not hear what they were saying so she tiptoed over to the door. From the sound of their voices and the slurring of their words, she suspected that the two of them had been nipping at the jug of whiskey all evening.

It was Buck's voice she first recognized as she stood there listening. "I swear I'll blow your God-damned brains out, Cody, if you go through that door tonight to pester that little gal. I mean it, and this is one time you won't bluff me out. You try it and you'll see," Buck told his buddy.

Aimee smiled smugly, for it was sustaining for her to know Buck was on her side.

Cody glared at Buck with disbelief washing over him. That sonofabitch really meant what he said, Cody realized, and he was just drunk enough to pull that trigger he was aiming directly at Cody's chest.

He did not know what had taken over in his old buddy, but he wasn't going to be stupid enough to try to find out or push him—not with the mood he was now in. Hell, there was no woman worth him getting his guts blown out for! Getting himself a woman was the least of his concerns, but this one had challenged him. He did have an awful ache in his groin and he had swelled with a fever of desire to have that pretty little thing in the next room. God, he'd been fired up all evening!

Right now, he realized he had to calm old Buck down if he

wanted to live to see a new day. Trying to sound far more casual than he was feeling right now, he gave out a chuckle, "Hell, Buck, I've decided I need some sleep, not a woman. Couldn't handle it tonight even if I wanted to. I'm too damned tired after the long day we've put in. I say we both get a little shut-eye."

He seemed sincere enough to Buck but he, of all people, knew Cody was not to be trusted. He said one thing and then did another. "Then you go on to bed, Cody. I—I ain't ready just yet."

"Suit yourself then. Figure this dude Fred to be gettin' here sometime tomorrow." Cody rose from the chair and slowly ambled over to set his glass down on the kitchen table.

Aimee stood there by the door for another brief moment, frozen and stunned by Cody's remarks. By the time she finally urged herself to go over toward the bed, the silence outside the door told her Cody had turned in for the night.

As she sunk down on the old bed, she prayed that she would be safe the rest of the night but wondered what tomorrow would hold for her.

Right now, she couldn't worry about tomorrow. All she could do was hope to make it through the rest of this night.

Chapter 48

Aimee stumbled back toward the bed and was stunned by the name she heard Cody mention to Buck. The remark he'd made about a man called Fred arriving here tomorrow was enough to make Aimee very alert, coming alive with speculation that the man could be Fred Bigler.

She would never forget the fury on his face the night of the Governor's Ball, when she'd rebuked him and his amorous advances there in the garden. Would a man go to these limits just because a woman had refused his kisses? she wondered. Until now, she had been thinking that this dastardly deed had been done for the price of a ransom, because she was the daughter of a wealthy vintner in this California valley. But perhaps she had been wrong. If Fred Bigler was at the bottom of this, then it was an act of revenge. Obviously, he was a very sick man and she had been right all along not to have invited his attentions as her father had expected her to do. Her instincts had been far more correct than her father's about this man. Now that she thought about it, she had not liked him from the first minute they'd met and his hand had held hers for that brief moment when they'd been introduced.

She was convinced that there had to be some substance to that particular impression one gets from that first encounter. Funny, now that she thought about it, how different that first impression had been when she'd gazed up into the eyes of Mano Mateo. There was an instant magnetic warmth, drawing her to him with such a force that she had helplessly surrendered.

Oh, God, she wished she'd never found out that he was anyone but Mark Perez. That was the magnificent man she'd fallen so hopelessly in love with and the man who still held her heart in his hands.

She might have denied it that last night they were together and she might do the same thing again if they should meet, but her lips would be lying if they spoke such false words. Never would her heart confess to such a lie!

There would be no sleep for her tonight, Aimee had already decided. Tonight she must think about the enemy she would face tomorrow, for now she realized it was to be a most vindictive man—Fred Bigler. She recalled his words of that night in the garden, that she would be sorry for acting as she had toward him. She should have taken him more seriously. Funny how you think of strange little things about someone later, as she was now, recalling various traits about Fred when he was around her. Never had she liked the way his beady little eyes had moved over her on the occasions they were together. An eerie feeling had always washed over her.

A resentfulness sparked in her now as she thought about all these things and what had happened to her this afternoon because her father had encouraged this scoundrel's attention. As smart as he was, Paul Aragon's judgment had been poor. She hated to fault her father, but if Bigler had not come into her life and been encouraged to call upon her, all this might not be her plight right now.

She could not help feeling a little angry toward her father as she was there in that shack held prisoner by two drunk men.

God only knew what fate lay ahead of her!

As miserably hot as she was, with no fresh air allowed to flow through the windows, she dared not remove her blouse and riding skirt. Since she could not sleep, she moved off the bed to slowly pace across the plank floor. But she did take the time to remove her fine leather boots, so she would not make any noise and alert the attention of the two outside the room. She could only pray that she did not pick up a splinter as she moved around. At least she did not have to rely upon the moonlight streaming through the window, since Buck had brought the kerosene lamp to the room.

As she moved back and forth, along one side of the room and down the other, she spied an old yellowed paper. Picking it up, she used it to vigorously fan herslf. How wonderful it felt as she enjoyed the little gusts of air caressing her warm flesh. Suddenly, that yellowed newspaper was the most precious thing in her possession.

For several minutes, she sat there on the dilapidated oak chair, fanning herself. Her mind mulled over things she'd never expected to be occupied with, but it also made Aimee realize that she had certainly led a very sheltered, pampered life. At this moment in time, she was going to have to stretch herself to think and feel in a most primitive way.

What, she pondered, could she find in this room that would serve as a weapon? She looked around and saw nothing. All her life she'd been told what a clever young lady she was, so where was all that ingenuity and resourcefulness right now? she chided herself.

When she demanded herself to carefully investigate the room in every nook and corner, she chanced to look under the bed. There, she found her weapon. It was a long wooden pole she judged to be about four or five feet long. It could serve as a grand club to do battle with the enemy outside her door and she knew it was enough to give a stunning blow to their heads. She moved it to the edge of the bed so that it would remain concealed from their eyes but handy for her hand to reach in a hurry, if she must use it.

This was enough to give her a small degree of courage. By now, she was like a hound dog sniffing out a squirrel in the woods. She scrutinized every inch of the plank floor. By the time she was sure she had covered every corner of that room, she had gathered together a huge rusty nail some three or four inches long and a rock with jagged edges.

Before she finally gave way to the weariness engulfing her, she found it amusing that such very simple things meant so much to her right now. A rock, nail, yellowed paper, and a wooden club of a pole were her cherished belongings.

She knew not how long she lay there in that smoldering heat, fanning herself, before she finally dropped the paper to fall into a deep, deep sleep.

Luckily for her, the two men on the other side of the door were sleeping as deeply, for they were numbed by all the whiskey they'd consumed.

By the time Ross Maynard rode up to the shack just outside Sacramento, back in the secluded wooded area where few settlers lived, he had already hired himself another lackey to drive his ransom note this evening to the Chateau L'Aragon. When that had been taken care of, he was ready to carry out the next step in this devious little scheme of his. If it all went according to his plans, he would be riding away from the state of California in another forty-eight hours as a very wealthy man. He was now churning with the wild anticipation of having his saddlebags filled with Aragon money and returning to Texas to enjoy a life of leisure.

One other tribute he planned to enjoy before he left this California countryside and that was the delectable charms of Mademoiselle Aimee Aragon.

He planned to leave no clues behind him when he left the

state, which meant he would have to take care of Cody and Buck before he settled up with them. They would not receive any more gold from him. The final payment they were expecting would not be gold, but a bullet in their backs.

Ross spurred the horse without any mercy as he galloped out of Sacramento, because the clouds looked threatening and he figured storms might be moving in over the coastline now.

An hour later, Ross emerged out of the wooded area into the small clearing where the shack was situated. He gave forth a wicked laugh, thinking how degrading it must be to the haughty Aimee to have to spend the night in such a place as this shack—and in the company of such a pair as Buck and Cody. He wondered if she had given way to the usual feminine panic of tears. He hoped so!

He hoped to see those flirting eyes of hers reduced to bloodshot weeping ones filled with panic. He wanted her to be wounded as painfully as she had stabbed his ego all those many weeks when he'd tried to play the role of the nice, gallant gentleman.

After he'd tethered his horse to the hitching post and walked down a dirt path that led to the steps of the shack, Ross tossed aside the cheroot he'd been puffing on.

As soon as he opened the door to walk into the front room, he heard the ear-piercing snoring of the two men. The air of the small quarters reeked of tobacco smoke and liquor. Moving on into the room, he found Buck curled up on a pallet of old ragged quilts there on the floor, and in the adjoining room, he saw Cody stretched out on a narrow cot.

God, they were a disgusting pair! A sharp qualm struck him and he wondered if he'd acted wisely in allowing such a dainty miss like Aimee to be at their mercy overnight. If they'd used her crudely or ruthlessly, she might not have survived such a night. An urgent need to check on her made him hastily turn away from the sight of Buck and Cody.

He unlocked the door, quietly opening it just enough to peer

382

inside the small room where the kerosene lamp was still burning dimly. Her clothes were still on as she lay there on her side, her lovely fair hair fanned out on the bed. There were no silk pillows resting underneath her head as he was sure she was used to in her fancy boudoir back at the Chateau L'Aragon. But she was sleeping and it seemed to be a peaceful sleep. He watched her sensuous breasts heave up and down in a normal tempo.

When he had satisfied himself beyond a shadow of a doubt that Aimee had not been used by the pair out there, he cautiously closed the door and locked it.

Now he must deal with the two out there. He knew he had to endure them another twenty-four hours, but hopefully that would pass quickly. In twenty-four hours, Ross Maynard figured he would have more gold in his coffer than he could have made in Texas in twenty-four years.

Paul Aragon would be more than willing to cough up a hefty sum to have his beloved daughter returned to him and Ross would willingly give her back for the sum of money he'd requested. Aimee meant nothing to him besides the money she could bring him and he wanted that moment to satisfy his evil lust before he took off for Texas.

He gave Buck a swift kick in his rump and walked over to the cot to give Cody a rough nudge in the ribs to bring him alive. Both men came alert with a dazed look on their faces as they stared up at him. A flowing stream of cusswords came from Cody as he sat up on the cot. Once again, Ross observed him, thinking what a disgusting sight he was!

Buck rose from the floor, scratching his head as he tried to make his eyes focus on the imposing figure towering above him. "Mornin', Mr. Bigler," Buck mumbled in a faltering voice as he was still feeling the drunken stupor from the night before.

"Good morning to you, Buck."

By now, Cody had managed to swing his husky body to the

383

side of the cot, and with great effort, he stood up.

"I see that the two of you managed to carry out the job I hired you to do. I've already checked to see how the young lady is. I was hoping that neither of you would have been foolish enough to use her solely for your own pleasure," Ross pointedly declared.

Buck quickly spoke up, "Oh no, sir, that little lady is just like she was when we took her."

"Be glad she is, my friend. If she had not been, you would be hanging from a rope right now. I would have seen to it." Ross's fierce eyes pierced the pair.

It was enough to convince Buck that he meant exactly what he said. Buck exchanged glances with his buddy Cody and Ross observed this.

He expected that Cody might have had some wild ideas about Aimee. He realized that he had to instill fear in him as he waited for the ransom money to come.

"I can't impress on the two of you how important it is to me that this young lady is not violated while I leave her in your care. If you do, then you will not receive one more penny from me. Do you understand me, Cody?"

"Sure! Sure I—we do," Cody assured him, daring not to look into those eyes of his.

"All right! This time tomorrow we shall all be a lot richer. The two of you can go your way and I shall go my way. There is no woman alive worth messing that up, eh?"

"Right, sir," Buck quickly chimed in. He would have eagerly agreed with anything this man was saying that would allow the young lady to be spared the brutal touch of Cody. He knew his buddy and what he was capable of with women. This pretty little lady was far too nice to have to suffer being degraded by the likes of his friend Cody.

"Glad to hear you say that, Buck. What about you, Cody?"

"Oh, yes, I agree with Buck," Cody stammered.

Ross did not believe that sonofabitch for a minute. But his

384

fierce eyes locked into Cody's as he prodded, "Somehow, Cody, you don't convince me you speak with sincerity. So I will warn you one more time to not cross me. If you do, you'll live to regret it."

Cody had never felt so threatened. The man he was looking at was dangerous, and Cody knew it!

Part Four

The Splendor of Love

A stand they must take,
these two zealous hearts!
Love's final quest,
they never shall part.

Sheila Northcott

Chapter 49

Beads of sweat spread over her forehead and down the sides of her face as Aimee awoke from her restless sleep. The rest of her body was drenched in perspiration. More than ever she realized what a luxury her baths were, with the perfumed oils and soap. She vowed if she ever got away from this miserable place and back to the Chateau L'Aragon, she would never complain about silly, mediocre things again.

She realized that she'd accepted all the luxuries of her life as natural and normal. Dear God, how little she truly knew about life! Now she suddenly realized how lucky she was to be the daughter of Paul and Lisette Aragon.

She arose to see that the dawn was breaking and it was cloudy. The skies were overcast and no bright sunshine was there outside her window when she slowly strolled over to look out. However, there was the pleasant sight of two strolling turtledoves just outside the windows, picking around in the tall grass surrounding the shack. As she stood there watching them, she heard the calling of a mockingbird over in one of the branches of the trees in the woods bordering the small clearing

389

where the shack stood.

As Aimee carefully surveyed the area now in the daylight hours, she saw some violet-colored wild verbenas there amid all the tall grass and weeds. Somehow, the sight of them and the doves lifted her spirits as well as her will. She did not feel as desolate and frightened anymore.

But all this was spoiled when she heard the clicking booted heels of someone leaving the cabin and when she saw the figure moving toward the hitching post, she recognized it as that of Fred Bigler. So she knew now who was the one responsible for her being here at this shack.

She gave out a soft moan of despair, "Oh, Papa, Papa, to think you encouraged this man to come calling on me when you would not have allowed Carlos Mateo's son to darken our door. Oh, dear God!"

She sunk down on the plank floor to give way to tears. Perhaps she was merely searching for some excuse to justify her feelings, but if only this stupid feud had not existed between their fathers, then maybe Mano would not have pretended to be someone other than himself.

She refused to believe that some of the words he'd so huskily told her in the heat of their passion were not sincere. Was she once again playing the fool? She didn't think so. Could a man's lips lie so convincingly? Could a man's arms hold a woman as his had held her unless they yearned to do so, pressing her so lovingly close to him as though he could not stand for her to be apart from him?

She recalled those jet-black eyes devouring her with the depth of his emotion as he let them slowly and sensuously dance over her. Could a man fake such a thing? she quizzed herself.

Maybe she'd never know the answer, but for now, she had to cling to something to give her courage to do what she must to be free of this prison. To think of Mano was the thing that gave her the courage she needed at this time. The other thing was this insane, wild idea that he would come to rescue her from this hell. Thoughts of Mano gave her strength.

She wanted to take that rock she'd found, slamming it with all the force within her against the window, but she knew that the noise would bring that pair of scoundrels in the next room upon her in a few seconds. She would be no match against the two of them. No, she must be patient and wait for the right moment, she urged herself.

On the other side of the room where Aimee was sequestered, the two men were having their own discussion about what they'd been told by Fred Bigler.

Buck was feeling greatly relieved as he stammered in that simpleton air of his, "God, Cody, I'm sure glad that fellow intends to turn her back to her folks once he gets his money. I'm surely glad to know that." He had a grin on his oafish face.

There was a smirk on Cody's face, but he didn't know whether or not he should make the effort to try to convince Buck the man was a liar. He felt it in his gut.

All that authority in Bigler's voice and his hints of threats had not impressed Cody. He still intended to take his pleasures with the beautiful girl before he left this place. All he had to do was keep old Buck cool and calm, so he didn't do something rash like blast his head off in an impulsive moment. This was Buck's nature and Cody knew it.

"Yeah, I'm glad, too, Buck, but what do you say we get us some grub? I'm hungry. How about you?" Cody inquired, rising up from the cot. Besides, he figured some food in his belly and some strong black coffee might help the miserable head he carried on his shoulders right now.

"I'm hungry, too, Cody, and I bet that little lady could use some food, too. She's a real lady, ain't she, Cody? Bet she lives in a fine house with servants and all. This must be a terrible thing for her to go through. Bet she's scared to death, Cody. She—she ain't like the women we know. You gotta' admit to that. I—I gotta say I feel damned bad about this—this job, Cody. Don't mind robbin' a man and the likes but I don't like doin' this to a fine lady like this one."

"Come on, Buck, let's fix some food and we'll talk about this later, eh?" Cody urged his buddy.

Cody realized that Buck was obviously beguiled by the fair-haired girl they held prisoner and he knew he was going to have to play him with caution if he didn't want to stir up a hornet's nest.

The two men fixed themselves a hearty breakfast, eating with relish. Buck appointed himself the one to serve Aimee her breakfast and Cody watched him go to the room with a plate ladened with eggs, ham, and his fresh baked biscuits. The eager, anxious expression on Buck's rugged face reminded him of a young lad taking his best girlfriend a bouquet of flowers.

Bigler had told them that they would be free to leave tomorrow when he returned to the cabin. Cody figured that he would restrain his lusty desires for the young lady until tonight, and then he'd make damned sure Buck was sleeping soundly.

All the sweet dreams Armand Aragon had allowed himself to enjoy the night before came to a stark reality the next morning when he happened to observe the most intimate scene in the gardens of the Chateau L'Aragon. He'd glanced out his window to see the lovely Jolie in the gardens in the early morning hours, hastily dressing himself in his usual workday garb so he could rush down the stairs to join her.

Never had Armand flung his clothes on so swiftly, dashing down the steps to rush out into his mother's gardens.

But just as he came to the trellis entwined with wisteria and was about to call out to Jolie, he saw his brother emerge through the arbor. He also called out to Jolie, and she came rushing across the thick carpeted lawn to go to him. Emile's hands reached out to take her dainty ones in his. Then he urged her gently to move closer to him and she did.

Armand stood there painfully watching his brother's head bend down to meet her lips with a kiss. He knew now that Jolie could never be his, for his brother had already claimed her. He moved slowly from the secluded spot behind the trellis to leave the garden. Any thoughts he might have had about Jolie there in the serene quiet of his mother's garden had to be forgotten forever.

He headed up the path that would lead him to the hillside trail to go to the winery. This was the life fate had surely deemed he should have, Armand told himself. It was a most fulfilling life, and perhaps he should have known he was merely dreaming to have thought anything would have come from that very brief encounter with Jolie last night. But he had dared to dream for one precious night and it had been truly wonderful.

By the time he reached the massive double doors of the stone-structured building and fumbled in his pocket for the key to fit into the heavy lock, he had accepted the reality he had just witnessed. The truth was he was happy for Emile that he'd found himself such a fine young lady as Jolie.

Just as he was about to insert the key in the heavy lock, he noticed the folded slip of paper secured in the iron handle attached to the heavy wooden door. After Armand read the scribbled note, he never turned the key in the lock. Instead, he turned hastily around to run down the trail he'd just traveled to get to the winery.

His heart was pounding wildly as he thought about his beautiful sister in the hands of such scoundrels as these men must be to snatch a lovely lady for a ransom. Such things should not be happening in this civilized countryside, but they obviously did. Any pain or heartache he might have been harboring about the lost love he'd been anticipating the night before was quickly forgotten.

As he neared the gateway of the stone-enclosed gardens of the estate, he heard the galloping hooves of a rider approaching. The sight of the fine stallion was quickly recognized as the one belonging to the man he'd first come to know as Mark Perez but who he now knew was Mano Mateo.

He had no time to waste on him, Armand decided. It was his father he urgently needed to see. These devils who had poor little Aimee in their custody were giving the Aragons little time to gather together a very hefty sum for their pickup this evening or else they promised to kill Aimee.

Right now, his father needed no encounter with the likes of Mateo. This ransom note would be enough to make him distraught, so Armand decided to linger there by the gate. He would tend to Mano and see that he rode away from the estate. No Mateo was needed at this harrowing time around the Chateau L'Aragon.

Armand stood, watching the high-spirited stallion approach him. Being an admirer of fine horses, he had to admit to himself that Mano's horse had to be the most magnificent beast he'd ever seen in his life. The Latin had an expertise in picking himself a fine animal.

As Mano yanked up on the reins to come to an abrupt halt, Armand called out a cool, casual greeting, "Good day, Mateo. What brings you to Chateau L'Aragon?" It was hard for Armand to be blunt and unfriendly to Mano, for he had genuinely liked him when he thought he was Mark Perez. He had been beholden to him for rescuing his sister that night so long ago. Now, as the two of them locked eyes with one another, Armand found it hard to believe that this man did not sincerely care for his sister, having witnessed them together in the days that followed his rescuing her and bringing her home safely and unharmed.

In that straightforward air of his, which Armand would have expected, Mano candidly answered, "I come to see Aimee, Armand. I—I care for her, and the name of Mateo can't change that." There, in his piercing black eyes, Armand saw the reflection of a pleading that convinced him Mano spoke the truth. Try as he might, Armand could not help but believe him!

"Aimee is not here, Mano. She has not been home now for over twenty-four hours," her brother told him. He took a couple of steps away from the gate to stand by the side of the stallion, where Mano still sat astride the saddle.

"Read this and you will understand what I am talking about. I just came across it stuck in the winery door. In fact, I've yet to show it to my father. He will be most upset, but then this family has not had a moment's peace since this all began."

An agony Mano had never known before seized him. As he read the note he felt like a dagger was turning in his gut. Every nerve in his firm muscled body tensed, his teeth clenching as he read the message. Never had he experienced such a fury as the one that was brewing in him by the time he handed it back to Armand.

If Armand had ever harbored any doubts that this man did not care for his sister, the truth became clearly evident now when he spoke with such absolute honesty, "We must find her, Armand, and we must get the one responsible for this act. The one picking up this ransom money must be followed tonight. I shall do that."

"You—you do care for Aimee very much, don't you? Father was wrong when he said you were playing Aimee for a little fool—for a family revenge?"

"He was never more wrong, Armand. There was never anything in my mind about a stupid family vendetta. I could never have cared less about that, Armand. I love Aimee—I have since the moment we met. Your sister means more to me than anything else in this whole crazy world."

Such a declaration was enough to convince Armand he meant exactly what he said. Besides the words he spoke, there was the look of anguish on Mano's face that was real and true.

The husky Frenchman gave him an understanding nod of his head. "Wait for me over at the edge of the clearing—there by the woods, Mano. I will come to you in an hour's time and tell you what my father's plans will be. I don't think that this is the time for the two of you to meet. But I do believe you, so I will come to you and tell you what my father decides to do," Armand said to him.

"I'll be there waiting for you, amigo." He turned Demonio

around to ride away. It really didn't matter what Paul Aragon decided in this matter, he thought to himself. He'd search this whole California countryside over until he found the woman he loved. Believing Armand to be a man of his word, he would wait to see what their plans were to rescue Aimee from the clutches of the bastard who'd done this dastardly deed.

Now he knew why he'd been so anxious to return to La Casa Grande and leave Half Moon Bay. Aimee was calling out to him to help her. It was her sweet, soft voice that was calling out to him.

He rode away from the country estate of the Aragon family to go to the spot in the woods where Armand would join him later. Never before had he felt the torture and fear that was flooding him now.

Silently, he prayed that she was safe and unharmed. He vowed, "Oh, *querida*, I promise you I'll save you."

Could his fervent vows carry over the distance dividing them and give her the courage and support she must surely be needing right now? he wondered.

God, he had to believe that they would or he'd go crazy with worry about her!

Chapter 50

Never could he remember such a thick, dense fog settled in over the hillsides and valleys here in San Jose, Mano thought, surveying the countryside. At Half Moon Bay this wasn't unusual but it was in this area. He was having a hellish time keeping track of the man he sought to follow. He would lose sight of him and luckily he would find the moving figure once again in the thick veil of swirling smoky fog.

He could not allow this pea soup haze to separate him from this man, who'd just picked up the ransom money for Aimee's safe return to the bosom of her family. Mano did not kid himself at all about the man he was now following. He was only the messenger and the carrier. The man he sought was now waiting for the money to be brought to him. That was the one he wanted.

The man was traveling to the north-northeast, and Mano figured it was around the Sacramento area he was heading.

Mano did not dare take his eyes off the man for a minute, for fear he would lose sight of him as he rode through the dense forest. Who was the one he was meeting to hand over the bounty he'd just collected from Paul Aragon for the release of his daughter? Mano pulsed with an insatiable, curious rage about this person.

For two long hours he trailed this fellow, and it was a draining, exhausting two hours for Mano. For a man with his impatient nature, it was a most trying time indeed.

Now the skies above him became more threatening. The rumblings of thunder could be heard across the way and flashes of lightning could be seen. These dark, gloomy skies had been hovering overhead ever since he'd left the woods near Chateau L'Aragon, after Armand had come to him to tell him what they planned to do about the message they'd received.

To wait out the time he must endure until the messenger was due to return to pick up the demanded ransom money, Mano had ridden back to La Casa Grande. However, he went no farther than the kitchen, securing some of Minerva's food to put in his saddlebags for his jaunt. Since there were a few hours to wait until darkness fell over the countryside, Mano indulged himself in the hearty meal Minerva had prepared for him.

"You take care, picaro," she'd cautioned him. "You don't go get yourself killed. But I know you must go to the poor little senorita and save her. What horrible, horrible people must have done this!"

"I plan to be very careful, Minerva. If I'm not, then I can't save Aimee and get her away from these varmints if I'm dead." Turning aside from that serious air, he reverted to that happy-go-lucky nature of his by teasing Minerva, "Besides, I want to be around for a long time to come so I can pester you, Minerva."

She'd tousled his black hair as she walked around the back of his chair, but there was nothing lighthearted or casual as she spoke to him, "I want you around, Mano, for a long, long time."

He turned around in his chair to gaze up into her warm, adoring eyes. This look of special love had been there in the old mestizo servant's eyes and face for as long as he could recall.

How comforting it had been to him throughout the years to always have her to count on in his times of need and stress. In her way, she had made up for the things he'd missed by not having a mother to gather him up in her arms and comfort him during his youth.

"For you, I shall be most careful and cautious, Minerva," he assured her, patting her wrinkled, rough hands.

He'd bid her farewell, his packet of food in his hand, to go back to the stable to start on his venture. It was to be the most challenging mission he'd ever set out on. He knew he would either be returning as the happiest man in California or he would be the most lost soul in all this world without Aimee by his side.

Destiny could not be so cruel to him! he told himself.

Aimee went through the ritual of eating the food Buck brought to her shortly after she'd seen Fred Bigler ride away from the shack. Maybe it was because she was famished from the tossing and turning she'd done during the night, but the food Buck had served her was tasty.

He was receptive to her plea that one of the small windows be opened to allow some fresh air to permeate the room. "Leave it to me, missy, and I'll get them nails out of there later and crack it a bit for you," he assured her.

"Oh, Buck, I would be ever so grateful to you. I'm—I'm not foolish enough to try to escape and go into that woods out there. How would a poor helpless miss like me possibly survive? Why, mercy, I would be committing myself to a sure death." She gave forth a most pathetic expression, which wrung Buck's heart out with compassion.

"I'm glad to hear you say that, miss, 'cause you are absolutely right. You'd not make it," Buck stammered in that faltering manner he assumed whenever he was as stimulated and affected as he was now by the lovely sight of Aimee Aragon.

"You've been most kind to me, Buck, and I thank you. I—I don't know what all this is about, and I shall not ask you to explain to me either, but I've done no one any harm to bring out such wrath. I can't imagine why anyone would hate me so much as to want to hurt me or my family so."

Dear God, she had a way about her that made Buck feel like the devil himself! So sweet and innocent she looked, sitting on the edge of the bed. So pure and childlike she appeared, clasping her dainty hands in her lap. Buck looked upon this fair-haired lady and wondered why in God's name he'd ever agreed to such a scheme as this. Feeling this way, he got angry and blamed Cody for pulling him into this shabby, seedy fiasco.

Buck was so affected by Aimee that he stood silently before her for a moment before he sought to speak. When he did, he could have been standing there making his confession before a preacher. "Miss, I'm not much—never have been, I'm sorry to say—but I can tell you this, and that is I ain't goin' to let anything happen to you while I'm around."

Those deep blue eyes of hers looked up at him and there was trust there. Buck saw it. Her voice was soft and sincere when she answered him, "I believe you, Buck. I truly do. There is good in you, Buck, and I see it there in your eyes."

A slow, lazy smile came to Buck's weathered face. She made him feel an exaltation he'd never known before. For a lady of quality to put her faith and trust in the likes of him was something Buck never expected to experience in his lifetime. Dear Lord, it was a glorious feeling, and he'd never forget this golden moment as long as he lived!

He swelled with an enormous pride and could think of nothing to say to her. So he just started to move backward toward the door. Overcome by the emotions he was feeling, he was like the bashful, embarrassed schoolboy as he once again stammered, "I'll—I'll get that window opened for you, Miss Aimee. As long as Cody don't find out, it will be all right."

"I don't want you to get in trouble with your friend, Buck," she told him. But as she said it, she knew that he was her only hope in escaping this place. She also knew that he was a simpleton who she had to use to gain her freedom.

"Don't you worry about that. Cody ain't always as smart as he thinks he is. I ain't as dumb as he figures me to be. Everything is going to be all right."

He left the room and Aimee was once again alone. Left by herself, she began to think, her thoughts drifting back to the happy times of her life. The happiest times had been those spent with Mano.

Mano Mateo! That devastating Latin, with his black roaming eyes, who could thrill her and excite her like no other man ever had. Mano, with his huge exploring hands, who could caress her and touch her in a way no other man had ever stimulated her.

It was Mano who had taken her through the threshold of sweet innocence, to know the exciting wonders of becoming a woman—a most sensuous woman! He'd sparked passions she did not know she possessed and he'd stirred a wild, exciting ecstasy she did not know was possible.

How could she ever rid herself of a man such as Mano? It was impossible and she knew it. As long as she lived and breathed, she could never be free of him.

A shadow moving outside her window caught her attention and thoughts of Mano were put aside for the moment. She saw it was the tall, lean figure of Buck doing exactly what he'd promised he'd do. He was going to release the nail so that the window might be raised. He gave her a broad grin as he went about the chore and she returned a smile of her own, giving him an understanding nod of her head.

When the job was finished and she saw his weathered hands raise the window a couple of inches, she rushed over to absorb the welcoming breeze the space allowed. Dear Lord, it felt wonderful!

Quietly, she murmured softly, "Oh, thank you, Buck. Thank you so very much!" She inhaled deeply of the light gust of refreshing air. But a noise just outside her door made her suddenly turn around, and Buck denoted the startled expression on her lovely face. Without any hesitation, he dropped the hammer to the ground and rushed to the front door of the shack.

Instinctively, he knew it had to be Cody at her door that would have made her react as she did. He swept through the door to find his buddy pacing along the plank floor.

"You weren't gone long, Buck. Thought you said you were going for a walk in the woods. Tired of the cabin, you told me," Cody muttered, trying to not reflect his disgruntled feelings that his cohort had appeared so soon. He was hoping Buck had slipped the flask out with him and had gone into the woods to sit out there, enjoying the whiskey.

Obviously he had figured Buck wrong, he realized. Actually, he hadn't been able to figure him out at all since they'd arrived here at the shack. He was not acting in his usual way. Last night, Buck had been far more in control than he was, and Cody had to admit that he had been the one drunk as a skunk.

"Ah, gosh, I decided I didn't want to walk in them woods and pick up a lot of ticks. Decided to save my energy."

"You are getting lazy, Buck."

"Guess you could be right, Cody. When this job is finished, I might just get very lazy, I'm thinking," Buck gave out a light chuckle. All the time he was engaging Cody in conversation, he was smugly thinking to himself that he was giving that sweet little lady a more pleasant feeling having that window ajar. The other gratifying thing to him right now was that his hasty return to the shack had kept Cody from trying to go through that door.

There was no doubt what Cody had on that mind of his, and by the Jesus, he was not going to get the job done, Buck firmly decided.

He had committed himself to protect the little Aimee, and if it meant that he had to kill Cody, then he was going to do it. At least, he could say that he'd done one decent, worthy act in his life. Even if Cody ended up killing him, he could die knowing that he had tried to protect the fine young lady. That would make him happy.

Buck watched Cody pace nervously around the room and knew the itch bothering him. When Cody got this way, he got mean. Buck knew well what a menacing bastard his buddy could be. To get Cody's thoughts off Aimee, Buck remarked, "Won't be too long now, Cody, before we can be on our way from the way this Bigler was talking this morning before he left. We'll have our saddlebags full of money and we can have ourselves some high living, right?"

"Right! That's for me—some high living with some real pretty ladies, good whiskey, and some high stakes poker games."

"Yeah, Cody. That sounds good to me, too," Buck chimed in. "Where—where do you want to head out for, Cody? Want to go to San Francisco? I'm—I'm a little tired of Sacramento."

Cody stood there thoughtfully for a moment before he spoke. "You know, I think you got a good idea there, Buck. Maybe we should go to San Francisco."

"Sounds good to me, Cody." By now, Buck had ambled over to the old wooden table to take a seat. He pulled out a deck of cards and started shuffling them. "Maybe we should do a little practicing, eh Cody?"

Reluctantly, Cody strolled over to the table and sat down. Might as well play cards, he decided, to pass some time. Buck was going to stick to him like a leech, and with him underfoot, he could hardly do what he ached to do with that pretty gal in the next room.

"Deal the cards, Buck," he told his pal.

Buck had a sly grin on his face, but Cody didn't suspect what he was thinking. Maybe Cody thought he was dumb but this was one time when he'd outfoxed him.

It had been a long time since Buck had felt so good about himself.

Chapter 51

Rain pelted the coastline of California and moved eastward to the inland area. The heavy moisture-ladened clouds hanging over the region of San Jose at dawn gave way to torrents of rain by midday. Rainy days always depressed Lisette but never as much as today. As hard as she tried, she could not settle herself into her daily routine.

When her son had come into the dining room as they were having their breakfast to show them the ransom note left at the winery, the rest of the morning had been like a foggy daze to Lisette.

Quickly, Paul had excused himself from the table to go into his study with Armand and Emile. There, the three of them had spent the next hour. It was only after they had emerged from the study that Paul came to her to explain exactly what was going on and the action they were preparing to take to rescue Aimee from her captors.

Suddenly, Lisette found herself all alone in the gloomy stone house as the men of the Aragon family left to go to the winery. Never had she felt so utterly deserted and miserable, with tension engulfing her. She sought the solace she needed in her little sewing room, and it was Jolie who came to her to console her and give her comfort.

She told herself that she would never forget how sweet and dear Aimee's little maid had been when she was so in need of understanding. The last thing in the world that she needed this harrowing day was the arrival of an unexpected guest.

When Hetty ushered Paul's sister, Denise, into her sewing room this stormy day, Lisette's grace and charm failed her. "*Mon Dieu*, Denise, what brings you to California?" she bluntly inquired.

The petite French lady swayed in that usual way of hers toward the floral overstuffed chair to sit down. She gave forth that engaging smile of hers as she exclaimed, "I would not call that a gracious welcome, Lisette."

Lisette felt very badly about her poor manners, quickly explaining the torment she was enduring at the moment. She also noted something else when she was explaining to Denise why she had been so rude. "You know that this is not my way. I am just so worried about Aimee that I am not myself."

Denise reached over to give her hand an affectionate pat of understanding. "I know that, Lisette. I am sorry that I did not have time to let you know I was coming."

Lisette looked at the lovely lady sitting there in her sewing room. Her delicate features looked strained and weary, but that could have been from her long journey across the vast ocean she'd just crossed. But there was more grey in that lovely, thick styled mass of Denise's hair. Her deep blue-amethyst eyes had no luster or bright vivacious sparkle to them, like those of the woman Lisette had always known. Something was wrong with Denise. She was ill, Lisette realized.

Denise was always a most perceptive person and she'd seen her sister-in-law carefully scrutinizing her. "You know why I've come, don't you, Lisette? I'm ill. To be completely honest with you, I am dying but I don't want Paul to know. As I've kept your secret all these years, I request that you keep mine."

Lisette gave her a nod of her head. "I won't say a word, Denise. May I ask . . . tell me, how long—?"

Denise interrupted her stammering query, "How long I have? Any time now, Lisette. I was told before I left Paris I might have four months, so as you can see by now I have only a few weeks. I had to come, Lisette. Surely you can understand that I wished to see my daughter one last time. How many people have the privilege to be forewarned?"

Lisette could hardly breathe and her heart was pounding erratically. "Will you tell her, Denise?"

"Heavens, no! Why would I dare do that, Lisette? You are the one who has been her mother all these years. I can never forget what you did for me. There I was, six months pregnant, and you came to Paris to attend the funeral of your father. You told me your sad news and I told you about my dilemma. We made our pact and we have both rejoiced in that secret pact all these years because it has given us all such joy and happiness, *n'est ce pas?*"

"Oh, *oui*, Denise, I—I have never regretted that binding secret we've shared throughout the years. I've prayed that you hadn't," Lisette gave out a sigh.

"Ah, Lisette, I love you so deeply for what you did to give my brother such happiness. Aimee is an Aragon. She is my daughter and Paul considers she is his and he is happy. You saved me in a time of great turmoil and torment. I shall love you until the day I die. I would never tell Aimee I was her mother and cause her pain. But I do wish to see her one last time." Tears flowed down the face of this lady who'd lived her life to the fullest. For a woman like Denise, whose beauty had always been so ravishing and alluring, she knew now that while it opened the door to the most lavishing pleasures, it also brought forth the price of endless pain.

"And I shall love you, Denise, until the day I die, because you gave me the most wonderful gift I've ever had. I love Aimee as much as the sons I've bore. Armand and Emile are so

406

dear to me, but in some ways, Aimee is even dearer."

The two women reached out to one another and locked in an embrace. For a long moment, there was no need for words to be spoken, for they understood the depth of emotions rushing through them. It was Lisette who broke the silence as she spoke softly to the sobbing Denise, "I'm so very glad you're here, Denise. I—I need you."

With tearstained eyes looking into Lisette's blue ones, Denise confessed, "I guess I just wanted to be with my family. I was scared." It was going to be much easier and more comforting for her to die here in this California countryside than it would have been if she were all alone in Paris. She found herself at peace, and this was what she had sought when she'd started out on this long, exhausting voyage across the seas.

She knew that she would see the lovely face of that daughter of hers one more time before she died. She just knew it! No harm would come to Aimee! Denise felt most strongly about that.

There was only one sad thought troubling Denise. It was that she would not be buried in the soil of her beloved France. But she would lay here at Chateau L'Aragon and her daughter could bring flowers to her grave. She knew Aimee had adored her as her *Tante* Denise and that was enough to bring joy to Denise's heart.

Darkness gathered over the California countryside, with the thick, heavy clouds still present. The heavy rain had now subsided and a light mist fell on the woods where Ross Maynard sat astride his horse, awaiting his messenger to arrive in the forest surrounding the shack. He had no intention of enlightening him about the shack a short distance away.

Besides, this secluded woods would provide the ideal surrounding for Ross to put a bullet in the messenger's back as he rode away with his reward for doing the chore for him. He had no intention of leaving behind any witnesses when he left this place to ride toward Texas—and that included Aimee Aragon.

He had purposely picked a young drifter to be his messenger, because he knew his absence from the nearby town would never be missed or investigated. As he waited there now impatiently, he could not even recall the young dude's name. It really didn't matter anyway.

Nervously, he pulled out his gold watch to check the time. If the man had picked up the ransom as scheduled and ridden directly to this appointed spot in the woods, he should be due to arrive by now. But Ross tried to remain calm by reminding himself that heavier storms could have been brewing southward this evening.

He dismounted from his horse, tying the reins to a sapling so he might stretch his legs to walk around. In the quietness of the woods, every little sound or movement could be heard. But the sound of approaching hooves was not to be heard by Ross as he was hoping.

Time seemed to drag this night. He could have sworn that a half hour had passed since he had last pulled out his pocket watch to check, but it had been a mere fifteen minutes.

He knew he was overanxious, but what he was asking himself now was what if the dude did not appear with the bounty? What did he do then? Did he just hightail it for Texas, leaving Aimee there at the shack with Buck and Cody? Perhaps that was what he should do. How long did he wait here, pacing in this damned damp woods? Was this scheme to go awry too?

After he had walked back and forth, making a path in the carpet of grass for what seemed like an eternity to Ross, a kind of panic set in.

In that same instant, his alert ears heard the welcoming sound of an approaching rider and he came alive. He moved back to the sapling where he'd secured his horse. It was a delight to his eyes to see the young fellow he'd just hired a couple of nights ago moving his horse through the trees. The grin on the man's face told Ross that everything had gone according to his plans. The bounty had been collected and the mission was successful.

That brought forth a broad smile on Ross's face as he greeted the young man. In less than some fifteen minutes, the two men had stood there in the woods, having a very brief conversation. Ross handed him his fee for the services performed.

The young drifter stood there, amazed that such a sum had been paid for a task that had proved to be so easy. He was in a state of complete bliss and exhilaration as he stammered his thanks to Ross.

"I don't reckon we'll be crossing paths again, sir, but I can tell you that you surely have made me one happy man. Guess I've got nothing else to say, so I'll be on my way so you can be on yours. Thanks again, sir," he told Ross, bubbling over with elation about such a hefty sum to stick in his pockets.

"Glad you're happy, son," Ross replied, thinking to himself that his happiness was going to be very short-lived.

He watched the young man mount up and spur the mare into action. When he had moved about twenty-five feet away from where Ross stood, Ross's pistol took aim and the trigger was pulled. The explosion echoed through the quietness of the woods and the young man fell to the ground. Cool and casually, Ross walked over to take back the money he'd paid the young man only moments ago.

Mounting his own horse, he was now ready to ride to the shack. The same fate that had befallen the young man there, lying on the earth of the woods, was what awaited Buck and Cody.

In the misting rains and gathering fog, Mano had lost sight of the rider he was trailing, but the explosion of gunfire made him halt Demonio. He was traveling too far to the east. The gunshot he'd heard made him veer back into that direction.

By the time he'd corrected his direction, getting on the trail that would lead him to the young man laying there on the ground with a bullet in his back, he had lost a good half hour. There was nothing this man could tell him, anyway, because he was dead.

Mano looked around the dense woods, pondering which direction he should take, for a black darkness now settled over the area. All he had to rely on was that rare instinct of his, which Phil Cabrillo swore he had. He prayed old Phil was right. There was no doubt in Mano's mind now that he was dealing with a cold-blooded killer.

He mounted back up on Demonio and set out on his quest. He only hoped that he was taking the right trail in this thick, dense forest of tall, towering trees. He heard the low moaning call of a night bird as he spurred Demonio into action. Over in a low-hanging branch of a pine tree was an owl hooting. Right now, he was calling on all the powers he possessed and all the wisdom he'd learned from old Phil to guide him to his beloved Aimee.

He had to find her before any harm came to her.

He reined Demonio to the north, hoping he was taking the right trail, which would lead him to the woman he desperately sought and whom he'd love all the days of his life.

Somehow, he knew he was going in the right direction, even though it was too dark to tell if a rider had recently come this way.

If Mano could have seen the trail, he would have been able to tell that Ross Maynard had been down this very same path a short while ago. But that was utterly impossible on a night like this, with no moon shining down and the skies so overcast with heavy clouds.

Mano veered to the east to get away from the thick covering

of underbrush. He could not have known it at that time but he had taken the wrong path to the cabin where Aimee was held a captive.

Ross Maynard had already arrived at the destination that Mano sought to free the lady he loved. He was now sitting at the old oak table with Buck and Cody, sharing a glass of whiskey with the pair.

"Guess it is time to pay you two the money I promised when we struck our deal, eh?" Ross said, giving forth a friendly, cordial smile.

"Guess so," Cody replied.

Buck watched the two of them, and something about the gent sitting there talking to Cody made him nervous. He didn't trust him. In that stammering voice of his, he abruptly declared, "I—I gotta go outside for a minute. All right?"

"Sure, Buck, you go ahead and go outside," Cody dismissed his oafish buddy. That blockhead was really not needed now, Cody told himself. He and Bigler could complete their deal, and it was probably best that Buck not be around. He'd give Buck a share to satisfy him and Cody figured he'd keep more than a fair share for himself. Buck was such a dumb idiot he'd never know that he'd been cheated.

As soon as Buck had gone out the door, Ross started pulling out the impressive bounty from his saddlebag to dole out to Cody his share for the job he'd done.

"God Almighty!" Cody gave out a sigh. "Never saw such a nice little bundle for such little work."

"Told you, Cody, that this was a job that required very little blood, sweat, or tears, didn't I?"

"You sure did, and now that I see this I damned well believe you! Lord!" Cody started fingering the bounty nervously. So engrossed was he in the fortune lying there on the table that Cody did not notice Ross's hand had not been idle. Now his hand was gripping his pistol and his finger was caressing the trigger.

411

Those beady eyes of his were looking at Cody's face. Without blinking an eyelash, Ross raised the pistol and aimed it directly at Cody. His finger pressed the trigger to ignite the explosion, and an acrid aroma permeated the small room.

An evil smirk creased Ross's face as he looked at the man slumped there at the table. Disgust washed over him.

Chapter 52

The heartless Ross Maynard sat for a moment, staring across the table at the still figure of Cody before he moved out of the chair to dim the lamplight. He felt no hint of remorse, for this was his unmerciful nature.

The roaring sound of the exploding pistol set forth a flood of panic in Aimee because she knew that Fred Bigler had returned to the shack. She'd stood with her ear pressed against the door to hear what they were discussing. She recognized the voice as belonging to the man she knew as Bigler, and she could also detect that he was having a discussion with Cody. Just before she'd gone back over to sit down on the bed for a brief moment, she'd not heard Buck joining in their conversation.

Now she could only pray that it was not Buck who had received that bullet, for then there would be no one to defend her as she felt certain he had done for the last forty-eight hours. She could only endure the tormenting mystery of who the victim was outside her door as she listened to the movement of shuffling feet around the room. Suddenly, she felt herself trembling, and as much as she tried to remain calm, she could not control herself.

She moved from the door over to the windows. Did she dare to open that window all the way and leap outside, or would the sound make Bigler rush into the room? She had to chance it, she told herself. If only she could get to the woods, she could hide from him, with the darkness helping to conceal her. But when she tried to force the window higher, it would not budge.

She didn't notice the figure in the shadows of the shrubs at the corner of the shack. He was trembling as violently as she was.

When Buck had excused himself from the presence of Ross and Cody, he'd sneaked away quietly to observe the pair there in the front room. He'd witnessed everything that had gone on, seeing the man he knew as Bigler kill Cody in cold blood. Buck had watched in shocked horror as he'd pulled the trigger with that evil smirk on his face, never even blinking an eye.

Now he knew why he had been so nervous and tense after Bigler had arrived. He wasn't so dumb—not half as dumb as poor old Cody had been tonight.

When he knew there was nothing more he could do for Cody, he'd slipped around the shack to get to the windows, so he could see if Bigler had come through the door of the room where Aimee was. If the bastard dared to lay a hand on her, Buck planned to use his pistol on him just like he'd used it on Cody.

Back in the woods, Mano heard the burst of gunfire across the way. The sound alerted him that he was slightly off the trail he sought to get to Aimee. It spurred him into quick action and Demonio sensed how his master wished him to perform. He moved accordingly, through the numerous trees of the forest at a much faster pace.

As black as the night was, Mano could tell that he was coming to a clearing and his hopes surged. In another few minutes he knew he was right and he halted Demonio, not wanting to alert anyone around the area of his approach.

Dismounting the stallion, he led Demonio with him as he moved noiselessly over the ground of the woods. His searching black eyes caught sight of a small cabin and he took notice of the three horses secured to the hitching post. So he was going to be dealing with three scoundrels to free the woman he loved!

It made him realize just how guarded and cunning he must be if he were to subdue all three of them. Securing Demonio to the trunk of a nearby tree, Mano decided to go the rest of the way on foot.

There was only a dim light in one of the rooms, Mano saw, so he moved to the back of the shack. When he saw that this part of the grounds gave no signs of a threat, he started to move around the corner, scrutinizing every inch of the area.

He stopped short, moving back around the corner. A tall, lean figure of a man stood there with a pistol poised ready to take aim.

As he moved up on the man, he heard the glorious sound of Aimee's voice speaking to someone inside the room. He could not hear each and every word she spoke, but he did hear her say, "You are a despicable bastard! Did you know that?"

That was his girl! He was overjoyed to hear the fire and spirit in that sweet, sweet voice of hers. His heart pounded wildly now, knowing she was not harmed in such a way to render her helpless. From the way she was speaking, she was far from helpless. He could even grin as he recalled that spitfire temper of hers. She was never more beautiful than she was when those deep blue-purple eyes were flashing with fire. He could envision that face, even though he couldn't see it.

Buck never knew what hit him from the back as he slumped to the ground, drowning in a pit of blackness. Mano figured he had just cut the odds down to two against one. He moved closer to the window as the man there with Aimee was giving forth an evil roar of laughter as he taunted her, "My, my, didn't know you had such strong feelings for old Cody in there. Last couple of days you got to feeling close to him, eh? He bragged about how he had a way with women."

Aimee glared at him as she hissed, "Shut your filthy mouth! So it was Cody you murdered?"

Ross took a couple of steps toward her to stand near the nightstand where the dimly lit lamp sat. "Yes, it was Cody, and I'll take care of Buck, too, Miss High and Mighty," he snarled at her. "You and your snobbish French airs need to be taught a lesson and taken down a notch or two. I'm not used to a woman turning her back on me like you did, Aimee Aragon."

She was in a dangerous position and she knew it. At this moment, she was too far from the edge of the bed where she'd placed the club of timber. "So that is what all this is about, Fred?" As she spoke she slowly moved from the foot of the bed around the corner, and Ross thought he detected fear in her reflection as she cowered away from him to put some distance between them. This was exactly what he wanted from Aimee. He wanted her to tremble and shrink with fright.

"It is a part of it, but not all by any means, sweetie."

It was hard for Mano to restrain himself, but he was glad he had prolonged the impulse to rush right into the house because he knew he would be facing only one man. What really shocked him was the man he was facing. While he had no admiration for the man he'd met there at his father's fiesta with some of his friends, he would never have expected him to pull such a dastardly act as this.

However, it mattered not to Mano who the man might have been. At that moment, he secretly vowed that he would kill him for what he'd done to Aimee.

He saw Fred moving toward Aimee with that vile, lustful look on his face and a lecherous glint in his eyes as he told her, "Well, sweetie, tonight is going to be a hell of a lot different than the night of the Governor's Ball. You see, I'm going to take my fill of you and you can't stop me."

However, it was not Aimee's protesting voice Ross was to hear but the deep, threatening voice of a very angry man just outside the window, his silver-plated pistol pointing directly at him. "All you'll get, amigo, is your gut filled with lead. Now, you do exactly as I tell you if you wish to live another second."

Aimee swelled with overwhelming elation that she felt giddy. She knew that voice. It could be no one but Mano standing out there in the darkness, so very near that she felt herself began to tremble with the happiness flooding her body and soul.

"Move away from the door, Bigler, and to the far corner of the room and, Aimee, you get out of the room. Come to me while I keep my pistol aimed at this bastardo's heart."

Ross knew this was a man who gave no quarter, so he dared not trifle with him as he saw that pistol pointed directly at him. The authority in that deep voice was enough to convince Maynard the man meant every word he spoke.

Like obedient children, Ross and Aimee did exactly as Mano demanded. After Aimee dashed through the door, Ross knew his life wouldn't be worth a cent once she was safely outside the shack and by Mano's side. His only chance lay in the next few minutes and he was a man desperate. When he heard Aimee lovingly greet the man standing out there in the dark, Ross figured her presence by his side would provide the moment's distraction he needed to reach out for the keroseme lamp and toss it into the feather bed. Immediately, the old mattress ignited and flames began to leap and blaze. Ross wasted no time getting out the door and to the back of the house.

No one had to tell Mano that he had allowed his eyes to stray from Bigler when he saw the rushing figure of Aimee stumbling across the grounds. When she had reached his side, he could not resist allowing one of his strong arms to snake out to clasp her to him. As he held her that brief second, he felt her trembling body. She seemed so fragile and weak. Mano pressed her closer and it was at that moment he failed to see Ross making a hasty getaway.

Mano had a decision to make and he made it without any hesitation. He held the women he loved now safely in his arms and he could not leave her alone to go chasing after Bigler. But that didn't mean Bigler wasn't going to pay the price for his sins.

But for now, Aimee and her well-being were the most important things.

When he'd last cast his black eyes upon her, she had glared at him with such fury. But now she was staring up at him with a look he'd never before seen on her lovely face as she remained silent.

All he could think was that what she had endured the last two days could have been enough to put her in a state of shock, but she hadn't sounded like that when she was bravely rebuking Bigler. For a brief moment, he just let his strong arms hold her close to him. He figured she had to see the deep love shining there in his eyes as he looked down at her.

As he held her, he heard the galloping hooves of Bigler's horse moving away as if demons were chasing him. Let the bastard think he was getting away, Mano told himself. Let him live in his fool's paradise. He didn't care how long it took, Mano vowed, but he would find him and deal with him just as soon as he had Aimee safely deposited back at Phil's cottage. It was far closer than the Chateau L'Aragon.

He was the first one to break their silence as he asked her, "Are you all right, *querida?*"

She wanted to shout out her joy of feeling his comforting arms around her. It was such a glorious feeling! How good it felt to be in his strong arms again, enclosed with such warmth! She cared not what his name was nor would she ever fret about that again as long as she lived. It was how he made her feel and how she felt about him that was important.

"I am fine, Mano, *mon cher*," she sighed. Her term of endearment meant everything to Mano and he did not question that she meant it. Aimee's eyes never lied, so he knew that she felt the same depth of love for him. This was all he needed to know to make him the happiest man on the face of the earth. Fred Bigler could wait, because he would be taken care of in due time.

A crooked grin creased his face and he swooped her up in his arms to walk to the spot where he had secured Demonio. He wanted to leave this place behind them just as soon as possible and he knew she had to feel the same way, too. But he could not resist tasting the sweet nectar of her lips as he carried her through the knee-high grass to the edge of the woods.

"I'll never let you go again, Aimee. I'll never let you walk away from me again as you did a few weeks ago," he huskily declared.

Overwhelming desire washed over her, and she knew how much she'd missed him and how lonely life had been without him there with her. "I'll never walk away again, Mano. I was a fool to do it that night."

As they came to the edge of the woods where Demonio was tethered and he swung her up on the huge stallion, he could not resist asking her, "Was it because you found out that I was Mano Mateo, instead of Mark Perez?"

As she had always been with him, she candidly answered, "That would not have mattered to me, Mano, for I loved you too much by that time. It was because I thought you were playing me for a fool, all for the sake of that stupid Aragon-Mateo feud. Being the reckless character you're reputed to be, I figured you were just having yourself another carefree escapade."

A smile came to his face and he was now astraddle the horse with his body pressing close to hers. His fingers flipped her long hair away from her cheek as his lips moved to caress her. "Ah, *chiquita*, I can honestly tell you that this reckless vagabond was conquered the first moment his eyes fell upon you. Never did I want to roam from you."

"Never?" Aimee taunted him playfully.

"Never! Do you mind if I keep you my captive the rest of our lives, Aimee?" His black eyes seared her with the passion engulfing him as they sat so close together atop Demonio.

She turned so that her lips could meet with his. She softly murmured, "I surrender to you, Mano, all my love for the rest of my life."

Chapter 53

Aimee's sensuous lips taunted him so closely that a blazing liquid fire flowed in his veins. He wanted nothing more than to pull her down from the saddle and lay there in the soft green grass to make love to her as she was inviting him to do. But a stronger force urged him to get her as far away from this area as possible. Then he would breathe easier. For her sake, he couldn't risk a bullet in the back from Bigler, leaving Aimee at his mercy once again.

So he had to soothe her as well as himself with only words of endearment and the look of love in his dark eyes. Demonio sensed the need for a swift departure and he broke into a wild gallop through the woods he'd traveled less than an hour ago.

Maybe it was because Aimee rode there with him on Demonio's back, but it seemed they covered the woods leading to the clearing on the other side much faster than he had when he was coming this way. Time passed so swiftly, they having just left the small little settlement of Birds Landing behind them. Mano had finally begun to relax. Now that he could breathe easier, he asked her if Bigler had dared to lay a hand on

421

her and was relieved to hear her declare he hadn't. She told him how she was taken captive by two men, obviously hired by Bigler to capture her when she was out on her afternoon ride across the countryside.

Mano listened as she told him about the night of the Governor's Ball and how she had refused Bigler's amorous efforts in the governor's gardens that night.

"For a man to do something as drastic as he did, he had to be insane, Mano. Many women refuse a man's kisses and it certainly doesn't drive them to do something so drastic," she'd pointed out to him.

"Oh, I don't question at all that he is a little insane, but it was more than that. It is surely true that his ego was wounded by your denial, but it was money, Aimee, that Bigler sought from your father to get you safely returned."

"Money?"

"Yes, there was a ransom note sent to your father and he paid it. The man picking up the bounty was the one I followed here to this area. I found the man dead, obviously after he'd handed over the loot to Bigler. I'll get your father's money, as well as Bigler, just as soon as I get you safely to a relative of mine who lives up on Half Moon Bay. Once you're there, I can get on the trail of Bigler as fast as possible. Then I'll get you home, *chiquita*. You understand, don't you? You will not object to that, will you?"

She found it most objectionable for him to leave her so soon now that they had found one another again. But she also admired him tremendously for seeking to avenge the evil done to her by Bigler and for going after the money he'd taken from her father. Paul Aragon would soon have to eat his words about Mano Mateo, she thought to herself.

"I will not object to being left at this relative of yours, Mano," she said sweetly. With a provocative purr in her voice, she murmured, "I will object violently, though, if you don't make love to me before you leave me again, *mon cher*. I want you, Mano. I want to feel your arms hold me as they've held me

422

before and I want to know that wonderful magic we shared. It seems to me like a lifetime has passed me by since we were together. I never knew whether I'd ever be this close to you again."

Mano was ignited by such an overwhelming flame of desire he was not about to deny her or himself one minute longer. He spotted a grove of willows a short distance away, in the valley they were now riding through.

In that husky voice of his, he whispered in her ear, "Oh, *chiquita, chiquita,* I will fill you with all the love overflowing in me. God, Aimee, time has been endless for me too."

By the time he'd reined Demonio into the secluded grove of willows, he was a man with a fever of blazing passion consuming his firm muscled body and Aimee sensed his wild excitement.

The wind rushing the willows and the bubbling currents of the creek were the only sounds invading the quiet of the valley's darkness. Eagerly, he lifted her down from the stallion's back. Without letting go of her hand, he grabbed for the rolled-up blanket there by his saddlebag. When he had spread it on the ground for them to lie on, he guided her down beside him.

A crooked grin was there on his handsome face as he jested with her, "Suppose we will ever enjoy the comfort of a bed, *querida?* Always, it seems we've found our paradise under the skies and on the earth of this California countryside. This has always told me that you are a woman of such great passion. You are a woman who has delighted me beyond my wildest dreams. You are the one I want to share my life with, Aimee." His hands were already removing the restraining blouse she wore, for his lips ached to take the pulsing nipples of her full, rounded breasts. Her pliant body yielded to his magnificent touch, undulating toward him so he could remove the blouse with ease. So masterful were those tanned hands of his, moving with such expertise, that she was soon free of not only her blouse but all of her clothes. She felt no shame as his black eyes danced over her nude body, for there was such adoration shining in them. What woman did not like to be worshipped as Mano was now doing? she thought to herself.

Her nimble fingers became as busy as his hands when they sought to relieve him of his shirt so she might caress his broad chest, with its clusters of black, curling ringlets. He loved the featherlike touches of her dainty fingertips as they trailed over his chest and down toward his waistline.

"Oh, God, *querida*, you bewitch me! No woman ever affected me as you have. No woman ever will!" His swelling body surged against her and he sought to aid her by removing his tight restraining pants.

An impassioned look was on her face as well as a smile as she watched him scramble to get off his pants and his boots.

She leaned over him, allowing her full breasts to touch lightly against his cheek. "No woman ever will again, Mano. I'm a most possessive woman."

He gave out a light laugh, "Not half as possessive as I am, *chiquita*."

Of course, this was exactly what she hoped he would say as she moved her satiny soft body over so that it pressed against his. His arms snaked out to enclose her and pull her over on top of him. He felt her smooth legs straddle him. He felt them clasp his muscled thighs and he pulsed with a searing fever that devoured his body.

He lifted her so that his lips might take one of her breasts. His other hand moved to take the other one, cupping it so he might caress it with his most sensuous touch.

He felt her body undulate with the wild pleasure he was stirring within her and he was delighted. By now he was also hearing her gasping little moans of pleasure as her body moved with mounting sensations. Her sensuous little body was stimulating him to heights of a raging passion he knew he could not control much longer.

He hoisted her upward to impale her on him, and as he did, he heard her sigh of excited pleasure. "Oh, *Mon Dieu*, Mano!

Mano!" she moaned with sweet anguish.

"I know, *chiquita!* I know, *mi vida!* It is *magnifico!*"

He moved his fine male body in the same sexual tempo as he had the night they had danced their exotic flamenco dance at La Casa Grande. She followed him as instinctively as she had that night, when she had never danced the flamenco before. With Mano, everything seemed to come naturally.

Destiny had surely deemed that they should be lovers, it would seem. Surely no other couple had ever come together and been bound together as they had been from the very beginning.

Mano's strong will was not all that strong and he knew it. With her tantalizing flesh teasing him unmercifully, he was finding himself helpless and weak to restrain himself any longer. He gave forth a mighty thrust and a moaning gasp as he buried himself deep within the velvet softness of her flesh. She pressed closer to him so that she might absorb the whole of him and be filled with his love. Oh, she was a greedy little vixen and he adored her!

He loved the way she abandoned herself to give her love to him, as she was now doing. God, he'd never experienced such a wild, savage ecstasy with any woman as he had with Aimee!

It was a most golden splendor they soared to as they ascended the heights of sensuous pleasure. He knew that she was feeling it, too.

On this lofty pinnacle they dwelled for a few brief, stimulating moments, in that lovers' rapture. Voicing her pleasure, Aimee clung to Mano as if she feared he would suddenly fade away and she would be left alone. Never did she want to be far from his side. After this night, she realized that he was her reason for living, and without him, she could not be whole. He was a part of her—body and soul!

She heaved a deep, exhausted sigh as they slowly descended down from the heavens they'd lingered in for one golden moment, "Oh, Lord, Mano, I never knew . . . I never imagined . . ."

Mano interrupted her before she could stammer out the rest of the words she was struggling to speak, "Oh, I know, *querida.* I know! It doesn't happen that often. I think that the gods smiled down on us, Aimee."

"You think so, Mano?" she asked in that soft voice of hers, which was now almost childlike in its innocence. She snuggled there in his arms and he thought to himself how petite and fragile she felt. He marveled about the fact that his huge male body did not devastate one so tiny as she was. He was also amazed that only a few minutes ago she was the most titillating, provocative woman, wickedly luring him to love her. Now she lay so still and cozy in the circle of his arm, like the innocent child he wanted to protect from all harm.

This was the excitement of Aimee Aragon that Mano Mateo had never found in any other woman he'd ever encountered. She was a woman most complex and puzzling, but she was a woman who would forever excite and delight a man like him.

Never would he be bored with her, for there would always be something to whet his interest. With Aimee, there would always be that element of the unexpected.

He turned this child-woman toward him as they both lay naked under the California black sky. The cool breeze rushing through the willows cooled their heated flesh. "I believe, Aimee, that a powerful force brought us together and that we will forever be bound together for all the days of our lives."

She lifted her head and her silvery-blond hair fanned out over his bare shoulders. Her deep blue eyes were shining brightly and a pleased smile was on her face as she looked down at him. "Oh, Mano, I feel such things are true. You make me most happy to know that you share such feeling. I feel that some things are meant to be."

He gave out a lighthearted chuckle, "Why, *chiquita*, I knew that from the beginning. You were my woman and I never doubted that for one minute. Our eyes spoke the words of our love when our lips remained silent. Such is the way of true lovers."

"Mano, I—I know now that I was so wrong to think you were using me for this silly family vendetta. It mattered no more to you than it did to me. Is it not so?"

"Never, Aimee. Someday I shall tell you many things that are in my heart and things I wish you to know. Tonight, I wish only to love you before I must leave you at Phil's cottage to go to seek my revenge with Fred Bigler. Now, that I must do and I trust you will understand that."

"I do, Mano, and I admire you for feeling that way."

Reluctantly, he released her from his arms, for he had to think in practical terms. He had to get her to Phil's cottage and that meant that Fred Bigler was going to be three hours ahead of him.

He gave her one last gentle, tender kiss before he softly whispered in her ear, *"Querida*, we must go. As much as I hate for this moment to end, it must. I have to get you to Half Moon Bay with Phil so I can start tracking Bigler. If I don't, I'll never get him."

"Then we shall go and I will count the minutes until you return to me," she declared, rising up to stand before him, looking like a divine goddess in her bold nude state. Without any hesitation on her part, she immediately started picking up her clothing and began to dress.

Mano did the same, as he allowed his eyes to wander over in her direction every now and then to admire the glorious sight of her. She had to be the most exciting, alluring lady in the whole world, he thought to himself as he pulled on his pants and buttoned up his shirt.

He wanted to get this whole business with Bigler over and done with so he and Aimee could go forward with their lives. He had not been able to tell her about his great plans for his own winery, the Golden Splendor. He had not even told her yet that he wanted her to share this future with him.

By the time he had pulled on his black leather boots, she was already standing before him with her clothes back on, as well as her brown leather boots.

427

"Well, Mano, I am ready!"

He grinned up at her, *"Chiquita,* a woman like you can make a man weary. I suspect you'll make an old man out of me in short time. After all, I have a few years on you."

She gave out a lighthearted giggle, "Ah, Mano, you have been a wonderful teacher. You've taught me well, Mano. You introduced me into a world I'd never imagined."

"If you say so, *chiquita.*" He looked at her, finding her so damned cute and seductive he realized he'd getter get her up on Demonio hastily and ride for Phil Cabrillo's cottage if he hoped to track down Fred Bigler.

He tried to ignore the beguiling little witch standing there so close to him, trying to control his hot-blooded Latin passion as he hoisted her up on Demonio. It was not so easy to do, though.

As he spurred Demonio into action, he found himself amused at the thought of Aimee and Phil meeting one another. What a pair they would make! He figured that the two of them would instantly like each other.

"I think you and my old Portuguese relative, Phil Cabrillo, will like one another, Aimee. He's a very down-to-earth old gentleman."

She turned to look at him and a smile creased her face. "I'm sure I will like him, Mano, because you do, and I sense the warmth in your voice when you speak of him. He is a special person in your life, *oui?*"

"Yes, *querida,* he is most special!" he confessed.

"Then I will like him," she assured him.

"And he will adore you, Aimee. But I must warn you that he is an earthy old gent and the Portuguese are a rare breed. My mother was Portuguese and I guess that is the explanation for the wild streak in me. At least, that is what my father has always led me to believe. I was my mother's son, not his. Mario, my brother, was always more to his liking."

She gave his cheek a gentle caress with her lips. "I think, maybe, your mother and I would have liked one another, Mano."

Now that he thought about it, Mano had to agree with her. Theresa and Aimee would have enjoyed one another's company very much. They would have understood each other.

He cocked his head to the side and grinned, "You know, *chiquita*, I think you are right! The two of you would have gotten along fabulously!"

He could not linger there with her any longer, as much as he wanted and yearned to do. "We must get going, Aimee. I must get you to Half Moon Bay."

She gave him a nod of her head, understanding what he was saying, but she could not deny that she would have liked to linger awhile.

It dawned on her that it had come as naturally for her to love Mano Mateo as it had to love Mark Perez. So what was in a name?

Chapter 54

Mano wondered, as they rode down the trail leading to Cabrillo's cottage, how she would react to such very humble surroundings. There were no servants nor would she be provided with a lady's maid as she was accustomed to in the palatial mansion at Chateau L'Aragon. He had faith in this lovely spirited lady, seeing how she had withstood the last harrowing forty-eight hours as the captive of Fred Bigler and his cohorts. He figured her to be a bold, gutsy lady!

As he had discovered when he'd first met her, even though she was the spoiled, pampered daughter of the wealthy vintner, Paul Aragon, she was also a lady of strong will and determination. This, he admired in her.

Being a man with a vivid imagination, he could envision the times she and Phil would share while he was away. He was certain she could be giggling alot about Phil's remarks and he would be roaring with laughter at some of her very candid retorts back to him. Knowing the two of them as he did, Mano could well imagine the camaraderie that would be formed between these two very volatile people.

As they rode toward Phil's cottage, he tried to prepare her for the old reprobate, Phil Cabrillo, because he did not want her to be stunned by their first encounter, especially when he must leave her there to seek out Fred Bigler.

"Please, *mon cher*, your relative and I shall get along just fine," she assured him. "You seem to hold him in such high esteem that I have no worries about how he and I will get along."

When they came down the trail to the hitching post in front of Phil's cottage, the two hounds were there to greet them with tails wagging. But this night Phil was not sitting on the narrow front porch and the house seemed deadly quiet as they walked up the path. Mano sensed that something was not right here.

When Mano and Aimee entered the front door, the odor of sickness assailed their nostrils. That was obvious when they both went into Phil's bedroom. The old Portuguese tried with labored effort to raise himself up in the bed. "Mano? That you?"

"It is. What ails you, Phil? Now, don't you tell me you're not sick." Mano rushed over to the bed. He turned to Aimee to declare, "Hell, he's burning up with fever!"

She did not answer him. Instead, she left the room to go to the kitchen. She returned to the room with a pan of water and cloths. "Bathe his face, Mano, and I'll get some water for him to drink. He needs to get some liquids into him."

Mano did as she had instructed him to do. She seemed to have such an air of authority about her he did not dare question her. When she had brought him the pan of water and cloths, he immediately started to apply them to Phil's face and throat.

"Oh, Mano, that feels so good," Phil gave out a groan of pleasant delight. Mano told him that it was his lady, Aimee, who had told him to apply the cooling cloths to his forehead. "You have yourself quite a lady there, Mano."

Mano took this moment to explain to Phil what he intended to do and why he must leave Aimee there with Phil. "I must get

431

this bastard, Phil, before he leaves the state. You can understand that? I didn't figure to find you this sick, I have to admit." There was a concerned look on Mano's face.

"Don't worry about me, my son. As long as I have a sweet lady like yours, I'm in good hands. You go and do what you must to avenge this young lady. She will take very good care of me."

"You never doubt that for a minute, Phil. I won't rest until I deal with this bastard. I've a suspicion that he won't linger long in California."

"Then you are wasting valuable time sitting here at my bedside, Mano. Get your butt out of here and leave me to Aimee's capable hands, eh?"

Mano looked down at his tousled grey hair, streaming onto his shoulders like the mane of a lion. As sick as he was, those expressive dark eyes of his were piercing Mano. Without any other words being spoken, Mano rose up from the side of the bed to seek out Aimee. She had been gone for a long time, he realized.

When he found her, she was in the small kitchen of the cottage stirring the contents of a pot steaming there on Phil's stove. The aroma of garlic and various herbs permeated the room, along with cubes of a beef steak she'd found in Phil's cupboards.

For a brief moment, he watched her moving around the tiny kitchen with such expertise, he was utterly amazed. He would never have imagined that this lovely lady could have been so handy in an ordinary kitchen as she obviously was.

"What are you brewing, my divine little witch?" he asked her.

"I am brewing a healing tonic for our good friend Phil," she declared, turning round to give Mano a most alluring smile.

"So, you have talents I've yet to discover, *chiquita?*"

"Ah, you have many things to discover about me, Mano Mateo. You actually know so little about me. I have many things to surprise you with. I think it shall take a lifetime, *mon cher.*"

He gave forth a lighthearted chuckle, "Ah, *querida,* I plan to spend a lifetime exploring the whole of you. You are very unpredictable, and that is what has held my interest. I could never have settled for an ordinary lady. Don't you know that? I am not an ordinary man, Aimee, either, but neither am I the reckless, irresponsible son of Carlos Mateo. It was a matter that I did not conform to the traditions of the stern Latin family. I am Latin and I am very proud of that, but there is a part of me that is Portuguese and that part I can not deny."

She grinned and it was a devious grin as she told him, "I think it must be that wild, crazy streak of Portuguese in you I find so irresistible, Mano."

"Why naturally, *chiquita!* From all I've heard, the French are a reckless breed, too. Is it not so?"

"Not necessarily so, Mano. My two brothers are the most serious young men you could possibly know. I was always different from the day I was born, I guess. I was always different from Emile and Armand, and I realized that by the time I was nine years old. Mama always told me that it was because I came to them so late in life and they pampered me. I was the only girl in the family. Somehow, I've always felt there was more to it than that."

He found what she was telling him most interesting, for it was another mutual bond they shared. He had always felt that he was different from the rest of the Mateo family.

"So what you are telling me is that you often felt apart from the rest of your family, Aimee?"

"I guess that is what I am saying."

"Then I guess that is why us two misfits were drawn to one another, eh?" he laughed.

He was most reluctant to take his leave of her but knew he must. He had wasted too much time already if he hoped to catch up with Bigler. He now had more than a good two hours ahead of him, Mano realized. A lot of distance could be covered in two hours time.

433

"I must go, *querida*. I don't want to, but I must. I pray you understand that I do not wish to leave you. God knows, I don't, but I must find this man and deal with him for my honor and yours."

"I know this, Mano, and I agree that you must go. I shall wait for your return. In the meanwhile, I will try to get your dear friend Phil well, *oui?*"

He smiled, *"Oui, mi vida."* He took her in his arms and held her for a long, lingering moment. His dark eyes danced over her lovingly before he sought to speak again. "Our children face a most hectic future, Aimee. They must speak Spanish, as well as French. I shall hope that they will be very intelligent children."

She gave out a lighthearted giggle, "They would have to be very smart, Mano, with parents like you and I, *n'est ce pas?*"

"Now what was that you said to me, Aimee?"

"I said is it not so?"

"I see that I must learn your language, Aimee. I shall enjoy teaching you my Latin ways. It should be a most wonderful, exciting life we shall live. It will never be dull."

"Never!" Her eyes sparkled with a hint of mischief as she declared to him, "I am a most willing pupil you must agree, *mon cher*. You have taught me well. The truth is, you spoiled me for any other man, Mano Mateo."

She stood there with her hands at her waistline, giving forth a look of faked indignation. He thought to himself she was the most intriguing little creature he had ever known. Women like Aimee Aragon were rare, indeed! They were those certain, particular women that men did not meet too often in a lifetime. He'd be the first to say that there were many beautiful women in this world—and he'd had several—but none possessed the special magic of one like Aimee.

Mano realized that if he lingered there at Phil's cottage any longer, he was going to be the helpless victim of her bewitching charms. He'd never manage to tear himself away from her.

With a look of anguish on his face, he declared, "I must go,

Aimee. I will leave you here with Phil and I shall know he's left in good hands."

"Go, Mano! Go and do what you must do, but hurry back here to Half Moon Bay to me," she told him with an impassioned look on her lovely face.

For one magical moment, he held her in his arms and kissed her sweet lips. She clung to him, knowing the danger he might be facing when he encountered Fred Bigler.

When he finally released her, she looked up at him to say, "I'll pray for you, Mano. I'll pray that you will come back to me here at Half Moon Bay."

"I'll come back, *querida*. I swear that to you! I have a whole lifetime planned for us. I have not had the opportunity to tell you, but I have bought for us a winery. It is a most beautiful place which I think you will love. The region is called the Valley of the Moon."

"Valley of the Moon? It sounds like a wonderful place, Mano. Hurry back to me so we can go there," she urged him.

"I will, Aimee. I promise that," he vowed as he turned to leave the room.

She watched him leave the small kitchen of Phil Cabrillo's humble cottage. Now that he was gone, she moved to check the broth she was brewing for the old gentleman in the bedroom.

Being a person guided by her impulses, she liked the old gentleman she'd met briefly. There was something about his dark eyes that reminded her of Mano as he'd gazed up at her. She couldn't determine whether it was the piercing quality, which seemed to bore right into her, or that glint of devilment that was part of his personality.

Just about the time she was ready to ladle up a bowl of the steaming hot broth to take to Phil, Mano reappeared in the kitchen. "I have said my good-bye to Phil. Told him I expected to see him up by the time I returned and ready to give me hell," he told her. She saw that Mano was having a difficult time trying to project that happy-go-lucky attitude of his. Mano found it impossible to pretend to be anything but his true self, and she knew that he was most reluctant to give her that final kiss and embrace before he went out the door to mount up on Demonio and ride away.

In a soft voice, she assured him she would have Phil well by the time he returned to the cottage. "I won't offer you any of my broth, for you might linger too long, *mon cher*. The sooner you leave the sooner you can return to me. Then you'll never leave my side again. This, Mano, is what I want."

He moved to take her in his arms. Never had he loved her more as his head bent to take one last kiss before he left her to seek his revenge for the two of them. His soul would find no rest until he settled the score between him and Fred Bigler.

It was a long, lingering kiss he took from the nectar of her sweet, sweet lips. He savored the flaming warmth of her curvy body encased in his arms. The memory of this moment would comfort him while he was away from her, because he knew not how many days and nights it might take for him to find the bastard he sought.

When he finally released his hold on her and he started to say farewell, her dainty fingers touched his lips and she shook her head, declaring, "No, no, never tell me good-bye! Just go, Mano. It will be easier for us both. Remember, I love you and I will be waiting impatiently for you to return."

He understood exactly what she was saying to him and a smile creased his handsome face as he quickly turned on his booted heels to walk out the door.

Theirs was an endless love. Now he knew why everything had been so different with Aimee Aragon than it had been with any other woman.

Chapter 55

Unmercifully, Ross Maynard had driven the mare he rode as he'd made his hasty, frenzied departure from the shack. In that darkness outside the windows of the cabin, he could not make out the threatening face of the man ordering him to move away and allow Aimee to leave the room, but he recognized that forceful, determined voice with that arrogant air of authority. He remembered their brief encounter at his father's dinner. It was Mano Mateo standing out there, ready to kill him for having wronged his woman.

There was no way Ross wanted to tangle with a man like Mateo, with his hot-blooded Latin temper, especially when a woman was involved. Especially when that woman was the beguiling, beautiful Aimee Aragon!

In his frenzy to be gone from the cabin and on his way to Sacramento, to gather together his belongings so he could leave this California countryside for Texas and forget that he had ever posed as a man named Fred Bigler, Ross had neglected to take the saddlebag there on the table, which contained the handsome bounty Paul Aragon had provided for the release of his beloved daughter. It was not to dawn on him that he had done just that until he had approached the small hamlet of Courtland, some forty miles south of Sacramento.

He yanked up on the reins of the mare, muttering a stream of cusswords that he had been so stupid. For several moments, he just sat there astride the mare, pondering what he should do. Should he ride on to Sacramento or go back, hoping that the saddlebag would still be there untouched by Mateo in his delight of rescuing his ladylove?

His greed finally won out and Ross turned the reins to return to the cottage, in that ray of hope that Mateo did not check out the saddlebag. There was too much to lose to not chance it, Ross convinced himself. There was a fortune in that saddlebag! His fortune and his future!

He rationalized that a couple of hours did not make that much difference in his plans. He had to figure that Mateo had taken care of old Buck, so he would pose no threat. He also reasoned that Mateo had headed back to San Mateo County with his beloved Aimee, so he posed no threat, either.

About the same moment Ross Maynard had made his decision to return to the scene of his crimes, Buck was just recovering from the astounding blow Mano's pistol had rendered to his head. He'd stumbled into the cabin to find it deserted except for the dead body of his old buddy Cody. He figured that he could at least give him a proper burial. It was a most laborious effort for Buck to carry forth his efforts to dig the proper grave for his buddy. His head was throbbing with pain and he felt an overwhelming weakness washing over him, so he had to stop from time to time to sit there on the ground to rest.

Finally, the task was accomplished and he staggered wearily to the cabin. There was one comforting thought for Buck and that was that the nice little lady was safely in the care of that dude he'd gotten one fleeting glance of before he crumpled to the ground. There was a fierce look in the man's black eyes that he didn't think he would ever forget as long as he lived.

When he managed to get back into the cabin, he did not seek the jug of whiskey but went to the kitchen to brew himself a very strong pot of coffee.

It was not until the coffee was brewed and he was sitting there at the old oak table, sipping it, that his weary eyes noticed the saddlebag. He reached out, pulling it toward him to examine. He suddenly became alive as he kept pulling out the bills, which represented a small fortune. As he began to count it out there on the table, he realized that Cody had lied to him about what they were getting for their services.

As Buck pulled the last pile of bills out of the saddlebag, he found a letter addressed to a Ross Maynard. Buck read it not only once, but twice. It was a most interesting letter from a lady this Ross Maynard had known back in the state of Texas. Buck might not have been the smartest fellow, but he had it all figured out that a Ross Maynard had come here to California and posed as a gent named Fred Bigler. He planned to cash in on that name before he returned to Texas.

Buck sat there, thinking out this whole game of insanity he and Cody had played with this silver-tongued dude from Texas. He had been using them, and now Buck suddenly realized that he'd never intended to allow them to live once they'd done his dirty work for him. Buck realized that he would never know what had happened during the time he was lost in that black bottomless pit, when the pistol barrel had slammed into his head, but it was obvious that Bigler—or Maynard—had left swiftly.

Buck knew his kind and he knew he would return. With that in mind, Buck became very alert and alive. He helped himself to another cup of coffee. It wasn't whiskey he needed right now, for if he were numbed, he would be as dead as poor old Cody who he'd just buried out there.

Buck wasn't the greedy individual Cody had been. He pulled a few hundred dollars from the bounty in the saddlebag to stuff in his pocket. Walking over to the kerosene lamp, he dimmed it. There was no need to linger here any longer; he should do as he'd been doing all his life. He'd best be drifting on. Hell, he'd been a drifter all his life and forever he would be!

He mounted up on his horse, leaving the little cabin in total darkness. But he had to say to himself, as he rode away, that something had come into his life that would forever change him. He had met a charming young lady who had pulled out certain qualities from him that he'd never before known were buried deep within him. She had been sweet and kind to him, and he had realized that she had ignited a courage from him he did not know he possessed. She would never know it, he realized, but she had taught him that he was a stronger man than he had credited himself to be. Buck rode away from that place convinced that he was going to make a better life for himself. He knew he could do it now!

He hoped she was happy now that she was safe. That was what he'd wanted for her from the moment he'd taken her that first tray of food in that miserably hot room of the cabin and she'd looked up at him with those lovely eyes of hers, pleading with him to help her. Dear God, there was no way he could have harmed a sweet, innocent miss like her, and that was what he had feared Cody was going to do!

God, he was glad it was all over! He was happy to be riding away at this late night hour. Soon there would be a new day dawning and Buck thought to himself that a new life was going to be dawning for him because he was going to make it happen that way.

With each new day's dawning since Denise had arrived at her brother's estate, Chateau L'Aragon, she was feeling weaker and more weary. She knew that she must make the most out of each day she had left. Her only prayer was that Aimee would return safely to her home before she died.

Yesterday, she had given Lisette a list of all her jewels, instructing her sister-in-law what she wished her to have and what she wanted Aimee to have. She noticed Lisette's look of disdain and aversion to what she was saying.

"Ah, Lisette, I understand that this is distasteful to you, but some things have to be said and I am just grateful that I've been given this opportunity that so many don't have. You have been the sister I never had. We have a bond, *n'est ce pas?* We have given one another such joy and pleasure. I die a most happy woman and that happiness is due mainly to you, Lisette. Think about what I am saying and then you will admit that I speak the truth. How many people can honestly say that?"

Never could she have been that risqué lady that Denise was and had always been since she'd first known her, but she had to admit that she was absolutely right about life. This was a quality that her daughter, Aimee, had inherited from Denise, for which Lisette was grateful.

While they sat on the terrace that golden autumn day, Denise sipping on her favorite white wine, she made one final request of her sister-in-law, "There is a spot I love here on your lovely estate, Lisette. There is a small grove of trees and the grass is so green. Wildflowers seem to flourish there and you know how I've always loved flowers. I adore that hillside. Paul has told me that there is no cemetery on these grounds, since no family member has ever died. I wish to be buried there on that hillside, just to the south of the winery where the lovely wilflowers grow. Will you tell Paul that?"

"Oh, *Mon Dieu,* Denise, I hate talking like this when I see you sitting there so alive and lovely,' Lisette sighed.

"Oh, Lisette, I know the burden I put on your shoulders, but you are a woman and I know you must understand. Can you imagine the effort it takes to make myself look this good? Don't you know that I only fight now to wait for Aimee's rèturn, so I may kiss her one last time and gaze on her lovely face and say to myself secretly that she is mine? That is the strength that keeps me going, Lisette! Only then shall I go peacefully if God grants me that reward."

Lisette knew that there were some who would have classified

Denise as a wanton woman if they'd known the life she'd lived in Paris as the demimonde, but she could not consider her sister-in-law a bad woman. Oh, it was true that she had always been a high-class courtesan, but Denise truly possessed a good heart.

She was grateful that she'd not destroyed the beautiful life of the baby who'd given such joy to her life—her Aimee! No, Lisette knew there was a kind, loving nature in Denise.

"This young man who has gone to rescue our Aimee, will he do it, Lisette?"

"Emile is convinced that he will, Denise. We must trust that he will, because the sheriff and his posse have done nothing for days. I feel that he will bring Aimee home to us," Lisette told her.

"Then I must believe that too," Denise replied. "I would like to meet this young man, Lisette."

"Oh, I pray you will, Denise. I truly pray that you do. I must confess to you that I like him very much. Paul and I did not agree about him at all. It was not the young man himself, but the matter that he happened to be the son of a man Paul detested throughout the years we've lived here. They have always been bitter enemies."

Denise shook her head as she scoffed her disgust, "Ah, that is absolutely foolish that two young people should pay the price for their two fathers' egos. I feel very sorry for these two young people. Paul is the fool!"

"I agree! I always have, Denise. But Paul can be a very hard man at times," Lisette told her sister-in-law.

"I can believe that and that is why I think you must surely be an angel, Lisette."

She recalled the fond memory she had of Mano Mateo, when she had thought him to be Mark Perez and he'd sat with her here on this same terrace awaiting Aimee's arrival downstairs.

"He was so gracious and pleasant and a most interesting conversationalist who would have impressed you, Denise. With all this charm, he is almost the most handsome young man I've ever seen in California or France," Lisette declared.

Denise already knew that it had been Mano Mateo who'd saved Aimee from an attack by some drifting scoundrel prowling the countryside. Angrily, she asked of her sister-in-law, "What is the matter with this stupid brother of mine? After all this and all these grand qualities, what should he possibly object to such a paragon seeking the affections of his daughter? I can now see why Paul and I never shared anything in common as we were growing up under the same roof."

There was an amused smile on Lisette's face, for she still saw the fire and spirit in the once-lovely lady and it gladdened her heart. She agreed wholeheartedly with her, she had to confess.

"I can't give you an answer, Denise, except what I have already told you about the feud existing between Paul and Carlos Mateo, which stems back to the time when we first arrived here in the valley." Leaning over to Denise, she declared excitedly, "Oh, you should see them together. They make the most magnificent couple, he with all that dark Latin handsomeness and those flashing black eyes and our Aimee with her golden-haired loveliness and that satiny gardenia complexion. You would have been as impressed as I was seeing the two of them together."

"Dear God, Lisette, you are exciting me just talking about such a man! It might just be the incentive I need to make me refuse to go when the time comes," she jested in a lighthearted air. No one realized more than Lisette how this miserable state of affairs had to gall the always-vivacious Denise. Better it would be for a woman like her that God should have taken her fast and saved her the misery of any lingering days when she could not enjoy the active, gay life she had always led. How she must abhor this miserable state of existence!

"Oh, Denise, I would believe that of you. I honestly would," Lisette laughed, trying to play the game with her if that is what she wished.

"Oh, I would, I swear. But to change the subject to another couple who I happened to observe the other afternoon as I was sitting there by my window, which I do quite often because your gardens are so beautiful, Lisette. I saw your son, Emile, embracing Aimee's little maid, Jolie. I would say that the two of them are very much in love."

Once again, Lisette grinned as she prepared to address Denise. She, too, had observed the young couple during one of their secret rendezvouses in her garden. She also thought the two of them made a most striking pair. She did not find it objectionable to have Jolie as her daughter-in-law if Emile came to them to declare his intentions of marrying her. But she knew that Paul would find it abhorrent.

These feelings she expressed to Denise, who was quick to reply with an indignant retort, "Then I think my brother better come out of the dark ages. He's due for a rude awakening, Lisette!"

"I couldn't agree with you more, Denise. I think he is to find this out very soon," Lisette remarked.

"Ah, but think of all the wonderful pleasure my dear brother had denied himself all these years by restricting himself. Paul is too rigid and strict with himself and his family. My heart has always gone out to you, my dear Lisette. When you've told me about all this rebelling my daughter has done, I find it gloriously amusing. I praise her for that!"

There was a tender, caring warmth in Lisette's eyes as she told her sister-in-law, "She is your daughter, Denise. She inherited that wonderful zest for life that has always been a part of you."

It was the grandest tribute she could have paid to Denise!

Chapter 56

When Aimee sat on the edge of Phil Cabrillo's bed and fed him the broth she'd just made, a new day was dawning over Half Moon Bay. But time was lost to her tonight, as it had been for several days now. The hands of a clock really didn't matter, she'd come to realize. Being a most persuasive young lady, she'd managed to get Phil to consume the entire bowl of broth, which she knew was bound to help the weak old gent lying there in the bed.

His dark brooding eyes told her he appreciated her kindness and that was all the thanks she wanted. She gave him a warm smile and a gentle pat on his shoulders to express to him she did care. "We'll have you well by the time Mano returns. I promised him that. Now I shall leave you to rest, because that is most important, too."

In a very weak, faltering voice, Phil managed to say, "You are as beautiful as you are sweet and kind. Mano is a blessed man."

Softly she whispered her thanks as she rose from the edge of the bed. As she quietly moved to leave the room, she heard the old Portuguese muttering to himself, "She is even more beautiful than you, Theresa."

For a moment, she lingered there in the doorway to look back at him. The fever was making him ramble on, she decided as she left the room. Only then did she decide to seek the comfort of the small cot she spied in the other room. How nice and peaceful it seemed to her to be here and away from that horrible place where she'd been. How wonderful that little narrow cot would feel to her tired body!

She wasted no time seeking the comfort it would offer her, and it was only when she had laid her bone-weary body down on the cot that she realized that this was where Mano must sleep when he was here. That thought made a calm serenity wash over her and she fell into a deep, peaceful sleep.

In the next room, Phil slept peacefully, too.

There was no peace in Ross Maynard as he backtracked over the many miles he'd just covered. But he couldn't turn his back on that much money left there at that cabin. He had to go back.

There was no peace in Mano as he rode in the early morning dawn. He knew the odds against him, and it was like trying to find a needle in a haystack. Somehow that instinct of his was guiding him back to the place where he'd found Aimee. The man whose head he'd slammed with the butt of his pistol might still be around, because Mano knew that he had not killed him. He'd violently stunned him and put him out of his way for the time he needed to eliminate the other two he'd thought he might be facing. As it had turned out, there was only one man he had to go against.

His only other recourse was to go to Sacramento in search of Bigler and, if necessary, demand an audience with the governor himself about his black sheep relative. Mano was prepared to do just that.

By the time he reached the remote, isolated spot where the

small cabin stood, some miles just south of Sacramento in the thick forest of trees, a new day was coming upon the countryside. There was that awesome quiet of the early morning hour. The only sound coming to Mano's ears was the calling of birds and the scampering creatures of the forest already alive to meet the new day.

Mano rode up to the cabin, tying Demonio to the hitching post. Ironically, he had to confess that it seemed so peaceful there now. He leaped down from the stallion, moving up the overgrown path of grass and weeds to go into the cabin.

He heard the trilling sound of a mockingbird calling over in the woods, and the grass was still damp from the morning dew. He found himself saying what a beautiful morning it was until he remembered the night before right here in this very same spot. So he did not allow himself to be disillusioned by the quietness.

The man he'd slammed with his pistol could still be lurking there in the cabin and one unguarded moment could be his downfall. So Mano moved slowly and cautiously around the corner of the cabin, which provided the concealing cover of the underbrush. He felt his pants being snagged by the thorns of the shrubs that had been allowed to grow rampant.

He passed the spot where he had sneaked up on the man outside the window of the room where Aimee had been kept captive. He no longer lay on the ground where he had fallen, so Mano became more wary as he moved slowly around the corner of the house. The man was not dead and he had not figured him to be.

As he cautiously entered the shack and guardedly explored each room, he found no one there. But he did spot the saddlebag there on the old oak table. It contained the loot Bigler had demanded in his ransom note. Mano examined the bag carefully. One part of his mission was now completed, he thought to himself. He could return this money to Paul Aragon. At least, Bigler had failed to accomplish his scheme to

447

feather his nest at Aragon's expense by using Aimee as the bait.

Tucked down at the very bottom of the saddlebag was a folded, worn letter, which was very interesting as he read it. It explained many things to him. Now he knew why he could not accept Fred Bigler as any relative of the very dignified, well-respected Governor Bigler that night when he'd met him at his father's fiesta. He didn't fit the mold.

He read the letter once and then he read it again. By the time he'd finished reading the letter the second time, he had the whole despicable plot of Fred Bigler's figured out. What a conniving, evil sonofabitch this man was! Mano thought to himself as he sat there. It was obvious that it was Ross Maynard from the state of Texas, merely posing as the relative of the governor who'd mysteriously arrived here in California. It was Ross Maynard who'd murdered the real Fred Bigler and assumed his identity.

The lady who'd written the letter was obviously a most intimate lady friend of Maynard's and she knew him quite well. She knew of his unsavory past and she knew of his plans once he'd arrived in California several months ago. It was also obvious that Maynard had led her to believe she was to share the luxurious life they would enjoy once he returned to Texas.

Mano folded the letter, tucked it in his shirt pocket, and gathered up the money in the saddlebag. He saw no need to linger there any longer as he rose from the table, leaving the saddlebag right where he'd found it.

Without any doubt in Mano's mind, Ross Maynard had rushed out of that cabin last night in dread fear for his life. This Maynard character was most likely figuring that he would be forgotten once Mano had Aimee safely away. A devious grin creased Mano's face as he moved toward the front door of the cabin. Maynard did not figure him right, however, thinking that he would turn his back on this and forget that there was a score to be settled.

Once again, he allowed his instinct to guide him as he went

to the hitching post and mounted Demonio. He was heading for Sacramento to turn this letter over to the governor and he suspected that it was there he would run into Maynard. He figured that Maynard would return there for a brief time before heading out to Texas.

It was in the direction of Sacramento he reined Demonio. In Maynard's swift departure, he'd not thought to gather up the saddlebag containing his loot. Thus Mano was certain that he would meet him on the trail, seeking to return.

Fate does strange tricks sometimes. For some unknown reason and in his frenzy to get back to the cabin to retrieve that rich saddlebag, Maynard had taken a side trail leading up to the back of the property where the cabin was situated. He had missed encountering Mano Mateo by less than ten minutes when he entered the cabin.

A raucous gale of laughter erupted from Maynard when he ambled into the front room of the cabin to find the saddlebag exactly in the spot where he'd left it. He gave forth an exuberant roar of joy, "God damn! Holy Jesus, it's still here!"

He rushed eagerly over to the table to grab it. Every fiber of his being was churning with the wildest anticipation as he sought to plunge his nervous fingers into the pouch. But the void and emptiness he touched sent him into a rage, which mounted into an explosive inferno. He went through the motions of examining the other portion, knowing that it, too, would be empty. The bastard had taken the money after all!

He gave way to the overwhelming rage boiling within him by kicking at the furniture and tossing any object his hands came in contact with. His ranting fury went on and on until he was drenched in his own sweat and gasping for breath.

As Mano had decided a brief time ago when he took his leave of the cabin, Maynard sat there considering that he had nothing there demanding that he stay any longer.

Moving like a man in a trance, he walked outside to mount his mare. Once he was sitting in the saddle, he reined his horse in the direction of Sacramento. Little did he know that he was trailing the man who had his loot in his possession.

Traveling along the countryside, Ross Maynard was only a half hour behind Mano, who was riding that same trail hellbent on finding the man only a short distance away from him. By now, the long trip to Half Moon Bay and the ride back to this area was taking its toll on Mano, who'd had no sleep for many hours now. He was wise enough to know it.

When he spotted the rippling little creek just off the lane he was traveling, he reasoned that he'd best stop for a while to bathe his face in the refreshing cool waters. He veered the reins to guide Demonio through the thick growth of greenery and brush.

Demonio seemed to enjoy the fresh, cooling waters of the stream as much as Mano. "We shall rest a spell, amigo. I am tired, too," Mano declared to his stallion.

This is what they did there by the secluded bank of the creek. He had not intended to give himself the luxury of a nap but nevertheless he dozed off. It was only the sounds of a rider going down the trail that made him come alive with a jerk as he sat up from the log he'd been leaning against.

Mano did not know how to explain it to himself but he sensed danger. Feeling so strongly as he did about it, he could not lightly shrug this strange rider aside. So he gathered up his gear, preparing to mount Demonio. The rider ahead of him could only be a short distance ahead, Mano figured as he spurred Demonio into action.

Across the way and along a hillside less than two miles from where Mano had sought his brief moment of rest on his way to Sacramento in search of Ross Maynard, another fellow had stopped on the trail to rest.

It was only after a few hours ride that Buck felt safe to take a break from the hard riding he had done when he'd left that shack back in the woods. It was a good feeling to not feel his heart pounding so fast, and he could finally relax as he led his

450

horse down the hillside to sit there and enjoy some hearty gulps of whiskey from the flask in his saddlebag. One or two swigs were never enough for Buck once he'd had that taste of whiskey. There had to always be another and another.

He had no inkling of when he'd become so numbed that he had dropped the flask from his hand and leaned down against the trunk of the tree where he'd sat down. A deep sleep came upon him. Unexpectedly, something roused him from his sleep and he couldn't explain the sudden flooding of fear that he felt. Maybe it was that he did not have his old buddy, Cody, riding with him. He had to admit that there was a certain security about having that hell raiser by his side when they'd drifted around the country.

Then he heard the galloping hooves of a horse moving swiftly along the trail.

As he looked upward from the hillside where he sat, he could have sworn it was Fred Bigler astride that galloping horse. Buck knew that he'd obviously returned to the shack to claim the money he'd left behind when he'd departed.

Suddenly a fury erupted in Buck when he thought about how Bigler had killed his buddy in cold blood and his evil, wicked intentions for that pretty little lady, Aimee. Buck mounted up on his horse with a sense of fierce revenge burning within him. The bastard deserved to be killed and what better way to do it than to be riding behind him. A rat like him deserved to be shot in the back. It was no more heartless than Bigler's act when he'd blasted the life out of Cody. Buck did not harbor any hard feelings for the man who'd slammed him on the head, however, because he knew that man had come to the cottage to rescue that nice Miss Aimee.

Before Buck could get himself up and alert enough to gather his gear to mount his horse, he observed another rider on the trail above the slope of the hillside. The rider astride the magnificent silver-grey beast, with its jet-black tail and mane, had to be the man who'd dealt him such a mighty blow on the

451

head, Buck figured.

As foggy as Buck's brain was at this minute, he just knew he was right. That formidable, dark-haired gent was on the track of old Fred Bigler. Buck grinned, knowing he would get him. He hoped he did!

He anxiously mounted his horse, spurring him into action. He did not want to miss this showdown. He had no doubt that justice would be doled out to that beady-eyed Bigler.

Chapter 57

Along that California back trail leading into the city of Sacramento, three men were now riding, following one another with less than a mile's distance dividing them. Ross Maynard was in the lead, with Mano trailing behind him. Buck followed Mano, who was not in Buck's sight now that they were riding into another wooded area.

Ross Maynard would never have heard the rider back on the lane he was traveling had he not been forced to stop there in the woods to relieve himself. It was only as he stood still there in the woods that his ears heard the sound of Demonio's fast-paced hooves beating down on the earth. His curiosity was whetted enough that he decided to linger there a while, allowing the strange rider to go on by. So he remained back in the concealing underbrush and thickets watchfully, waiting to see the rider and wondering if he would recognize him.

Mano had slowed down Demonio's pace about a fourth of a mile back on the trail when he caught sight of a swinging branch from one of the young saplings. He had to conclude that a rider had come this way a short time ago, brushing the low-hanging branch just hard enough to make it break the bark.

So he slowly scrutinized the area along the trail with more caution, instead of so much haste. Demonio didn't seem to understand his master's restraining hold on the reins, doing some high-spirited rebellion until Mano demanded that he obey him.

As Mano slowed his pace, Buck had begun to close the gap that divided them. When the fine grey stallion with Mano astride him came into view, he also halted up on the reins of his horse. For some unknown reason, Buck veered to the right of the trail, for he was curious about the dark, swarthy gent moving so slowly and gazing down at the leaf-covered lane. What was he checking out? Buck wondered. Whatever it was, Buck decided to move a distance away and around him. He wanted no part of this hot-blooded Latin who might turn around to see him trailing him.

He set his pace in unison with Mano's, catching fleeting glimpses of him through the dense cover of the numerous trees there in the woods. Suddenly, Mano halted his stallion and dismounted. Buck watched as Mano plucked something from one of the thorny bushes. It looked like a small shred of material.

In one flashing second, which happened so quickly, Buck was hardly aware of his reaction and what his eyes beheld. The ray of light from the sun seemed to focus in through the branches of the high treetops on the silver barrel of a pistol, poised and aimed at Mano. This was what Buck observed.

Ross had no idea that Buck stood less than thirty feet to the right of him in the cover of the thicket. But he did recognize the tall, towering figure of the son of Carlos Mateo. Sweet Jesus, he was the last person he'd expected to see when he'd hidden back there in the underbrush!

Ross never expected to be so damned lucky after so much had gone wrong for him. Now he would finally have the satisfaction of killing this bastard, at least before he took off for Texas where his luck seem to run better. California had put a hex on him, he had come to believe.

His finger teased the trigger of his gun and he had a devious grin on his face as he anticipated pulling that trigger. In a way, it would be the greatest satisfaction to know that he would be denying Aimee of her Latin lover as she had denied him of the pleasure he'd intended to have with her.

With these thoughts churning within him, his whole body began to pulse with a wild excitement. As far away as Buck stood, he could see the evil intent on Bigler's face. He had never hated a sonofabitch in all his life as he hated this man. While he had done a lot of things in his life that he could not be proud about, he'd never been a killer. This day he was going to add that crime to the others. His hand went to his holster.

The woods rang out with two exploding shots of gunfire. Ross had taken his aim, and he knew as he was about to pull the trigger, that his bullet would hit his target. But in that last split second, the sharp cracking of a branch caused his hand to move ever so slightly. It was enough to miss Mano by only a hairsbreadth.

It was enough to make Mano dive for the ground, rolling over to pull his pistol hastily out of his holster. That bullet was meant for him and he had no doubt about that, but his keen ears had heard two explosions. They had happened in a swift sequence. Who had shot that second blast of gunfire? he wondered.

Every fiber of his muscled body was alive and alert as his black eyes anxiously danced around the wood surrounding him. He saw nothing, but Buck saw him and the menacing look in his dark eyes.

He knew no other way to make his presence known than to yell out to him, "I took care of him. He's dead." Buck could only hope that this would be enough to ease his itchy trigger finger. The lean, lanky figure of Buck slowly emerged through the thicket to amble up to Mano, who was now raising himself up from the ground.

"That bastard Bigler deserved killing and it was right that I be the one," Buck declared as he placed his gun back in the holster.

"Well, I owe you my life. That bullet was for me," Mano replied. "I thank you, amigo." By now, he was standing there beside the man who'd just saved his life. His eyes were now busily surveying the man's face.

A slow, easy grin came to Buck's face as he said, "You are the one who gave my head a hell of a blow. Can't say I blame you, though, not for a sweet little miss like Miss Aimee."

"So you were the one standing outside the window?"

"I was, and for a very good reason. I was determined that that no-good Cody was going to do her no harm. You see, I came to think most highly of her. She was a fine little miss and I might have agreed to the deal this Bigler made with me and Cody to abduct her, but damned if I didn't regret it later. Once we had her and I knew what was going on in Cody's head, I was determined that he wasn't going to touch her if I had to kill him."

"Were you the one who killed this Cody?" Mano asked him.

"Hell, no. That Bigler did it and in cold blood, too. I'll tell you something, mister, I've been a hell raiser and I've swindled a lot of dudes, but I never killed anyone until today."

"So Bigler hired you and this Cody to kidnap Aimee and hold her until he collected the ransom, is that right?"

"That's right. He approached us one night a few weeks ago in a tavern where me and Cody always go to do our drinking and gambling. We struck a deal with him. Seemed to be a simple deal to make a hell of a lot of money. But I know now that he never intended to settle up with us. He came to that cabin that night to kill us both. God knows what he had in mind for Miss Aimee."

456

Buck told him how he'd gotten squirmy after Bigler had arrived at the cabin so he'd gone outside, using the excuse he needed to relieve himself. It was while Buck was outside that Bigler killed Cody and Buck had heard the shot.

"I rushed around the house to get to Miss Aimee's windows so I could see if Bigler was going to come through that door. That's why I was there when you happened on the scene. I was just about ready to blast him when you gave me that slam on the head."

"I am sorry, amigo. I truly am, but at that point, I figured to be up against three. I couldn't take the time to ask any questions," Mano grinned.

"All's forgiven. I'm glad you came when you did and got Miss Aimee away from there. I—I only hope she'll find it in that sweet heart of hers to forgive me for having any part of something that caused her so much trouble."

"I imagine that Aimee has suspected how you protected her and I'll be sure to tell her you wish her forgiveness," Mano assured him. "By the way, I think by now I should know your name. I am Mano Mateo."

"Just tell her Buck is sorry. Since our paths will never cross again, I will tell you that it's my pleasure to shake hands with such a gentleman as you, Mano Mateo. It's not something I've done, shaking hands with a real gentleman. Just call me Buck," he said with a broad smile on his face.

"Well, Buck, you'll always be remembered by me. Before we do part company, do you think we might just bury this vermin you killed?" Mano saw no point in lingering any longer here, for he was anxious to return to Aimee waiting for him back at Phil's cottage.

"Yeah, you got a fine young lady waiting for you back there. I'll tend to that dirty job. It's only fitting I do it. I owe old Cody that much. You be on your way back to that nice little lady. I got no one waiting for me."

Mano extended his hand to Buck in a final gesture of

457

farewell. He understood what he was trying to tell him and he accepted his offer.

"Adios, amigo, and God be with you, Buck," Mano declared as he turned to mount Demonio and ride in the direction of Half Moon Bay.

Buck watched him go and he felt happy. Miss Aimee had herself one fine man there. He went to untie the reins of his own horse, and as he walked along the spot where the lifeless figure of Ross Maynard lay, Buck looked down on him, feeling no qualm of conscience about his deed.

"You're not worth my effort to bury you, you bastard," Buck spit out as he moved on by to get his horse.

So he left the spot to ride on through the woods to his unknown destination.

As Ross Maynard had left his victim in an isolated spot in the Texas hill country when he'd murdered the young Fred Bigler, the same was to be his fate in the secluded woods of California.

Ironically, the dumb oaf of a drifter, Buck, had been Ross Maynard's jury and judge. As Buck had ridden away across the hills and valleys, he broke into a gale of laughter, recalling how that Bigler had smirked at him a couple of times when he'd been around him.

Yes, indeed, justice had prevailed!

All the lights of the house had dimmed except for those in the upstairs bedroom occupied by Paul and Lisette Aragon. Lisette was voicing her fears to Paul that Denise would not last too many more days. "She grows weaker all the time. Only one thing is making her hold on, Paul, and that is to see Aimee again. But Paul, my dear, I think you should prepare that spot she'd spoken of up on the hillside where she'd like to be buried. I really think you and the boys should do that."

"I will see to that tomorrow. Damned, I should have sent Emile or Armand with that—that Mano. Why I allowed Emile to talk me into such a stupid plan I'll never know. It should be an Aragon going to rescue my daughter and avenge this wrong, not a Mateo," Paul muttered as he paced the room nervously.

Lisette knew there was nothing she could say when he was like this, so she sat there quietly, allowing him to fuss and fume.

"We all sit back here wondering and worrying and still he doesn't return with our Aimee. How do we know that he is worth our trust? Tell me, Lisette, eh?"

"I have faith in him, Paul. I have complete faith in Mano because I saw the love in his eyes for her when they were together. You could have seen it, too, if you had not been so stubborn and refused to admit it to yourself," she told him in a soft but candid manner.

A frown of resentment clouded Paul's face and he stopped his pacing to glare at her. "*Mon Dieu*, that Mateo charm has infected you as it had Aimee. I don't understand you women at all."

Lisette could not control a girlish giggle breaking forth and this irritated Paul all the more. "Ah, *mon cher*, we women are so very simple to understand, really. It is *magnifique* when a woman finds a man who is so very willing to show how much he adores her. Aimee found this in Mano Mateo, so it was very understandable why she gave her heart to him and fought you so much about Fred Bigler." She watched his reaction to what she had said, because she hoped to mellow that hard shell of his when their son Emile came to them to tell them of his desire to marry Jolie.

"Paul, we can't pick the mates for our children. Did your parents pick me? I can answer that for you. They did not!"

Paul began to squirm as he mumbled in a faltering voice, "They did not refuse me, though. We—we married, didn't we?"

An amused smile broke on her face as she laughed, "Oh, Paul, what a feeble excuse you are making to avoid the truth!

They did not greet me with open arms, as I vividly recall." She motioned him to come to bed, and as he slowly did as she requested, she confidently assured him, "Mano will bring our daughter home, Paul. You wait and see!"

How could he possibly doubt such confidence in his devoted Lisette?

Chapter 58

A short distance away from the hillside of the Aragon estates, in the lush valley where La Casa Grande was situated, lights beamed out of the double windows of Carlos's study as he, too, paced the carpeted floor, ranting out his rage to his son Mario, "I find this hard to believe, Mario."

"But it is true, Father. You know how gossip travels around this countryside. I've heard it from more than one source, and Mano has admitted his great affection for Aimee Aragon. So I fear you will have to accept it, as will Paul Aragon. Mano and Aimee are very much alike. Both of them are very strong-willed, determined individuals."

"*Dios,* I'll never accept an Aragon as my daughter-in-law!"

"I'm afraid you won't have much to say about it, Father. Nothing you can do would stop Mano from marrying her," Mario declared in a blunt tone, which surprised him a few minutes later. Carlos flinched at the surprising arrogance of Mario to dare speak to him in such a manner.

Yet, he admired this spirit of daring and courage in his older son. This was a trait he'd seen sadly lacking in Mario throughout the years, while Carlos had found Mano to have inherited more than his share of bravado.

There was an awesome silence in the study for a moment before Carlos sought to speak in that deep, impressive voice of his. Those aristocratic features of his gave no hint of his innermost thoughts, though. "No, I suppose I can't stop him, Mario, but I still don't have to accept this woman."

Once again, Mario replied to his father in that same assured tone of voice, "This woman as you call her, Father, is a young lady of astounding beauty and intelligence. She is a lady of quality, who would do this family proud if she does Mano the honor of becoming his bride."

Without further ado, Mario turned to walk out of the study without looking back to see if it met his father's approval or not. The truth was Mario truly did not care!

Carlos stood there slightly puzzled by Mario's overwhelming defense of this lady, Aimee Aragon. One might think that Mario was in love with her, too, Carlos thought to himself.

Obviously, she was surely a young enchantress for men to worship her so much!

Carlos Mateo could not deny that he now found himself curious about this young French mademoiselle, and that was quite an admission for the uncompromising Carlos.

Now that he was there in the quiet solitude of his study, since his oldest son had marched out of the room to leave him alone, Carlos became quite thoughtful about things of the past. Perhaps his sons were more like him than he'd thought! When he recalled those days when he was a young man, he remembered how he had not found the young ladies his father had chosen for him to escort to be to his liking. By the time he'd gone from twenty to twenty-five years of age and there had been no serious romance in his life, he recalled how his father had become very irritated with his lack of interest in the lovely senoritas of his friends' families.

Never had it been a matter of no interest on Carlos's part, but merely that none of the lovely senoritas attracted him or held his interest.

It was only when that wild, fiery Theresa came into his life that he was flamed with desire as he'd never been affected before. Never had he gazed on more glorious beauty than he beheld in those flashing black eyes of hers, and her skin reminded him of rich deep gold satin. Those lush, sensuous lips of hers were so inviting it was enough to drive any man crazy and it certainly did just that to Carlos.

He would have defied his father and the whole world to possess this very bewitching woman with that Portuguese blood flowing within her. Carlos recalled all the violent arguments he'd had with his father over this woman, but in the end, Carlos had his way, assuring his father that he was a strong man and she would bend to his will and their ways.

In years to come, Carlos would be reminded of his father's sage words of wisdom when he'd told him, "No, she will not, son. Her ways are different than ours and never will she yield to you as you're thinking. In the end, it will only bring heartache and sorrow to both of you."

How right he had been! Carlos had realized when it was too late to do anything about it. Never would she allow herself to completely surrender to him, even though she'd given him two magnificent sons. That stubborn pride of his would never allow him to say he was sorry when he knew he'd been at fault and overbearing. Theresa would be crushed and hurt, and he'd watch as that hurt festered and grew like a cancer in her.

He'd always known why she sought the refuge up at Half Moon Bay with this relative of hers, Phil Cabrillo. God, how it had galled him that she wished to leave the fine mansion he'd provided for her to go to that humble cottage of old Phil's. For all the luxury he had and could provide for her, it was obvious to Carlos that none of this meant anything to her.

As crazy as it all was, he admired her tremendously, for she was that rare breed of woman he knew he'd never meet again. It was the reason that he had never sought another wife after she'd died. God knows, he'd had many opportunities to have his pick, being the prominent, wealthy man he was in the county.

Perhaps neither of his sons would have suspected him of being such a sentimental gentleman, but he was. It was just a part of himself that he had kept locked deep within him.

This was a rare night for Carlos. He found himself a little perplexed by the thoughts and feelings rushing through him like a parade of all the years past and gone forever. He was not a man who allowed himself to dwell on the past. Silly sentiment was not the way he'd been brought up by that strict Latin family of his. A young man did not give way to tears as the foolish female might. A young man must always show strength and control, so his father had told him for as long as he could remember.

Well, there would be no tears for Carlos, for they had been shed in the privacy of his bedroom long ago, but he did amble over to the teakwood liquor chest to get himself some of the brandy he kept there. When he had filled the cut-crystal glass, he moved back over to sit down in the leather-covered chair, sipping leisurely on the brandy and thinking about the pleasant times of his life.

He recalled the most wonderful, sweetest memories he'd shared with his beautiful Theresa. When he had finished the glass of brandy, he placed it over on the table. Such a very peaceful sleep fell over him that he remained there in his study the rest of the night.

It was not until the dawn was breaking that Carlos was roused up out of the leather chair to realize what he had done. Quietly, he slipped out of his study and up the stairs to go to his bedroom. Maybe Theresa had come to him in that late night hour and waved that magic wand over him, for he had not felt so serenely peaceful in many, many years. The feeling was so good that Carlos wanted it to remain with him the rest of his life.

No bitterness remained within him. He was free of all of it that had lain there for years. Dear God, what an absolutely glorious feeling it was! Never before had he realized how he'd allowed it to cripple him, but never again would that happen, he vowed.

He also vowed that when Mano returned to La Casa Grande, he would open his arms to him as he never had before. Carlos realized now that he had cheated himself of the greatest love he could have had in his lifetime—the love of his son!

Mario would also be aware of this new Carlos Mateo, and all would be well here at La Casa Grande. Yes, finally all would be healed!

Now his eyes did mist with tears, but he was not ashamed of those tears as he would have been at one time. He could only ask himself why it had taken a lifetime to finally become so wise to the splendor of truth.

A few misting tears fell from the eyes of another elderly gent this same night, and his grey mane of hair was as thick as Carlos Mateo's. He'd never known a lady as grand as the one who had given him such devoted, generous care as Aimee Aragon had the last day and night. Phil Cabrillo knew he would never forget her generous efforts. What was more impressive to him was the fact that she was the daughter of a wealthy vintner, and yet, she had not resented the fact that Mano had left her behind to care for an ailing old man like him! God, what a jewel he had!

He better never hear of Mano treating her badly, Phil thought to himself as he lay there in his bed that night. It was funny that the two of them had been able to carry on such conversations as they'd enjoyed in this brief period of time. She'd told him all about herself and her tour in Paris, and he had been just as eager to tell her about his life here at Half Moon Bay.

In a tone he took as genuine, she exclaimed, "I find you one of the most fascinating men I've ever met, Phil Cabrillo!"

He never doubted for a minute that she meant exactly what she said.

A slow, pleased grin came to his weathered face and his dark eyes twinkled so much like Mano's that they held Aimee entranced as she looked at him. Mano was as dark in his coloring as Phil. In that deep, melodic voice of his, Phil declared, "I find I share a mutual feeling about you, my little Aimee. I find you the most fascinating young lady I've ever met. Now, while you might not think so looking at this old man I am, there was a time when I had a few ladies fawning over me."

"Oh, I've no doubt about that at all, monsieur. The striking features of your face haven't faded with age. Not at all! There's so much about you that reminds me of Mano."

Phil studied her carefully and he saw that she was a very perceptive young woman. There was far more to this young woman than just a beautiful face and figure. She sought to look beyond the ordinary, and he knew she had measured him as he had her since the two of them had been here in the cottage alone.

"You think so, eh? Well, I would be very proud to think that. I adored his dear mother and she was Portuguese as I am, so perhaps since we are kin that explains that."

"Well, I know one thing, and that is that Mano holds you in high regards. He talks of you and his fond memories of his visits here at Half Moon Bay."

Phil gave her a nod of his head, for he knew what Mano's visits here had meant to the two of them—him as well as Mano.

It was only after she had bid him good night that the mist of tears had come to Phil's eyes. Looking out his bedroom window, he could view her graceful figure moving back and forth across the front porch. He knew she had sought the solitude of the darkness there to think about Mano, hoping she could see him riding up to the cottage. She was yearning for the sight of the man she loved, Phil knew.

He was feeling the same way but for different reasons. He could not help being apprehensive about what was happening to Mano, wherever he was. So Phil could only pray that he was

466

all right and soon would be galloping down that narrow lane leading up to the cottage.

As Mano was on his mind tonight, so was Theresa. Would she have approved of everything he'd done? God, he hoped so! She could never say he had not tried to warn her when she sought to marry Carlos. He had talked until he was hoarse, but she was so determined to have her way and in the end she had had it. Phil could understand her girlish daydreams of marrying a wealthy man who would give her all the fine things in life. He understood her yearning to have the fancy gowns, exquisite jewels, and a grand home.

It seemed like yesterday that the two of them had sat on the same porch where Aimee was now sitting. Theresa had sat there in the moonlight, with her curly black hair falling down over her face and her feet bare. The full gathered skirt she had worn was one she had made, as well as the simple batiste blouse.

Phil had told her, hoping to warn her, "For all these wonderful luxuries you would be getting, you must be prepared to sacrifice other things, Theresa. Do you think you would be willing to do this?"

Her curly head had turned to look at him. She had given forth a soft little laugh as she inquired of him, "I have nothing, so what could I possibly sacrifice, eh?"

Ah, how young she had been that night and how naive she was!

"Your wild, wonderful spirit, my dear Theresa! That is what you would have to deny and I don't think you could ever do it," Cabrillo had declared.

"Carlos loves me the way I am. He has told me so many times," she'd haughtily retorted.

"Maybe he says that now, but will he feel this way after he has married you, Theresa? What happens if he demands that you become the conventional Latin wife who is subservient to her husband? In the Spanish home, the husband is the master. This I know!"

She had leaped up from the porch and given out a lighthearted giggle, "Ah, I love Carlos very much, but no man could ever master me as you know."

Phil Cabrillo had to agree with her about that and this was what had troubled him so deeply that night so long ago. As she had declared that night before she and Carlos had married, Carlos never mastered her.

The marriage was doomed before it had begun, and Cabrillo knew it!

Chapter 59

A dazzling display of lightning shot across the late summer sky as Mano rode through the woods after he'd said his farewell to old Buck. As he had emerged from the woods into the clearing, he was a man feeling in the highest spirits. He had tasted the gratifying reward of his revenge for the man who had wronged his ladylove, and yet fate had deemed that he was not the one to have killed this Ross Maynard. Buck had done this. Ross Maynard had been justly punished.

Now the only thing occupying his thoughts was just getting back to Half Moon Bay to join Aimee. After a good night's sleep there at Phil's cottage, which he sorely needed, he would take Aimee home to San Mateo County. But once they arrived there, Mano was going to let his own father and Aimee's father know that no longer would they stand in the way of his and Aimee's happiness. She would be his bride—come heaven or hell!

All he had to do was think about seeing her lovely face and kissing those honey-sweet lips to urge him to spur Demonio into a swifter pace. He was riding toward his woman and his future, he told himself. With Aimee by his side, they were going to build themselves a wonderful future here in this California valley.

He rode through the night, indulging himself in his daydreams about the future. He realized now how things of the past could have a most significant meaning someday. Now he knew why he'd purchased a most magnificent oriental blue sapphire when he'd gone on one of his adventures and shipped out on a packet. At the time, he'd impulsively purchased the gem from a merchant in the foreign port his ship had stopped over in for a few days. This exquisite jewel would be his bride's ring. He could not have known some five years ago that he would find a girl and fall desperately in love with her and her glorious eyes would shine with as much blue-fire brilliance.

He also had some very definite thoughts about the wedding they would have. He wanted no grand, showy wedding, which would only end up being a boring, monotonous affair. He had no need for all that flair and he hoped Aimee would share this feeling. Somehow, he felt she would!

Dear God, he felt a sudden assault of weariness engulf him, and he had to admit he had the right to feel this way. But for the fact that he wanted to be with Aimee so much, he would have lain down on that cool, damp ground and fallen asleep.

As suddenly, he realized that he must be getting near Half Moon Bay, for the air seemed heavy with the moisture drifting in over the California coastline. He could feel it. So often when he was spending time there at Phil's cottage, he would wake up in the morning to be greeted by that haze and fog that seemed to invade the countryside until the sun came up to burn it all away.

The area up there was so different than the area in San Mateo County, with its hills and valleys, that Mano had been fascinated by it all.

Aimee was now sharing those same feelings as she stayed there with Phil, awaiting Mano's return. For some unknown reason, she seemed to wake up much earlier than she did back at Chateau L'Aragon. This morning was no different.

She wore one of Phil's old faded blue shirts as a nightgown, because she had washed her undergarments yesterday and this was all she had in her possession except for the divided riding skirt and the blouse she'd been wearing the day she was abducted.

She found it amusing when she thought of all the clothes there in her armoire back at her home. It also made her realize that one could do with a lot less if they must.

Dear Lord, there had been no luxury of a sweet-smelling bath nor had she enjoyed the pleasure of her silver-blond hair being cleansed.

As she stood there on Phil's porch, looking over the grass ladened with a heavy dew and misty fog, insidiously creeping nearer and nearer to the cottage, she remembered that Phil had mentioned a little cove that veered off the bay a short distance away. How marvelous it would be to give herself a bath in that stream and wash her hair before Mano returned! But she knew not the direction to go to get there, so she must ask Phil.

First, she must prepare breakfast for Phil, and then she would seek out this little stream she'd heard him speak about in their numerous conversations since Mano had left.

Phil could see her moving around the cottage in that bobtailed shirt of his, and all he could say was it was a good thing he was as old and as ill as he was. He had to admit he might not be able to restrain his own male lusty desires at the sight she presented. It was enough to make him wish that he were young and randy again. God, he wished it were possible to live his life all over again!

She sang a lively little French tune as she busily moved around his small kitchen, and he sat there in his bed, watching her with an admiring eye as she bent over in his shirt, which hardly covered her firm little behind.

When she came bouncing into his bedroom with a tray bearing his breakfast, which smelled so delightful, Phil sought to tease her, 'I didn't know that pampered young ladies like you were such good cooks."

"Ah, monsieur, it just goes to show you how we can surprise you, *oui?*" she grinned as she set the tray before him. Phil knew he was getting well when he found himself ogling her shapely legs being displayed by the short faded shirt she was wearing.

She noticed the path of his appraising black eyes and found it amusing. She gave out a soft little laugh and declared, "Now, I surely know, Phil Cabrillo, where Mano gets his devilish ways. It was from you!"

Sheepishly, he gazed up into those all-knowing deep blue eyes locking with his. They understood one another instantly. Those eyes of hers pierced him to the core of his being and there was a strange spell falling over the old Portuguese. Yet, the feeling was as old as the ages, and Phil understood it and was guided by it. It was the way of his people and his heritage. Some might find it strange, but Phil felt it to be the right time.

"Sit down, Aimee. Keep me company while I eat this fine food you're prepared for me."

Instinctively, she knew he was going to talk to her in a most confidential way, so she excused herself for a moment to pour herself another cup of coffee. When she returned to the bedroom, she smiled warmly, "Now, monsieur, I shall enjoy my coffee while you enjoy your breakfast, and then we shall talk, *n'est ce pas?*"

"Yes, little one, we shall talk," he grinned. He ate with relish of the food, just as he had lived his whole life with relish and exuberance. When he had finished eating and Aimee saw that his cup needed refilling, she rushed back into the kitchen to fill it.

"Now, we talk, *oui?*" she prodded the elderly old man propped up in the bed.

His weathered, wrinkled hands moved up to brush aside the straying grey hair falling over his forehead. She sensed a reluctance plaguing him. If she could have read his thoughts at that moment, she would have known that Phil had to face the possibility that Mano might not return to this cottage for her. Someone had to know, he reasoned. If something should happen to him, then the secret would be forever buried. This could not be!

"You, little Aimee, you are the only one to know what I am about to tell you. This must tell you how much I trust you. While I might feel as young as springtime this morn, I accept that I am an old man. There was a reason why Mano was always drawn up here to Half Moon Bay and it was the same reason his mother came here for her solace. It is true I am a relative, but what no one ever knew was how close a relative I am. I was guilty of making a pact with Theresa. I regretted it later, but it was too late by then. You see, Aimee, I was Theresa's father. Mano is my grandson, and there have been many times when I've cussed her for making that evil pact. God, you can't imagine how I've hurt to tell him that he was my grandson!" So expressive was his face as he spoke.

"Oh, how you must have suffered!" Aimee sighed, looking at the pained face of Phil.

"I won't deny that, but I honored a vow I made to my daughter. What else could I do?"

"Forgive me for what I am about to say, but I feel your daughter Theresa was most selfish to ask of you what she did," Aimee asserted in that impulsive, honest way of hers.

Phil reached out to take her hand, holding it there in his rough, wrinkled one for a moment before he spoke, "You are right, Aimee. Theresa was greedy and selfish. This is why happiness was never to be hers. I loved her dearly but I saw the truth before she died."

"Oh, Phil Cabrillo, I am so glad I have had the privilege to know you," Aimee sighed. "You are truly a most remarkable man!"

A deep voice echoed behind her, "And so am I!" She turned to see Mano standing there in the threshold, and it was obvious he had heard Phil's startling relevation. "Aimee's sentiments are mine, Grandfather," Mano declared with the hint of tears

473

coming to his eyes, and he allowed them to flow without any shame that Aimee was sitting there observing him. Seeing this man she loved being able to feel such depths of emotion endeared him to her all the more.

Then she chanced to turn to look at old Phil Cabrillo's face and there she saw the same overwhelming display of love and emotion.

What a very special moment this was in both of their lives, and she felt like she was intruding by being there. She gave them both a smile as she rose from her chair. "I shall see you two later, *oui?*" She moved to go to Mano, flinging her arms around his neck for the kiss she'd yearned for so desperately. He forgot everything in that one brief moment to kiss her lips, allowing them to tell her how glad he was to be back.

Both of the men in the room admired her understanding that this was a time for the two of them to be alone. Their admiration mounted to a new height for this remarkable woman, Aimee Aragon.

No one had to tell Mano Mateo that he had to be the luckiest hombre in the whole world to have won the heart and love of such a lady. When he finally sought to release her, he whispered tenderly in her ear, "I'll join you shortly, *mi vida.*"

"I shall be waiting for you, *mon cher.*"

Phil's eyes watched the young couple so much in love with one another. Oh, if only his Theresa could have known a love like theirs, how happy he would have been for her! Mano and Aimee were right for one another. It had not been the case with Theresa and Carlos.

To break the tenseness of the situation he and his grandson found themselves in, Phil sought to create some lightheartedness. He had listened to Mano speak his words of endearment in his language, being of Spanish heritage, while Aimee, in turn, had spoken the French language of her family and background.

"I pity your poor children. They are going to be much confused, I think. They will be speaking French and Spanish,

474

with a little English thrown in, too," he chuckled.

By now, Mano had released Aimee from his arms and she had made a quick departure. Now he sauntered over to the bed where the old man lay there propped up on the pillows, a glint of mischief in his dark, dancing eyes. "And perhaps there will be a little Portuguese thrown in too, *si?*"

With a searching look on his face, as if to measure Mano's true feelings about the startling revelation he'd just confessed to Aimee, Phil replied, "Well, if I have the chance, I shall surely teach them a little Portuguese."

By now Mano had reached the bed and he'd taken Phil's tanned, wrinkled hand in his strong one. "Oh, you'll have the chance." He looked down at the old man and now he knew and understood so much that had puzzled him all his life.

It was a moment where words were not necessary, and so he bent over to embrace Phil Cabrillo in his firm muscled arms. "Now I know why I've always loved you so and came here to Half Moon Bay. I find it so easy to say to you your rightful title—Grandfather. I'm just sorry I didn't know it years ago."

He felt the old man's body shake with his sobs as he confessed to Mano, "I am sorry, too, Mano, but I had given my word to Theresa. But I shall enjoy the rest of my days hearing you call me grandfather. I can't think of anything that would make me happier, my boy."

It was a golden moment in life that both of them would remember forever!

Chapter 60

By the time Mano left his grandfather, he was a young man reflecting on the years of his past and the years of his future. Without a shadow of a doubt, he was a man prideful of his heritage—the Spanish and the Portuguese. He admired no one more on the face of this earth than he did that old Portuguese fisherman he'd just left.

To be the grandson of such a man as Phil Cabrillo and the son of such a man as Carlos Mateo was enough to make any man hold his head high with pride, Mano considered. As he had never felt before in his whole life, he now felt a great compassion for his father, as strange as it might seem. The misguided love he'd harbored for his mother was not deserved. He realized that now. He had been wrong to have had such disillusions about her. She had not deserved it! She had deceived and lied to her husband, and Mano found that despicable, comparing her to the woman he loved. She had denied a father who did not deserve to be used so sorely but who loved her so much that he was willing to go along with her scheming ways to please her. No, she was not a woman to be admired or respected! Now Mano did not!

It was very understandable to Mano why she had never been a happy, contented person, for she was living a lie. As a man deeply in love with a woman, as he was with Aimee, he could well understand and sympathize with his father and the frustrations he must have endured living with such a woman.

From all the things his grandfather had told him in that short half hour they talked, Theresa played her little game of deception with Carlos from the moment they chanced to meet and he fell helplessly in love with her. None of Phil's warnings made an impact on her, for she was hell-bent on becoming the wife of a wealthy man like Carlos Mateo. It mattered not to her about anyone else, as long as she had her way. Mano called that a very self-centered, selfish woman, who was willing to sacrifice her father, her husband, and her sons.

He realized that he had wasted too much time in his twenty-five years of life idolizing the wrong person. From this day forward, he would not do that anymore!

Now he went to find a woman worthy of his respect and admiration, a woman who gave her whole love so unselfishly to the man she loved. He felt himself so lucky to be that man. With a woman like Aimee, a man could have all his dreams come true. Right now, he felt like he owned the whole world and there was no one he envied.

He knew the spot she liked near the woods, where the wildflowers grew, and he suspected that was where he would find her strolling. As he opened the gate, he had to push the two over-eager hounddogs back as they insisted on following him out the gate.

"Sorry, I don't wish your company right now. Get back!" Mano demanded of the two hounds. He slipped through the gate and secured the lock. All the weariness left him as he strolled along the path that he knew would lead him to that silver-haired enchantress out there somewhere in the woods. All that golden loveliness of hers, as he stood there in the bedroom listening to Phil talking to her, was enough to fire him with the wildest desires. When she had turned to see him standing there and her lovely face looked up at him with that radiant, glowing smile, he'd never viewed anyone as breathtakingly beautiful as Aimee Aragon. She had to be the most exquisite female in the whole world, Mano thought to himself as he moved toward the woods.

At least, she was as far as he was concerned!

He did not have to wander too far into the woods before he caught sight of her. As he had suspected, she was picking the wild verbenas growing there in their lovely shades of red and purple around a huge boulder, where wild ferns also flourished in the woods.

He stood for a moment to savor the sight of her, for she made a most alluring vision for his eyes, with those firm rounded hips of hers so delightfully displayed. He moved quietly up to where she stood, completely engrossed in the chore of plucking the flowers. When he stood there directly behind her, his hands reached out to clasp her wasplike waist.

Aimee gave out a startled jerk as she turned to face him. "Mano! You should not scare someone like that!" she declared as she dropped all the flowers she'd been picking to allow her hands to reach up to encircle his neck. "I missed you, *mon cher.* I missed you terribly!"

"No longer will you miss me or want me, *querida.* In fact, I intend to stay so close to you that you will become bored and tell me to leave," he declared as his hands held her firmly at the waist. There was a warm glow of passion in his dark eyes as they danced over her face.

"Oh, you think so? Try me, Mano Mateo!" she giggled as she challenged him, allowing her body to sway invitingly closer to his firm muscled one.

He looked down to see the flirting gleam in those lovely blue eyes of hers and he was most assuredly affected by the supple curves of her body pressing against the front of him. He grinned as he gave her tiny body an eager yank to draw her even closer. "You have to be a witch, Aimee Aragon, for you

478

have the power to cast a spell on me whenever it suits your fancy, it seems."

Her eyes met his, daring and bold. "You, Mano Mateo, are a Latin *gredin!*"

"*Gredin?* Now what is this you are calling me, *chiquita?*" he teased her.

"You are a scoundrel who makes me feel so wicked like a witch!"

"I do this to you?" he quizzed her, pretending to be utterly innocent and displaying an expression of surprise.

"Oh, don't you dare play such a game with me, Mano. you know exactly what you do to me. You have from the first moment we met. I've—I've never tried to deny it. That is not my way, and you also know that."

Before he allowed his lips to take those half-opened ones of hers inviting him to kiss them, he whispered tenderly to her, "I know, Aimee, and that is what made you so wonderful. That is what made you like no other woman I've ever known."

By now his lips were touching hers and no other words were necessary. The touch of his caress spoke for him and Aimee gave herself up to the sweet, searing heat of his passion seeking to consume her. His hands still had that special magical touch and his sensuous male body flamed her with the same wonderful, wild desire that knew no boundary. She eagerly invited him to take her once again to those lofty heights of ecstasy only he could carry her to.

As they had danced that night at his father's fiesta in unison, they now sunk down to the damp, dewy grass as though their bodies were already fused.

In that deep voice of his, Mano was already moaning his words of endearment to her, for he loved this woman so much that to declare his love for her was like breathing. She was his reason to live. She was everything he'd ever dreamed about finding in a woman!

He heard her gasps of pleasure as his huge hands began to release the restraining garments of clothing she wore and he felt the exciting arching of her tiny body pressing to be closer to him, firing him to a blazing peak of passion.

"Oh, Mano! Mano!" she sighed in the sweet agony rushing over her.

"I know, *querida*," he soothed her as he anxiously tried to rid himself of the clothes he wore.

By the time he had removed all his clothing and his naked body could feel the soft satiny flesh of Aimee, he was experiencing the most terrific, tantalizing sensations. He pulled her over so her tiny body could press his broad chest and her shapely legs could enclose his firm muscled thighs. His eyes could now look up at her lovely, impassioned face as she towered above him.

The sensuous mounds of her breasts were there for his eyes to worship before his lips sought to take the inviting nipples to tease. He knew the sensations he could stir, and the pleasure he created for her gave him the same exaltation.

Her undulating body told him this a few moments later as she moved with the same erotic motions as that night when they danced the flamenco dance, which was very suggestive and seductive.

He adored the way she allowed him to guide her as they made love. Yet, she also had to sense that he tried desperately to please her. Dear God, he had to confess that never had he tried to please a woman like he had Aimee!

The sweet, glorious rapture was now to such a peak that he could no longer hold back the floodgates. The surging currents of passion were too fierce and mighty and demanded release. He gave out a mighty gasp as he felt her fingers press against his back as she gave forth a breathless sigh of pleasure.

Aimee felt herself swept away by the force and power of Mano. He was like the majestic eagle soaring up to the heights of the heavens. She willingly allowed herself to be carried along to that zenith of rapture.

Once the fury of their passion was spent, they lingered there in one another's arms in a sweet, silent serenity. At that particular moment, there was no need for words to be spoken. Mano's arms, lips, and magnificent male body had told Aimee of his need and love for her. He fulfilled her so completely with his all-consuming love. The same was true for Mano. He knew she must love him as desperately and deeply as he loved her to surrender herself with such wonderful, wild abandonment.

His sensuous lips lightly touched her cheek as he finally whispered in her ear, "Do you suppose we'll ever know the comfort and joy of a soft bed, *mi vida?* Perhaps we'll have that to anticipate on our honeymoon, *si?*"

She turned languorously in his arms and her deep blue eyes twinkled deviously as she purred softly, "Our honeymoon, Mano?"

He laughed huskily, "Hell yes, our honeymoon! You don't think for a minute that I'm going to let you get away from me again, do you? Damned right, there's to be a wedding, my beautiful Aimee—yours and mine. I might add, it will be taking place quickly, for I am impatient. There'll be no long engagements for you and me, Aimee Aragon. I have no need for some grand flamboyant affair for the pleasures of others. I want only that you become my wife. That is all that matters to me."

Her arms encircled his neck and her fingers trailed up to caress his black hair with tender touches. "I adore you, Mano. I have no need to impress anyone with a grand wedding, as you call it. I would truthfully find it terribly dull and boring. I wish only to be your wife, so that we can go to this place you spoke about—this Valley of the Moon."

He hugged her closer to him, happily declaring, "Oh, *chiquita,* I was hoping you would feel this way. But I also know how much young ladies want a stupendous wedding with all the pomp and such."

"But I am not like most young ladies, Mano. Did you not tell me that?"

"I did, and it is why I fell hopelessly in love with you the moment I laid eyes on you that first night. You were like no other woman I'd ever met and I'd be willing to wager I'll be telling you this same thing many years from now."

"Oh, *mon cher*, I assure you that this is probably going to be true. My father was always exasperated because I didn't behave as the other young ladies my age."

Just before his lips claimed hers in a kiss, he declared to her, "Ah, *querida*, I am not your father and I adore the way you behave, just as long as it's me you're with."

She giggled and snuggled closer to his firm, forceful body. "Am I to have to put up with a jealous husband?"

He gave out a deep husky laugh as his strong arms claimed her once again. "You can be assured, *mi vida*, that I shall be a most jealous husband and a most possessive one, too."

A sly smile broke on her lovely face because he had told her how much he adored her!

Chapter 61

When Mano finally sought the comfort of a bed, he suddenly realized just how he had played his strength and indomitable will to accomplish the mission he'd set out to do when he'd left San Mateo County a few days ago. The tracking of Bigler's messenger for the ransom money had allowed him no time for sleep. Once he'd rescued Aimee, placing her here at Phil's cottage before he'd hit the trail again, he'd also allowed himself no luxury of sleep.

By the time he'd traveled down the same trail to return to the shack where Aimee was held captive and search for clues, another day was spent. The strange turn of events involving the drifter Buck had simplified his search for Fred Bigler, which could have gone on for an endless number of days and nights. Lady Luck had been with him, it seemed.

With that score settled once and for all, he was happy to say, he was free to return to Aimee on the same day. He was beholden to old Buck for ridding him and the world of the likes of Fred Bigler or Ross Maynard, whichever name he chose to be known by.

Those fleeting moments after he'd lain his head on the soft pillow on the narrow cot in Cabrillo's small back room, he was convinced that he'd inherited that sharp instinct of old Phil. Never had Mano been more at peace with himself and his life. Now he was enlightened about the things in his life that had troubled him for so long. He had the woman he loved back with him, a grandfather he already loved, and a father he now understood. Their love could now grow. A deep, deep sleep rushed over him like a fierce tide of the ocean lapping at the California shores.

Aimee had given him a tender kiss as she'd escorted him to the small door, closing it on him. "Sleep, Mano, before you fall flat on your face. You're strong, *mon cher*, but you're not invincible."

He gave her a grin and an agreeing nod of his black head as he turned to make straight for the cot. Like an obedient child, he did as she'd requested as soon as he had removed his shirt and pants. With a lazy yank or two, he removed his dirt-covered boots and let them drop to the floor. She was right that he was ready to fall on his face!

Aimee barely had time to turn away from the door and walk down the narrow little hallway when she caught sight of a shadowy movement through the doorway of Phil's bedroom. She went to peer into the room to satisfy her curiosity and check on the elderly Cabrillo. What she saw made her stiffen and place her hands at her waistline as she admonished the old man, "Now, just what in the devil do you think you are up to? You just take those clothes off and get back into that nightshirt. I haven't worked myself silly for you to undo it all by acting foolish!"

Phil stood there buckling his belt, turning to look in her direction as he continued to fumble with it. His dark eyes glared up at her as she stood there like a mother hen protecting her young. That determined look on her face and her hands placed firmly at her waist would give one the impression she meant every word she was speaking.

She looked so adorable and cute that Phil could hardly suppress the amused smile coming to his wrinkled face. But she wasn't going to boss him. That cantankerous old Portuguese had never allowed any woman to boss him, and he was far too old to change his ways now.

"I will not put my nightshirt back on, missy. I'm through with this bed. You've done healed me of what ailed me."

She raised a skeptical fine-arched brow and a sly smile came to her face as she accused him, "Monsieur, you and I both know what this is all about. You are still weak and we both know that, *oui?*"

That little minx was just too damned smart, Phil thought to himself. She'd seen right through him with those all-knowing eyes of hers. She stood there in the doorway with such a stubborn look on her face he rather doubted that she'd allow him to leave the room if she set her mind to it.

"I'll make a deal with you. I'll walk around the house a little, and if I begin to feel too weak, then I'll get back in my nightshirt, all right?" Phil parried with her, and those dark eyes of his were as persuasive as his grandson's.

"I can't cope with two husky men falling on their faces." She shrugged her shoulders as she relented to his suggestion. As her swishing skirts swayed when she moved to leave the room, he heard her mutter, "Oh, now I know where Mano gets that headstrong way of his!"

Nothing could have pleased Phil Cabrillo more than to hear her compare his grandson to him. Now he did not restrain the smug smile coming to his face as he pushed the thick grey hair away from his eyes.

Ah, Mano had himself a lot of woman in this one! What a happy and hectic life they would have!

Twelve hours would pass before Mano awoke from his sleep, and when he finally did stir, opening his eyes sluggishly, it was the lovely vision of Aimee his eyes beheld. She stood there by

485

the cot, her deep amethyst-blue eyes worshipping the sight of him. "Good afternoon, sleepyhead! You've just enjoyed a whole twelve hours of sleep. You see, you needed it!"

There was a twinkle in her eyes and he lay there giving forth a boyish grin. "You were right, *chiquita!* It was a very tired hombre that hit this bed."

"I know."

"I will admit that you are a very smart young lady. I confess to you that I didn't realize how weary I was." His hands reached out to take hers.

She sunk down on the bed beside him. "I've some warm food waiting for you. I am happy to tell you that your grandfather ate heartily and is now down by the stream fishing for our dinner tonight. Is that not wonderful?"

"You have magical powers, *mi vida!* You have obviously made him well," Mano declared as he sat up in the bed.

"Ah, he is a most impossible man to control. I could not keep him in bed yesterday after you arrived and went to this room to sleep. He was up dressing himself and defying my orders to get back in the bed."

Mano gave out a deep, throaty laugh, "He always was a stubborn old cuss and I imagine he always will be. I bet he stayed up, too, didn't he?"

"You know he did, and I have to admit he was walking as lively as ever this morning. Such a breakfast he put away, I could not believe it!"

Mano remarked that she'd probably spoiled him with all her fine cooking and he was going to be sorry to see her go.

"When will we be leaving for home, Mano?"

"In the morning, *querida*. I figure we need to ease the minds of some worried, concerned people back there at the Chateau L'Aragon, *si?*"

"Oh, yes. I hate to think of the sleepless nights they've endured over all this," she sighed solemnly.

He apologized for sleeping so much of the day away but promised her she would be back at the Chateau L'Aragon before nightfall tomorrow. "But I have no intentions of allowing you to stay there very long, Aimee Aragon," he lightheartedly teased her. It brought back a smile to her face.

"Oh, so you are already starting to play the role of lord and master, Monsieur Mateo?"

He did not answer her. Instead, he gave a tug on her hands strong enough to pull her down to join him there on the bed.

As his lips were enjoying the sweet nectar of her parted ones, she let out a shriek of panic, pushing frantically on Mano's chest and urging him to let her up. Her nose had smelled the burning aroma of the food she'd left on the stove when she'd come to check on Mano. He'd proven to be such a distracting force she'd forgotten about her cooking.

Mano had a stunned look on his face, for she did not take the time to explain as she rushed out of the room. He leaped off the cot and began to pull on his pants, muttering, "What in the hell hit her?"

Hastily, he put on his shirt, rushing out of the room in his bare feet to go in search of her and find out what had interrupted his kiss.

As soon as he entered the kitchen, he saw the dilemma she'd gone to face. Smoke circled up from the cast-iron pot and the smell of burned beans permeated the small room. She was surveying the contents and that soft voice of hers was spouting a string of cusswords.

"Shame on you, *chiquita*. Such words coming from your sweet mouth," he laughed, trying to cajole her.

"Shame on you, Mano Mateo, for making me forget the food. This just happened to be the meal I've been preparing for your enjoyment," she retorted as she brushed a stray wisp of her fair hair away from her forehead.

He walked across the room to examine the pot. "All is not lost here." He recalled one day in the kitchen at the ranch, when Minerva had burned a pot of beans cooking on her stove and he'd seen her scoop out the top of them to put in another pan, adding some more water.

He took charge of the situation and instructed her to get another pan. He left the layer of beans seared in the bottom of the pot. Aimee watched as he added some water to the salvaged portion. An amazed expression came to her face and she told him, "Once again, you have amazed me, Mano."

A crooked grin broke out on his face. Smugly, he declared to her, "Oh, I vow I'll never cease to amaze you."

It was at this moment that Phil Cabrillo entered the kitchen with the magnificent catch he'd made in the small creek where he had been fishing. "A grand dinner the three of us will enjoy tonight, eh? Grab us a couple of knives, Mano my boy." As his grandfather requested, he followed him out the back door, taking no time to come back to get his boots.

As the two of them sat outside on an old wooden bench to clean and scale the fish, Phil happened to notice Mano's feet. He'd not been around Mano as a young barefoot boy but he could look at him now and imagine the kind of lad he had been. At last, he was being rewarded!

It had been a wonderful blessing he'd received, Phil thought to himself as they shared this moment together.

Mano had no idea of the private musings of old Phil but he knew he was certainly feeling like his old self again. This pleased Mano, since he and Aimee were due to leave the first thing in the morning.

As they cleaned the fish, they talked of many things. Mano had a boyish grin on his face as he spoke of his plans to marry Aimee just as soon as possible.

"You'd be a fool to not rush that pretty lady into a wedding. I wholeheartedly approve of your plans. Are you prepared for her father's refusal, my boy?" his grandfather asked him.

"I would hope for his blessing, but with or without it, Aimee will be my bride, Grandfather. No one is going to prevent that." His black eyes flashed bright with firm determination.

"And Aimee feels as strongly?"

"I am sure she does."

Phil smiled as he patted his grandson's shoulder, telling

Mano, "I've no doubt that she loves you very much. You see, we talked often while you were away. I'm just glad you think she feels as strongly as you about her father's possible objecting to a marriage."

A few hours later the three of them sat down to the grand dinner Phil had assured them they'd have. It was a festive occasion, with a lot of gaiety and laughter.

After the meal was over, Phil sung some Portuguese songs while Mano strummed the guitar and Aimee delightfully applauded the two of them. From his jolly air and gay laughter, Aimee or Mano did not suspect how sad Phil was feeling about their departure early in the morning.

His cottage would seem very quiet and dull without Aimee and her soft gay laughter. It would seem strange for a day or two not to see her feisty figure and beautiful face.

The hour was late when they finally said good night and dawn was only a few hours away. But as the evening was coming to an end, Aimee had kissed him on the cheek and declared, "Well, you will just have to spend some of the winter months with us up this place, Valley of the Moon. Won't he, Mano?"

"I'd already planned on that," Mano grinned.

"We'll see," Phil remarked, trying not to show how pleased he was by the invitation.

It gave him something to look forward to now that he knew he would not be having Mano spend so much time at his cottage. It eased some of the sadness weighing on him, knowing he'd have to watch them leave in the morning.

Chapter 62

They galloped across the coastline of San Francisco Bay for several miles. A striking pair they made, and the people of the fishing villages they passed threw their hands up to give them a friendly wave. Some just stopped by the side of the dirt road to watch the pair ride by them—the tall, dark Latin gentleman astride the grey dappled thoroughbred and his beautiful companion riding in front of him, her glorious blond hair flying back wildly as they traveled swiftly down the road.

It was exciting and thrilling to travel this way back home with Mano. The last time she had traveled this way she had been filled with fright and uncertainty of what fate had in store for her in the company of Cody and Buck.

The time went by so fast that she could not believe the sight she was suddenly viewing over in the distance was the outskirts of San Jose. She knew that Chateau L'Aragon lay just beyond there. Mano was a man of his word and he would be getting her back home before nightfall, just as he'd promised.

He chanced to turn in her direction. She looked so breathtakingly beautiful he swelled with instant desire for her.

She wore such a happy, excited expression and he realized how elated she was to be coming home.

Compassion and tenderness washed over him when he thought about the horrible ordeal she'd endured as the captive of Cody and Buck. But she had only sobbed in his arms that first night when he'd rescued her. It would seem that she'd put the whole miserable episode behind her once they'd arrived at Phil's cottage.

Perhaps she had been raised as the pampered daughter of Paul Aragon, but one would never suspect it from the way she'd labored over Phil's old stove and cleaned his humble cottage up at Half Moon Bay. He loved and admired her all the more for being like that.

Not once had he heard her cry or moan about the fact that she'd had only the one change of clothing, which was what she'd worn the day of her abduction. A pair of Phil's old pants and his old faded shirt were the change of clothing she wore while her one outfit was constantly washed.

It was Phil's old shirt she'd worn last night while they had dined, so that her one outfit could dry and be ready for her to wear home the next morning.

"You are very beautiful when you are happy, *querida*. I've never seen anything more lovely than you are at this moment. I never shall," he declared in a warm, passionate voice.

Her eyes gazed over at him, reminding Mano of exquisite gems as they sparkled in the bright California sunshine. "You say the sweetest things, Mano. Perhaps that's how you won this heart of mine so completely."

He gave out a deep roar of laughter, "Oh, no, it was far more than the words I spoke to you, *querida*. You knew that no other man would ever love you as much as I love you. Is that not so?" His eyes locked into hers.

"It is so, *mon cher*," she willingly confessed to him.

Mano suddenly recognized exactly where they were, declaring to her that they were almost home now. He also observed the sun sinking lower in the sky. The magnificent purple blending into the rose and gold in the western horizon could have been his lady's lovely eyes.

As they rode up the winding hillside, which would bring them up to the stone wall surrounding the grounds of Aimee's home, Mano was filled with a wave of sadness to have to be parted from her even for the short time he would have to endure.

As they arrived at the entrance gate and Mano had secured his horse to the hitching post, there seemed to be no activity around the estate. He assumed that everyone had left the winery for the day, going to their home for the evening meal.

With autumn approaching, the days were growing much shorter now, so Aragon's hired hands did not labor as long in the winery as they did in his vineyards. It was the same over at La Casa Grande, but Mano knew that their evening meal was always held at that appointed hour regardless of the season or when the sun set.

But he suspected that here at the Chateau L'Aragon it might be different and he figured that they were going to be interrupting the dinner hour. But he also knew that it would be a most joyous interruption to the family to see their lovely daughter, safe and sound.

As he helped Aimee from his horse and their bodies brushed against one another, he felt the overwhelming need to declare to her, "I can't wait long for you, *mi vida*. Please don't ask me to. To leave you tonight is going to be sheer hell!"

Her hand went up to his tanned cheeks and she murmured softly, assuring him, "Oh, Mano, Mano, *mon cher*, you will be no more miserable than I will be. We will not let that happen to us. I am as anxious as you are that we shall be together forever, never separated again."

He was a man assured by her words. After all, Aimee had never lied to him. Her blunt honesty had been one of the things that had impressed him from the very first time they had met.

"That's all I need to hear from you, *chiquita*," he said with a pleased smile on his handsome face as he led her through the gate and up the flagstone walk toward the entrance of the two-story stone house.

It was Hetty who ushered them through the door and excitedly greeted Aimee by throwing her arms around her, exclaiming her delight to see her safely home. "We've all been so worried about you, mademoiselle."

"It's wonderful to be home again, Hetty."

"Oh, what a grand night this is going to be. Everyone is gathered now in the parlor having a glass of wine, waiting for my call for dinner." She gave Aimee a wink of her eye as she told her, "I'll hold it up for a minute or two. I feel there will be a call for a welcoming home toast to you before anyone wishes to eat their dinner, eh?"

"I am sure you are right, Hetty. We'll go on in then," Aimee smiled, patting the housekeeper's shoulder. Mano stood there, observing the warmth between the two of them, and he was reminded of the warmth that existed between him and Minerva over at La Casa Grande.

When the two of them walked into the elegant parlor, it was a moment Mano would never forget for the rest of his life. The excited dark eyes of her two brothers lit up as they turned to see their sister. Paul Aragon was standing there by the fireplace, and his aristocratic features turned from a stern, serious air to overwhelming pleasure as he stared at Aimee. It was only as he hastily glanced at Mano that the expression changed.

But it was Lisette Aragon who rose from the settee, shrieking her daughter's name as she grabbed her in her arms. As they embraced, Mano noticed another guest in the room, whom Aimee had not yet seen. It was she who held his attention completely. Her eyes entranced him as he gave her a warm, friendly smile, which she returned. She sat in the rose brocade overstuffed chair, her dainty feet propped up on a footstool covered in the same fabric.

Her dark auburn hair was attractively streaked with grey. She wore it piled high atop her head with wisps teasing her temples. She did not have to be standing up for Mano to know that she was a petite lady.

She tilted her head, as if she were surveying him most carefully, but he saw the hint of the vivacious lady she must have once been in her amethyst eyes, enhanced by the magnificent teardrop earrings of the same color dangling from her ears.

No one had to tell Mano that the exquisite blue-violet silk dressing gown she wore, with its French lace collar, was very costly. She looked very attractive in it.

It was not until Aimee had been generously embraced by her mother, father, and two brothers that her eyes glanced over in the corner to see the lady Mano had been staring at.

He did not have long to wait as he heard his beloved Aimee give out a wild shriek of delight, rushing over to the lady sitting in the chair, "*Mon Dieu, Tante* Denise, what a wonderful homecoming to find you here! I can't believe it!"

The two hugged and kissed one another. "Believe it, *ma petite*. I am here just waiting for you to return." As they embraced, it was Aimee's *Tante* Denise whose face Mano saw, for Aimee's back was turned toward him. As he stood there observing the two of them together, he knew who Aimee looked like. It was not Paul Aragon or his wife, Lisette. It was her aunt.

As Hetty had said, it was a most gala occasion that evening at the Chateau L'Aragon. Mano had not expected to remain for the dinner hour. While Paul Aragon had graciously thanked him for the rescue of his daughter, it was the rest of the family who'd insisted he remain to share the dinner hour with them. No one was more insistent that he stay than her aunt from France, so he agreed.

Mano enjoyed himself tremendously except on those rare occasions he chanced to glance in Paul Aragon's direction and saw his disapproving eyes upon him.

After the dinner hour was over and the group was about to return to the Aragon parlor, Mano decided to take his leave to travel on to La Casa Grande. It was not going to matter whether it was tonight or tomorrow, he was not going to have Aragon's blessing to marry his daughter, he decided.

Perhaps it was the look on his face and the tense feeling in his strong hand as he held hers when they were walking back into the parlor, which prompted Aimee to blurt out, "Papa, I think Mano has an announcement to make and I can't see any reason why it should be delayed."

His black eyes darted down at hers to see a devious glint of mischief there, as if she were daring him. He swelled with pride and love for her. Arrogance and his proud Mateo spirit mounted as he turned from her to meet the eyes of her father. He would not plead or beg for her hand. No, he would merely state his intentions to Paul Aragon. This was exactly what he sought to do as he declared, in a very firm, determined voice, "Yes, Senor Aragon, what Aimee says is true. I intend to marry your daughter. We love one another very much. We always have and we always will."

While Paul stood for a moment without making a reply, a soft accented voice declared enthusiastically, "Ah, *magnifique!*" It mattered not to Aimee's aunt that her brother glared at her disapprovingly.

Trying to gain control of himself, Paul suggested that Mano return to the chateau tomorrow so that they might discuss this matter.

"Oh, I shall, sir." He now turned his attention to Aimee, requesting that she accompany him to the door. In turn, he bid good night to Lisette Aragon, Emile, and Armand. It was Aimee's aunt he said farewell to last as he held Aimee's hand. "Now I know why she talks about you all the time."

Denise looked up at his handsome face and she was carried back to yesteryears. Dear God, he was a handsome devil! In that moment, she wished she could have lived her whole life over again! She envied Aimee! But then, how many women could look back and say that they'd lived and enjoyed life to the fullest as she had? Poor Lisette could surely not do it, for if the truth were to be told, Denise imagined life with her brother Paul had been very dull and boring most of the time.

Ah, no, never would she have traded places with the dear, sweet ladies like her sister-in-law! Now, Aimee would be different. If she had ever met a man like this Mano and she had loved him and he had loved her, as these two obviously did, then she would have settled for that.

Mano was the one now pondering the message given to him by the little French lady as she merely gave him an approving nod of her head as her gesture of farewell when he and Aimee turned to leave the parlor. She liked him! Mano felt.

As he took a final kiss from Aimee's lips, he could not resist telling her before he left, "I find your aunt a most adorable lady."

"I love her too, so very much."

"I can see why you would, *querida*. The two of you are so much alike."

"That is interesting you would say that, Mano, since this is the first time you have met her. Would you think I was crazy if I told you that I feel closer to her than I do my own mother?"

"No, *chiquita*, I would not think you crazy at all," he told her. He dared not tell her why he so instinctively felt as he did. It was best that he now take his leave.

All the way to La Casa Grande, Mano was engulfed by the strangest feeling about this lady he'd met tonight. This woman from France certainly intrigued him!

Chapter 63

For hours they talked, sipping from their glasses of wine as they had done during those months when Aimee had been in Paris. They laughed and giggled together as her aunt told her about the various episodes of her life since they'd last seen one another. Aimee told her about Mano and their plans to marry. She told her about this lovely place up in Valley of the Moon where Mano planned they would live and build their winery.

"Promise me, *cherie,* that you will let nothing stop you from marrying this wonderful man who obviously loves you so very much. I mean nothing!"

"Oh, that is an easy promise to make and keep, *Tante* Denise."

"I am going to test you, *ma petite,* about that. Are you sure you can keep this promise to me?"

Aimee grinned, "Absolutely sure! Nothing will stop me from marrying Mano."

"Good! This is the only thing I will ever ask of you as long as I live. I like your Mano, and to delay such a love can be a disaster. Marry him, Aimee, and let nothing delay it. You promise me?"

"I swear to you, *Tante* Denise, that I shall marry Mano within a week's time. Now does that satisfy you?" she gave a soft little laugh.

"I am satisfied; I am happy. Now, *ma petite*, I am very tired and very sleepy. Shall we kiss and call it a night?"

They kissed, but for some strange reason, Aimee sought to cling to her in their embrace. "I love you, *Tante* Denise, and I always will. To let you know just how much I love you I think I shall tell Mano that our first daughter shall be named Denise, after you."

This was more than Denise could endure without tears flowing down her pale cheeks. "Ah, *cherie*, this is the greatest honor you could ever pay me and you've made me the most happy lady tonight." She gave out one of those little delightful gales of laughter Aimee fondly recalled from the past.

"Now, to bed with you, and remember your promise to me, Aimee, *ma petite*," Denise urged her daughter, for she found herself weakening.

The two of them gave forth a duet of soft laughter as Aimee bent down to embrace her aunt and kiss her on the cheek. "I am so very happy you came to us, *Tante* Denise! I hope you rest well tonight."

As the two of them released one another, Denise declared, "Oh, I shall rest very well now that you are safely back home. Now, you go to bed and sleep, *ma cherie*. You've had a long day and night, eh?"

"Ah, my bed is going to feel so wonderful," Aimee sighed as she turned to bounce out of the room. Just before she went out the door, she turned to look at her beloved aunt once more before shutting the door. "Oh, I'm glad you came! I've missed you, you know!"

Denise was doing a battle to restrain the tears beginning to form in her eyes, but she managed to smile as she told her daughter, "And I missed you so very much, *ma petite*. But our wonderful memories helped me when I got lonely for you, Aimee. Wonderful memories are a treasure, *oui?*"

"*Oui, Tante* Denise. Good night!" Like a beautiful butterfly in flight, she was gone and the door was closed. There was no longer a need for Denise to hold back her tears and she gave way to them. She walked slowly to the window and pulled back the sheers, looking at the dark sky with the twinkling stars and the moon shining down on Lisette's lovely garden. She opened the window to absorb the glorious fragrance of the array of flowers blooming in the garden.

A part of her was so very tempted to tell her daughter the truth, which had been concealed all these many years, but she hadn't. Now she was glad and proud of herself for this last noble act of her life. Now that responsibility lay in Lisette's gentle hands if she chose to do so. What was she to gain now if she had told Aimee? If ever she would have told her, it should have been during those many months that Aimee was in Paris staying with her. Then was the time, but she had let it slip through her fingers. She had had her golden opportunity, and Aimee would have accepted the truth or she would have rejected her.

Denise knew now why she hadn't done so. She could not have endured Aimee's rejection and disgust for her. Slowly, she sunk down on the bed and removed her soft satin slippers. Propping herself up on the mountain of pillows, she reached over to dim the lamp on the nightstand. It dawned on her how weary she was just from the effort to dim the lamp.

She closed her eyes but sleep did not come. What did come to her, as she lay quietly there in the darkness, was a parade of her life. Visions and images of the past ambled by in her thoughts, and there was no inkling of time as far as Denise was concerned. But a most marvelous peace and serenity engulfed her as she thought finally of this time and this particular moment she'd just spent with her daughter.

When sleep did come, it was the most peaceful and the

deepest sleep Denise had ever known, so she did not fight it but willingly surrendered to it.

The next day, all the mysteries and puzzles were cleared up for Aimee. When she'd left her *Tante* Denise's room, she had been troubled by the feel of the delicate, frail body she'd embraced. Her aunt was ill—very ill, Aïmee realized.

As weary as she was, sleep would not come because her thoughts were whirling with disturbing musings. A foreboding that her aunt had sought to come to Chateau L'Aragon to die struck Aimee like a bolt of lightning. Denise had not wanted to die alone in Paris without any of her family there with her.

Aimee knew instinctively that her aunt had little time left, which was why she was making a point in drawing a promise from her tonight that she would marry her young man and let nothing delay her wedding.

There in the darkness of her room, Aimee looked out her window into the blackness outside. To the quietness surrounding her, Aimee whispered that vow again, "Oh, never you fear, my dear *Tante* Denise, nothing shall keep me from becoming Mano's wife. Nothing!"

It was a bittersweet atmosphere that hung over Chateau L'Aragon the following week after Aimee had returned to her home. Her aunt had died during the night and Aimee's instincts had been correct. She realized it was a strange revelation she'd experienced. She sought to discuss it with no one but her dear friend and maid, Jolie, that next day. It was Jolie who had discovered Aimee's aunt had expired during the night.

"She knew she was dying, mademoiselle. I heard her and your mother talking one day out on the terrace. She waited only for your return. I heard her say so. You came home last night, so she was too weary to keep fighting for her life. She was ready to go after she saw you, I think," Jolie told her.

"I think you are right, Jolie. So I must do as she requested me to and defy all the conventional traditions of this family. I shall marry before the week is over," Aimee declared to her startled maid.

As Denise had wished, she was buried on the tranquil verdant slope of ground where an old live oak stood to give a comfortable shade to her grave. A lovely garden of wildflowers flourished by the site, which Denise would have liked because of their brilliant color.

It was only the family who attended the private service held for Paul's sister except for Mano Mateo. It was he who was standing by Aimee's side when she announced to her father, later that evening in the parlor, her intentions to marry Mano in a few days.

Paul gasped in a state of shock, "Dear God, are you crazy? This would be unheard of at a time like this! I will not permit it! I can't believe you would dishonor the name of Aragon like this!" Never had Lisette seen her husband so furious as she stared up at his flushed, rosy face.

"Ah, Papa, that is where you are wrong. I am honoring the Aragon name by keeping a promise I made to my aunt the night she died. Her last words were that she wished me to marry Mano immediately and let nothing—absolutely nothing—stand in my way. This I shall do!" She took Mano's arm and led him out of the room into the hallway toward the front door.

It was not until they were in the gardens with the moonlight gleaming down on her silvery-blond hair, that Mano voiced his overwhelming admiration and pride in her. "Ah, *querida*, how wonderful you are! I have myself a very brave, courageous senorita. You are going to keep me on my toes, I'm thinking," he teased her. She turned to see the devious gleam in his black eyes.

"You can be assured I will. I guess you know that there is no getting out of it now, Mano Mateo. I shall be Senora Mateo before the week is over or I'll swear my *Tante* Denise will haunt you forever."

"Oh, *chiquita*, I can believe you. Truly I can! I surrender to your demands," he grinned, giving forth a dramatic gesture of his hands in submission.

They both broke into lighthearted, gay laughter as they came together in a loving embrace. That warm intimacy was theirs as they clung together.

It was Aimee who finally pushed away from his broad chest, gazing up at his face to inquire, "What about your family, Mano, what about your father?"

"What about my father?" He continued to lightly kiss her cheek and his nose nuzzled the sweet fragrance of her golden hair.

"Have you told him about our plans to be married?"

A grin was on his face as he looked down at her. "It has been discussed and settled once and for all, *chiquita*."

"You—you make it sound so simple and uncomplicated, Mano, when I happen to know that your father would never give such hasty approval to you marrying an Aragon. What kind of magic did you use on him, I'd like to know?"

There was a bit of the devil in those black eyes of his and she saw it instantly even before he began to explain. "I simply told him that I was going to marry the lady who carried his grandchild." He felt her petite body stiffen immediately against him.

"You what? You—you told him I was pregnant? Mano!" she shrieked. He sensed that she was preparing to slap him and he reached out to grab her arm with a lightning motion.

"You are insufferable, Mano, and the most conceited man I've ever known!"

He still wore that grin of mischief on his handsome face. "But it worked, *querida*. Besides, how do you know that I was telling a lie? I might just be right, you know. Do you dare to deny that, eh?"

Meekly, she had to confess that he spoke the truth. She allowed his arms to hold her as she became suddenly quiet and thoughtful.

When Mano would have prodded Aimee to ask what was troubling her, she abruptly came alive in that spirited way of hers. "You are incorrigible, Mano Mateo, but I love you with all my heart and I guess you know that."

"I do, *querida,* and I always have. It has nothing to do with conceit." There was nothing light or frivolous about his manner as he now spoke to her. He spoke from his heart in truth and sincerity. "As a man, I'd always had visions of the woman I'd love all my life. Until I met you, I'd never hoped to find such a goddess, so I'd expected to remain a bachelor for a long, long time."

She stood up on tiptoe to plant a kiss on his cheek, declaring, "Oh, Mano, I'm so glad I changed your mind about that. Your bachelor days are numbered, *mon cher.* The end of the week will be here before we know it."

So it was, and there was no time to prepare for any grand or formal wedding, which the two of them did not wish to endure anyway. There was no time for a seamstress to stitch Aimee a fancy wedding gown, but it thrilled Lisette that Aimee excitedly wished to wear the gown she'd worn when she'd married Paul Aragon. It was a lovely white satin gown with white gauze trimming. There was a delicate lace veil, which hardly covered Aimee's head and trailed to her shoulders.

She confessed that she liked the styling of Lisette's gown better than the wedding gowns now in fashion, with their high necks and long sleeves. Lisette's gown had short puffed sleeves and a décolleté neckline. She also preferred the short lacy veil to the long tulle train they were now wearing.

"The orange blossoms for the bride's bouquet is an old French tradition. Did you know that, *ma petite?*" Lisette asked her.

"No, I did not, but I love those beautiful white roses in your garden, Mother. That is what I will carry for my bouquet."

"And you will be the most beautiful bride in the whole world, my angel," Lisette declared, kissing her daughter on the cheek. As she kissed her, she thought about her sister-in-law, Denise, and was eternally grateful that she had not told Aimee the truth the night she died.

As Aimee had vowed, her wedding took place there in the parlor of the Chateau L'Aragon. It was a very simple, private wedding, but to Aimee and Mano it was exactly as they had hoped it would be, with only their families gathered there in the parlor.

Aimee felt the presence of her *Tante* Denise there with her, approving wholeheartedly. After all, she and her *Tante* Denise had never been the conventional type of ladies. She knew that there would be those neighbors in the California countryside and valley who would ridicule and gossip about this strange, scandalous behavior of hers to marry so soon after her aunt's death. But she and *Tante* Denise knew there was no disgrace or dishonor to what she'd sought to do.

Besides, she was leaving this valley to go with Mano to Valley of the Moon, where they would seek their future and grow their grapes. She was now seized with the same challenge and excitement as Mano when he talked about this land and the winery, Golden Splendor.

After the brief wedding ceremony and festive, sumptuous lunch, served in the dining room aglow with urns filled with colorful flowers from Lisette's garden, Mano's black eyes sent the message to Aimee that it was time they made their departure. She silently slipped out of the room to rush upstairs and change into her riding skirt and jacket.

There, as she changed her clothes and finished packing the valise, Jolie helped her. "I shall miss you, mademoiselle. But I am happy for you. I hope you will be as happy when I tell you that Emile and I will be married in late autumn." She gave out one of her soft little giggles as she confessed to Aimee, "Emile figures that you have now mellowed his father. I pray that is so."

Aimee embraced her warmly, "I'm sure I have. My goodness, it was a miracle to see him and Carlos Mateo actually enjoying themselves, laughing and talking together like old friends. Love is a wonderful thing, Jolie! Amazing things can happen, *n'est ce pas?*"

"Ah, *oui*, mademoiselle!"

A short time later, Jolie watched her fair-haired little mistress ride away with her new husband. She stood at the window with tears of sadness and joy flowing down her cheeks. Others there at the Chateau L'Aragon were shedding their tears of sadness and happiness. The two husky brothers, Armand and Emile, were affected by the sight of their lovely sister becoming the bride of Mano Mateo.

The glorious sight of his daughter as a bride, so radiant and breathtakingly lovely, brought a mist to Paul Aragon's eyes. He swelled with overwhelming pride.

Lisette gleamed with a motherly pride, for she knew she was the only mother Aimee had ever known. It did not matter that Denise had given birth to her, for it was she who had raised her and cared for her. Aimee would never forget that, even if she knew the truth.

Long after Carlos and Mario Mateo had arrived back at La Casa Grande, Carlos remained in his study, enjoying a brandy and thinking about this memorable day. He was glad that he'd given Mano his mother's plain gold ring to slip on Aimee's finger. He was glad he'd not given it to Theresa. He knew Mano had been overcome with emotion that his father wanted him to give to his bride the wedding band that had belonged to Carlos's mother.

As they traveled toward their new home, Aimee declared her pleasant delight about Mano's father gifting him with such a cherished treasure. Mano's grandmother's ring was special to her. "I love it, Mano. I shall wear it always," she'd told her husband.

"On your dainty finger is where it belongs, *querida*, and I'm proud that my father thought so."

They rode on by the Half Moon Bay area, and Mano suddenly realized what a very long day it had been for his bride. It was going to be a few more hours before they reached their destination.

After all, he thought to himself, their bower of lovemaking had always been the California earth and the roof over their heads had been the starlit night with the bright moon shining down on them.

Knowing his ladylove so well, he felt like she would have no objection to what he was about to suggest.

When he abruptly halted Demonio, Aimee pulled up on the reins of Lady, her palomino. Boldly, he made his suggestion and she eagerly accepted. "Lord, Mano, I wondered if we were going to ride all night long."

He leaped off the horse, roaring with laughter as he moved around Demonio to help her off the palomino. "No, *mi vida*, I have no intentions of riding all night long on my honeymoon."

He lifted her down to stand there beside him on the thick carpet of grass. She surveyed the spot he had picked and found it to her liking. Somewhere over in the distance, she heard the sounds of a bubbling stream of water. Within the secluded privacy of the grove of trees it seemed to her the rest of the world was blocked out. The only intruders were the moon up above and the millions of stars shining just for them.

To be here in this glorious setting with the handsome man standing by her side was heavenly. It was all she'd ever yearned for and now it was hers.

With an impish grin on her lovely face, she declared to her husband, "Mano, it is going to be awfully hard to get accustomed to sleeping in a bed with you. Did you know that?"

He laughed as he looked at the adorable little minx standing there before him, completely beguiling him with her seductive charm. He had to be the luckiest man in the whole world.

"It matters not to me, *querida*, where we sleep, as long as you are by my side. But right now, sleep is not exactly what I have on my mind."

She gave forth a soft, lilting laugh because sleep was not exactly what she had on her mind, either. Together, they lay down on the soft bed of grass. As long as the stars had been there in the heavens, sparkling brightly night after night, and the moon had been there shining down on this countryside, they knew that their love would last eternally.

A glorious, golden splendor was theirs this night!

FIERY ROMANCE
From Zebra Books

SATIN SECRET (2116, $3.95)
by Emma Merritt

After young Marta Carolina had been attacked by pirates, shipwrecked, and beset by Indians, she was convinced the New World brought nothing but tragedy . . . until William Dare rescued her. The rugged American made her feel warm, protected, secure—and hungry for a fulfillment she could not name!

CAPTIVE SURRENDER (1986, $3.95)
by Michalann Perry

Gentle Fawn should have been celebrating her newfound joy as a bride, but when both her husband and father were killed in battle, the young Indian maiden vowed revenge. She charged into the fray—yet once she caught sight of the piercing blue gaze of her enemy, she knew that she could never kill him. The handsome white man stirred a longing deep within her soul . . . and a passion she'd never experienced before.

PASSION'S JOY (2205, $3.95)
by Jennifer Horsman

Dressed as a young boy, stunning Joy Claret refused to think what would happen were she to get caught at what she was really doing: leading slaves to liberty on the Underground Railroad. Then the roughly masculine Ram Barrington stood in her path and the blue-eyed girl couldn't help but panic. Before she could fight him, she was locked in an embrace that could end only with her surrender to PASSION'S JOY.

TEXAS TRIUMPH (2009, $3.95)
by Victoria Thompson

Nothing is more important to the determined Rachel McKinsey than the Circle M—and if it meant marrying her foreman to scare off rustlers, she would do it. Yet the gorgeous rancher felt a secret thrill that the towering Cole Elliot was to be her man—and despite her plan that they be business partners, all she truly desired was a glorious consummation of their vows.

PASSION'S PARADISE (1618, $3.75)
by Sonya T. Pelton

When she is kidnapped by the cruel, captivating Captain Ty, fair-haired Angel Sherwood fears not for her life, but for her honor! Yet she can't help but be warmed by his manly touch, and secretly longs for PASSION'S PARADISE.

Available wherever paperbacks are sold, or order direct from the Publisher. Send cover price plus 50¢ per copy for mailing and handling to Zebra Books, Dept. 2424, 475 Park Avenue South, New York, N.Y. 10016. Residents of New York, New Jersey and Pennsylvania must include sales tax. DO NOT SEND CASH.

EXHILARATING ROMANCE
From Zebra Books

GOLDEN PARADISE   (2007, $3.95)
by Constance O'Banyon
Desperate for money, the beautiful and innocent Valentina Barrett finds
work as a veiled dancer, "Jordanna," at San Francisco's notorious Crystal
Palace. There she falls in love with handsome, wealthy Marquis Vincente—
a man she knew she could never trust as Valentina — but who Jordanna
can't resist making her lover and reveling in love's GOLDEN PARADISE.

SAVAGE SPLENDOR   (1855, $3.95)
by Constance O'Banyon
By day Mara questioned her decision to remain in her husband's world. But
by night, when Tajarez crushed her in his strong, muscular arms, taking her
to the peaks of rapture, she knew she could never live without him.

TEXAS TRIUMPH   (2009, $3.95)
by Victoria Thompson
Nothing is more important to the determined Rachel McKinsey than the
Circle M — and if it meant marrying her foreman to scare off rustlers, she
would do it. Yet the gorgeous rancher feels a secret thrill that the towering
Cole Elliot is to be her man — and despite her plan that they be business
partners, all she truly desires is a glorious consummation of their vows.

KIMBERLY'S KISS   (2184, $3.95)
by Kathleen Drymon
As a girl, Kimberly Davonwoods had spent her days racing her horse, per-
fecting her fencing, and roaming London's byways disguised as a boy. Then
at nineteen the raven-haired beauty was forced to marry a complete stranger. Though the hot-tempered adventuress vowed to escape her new husband, she never dreamed that he would use the sweet chains of ecstasy to
keep her from ever wanting to leave his side!

FOREVER FANCY   (2185, $3.95)
by Jean Haught
After she killed a man in self-defense, alluring Fancy Broussard had no
choice but to flee Clarence, Missouri. She sneaked aboard a private railcar,
plotting to distract its owner with her womanly charms. Then the dashing
Rafe Taggart strode into his compartment . . . and the frightened girl was
swept up in a whirlwind of passion that flared into an undeniable, unstop-
pable prelude to ecstasy!

*Available wherever paperbacks are sold, or order direct from the
Publisher. Send cover price plus 50¢ per copy for mailing and handling to Zebra Books, Dept. 2424, 475 Park Avenue South, New
York, N.Y. 10016. Residents of New York, New Jersey and Pennsylvania must include sales tax. DO NOT SEND CASH.*